To Caro

Daydreams, Moonbeams and Wings Over the Common

(From the Tail of a Magpie!)

By Louisa Middleton-Blake

Louisa Middleton-Blake

PublishAmerica
Baltimore

ISBN: 1-4137-4982-8
PUBLISHED BY PUBLISHAMERICA, LLLP
www.publishamerica.com
Baltimore

Printed in the United States of America

Dedication

I dedicate my story to the memory of my father, who endured great patience, especially during Maggie's "growing pains," and for his love of nature and wildlife, which was to inspire me right from early childhood. To my dear cousin Fiona, sadly missed, who as a fellow author encouraged me to write this story; and also no longer with us, my good friend Doreen, who was very persistent (over a glass of sherry—or two!) that I should follow my dreams and adapt them on paper.

The story is also dedicated to my lovely companions, Katie and Hattie, my two dogs, and Humphrey, my pony. They too have passed on, but are forever in my thoughts. And of course, last, but not least, I owe everything to Maggie (my co-author) for setting the story in motion in the first place, because without him, there would be no story to tell!

Long may all the birds of the world continue to grace the skies!

Acknowledgements

Many thanks go to my son, Adam, my chief draft sub-editor, who spent many hours rearranging some of the sentences and a few other minor alterations; and not forgetting my talented "artist," brother Derek, who designed, painted and airbrushed my "dream" cover pictures, and also the magpie chapter illustrations.

I am deeply grateful to all my relatives and friends who supported me these past few years during my times of stress through personal upsets, as they helped me through the long, dark tunnel until I came once more into the light. Not letting me off so lightly, they urged me on (kicking and screaming!) to complete this project.

Last (but not least), I owe everything to my poor long-suffering mother, who had to endure "not very punctual meals—not enough cups of tea—and too many late nights!"

Table of Contents

Introduction
In the Beginning

"Do you think he will return?" asked Doreen as she sipped her favourite sherry. She raised the question as we both sat opposite one another at the large, beautifully polished oak table, which was situated in the kitchen.

The kitchen was always regarded as "the conference room" when friends called in to discuss their latest projects or holiday arrangements or to air their views, and more often than not, problems were solved over endless mugs of coffee or cups of tea; but whenever Doreen came to visit, it usually meant a glass or two of sherry.

Looking intently into my face, Doreen continued with the inquisition. "And what if he decides to stay away for good? You may never see him again!" she said, peering at me over the top of her glass. "When did you last see him?" she asked, looking very concerned. "I mean, you've done everything you can for him. You've given him a comfortable home, he's had a good life with you, and you've always fed him well, not to mention all the freedom to go almost everywhere he wants to."

"Yes, I know," I sighed, looking down into my empty glass.

"So how long has he been living with you now?"

"Well, let me see now, in this house it's about a year, or a bit over I suppose," I said, reaching for the bottle of sherry, which was by now almost as empty as my glass. I made a mental note to replace it with another one before Doreen's next visit.

"He was with me for at least a year before that in Sussex, so that makes it about two years in all," I said. Doreen extended out her glass for me to top it up for her, and as she held the thin stem between her slender fingers, I could see that she was about to dish up one of her wild ideas or make a hugely impossible suggestion. It was the look on her face that told me so.

"Why don't you write about his extraordinary life, and about all those mischievous things he did?" she asked with a hint of a glint in her eye as she waited for my reaction.

I leaned forward in my chair and almost choked on my drink at the very thought of even taking on such an awesome task. I gave her a quizzical look as I shakily topped up my own glass. "You can't be serious! Now what purpose would I want to do that for?" I asked her. "And another thing…not only *where* am I going to find the time to do such a thing, but *who* on earth would be interested in reading about him anyway?" There was a slight pause before she answered me.

"Well, you could do a little each day, bit by bit. And yes, I agree that it might take you some time to complete it, but I really do think it would be well worth having a go. I'm sure lots of people would love to read about him because he was so unusual and the things he got up to were almost unreal. You could say that he was quite a loveable rogue in a way, I mean, he could make you laugh when he was acting up funny and being quite comical, now couldn't he?"

"Yes, I know!" I said brightly, remembering the happier times.

"And then he could make you cry when he was in one of his evil moods…and he could really hurt if he decided to attack you!" said Doreen on a more sinister note.

"Yes, I know!" I groaned, remembering the darker side of him, but before I could give my excuses for why I shouldn't take on this mammoth project, she carried on with her final list of reasons of why I should do it.

"He was definitely a one-off sort of character that you just couldn't forget or dismiss in a hurry, and because so many people talked about him and his exploits, and got to know about him, that many of their friends also wanted to come just to see him for themselves…didn't they? So I think personally that this is a good enough reason to write about him."

I laughed at her last comment, as I could visualize droves of people lining up at the front door demanding to see the great performer himself, and I smiled inwardly at her audacious suggestion to me that I should put down on paper his life story and the impact he made on the family and friends.

"Yes," I said, "I suppose you are right in some ways, and I can't fault your description of him, but he leaves such a trail of destruction behind him," I said, "and lots of angry people too. They might think I've got a bit of a nerve if I portray him as a hero or something."

I could see that Doreen wasn't going to back down, so I tried to humour her.

"Okay!" I said, "I might just think about it, but it would take me an awfully long time."

We carried on talking for a while about the possibility of the story, sifting through details and exchanging anecdotes until the bottle of sherry was finally emptied, and as if right on cue, Doreen's husband Wilf arrived back from his trip to the local library. He came in and joined us at the table, but he had no idea about our topic of conversation, and after a mug of steaming hot coffee, followed by a large wedge of Victoria sponge filled with fresh strawberries and thick cream, they both left. I waved them off from the front porch, and watched as their car sped up the drive and out of sight.

Returning to the kitchen and in deep thought after listening to Doreen's words of wisdom, I picked up the empty sherry bottle and placed it in the waste bottle bin. Before discarding it, however, I had managed to squeeze out a few drops from the remainder of the intoxicating liquid into my glass. Clutching it tightly, I made my way back into the hall towards the stairs. Reaching the staircase, I clasped the bannister and stumbled awkwardly on the first step, almost losing my footing. Steadying myself, I made my way upstairs to my bedroom, taking great care not to spill the drink, even though it barely covered the bottom of my glass.

My intention was to find a certain photo album and to look for a particular photograph of the "amusing character" who was the object of my earlier discussion with Doreen.

Throwing off the very old flower-patterned cover to the equally very old tin trunk where I stored the photo albums, I carefully lifted the hinged lid and took out each album. Right at the bottom of the trunk I found the volume I was searching for. As I opened it up, a single photo slipped out and fell to the floor, and when I picked it up and turned it over, there, staring back at me, was the culprit in question!

Now you might well be forgiven for thinking that my good friend Doreen and I had just been discussing the whereabouts of an unfaithful husband (or even a two-timing boyfriend), but that wasn't the case. We were actually talking about a very remarkable, and also a very talented (in his own special way) black and white bird, which may sound a bit insignificant, but the impact that he made on myself, the family, and other "humans" was really quite extraordinary and unforgettable.

This particular bird ended up in the realm of "humans," instead of his own kind, through a near brush with death, and I happened to be there at the right time to rescue him. Now I was gazing at just one of the few photographs I was able to take of him, due to the fact that he was not just camera shy, but had an aversion of them, bordering on hatred, and would attack any type of camera if he saw one pointed in his direction. It was almost impossible to take photos of him. But now I was concentrating on this one particular picture I held in my hand. I was not to know that in just a very short while, a very strange and inexplicable event in my life was about to take place.

Taking the photo with me with a certain amount of trepidation, coupled with an impending hangover threatening to appear at any moment, like an unwanted party pooper, I sat myself down in my comfortable bedroom chair and waited for inspiration to flow and gush over me like a glorious waterfall.

This particular chair was situated in a quiet, peaceful corner, where I was able to sit and contemplate about nice, or even serious, things. I gradually drifted into a sort of daydream, with the photo in one hand and the last precious dregs of the sherry in the other.

These odd moments of relaxation were quite rare these days, what with so much work to be done indoors and outdoors. I always kept myself pretty busy, but on this particular day, I was able to snatch the whole afternoon to myself. The rest of the family had taken themselves off for a pleasure trip to go sight-seeing and to explore fresh new territories through the Welsh hills, probably to end up at one of our favourite local coves along the coast.

As I sat in the chair, just blissfully meditating, memories started to flood over me. At first, they started to form as colourful pictures in my subconscious state, and events started to flow like a slow-moving glacier, and then gradually getting stronger and breathtakingly fresher, like the sudden coolness of a peppermint. A peppermint dream I call it, and a dream which appears to you as clear and sharp as a quartz crystal.

Whilst past events appeared in my mind like a motion picture, I decided that now was the time to make a few notes, before all the images that were hurtling about inside my head finally disappeared in a puff of smoke, making it almost impossible to grasp them again.

I moved from my comfortable chair over to the small desk by the window, where my computer, along with various bits of paper, envelopes pens, paper clips, stapler, sellotape, and files were kept.

Taking one more sip from my glass with my head now in an almost permanent fuzzy haze, I placed the photograph of the bird on my paper stand, which is positioned on the right-hand side of my computer, with its large, chunky, bulldog-type clip at the top (which I can fix my worksheets or other bits and bobs to), and set it alongside pictures brought back by my brother (on one of his many visits to the United States and Canada) of Native Americans.

I lodged the photo between an enlarged copy of a printed picture of Curly, who was a very handsome, very famous, Crow Indian scout, wearing the magnificent White Swan buffalo robe and on the other side of the stand, but just in front of Curly's picture, is a postcard-sized photo of a Spokane tribesman, by the appropriate name of Bird Rattle. His weather-worn granite features and his piercing dark eyes seemed to look straight at you, as if he was trying to convey his own spiritual message from a bygone age. I sometimes wonder what these great mystics and shamans of the past would think of our lifestyle of today. Do we not appreciate what we once had? Or are we expecting too much for what we could have in the future? And at what cost? Anyway, my picture of the bird, (which showed him perched at the top and on the left-hand side of his cage) was now sandwiched between a Crow, a White Swan, and a Bird Rattle — so he stood in very good company.

Bringing my thoughts sharply back to the present and grabbing a biro from the brass stand, where I kept a variety of pens and pencils, and opening up my jotting pad, I started to scribble some notes. At the top of the page, I wrote the words in big bold letters: MAGGIE THE

MAGPIE! because unless it wasn't already obvious, that's what this black and white bird happened to be. He was a common, everyday magpie, and Maggie was the name which was given to him by myself and the family. In fact, he turned out to be a very remarkable, and at times quite a talented, magpie.

After about an hour of intense writing, I laid the biro down and scrutinized the short piece I had already written.

"Hey, not bad at all!" I said out loud to myself rather smugly.

"Rubbish!...complete rubbish!" croaked a harsh, ear jangling voice that sounded chillingly inhuman.

Alarmed, my body jerked into action, and my arms flew up into the air at the suddenness of this unnatural sound. As I swung round in my chair to see where the voice was coming from, I knocked the thin-stemmed sherry glass off the desk and onto the carpet, and although it had a soft landing, the stem broke in two. I bent down to retrieve it, being thankful that at least it was empty and I wouldn't have to do any mopping up.

Oh dear!...I must have had one too many, and now I was hearing things!

Staggering awkwardly over to the window, I looked out across the valley and noted that the hills *did* look rather misty and rolling, and the trees *did* look as though they were moving across the landscape, and the fields *did* look as though they swaying up and down, as though they were dancing a waltz! Yes, that was it! It must have been that last top-up I had! Serves me right!

Then it was as though a whole symphony of bird sounds suddenly surrounded me about the room, mingling into all sorts of strange and weird noises, and they were getting louder and louder and almost driving me mad, until gradually they were transformed from what I can only describe as a concoction of "bird language" and into a strange, jumbled up composition of human speech, or at least some sort of an attempt at it!

"Utter *nonsense!*...completely *boring!*...lacking *colour!*...oh so very *twee!*...and a pack of *lies!*" hissed that menacing voice again.

Dumbfounded at this sudden outburst, I spun round to look towards the door to see if somebody was there after all and purely out to make fun of me. It couldn't be a member of the family, because they were not due back home yet, and besides, none of them would speak in this strange unnatural weird voice or in such a crude and coarse manner anyway.

The truth of the matter was that there was nobody there at all, and I was beginning to feel more than just a little uneasy, and not only that, I was now hearing things as well.

I promised myself faithfully; "I shall *never* touch a drop of sherry again!…*never, ever, ever*…or at least…*not in the early afternoon!*"

I slumped down again into my chair, then leaning forward over my desk, I stared hard at the photo of Maggie, and at first glance it didn't appear to be any different. Then, squinting hard at the photo, I did a double-take as the hazy image of the bird cleared. Did I detect a slight movement of his head?…a quick blink of an eye?…and didn't his beak look just a little bit odd, as though stretched into almost a grin? (or was it a grimace?) And to cap it all he was now perched on the *right-hand* side of the cage instead of the *left!*

"Were you speaking to me?" I asked, stupidly and in a very shaky, slightly high-pitched voice, which sounded more like a squeaky mouse caught in a trap.

"But of course, ducky!" came the reply. "Who else could it be?…my little chickadee!"

"But how on earth can that possibly be?…am I going nutty or something?" I asked, in a slightly lower, more confident tone of voice. "After all," I added, surprised that my speech was now beginning to lose its slur, "you're just a photo, and I've never heard you speak in real life before, even though I tried to teach you to speak a few simple words…. So why are you bothering to talk to me now?"

Before the image of Maggie could answer me, I thought I heard a sound behind me. I turned round, half expecting to see someone appear unexpectedly at the door and catch me out talking to myself, in which case if they did, then they would undoubtedly think that I'd strayed well off course from the path of sanity, and had slipped over the edge, straight into the "wonky-tonky land of happy talk." But thank goodness, apart from the talking picture, I was completely alone.

"Well now, nutty you may be, but if you are, then all I can say is this; just watch out for them squirrels, or any other nut fanciers, but let me tell you another all-important thing, since you have slapped me picture beside those 'wise boys' (otherwise known to us with feathers as 'The Guardians of All Natural Things') it's created a bit o' magic, no less," he said. "An' whilst we're on the subject of truth tellin', you've told a bit of an ol' porky pie when you says about me in your very own words: 'you managed to turn our lives *upside down* and *inside out!*' Now if the truth be known, 'tis t'other ways around and about, and not only that," he continued, "you even admit that you took me all the ways from the South of England to end up here, in a strange place called West Wales, and that, to me, is a very topsy turvy thing to be doin' to anyone as delicate and precious as me!"

"What an odd way of talking," I said, "and you can't even spell properly, let alone your grammar."

"I think I speaks very well," he said, "an' me spellin' ain't that bad, an' considerin' I was able to speak the language of 'bird' only just a few suns and moons after breakin' out of me shell, an' I bet it took *you* a whole lot longer to learn your funny way of speech after *you'd* hatched out. An' then to top it all, and as if I hadn't had enough to be puttin' up with, then blow me down an' stick me up again, I 'ad to begin learnin' the ways and speakin' the speech of the Pinkies, which I think is pretty damn impressive! An' talkin' of grammar an' all that higgledy-piggledy stuff, you ain't so hot on it either!" he said with a scoff.

"Well, I have to admit that I'm not the most eloquent of writers in the world; but....!"

"Wot's *'elyqwint'* mean?" he interrupted, holding his head on one side.

"Oh never mind about that, you wouldn't understand if I told you anyway!" I said.

"An' another thing!" he said, dismissing my last comment; "does that mean that every little word I utters, an' every little comment I makes, you're going to hold to ransom an' stoppin' me in me tracks before I can even start?"

"You talk too much, Maggie, once you get going!" I laughed, not expecting this last comment and question; so I answered, "Maybe I will hold some of your words to ransom, but I won't stop you in your tracks. And as to your comment about me being hatched out, I will have you know that I wasn't hatched out; I was born! And what on earth are *'Pinkies?'"*

"Pinkies is wot I calls you humans," he answered crossly.

14

"So now that you've made your point, what do you want to do then?" I asked him.

"You do your bits of story," he said, "an' then I'll do mine, so then everyone will know what the *real* truth is all about!"

I could tell by the tone of his harsh croaking voice that I would have to choose my words very carefully. "So you want to tell me your own story whilst I write it down for you and then to add it to mine?…is that what you are trying to tell me?" I asked.

"I'm not *trying* to tell you," he said, narrowing his eyes. "I *am* tellin' you!"

At this point, I was beginning to wonder if Maggie wasn't smarter than the average magpie after all! "As long as you agree that I will begin with my part of the story first, and then you can tell me everything you want to about your own story," I said guardedly.

"Why can't we start with mine first?" he whined as he drooped his head and tried to put on a pitiful look for my benefit; so I chose my answer with a different approach.

"Well, to begin with," I said, "I was born many years before you were even a twinkle in your dad's eye and hatched out of an egg, and if it wasn't for me saving you from being killed by two hungry crows, then you wouldn't be here at all, so I've got to begin with how things started; or to put it another way; haven't you heard of 'putting the cart before the horse'?" I asked him.

"Haven't you heard of 'the chicken before the egg'?" he replied tersely, snapping his beak with sharp clicks.

"*Touché!*"

"Which one of us said that?" I asked, confused and taken off guard.

"I did!" said the bird in a sing-songy voice.

After a few moments of silence, I said, "Right then, Maggie, I will now continue with my part of the story, starting right back to when I was young, and then how I found you, and you will have to let me know what you want to say for your part, and relating as far back as you can remember about yourself. Do you agree to this?"

"But of course!" he said on a happier note. "And not only that, I can tell you all about my ancient ancestors, which is more than you can say, seein' as you humans don't even go as far back in the world like wot us birds do!…an' have I got some goodly surprises for you in store!"

15

I was beginning to feel I was under a bit of pressure with my co-author.

"I can't wait!" I said sarcastically. "So let's get started...shall we? But before we do, how are you going to dictate, or tell me your story?"

"Ah, well!" he said, "I will tell you everything through thought transference from either my picture (wot you're talking with now, incidentally) or through these ancient guardians wot are wearin' the sacred feathers about their persons. An' just one other thing whilst we're about it, this will be the last time wot you will be able to converse with me by talk sounds; the rest of it will be put into your 'ead all silent like!"

"Just as long as you watch your language, because if you don't, and you say something *really* bad, then there's one thing I can do to stop you," I said.

"Oh yeh!" he said, "how's you goin' to do *that* then?"

"You see this?" I said, pointing to the delete button on the computer; "any nonsense from you, then all I have to do is to press this button, and it will delete everything you have said, so you'd better behave!"

"Wot's delete?" Maggie asked, nearly falling out of the picture as he craned his neck to see the button.

"Just a minute!" I said as I leafed through the large dictionary next to the computer. "Ah!...here we are!...it actually means 'to remove or erase,' or in other words, 'to get rid of.'"

He cocked his head on one side and said, "Wot's *erase?*"

"Perhaps you'd better invest in your own dictionary," I said.

"Wot's *invest?*" asked this increasingly irritating bird.

"Oh now you're just being awkward!" I said and snapped the book shut, making him jerk back into the picture again.

So this was to be our mutual agreement. As long as Maggie was reasonable with his rather quaint language, I would write both of our stories down, and there would be no further communication verbally between us, but because he is so unpredictable, I have no idea in advance of what he going to say, which should be interesting, if not a little unnerving!

This is how we began our tale (or tail, in Maggie's case), but before I sat at the computer with my notes to start my typing, I decided to turn Maggie's photo the other way round, so that he couldn't see exactly how I was going to start the story.

"Drat and botheration!" I said to myself. Why on earth had I forgotten to ask him where he was right now—in the flesh, that is (or should I say, in the feathers and wings?)—and I should have asked him the rather delicate question as to whether he was "male or a female," or perhaps I could have asked him in his own manner "if he laid eggs…or did he make them?"

Oh well, it's too late now!

Never mind, no doubt I shall find out later on—perhaps!

For those who are not too familiar with magpies, I will give you a short description of them so that you have some idea about their looks and their behaviour.

When on the ground, they look like posh gentlemen, strutting and swaggering about in their dapper black suit'n'tails and their snowy white shirt fronts, with their smart fitted waistcoats. I think a pair of spats and a top hat would definitely compliment their outfit.

They certainly suffer from a personality disorder. One minute they are quite charming (on a good day, if you're lucky!); and the next minute alarming (on a bad day, when there's nothing better to do!); also very clever (most of the time!); deceitful (often!); bold (nearly always!); cunning (all of the time!); loving (sparingly!); and hateful (excessively and indulgently!); hot and cold (frequently!); playful (occasionally and in very small doses!); and clowning (sometimes, when in the mood!).

They could be described as the "jokers in the pack," blissfully ignorant of their comical image.

They are the "Scrooge" or "arch villain" of the bird world. I am pretty sure that the Ten Commandments were made for magpies to break—in no uncertain terms—and one of Maggie's very own favourite pastimes is to bend as many rules as possible. But to give them their due, magpies do possess at least one endearing feature, as they are very devoted to their spouses and children, and usually they stick to one mate for life, and they can be quite affectionate towards their partners by preening them gently with their beaks, and they are sometimes seen cuddling up closely to them.

The magpies were also thought to be linked with witchcraft and magicians, and this was because they build their nests, usually with the branches from thorn bushes, with one guarded entrance which is dome shaped, and it was a popular belief that the thorn bushes protected doorways to the spirit world and led to the secret realm of the *faerie*.

Another interesting story told about the magpies, and maybe the reason why they are regarded as unlucky, is because the magpie was the only bird that stubbornly refused to enter inside of Noah's Ark and ended up by perching on the roof! Trust a magpie to talk its way out of obeying a command! This description bears a strong resemblance to Maggie's own stubborn, and excruciatingly contrary, nature.

So that's putting their description in a nutshell!

I do believe the environment Maggie was hatched in has something to do with his split personality.

The gorse, which grows thickly on the common, gives him his prickly sense of humour and sometimes his bad temper. The sweet-scented thyme gives him his more gentle and loving nature—very rare of course! The basking adder inspires his slippery evil ways, whilst the grand old windmill presiding in it's glory, now silent and still, and overlooking the trees where he was first rescued, probably influences his "this way…that way' mood swings.

It was this very same windmill which was almost destroyed many years ago, and it happened on one memorable stormy day.

As Mother was riding home on her bicycle, trying desperately to battle against the furious gale and lashing rain, she was just passing the common where the windmill stood. She was suddenly aware of a strange sound, and on looking up towards the windmill, she was horrified to see the sails whirling round at an alarming rate. Then as she watched, dumbfounded, she saw the great sails spin off in all directions.

Several years passed before the sails were finally repaired.

Just like the windmill, Maggie too would find himself struggling against the "elements of life."

At the end of each chapter, I have allowed Maggie to write his own account of his life with us, in his own words (as agreed by me), which can sometimes be very rude, and his language can be exasperatingly coarse, for which I do apologise, but it is only fair to let him tell his own story, in his own way. His vocabulary (with grammatical errors pouring off his tongue like water from a tap) and his comical way of talking can be very confusing—somewhat weird at times. You will learn how he calls humans Pinkies, whilst nests and houses are referred to as Klakkies, and dogs are known as earth runners, and cats are called earth whisperers, along with many more strange and wonderful words. To make things a bit easier, I do sometimes revert back to our human language.

Maggie also recalls some of the Magpie Folklore (or Bird Lore, to be precise) and little stories told to Maggie and his brothers and sisters by his parents and other birds he meets on his journeys, which sometimes includes their very own songs and verses.

As he glides and swoops through the first year of his life, he learns more about the ancestry of birds, and about gods, goddesses, and the evolution of a certain kind of fairies (yes....I did say *fairies!*). An important point to remember is that both *fairies* and *birds* possess wings! And another thing—do we not put a *"fairy"* on the top of the Christmas tree along with the *"fairy"* lights?…and what about those nice little *"fairy"* cakes?

Earlier on, Maggie did tell me that these creatures were actually called *faerlingers* in the bird world and not *fairies*, but these faerlingers (who were creatures of the "other world," as he put it) were probably related quite closely to fairies of the human realm.

Eventually, after much argument and many tantrums, he allowed me to call them fairies!

You will share his great courage, and of his aspirations to conquer and control every situation and almost everything and everyone he came across, and how he tries to blend in with his new environment, with a few mishaps along the way, until he finally arrives with us in Wales, and how he really *did* "turn our lives upside down and inside out!"

After reading Maggie's story, I doubt that you will ever look at a magpie (or any other bird) in the same way again....*ever!*

So here we have a colourful mix...a cup full of facts—as told by me—gently stirred with a basin full of fiction—as told by Maggie!

– Chapter One –
Shell Shock

Now before I begin Maggie's story, let me take you back on a brief journey into the past, about the picturesque countryside where he was hatched.

Many years ago, it was on this very well known common, which is covered to this day with a network of ancient pathways, well used and trodden down through the centuries by man and beast, where our ancestors lived on a meagre existence tending small herds of animals. But before their arrival, dark days hung over the land as tall trees dominated the whole area until they were cut down to make clearings for the animals, and also to construct dwelling places.

In medieval times, peasants were given the rights to graze their animals on the land, and they were able to make wicker-type fencing from split willow bark so that they could pen their stock in to stop them from roaming. They lit fires at night to keep wolves at bay as well as for cooking their meat on. Times were very hard, and food was not easy to find, so they would have to hunt for even the smaller mammals by trapping and snaring them, including hedgehogs, dormice, rabbits and hares. Small songbirds were a delicacy too. Much bigger game meant hunting deer and wild boar in nearby forests, which took a lot of skill and courage to stalk these larger animals, as they could turn on the hunter and attack, especially the wild boar, as this was indeed a very dangerous animal to approach. Once caught and killed, these big animals would have to be cut into large sections and then carried back to the camp. If they managed to drag the animal back whole, they could then be skinned, ready to be used for either clothing or bedding.

In the cold ashes of the burnt out fires, the chieftains or the soothsayers of the camp would carve out the image of the mother Earth Goddess, and as the wind blew the ashes towards the four directions. North, South, East and West, this would then supposedly promote good crops and healthy animals, and wild herbs would grow prolifically to be harvested and then made into potions and medicines used by the herbalists. They also carried out other ancient rituals to ensure an abundance of nuts and fruit, which grew along the hedgerows on the land and in the forests, to add to their food stores, which would help to sustain them through the cold winter months. Little wooden effigies were also carved out and buried beneath the trees. This was done to appease their gods and goddesses, to help protect them from all ills and evil forces.

The peasants built long dwelling huts (or crofts) which were mostly made from coppiced willow tree branches, and these were then covered in bracken, followed by dried grasses and rushes, and then soft green moss, and finally covered over by clods of earth, or sometimes they would use dried goats skins, or from the animals brought back to the settlement after the hunt. These pelts, which also came from their small flocks of sheep, were crudely stitched together to make clothes and footwear.

The women had their own chores, and they swept the inside of their homes with brooms made from gorse or willow twigs, and then they strew dried flowers and herbs about the floor (which they had gathered on the common or in the woods) to help keep ticks and fleas away, as well as making the homes smell sweeter! Their beds (or pallets) were made from bracken and straw piled high, and then sheep, goat, or other animals skins were placed on top.

The womenfolk were also sent out to collect hazel nuts from the hedgerow, and then in round clay pots, they pounded the nuts into a fine powder, and then they mixed this with a small amount of animal fat, then with a few drops of goat's or sheep's milk, they formed the mixture into a dough. The dough was flattened into small pancakes and finally baked on the fire. When the pancakes were cooked, they trickled some honey onto them to make a very tasty sweet dish.

Stinging nettles were gathered as an important food source and cooked as a vegetable. Stinging nettles were also used to brew an inferior "poor man's ale," which was like a very light refreshing lager. Hops were grown and picked to assist with the brewing.

Bees honey, and the flowers of the gorse, helped to make a potent drink of mead, They picked crab apples, which grew in an abundance on the common, to make a very "rough" cider. They also bartered some of their crops with woad traders, who grew and harvested the yellow-flowered plants, which they boiled down to turn them into a blue dye. It could either be made into a sky-blue or a deep indigo colour. It was used not only for dying their clothes, but the men also painted their faces with it. This wasn't done to frighten off their enemies, as these were reasonably peaceful times, but it was used by the strongest, bravest, and fastest hunters of the group, to be painted on their faces and bodies as a camouflage whilst they hunted the deer and wild boar of the forest.

Brown-eyed, tousle-haired children scurried about the common like little rabbits, almost camouflaged by their drab clothes and their darkened skin from earth and smoke stains.

These children of the camp also played a very important role in the survival of the group. The younger children looked after the chickens and collected the eggs, which were then stored in holes dug out in the ground and then covered over with straw to keep them fresh and cool. They were also in charge of the small flock of sheep, and also the goats that roamed freely about the common. When they were finally able to catch the frisky nanny goats, the children then had to milk them.

The children learned to communicate by sign language from a very early age, which was passed down to them from generation to generation, and was widely used by the boys who used it for very special purposes, and they also learned different bird and animal sounds for communication.

The girls helped their mothers with household duties, and they learned to cook and sew clothes as well as helping to look after the younger children.

The older boys, who were agile enough, climbed to the tops of the surrounding trees, which bordered the common and linked up to larger forest areas. Once positioned at strategic points, they were able to survey for long distances, and from the tree tops they could see if strangers were approaching their camp, or if herds of deer or other game could be spotted, and they would then pass on the appropriate bird or animal sounds to tell the others what they could see, and this would indicate if a course of action was needed.

If they saw strangers nearing their camp, they would give a wolf howl to alert the elders to prepare for a possible confrontation, which could end up as a skirmish if the strangers were hostile, but fortunately this didn't happen very often, as most of them were only passing through in a northerly direction.

If the boys could see herds of deer or boar grazing in the forest, they would make the sound of rutting deer, which was not so easy to imitate, but if they could see or hear grouse or partridge pecking about the forest floor, they would make the croaking sound of a raven to indicate that game birds were there to be caught.

The most efficient and hard working young boys were awarded with feathers to wear on their belts, like medals, or twisted and plaited into their hair. If they were good at finding things, they were given magpie feathers to wear, and the most intelligent and brave boys were given raven feathers, which they were very proud of displaying to their less fortunate siblings.

Ravens were also kept as pets and protectors of the camp. A fledgling would be chosen and taken from its nest by the soothsayer, who would then rear it until it was old enough to train for different tasks, and one of them was for it to give a call of alarm if danger approached. The raven was regarded as a sacred bird and was thought to bring good luck, and many of them outlived their keepers.

Many children living on the common perished at an early age from dreadful fevers or terrible accidents from either falling out of the trees, or whilst out hunting with their elders, and only the strongest, quick witted, and fittest, were able to survive. But later on, when an unknown ague almost wiped out the entire camp, the small group moved on to fresh pastures to start a new settlement.

This hard and difficult way of life was carried on throughout the long history of the common in those earlier years as settlers came and went.

There was also a much darker side to the north side of the common during the sixteenth and seventeenth century, as vagabonds, poachers, highwaymen, and other villains were often hanged there and left dangling on the gibbet for an awfully long time to deter other law breakers as the crows pecked about at the decomposing bodies.

The last known hanging on the common was in the year seventeen thirty four, when a pedlar named Jacob Harris murdered the landlord and his wife at a local inn called the Royal Oak. He also attacked the maid, who unfortunately stumbled upon the murder, but she somehow managed to escape and ran for help.

Jacob Harris was finally caught and then executed at Horsham. They took his body and hung it on a gibbet on the common, ironically close to the scene of his crime.

The hanging post still survives today, and it is known as Jacob's Post.

On a designated site on the south side of the common, a long oblong plinth has been placed to mark it as being the very centre of Sussex.

Mother used to play here with her brothers and sisters, and they often saw adders on the path basking in the sun. They would dare one another to see how near they could get to the coiled up reptiles, and sometimes the boys would tease them with a stick, which wasn't too clever, because these particular snakes had a poisonous venom, but it didn't seem to worry the children too much.

Travelling gypsies also took over the common, where they would set up camp from time to time.

They would arrive in their brightly coloured horse-drawn caravans pulled by their ponies, which were usually of the black and white piebald, or brown and white skewbald kind, and sometimes they had little dogs trotting alongside. They always seemed to keep to themselves, not bothering anybody, and going about their daily lives.

The gypsies always appeared to be very happy folk, and often they would dance and sing around their camp fires. The men would play accordions and mouth organs, and the girls swirled and danced whilst shaking their tambourines, and the smaller girls joined in, clapping and jigging up and down, with little bells on their ankles and fingers, which jingled away as they danced. Young boys joined in the music, making tunes on their penny whistles, and there was even an old organ-grinder with a little pet monkey, which was dressed up in a little red uniform and a tiny pillbox hat on his head. Laughter, singing, and the colourful dancers brought life to the common, as their music and voices rang out.

Mother and the other children used to see the women picking bunches of heather, which they sold from door to door, along with great big sturdy wooden clothes pegs, which they made as they sat together in groups outside their caravans, chatting and laughing amongst themselves whilst they exchanged gossip and told stories. The women used to hang their washing out over the gorse bushes, and in the winter, small gypsy children could be seen running about the common with no shoes and socks on, even when the ground was covered in frost or cold white snow! They never seemed to worry about the weather.

Sometimes, they would knock on Grandma's back door to ask her if they could have some water to fill their cans with, which she did gladly. Owing to her compassionate nature, especially towards others who were worse off than herself, she would insist on giving them her last slice of bread, if she thought that "a poor soul's needs were greater than hers." Many's the time that an old tramp would turn up on her doorstep begging her for a slice of bread or hot water to fill a mug or a flask to make tea with, and often as not, they were given not only a flask or mug of tea (or sometimes cocoa), but she would send them on their way with a ham sandwich, together with a large slice of cake to go with it!

Just like the gypsies, the old tramps would wander off to the common, where they would have to sleep out rough under the stars, and sometimes they were found curled up and fast asleep in an old wooden bus shelter or barn situated near the road.

One day, as Mother was walking across the common with the family's dog, Gyp, she was approached by a "tall, dark-skinned gypsy, who had a thick, black, drooping moustache!" she recalled. He then offered to buy Gyp off her "for a few shillings!" But of course, she declined his offer, and thinking that the man might try to snatch the dog from her, she ran off home as fast as she could, with Gyp hard on her heels!

Gyp was not just a pet. Being a terrier-type dog of a "mixed" breed, he was a possessive "guardian" to the children, and he would protect them with his life in any event, if the occasion arose.

The gypsies didn't stay long, and they vanished almost in the same way that they'd mysteriously arrived, and the only evidence of their occupation on the common were the small telltale black patches on the ground where their camp fires had been.

They would return again — one day!

The common was used for another purpose, when a good many years earlier, and the first World War had started, trenches where dug out by the troops, and evidence of these trenches can still be seen today, even though they had all been filled in so many years ago.

During the second world war, incendiary bombs were dropped all over the countryside.

After the war, our granddad (Mother's father) rode to the common on his old black bicycle, and with a large bag strapped to his bike, he collected up as many spent shells of the incendiary bombs as he could and rode back home with them.

In his large work shed, he set to work on the shells and cleverly turned them all into money boxes for his grandchildren. They were lovely and shiny, and the bases were made up with circular pieces of carved wood. They all had large slits cut out at the top where you could put your pocket money, such as sixpences, threepenny bits, farthings (with my favourite bird, the wren, on it), and when you were really lucky, half crowns!

I used my money to save up for horse riding lessons, but my brother usually spent his as soon as he got it!

During the second world war, it was on one particular day when my mother and her brothers and sisters (by now in their late teens and early twenties) witnessed a plane shot down.

There had been a particularly fierce "dog fight" which was taking place overhead, and fought between a single Spitfire and a Messershmidt. There was a hit, and the stricken aircraft went spiralling out of control, belching thick smoke as it went somewhere out of sight. Realising it was the enemy aircraft which had been hit, they all rushed with great excitement to the common, to experience for themselves what the enemy (a "German") really looked like. They watched in wonderment to see the airman's parachute open and slowly float to the ground, like a seed from a dandelion head. In reality, the shape of a man they were confronted with, standing there before them, looked more like a newly sculptured statue or a clay figure just taken out of its mould, but some time afterwards, one of the boys said that he looked just like a "chocolate soldier!" due to his muddy coating.

The young German airman was far from their expectations of what they thought the enemy should look like. Instead of a large, very aggressive, arrogant being, he appeared to them more like a mirrored image of themselves (apart from his pewter colouration), and as they stood in silence, their exuberance soon turned to pity. He was a tall, thin, short cropped, blond-haired youth, who looked about their own age and certainly didn't look old enough to be flying planes about the skies, let alone engaging in air battles. His frightened, shocked, and bewildered eyes stared back at them from his pallid, smoke-stained face, making him look more frightened than the onlookers! His airman's uniform was flecked with dried bracken fronds and bits of gorse, and his once shiny boots were caked with mud, as it had rained heavily the night before, turning much of the common to slush. Then quite suddenly, and to the surprise of his audience, he uttered in a very croaky voice, "Bitte, konnen Sie mir helfen, und wo bin ich?" or "Can you help me please, and where am I?" After which, the young man staggered forward a few steps, his legs buckled under him and he fell into a kneeling position.

Before passing out into a dead faint, and probably realizing that this small group of young villagers were actually offering him their token gesture of help, his last words were, "Gott sei Dank!" or "Thank God!"

Somebody suggested that he probably wanted to say something like "All I want to do is to go home, so that I can carry on working in my dad's sausage making factory!…if it's still standing!"

The story goes that the airman was on a special mission to seek out all the secretly located airfields, which were dotted around the countryside over Sussex and Kent, and that probably this particular area he was seeking out was just one of a selected few locations used as "decoy" airfields to confuse the enemy.

Mother, and the rest of the family, were later told that he had made a full recovery at the local Cottage Hospital. Secretly, they were glad.

There was a slight twist to the story. About six months or so later, a Polish airman, believed to be the same one who shot down the German pilot, was blasted out of the skies by a German fighter plane. The stricken Spitfire was seen to head somewhere towards the South Downs, and the young Pole landed very shaken, but safely, in the trees at the top of our road where we used to live as children. My brother, then only about four years old at the time, was taken by Granddad, after hurriedly gulping down their tea and marmalade toast, to witness the airman being cut down from the firm, unrelenting grasp of the branches by the local fire service crew. Tugging urgently at his Granddad's sleeve, he pointed a greasy, marmalade-sticky little index finger towards the ungainly figure hanging from the trees, and in a shrill, loud, questioning voice, and much to the embarrassment of his Our mother, he exclaimed, "Ooh, look Granddad! Isn't that Father Christmas!?...where's the reindeer!?...where's his sledge!?...where's my presents?"

Somewhere, there must be a moral in this story!

When we were quite young (I was about six years old, and my brother was about ten), my brother and I used to get up at the crack of dawn, and we would take ourselves off on a nature ramble across the common.

Setting off from the home of our grandparents' house (that is to say on my mother's side, and they lived just half a mile from the common), we would be extra careful not to disturb anyone in the household. These long rambles were going to be our "big adventures" to start off the long summer holidays from school. What bliss! My brother, being four years my senior, always took command and led the way to the first section of the common, as it's made up into five sections and divided by one major road.

The road we walked along was very quiet and twisty, and as we made our way under a canopy of oak and beech trees, standing majestically tall above us, they silently witnessed our passing beneath their interlocking branches, in much the same way as they had looked on, or acted as, a shelter from heavy rainfalls for our parents and perhaps even our grandparents many years ago.

We were always warned never to stand under trees in a thunderstorm, in case they were struck by lightening. These great giants, right from their early beginnings as young saplings, were perhaps already in the process of storing their own memories, locked deep down within their roots, relating to past events from a bygone age. I guess they could tell us many interesting stories if they could only talk!

Tales of war and peace, happiness and sadness, good deeds and bad deeds, and all of these things coded discreetly in the circles of their trunks, and perhaps casting off their own secret runes as the centuries rolled by, just waiting to be discovered and deciphered. Are these secrets lost when the magnificent trees are indiscriminately felled by man to be used for our everyday use? Or could it be that all these stories of our past, and other great things yet to be told, are meant to be related to us after all?...as these wonderful trees are, in the end, turned into paper to receive the written word.

This could be a case of "what goes around, comes around!"

We were fortunately lucky on these long walks, as there wouldn't be much traffic at five in the morning, and eventually, when we arrived at our destination just as the dawn was breaking, we always stopped and gazed in wonderment as the common unfolded before us into a truly magical place.

Standing out proudly in the mist, as it had done so over many years past, was the very majestic white windmill, flanked by tall green conifers, adding protection and acting as guardians to the surrounding countryside.

The early morning mist created an eerie silence, making the sharp honed senses more aware of the visual beauty to the scene opening up as we entered the unknown.

As we trod the path carefully, avoiding the rare heath spotted orchids, and brushed against young sapling silver birch trees, their thin hanging branches dripped with diamond-like dew drops.

Could these birch trees be the same ones that Maggie's ancestors built their nests in?

Little rabbits scuttled along their sugar-scented paths (sweet smelling to their twitching noses) looking for fresh new shoots to nibble on. We tried to catch them, but of course we never did, and we watched them as they disappeared into the distance with their little white puff-ball tails bobbing up and down.

Busy little spiders could be seen weaving intricate patterns with their webs, festooned with droplets like little crystals. Their little spinnerets, delicately working with silken threads, weaving their spells, spinning their dreams, casting nets for the unwary victim, the early morning mist catching each one in the pale sunlight, giving the appearance of chains of fairy-like Christmas decorations, forming a fine hairnet over the common, and becoming almost invisible during the oncoming daylight.

Our hot breath created little puffs of steam, rising in the crisp morning air.

As the sun began to warm the earth, the air became perfumed with the scent from the gorse blossom, like honey and almond—very intoxicating! Silver studded blue butterflies drifted up as we disturbed them from the tall grasses in front of us as we approached them.

Making our way silently, with the ancient white windmill now behind us, our path led us down a gentle slope towards the copse where the bluebells in the dell formed a magic blue carpet, enticing us to pick bunches of them to take home for our mother and Grandma.

Down by the dew pond, dragonflies jerked and hovered on their iridescent, delicately patterned wings. True "fairies of the glen!"

There seemed to be a certain atmosphere surrounding us, a moment of timelessness, where time seemed to stand still and hold its breath.

We would then double back across the common and take the path which led us past the pub called The Horns Lodge—which was also Mother's birthplace—and then finally back home to Grandma's house.

Mother lived in this very old pub with her grandparents, her mother, and her older brother, whilst her father was away in service with the navy during the first world war.

It was also here that our grandma kept two rather unusual pets when she was a young girl. One of these was a jackdaw, who used to fly onto our grandma's bedroom window sill and call out, "Get up Bessie! Get up!"—and the other pet was a white rat!

The white rat had to be kept in a nearby barn where Grandma used to feed and play with it, as she was strictly forbidden to keep it indoors!

Her mother told her that she'd "seen enough rats getting drunk at the bar each night!"

They obviously didn't have a "pub cat!"

The pub was owned by her grandfather, who became a widower when he was still quite a youngish man in his early fifties, and he became very well known with the locals as a water diviner.

Using a fork-shaped hazel twig, he would go out on a search for underground springs, and when the hazel twig flipped over in his hands, pointing towards a particular spot on the ground, then he knew he'd found water, so this enabled people in the village to dig their own wells. His pastime served as a very useful purpose, and he was in great demand.

The pub had its own well, which was situated on the opposite side of the road, and it served the whole village, as well as the pub, with their water supply. The villagers had to collect the water in buckets, which were carried on a wooden yoke across their shoulders.

There was one mystery created with the hazel twig which has never been solved. It seems that great-grandfather had detected some form of liquid, which ran deep underground, like a stream, and it followed for some considerable distance from the common right to the foot of the South Downs, and although it was liquid, it wasn't water, because the hazel twig bent over in the opposite direction!

The word *OIL* was banded about amongst the eager relatives, who could visualize "pound" signs…*many* of them!…and nice fat bank accounts…but unfortunately that was all pure, imaginative speculation!

Just along the road from The Horns Lodge, there was a tall hedge skirting farm fields which were reported to be haunted. There was an old wooden five-bar gate leading into the haunted fields where

Mother used to sit on the top bar of the gate on quiet summer evenings whilst waiting for one of her friends from the Girl Guides.

Mother told us that once, when she was sitting on this gate waiting for her friend, she heard footsteps coming towards her along the road, but as they drew nearer, there was absolutely no sign of anybody there, and what with the sound of raindrops dripping off the trees all about her, it made the atmosphere very spooky!

On another occasion, when Mother and her friend were walking one evening along the same stretch of road, they both heard somebody walking directly behind them (or so they thought) but when they simultaneously stepped to one side to let whoever it was pass by, it was only then that they realized there was nobody there at all!

Everyone thought that Mother was either mad or very brave!

We thought she was the latter!

I often reflect on the days when we were so young and everything seemed to hold a certain kind of mystery and magic, especially on a quiet early morning, with just the natural sounds of nature. This common is a very special place for me, and even as the years seemed to quickly roll by, I still enjoy walking there, even if it has become much busier and somewhat noisier!

Now that you have a small insight to Maggie's common, and I can only admire your patience at arriving at this point without being too "bored," as Maggie would say, I will now begin to tell you how he first appeared.

It was during this summer concerning our story, that Mother Nature took it into her kind heart to touch the earth with her warm breath, allowing an abundance of insects to thrive, which in turn helped the parent birds to feed their hungry little fledglings, when Maggie made his dramatic entrance into our lives on a bright and beautiful sunny Sunday afternoon.

The date was May 17, 1992, to be precise. In fact, on reflection, his ungainly (but rather premature) appearance on terra firma could easily be compared to that of the now famous *Mr. Bean*, as seen on T.V., who appears on earth in a beam of light, accompanied by a heavenly choir.

In comparison, Maggie's spotlight was a beam of sunlight filtering through a canopy of silver birch trees in a little sheltered copse, and he had only the sound of birdsong to accompany his entrance, but luckily for him, he had landed right in line with where I walk our two dogs, Katie, my black ten-year-old retriever-cross bitch, and Hattie, my mother's miniature white poodle.

On this particular Sunday afternoon, I suppose because of the exceptionally good weather, the car park at the entrance to the common soon became filled with dog owners eager to exercise their pooches, as well as themselves.

As cars arrived, pulling up to park in their usual favourite space, in a cloud of dust caused by the parched earth, the doors opened, and high spirited dogs leapt out of their doting owners' cars, springing about all over the place with great excitement, as though they'd never tasted freedom before.

All types of breeds; little dogs, big dogs, fat ones, thin ones, old and young; tails wagging; little Dachshunds looking like hairy millipedes, with their back legs goose-stepping, trying to keep up with the front legs, and just as eager to join their friends, the Great Danes, who bounded along like rocking horses.

After the usual cheery greetings from other walkers, accompanied by very impatient hounds, whose long pink tongues lolled out of the sides of their grinning mouths, and their expectant eyes pleading with their owners as though they were trying to say, "Come on, you lot!…can't stop!…all those lovely bunnies to chase!…quick!…lets get going!" Then with the usual quick leg lift, and they were off into the distance like hounds after a fox, whilst some of the owners, who had their dogs on leashes, were having their arms pulled out of their sockets as they galloped off after them trying to keep up, whilst others, whose dogs were off their leads, followed at a more leisurely pace!

After all the other dogs and owners had disappeared along their chosen paths, it was now our turn to choose a route.

Donning my wellies, I carefully picked my way through the steaming, freshly deposited doggy poo's.

A little further on, the ground was less hazardous and there were no more nasty little squidgy stepping stones. Although the ground was baked dry, my cumbersome boots added some protection against any encounters with an unwary basking adder, which has been known to happen, particularly on hot summer days. Only last year, a poor Great Dane was bitten by an adder, and although the dog was rushed to the vet to be injected with an antidote, it died after suffering a massive heart attack, so you can never be too sure.

Our particular route was over rough ground in some places, and the grass was tufted and coarse on the top of the banks, left over from the trenches dug out during the war. The prickly gorse bushes could be a bit of a hazard if you brushed against them with bare skin, and there were many gorse bushes growing on this part of the common.

The air was charged with bird sound, and the bluebells growing on the slope leading down into the woods had since passed their smell-by date. Bees flew lazily amongst the heather and gorse, conveying their presence with their hypnotic hum.

Katie led the way, her black tail held high, waving above the bracken, looking like the periscope from a submarine. All around could be heard the distressed calls of magpies, followed by the croaking calls from the scavenging crows.

As we walked to the edge of the copse, and about to enter under the cool shade of the trees, there was a sudden whoosh of air, followed by a fuzzy-like ball of black and white, which landed just a few feet in front of me, and this black and white ball was immediately followed by two wicked-looking big black crows. In an instant, they found their backsides were momentarily attached to the end of my boot, whereby they suddenly regained height into the blue yonder from whence they came, like two scud missiles, before they could even consider what launched them!

After making sure the coast was well clear of these scavengers, I returned to inspect the little casualty, who was by now lying in a pathetic heap at the edge of the path. Just a few minutes earlier, or a minute or two later, and there wouldn't have been a story to tell of

Maggie the magpie, as he would, without doubt, have ended up as "Mr. and Mrs. Crow's Takeaway!" that fateful Sunday afternoon.

Picking the poor bedraggled little creature up, I discovered that it could only be a week or two old, as he had a rounded stumpy rear end, where, at a later date, a most beautiful tail would grow, and he had a wide ugly beak which gave him the appearance of Daffy Duck. He didn't look all sweet or cute and cuddly like an adorable puppy, or soft and fluffy like a little kitten, but just sort of grotesque, podgy, but oh so very vulnerable!

I refer to *"him"* and not *"her"* as we do not know up to the present time, whether it's a boy or a girl magpie.

His eyes were closed and he was panting; the poor little thing was obviously in deep shock. As I picked him up off the ground, I noticed his floppy little left wing had been damaged, probably by the crows' big strong beaks as they pulled him out of his nest, and I was horrified to discover just below the tree, where his nest must have been, the grizzly remains of two of his unfortunate siblings. Looking up towards the canopy of the trees, it didn't take me long to fathom out that there was no way that I could have returned the chick to its nest, and it was nowhere near old enough to leave the nest yet. If I'd just left it there in the hope that its parents would return to feed it, then its chances of survival from predators was very slim. There was no alternative just at that moment; the baby magpie would just have to be taken home.

I carried him very gently back to the car, whilst the patient dogs, wondering what all the fuss was about, obediently brought up the rear, probably trying to fathom out why their usual long run had quite abruptly been cut short.

I placed the little bird very carefully in the boot of the car, and the two dogs were for once allowed the luxury of sitting on the back seat.

Maggie was now on his way to his new home!

We duly arrived at my parents' house, as I was living with them at that time, having recently separated from my husband.

I made a thorough search of the house to find something suitable to use as a temporary nest for the little magpie, and eventually found an old shoe box, which was stored on the top shelf of my bedroom cupboard. I then placed a folded page from the daily newspaper in the bottom of the box, and then I gently popped the casualty in.

He was still very floppy and wheezy, and his eyes were shut tight, and when he did open them for just a few seconds, they were looking a little opaque, which I thought wasn't a good sign at all. The prospects of surviving this terrible ordeal looked pretty bleak for the injured fledgling.

As it was still quite early in the evening, I had to make a decision about what I could feed the baby bird with. I knew this wasn't going to be an easy task. Should I go and dig the front garden up for worms?…or what?

No!…it would be much easier to pop down to the local butcher's shop and buy a pack of minced meat! Which of course is what I had decided to do.

The poor little thing wasn't at all interested in food, as he was still traumatized. I thought that the best thing to do was to take him upstairs where I could keep a watchful eye on him.

As I placed him carefully on top of the dressing table, I noticed how very pathetic and forlorn he looked, almost as if he had entered into another world, or onto a different level of existence, or was this just my imagination running riot?

This was truly one sorrowful little bird, and I did not expect him to survive the night.

- Chapter One and a Half -
Over to Maggie

*…for a bird of the air shall carry the voice,
and that which hath wings shall tell the matter.*

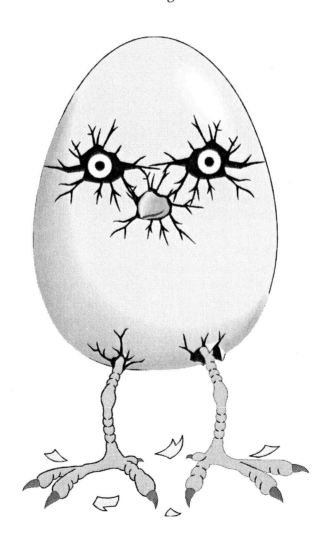

You could have struck me down with a feather (pardon the pun!)—there I woz, waitin' for me next nosh to arrive with me brothers and sisters, all nestled up snug and warm in the comfy little klakki ("nest" to you pinkies, as we wot lives on the wing call you wot is known as "human beans"), when these two big black beakies blotted out the sun, hollerin' out in gravely gruff voices:

Yum!… Yum!… Yum!…
You little fat scums!…
We'll carry you off,
To fill our skillies' tum tums!

This meant that us lot were potentially on their very own nursery's "menu of the day."

Now "skillies" means "fledglings" to the beakies, and beakies means "crows," as that's wot these black beasties are called in these parts of Mother Earth.

Look!… I was only hatched out not so long ago, an' I almost remember it quite vividly!… Yes!… *Really*! Well, at least I remember a bit about it all, when I did eventually crack myself out of that stuffy ol' shell of mine an' managed to shake those splinterin' fragments off me delicate little bum! Although I couldn't see for a good long time, I knew there were six or seven others, an' all of 'em just like me, sittin' tight as a snipe in our klakki.

We were all quite happy, being stuffed full of grub the whole sunlight-time long, by our egg maker (Pa) and egg layer (Ma), until one sunrise, everything changed.

There I was, enjoying myself with all the others, when suddenly these two big nasty black beakies arrived on the scene and started to yank me brothers and sisters out of the klakki, one by one, and in no time at all, it was almost empty!… Except for little ol' me. Then, when they returned for their last visit, they both looked hard and pointed their beaks in my direction, and when they spoke in turn, sayin', "Yes!… Yes!… Yes, little snitchy snack!… You're next!" I think that meant me!

I woz rather hoping that they were going to take me on a holiday, but oh dear me no, their idea woz that they were going to split me three ways and then to feed me in handy little strips to their own precious little hatchlings!

I thought it best to try and humour them, so I starts off with saying to them, "Who, in the name of the Grand Eagle, do you think you're feather dusting here? Well, let me tell you right now, buzzard buster!... I'm a one-hundred-per-cent recycled Bird o' Paradise!... That's what I am! And as for you!... Why!... You're just a couple of Lyrebirds!... Get it?... *Couple of liar birds?!*—Oh well!... Please yerselves then!"

If looks could kill, then I'm not here anymore.

I tries another soothing approach. So I sez to them, "Listen, me lovely black gladiators, good kind sirs, give us a break! You've just got to face facts, now at the end of the sundown, you wouldn't get much loose change after pluckin' an' scatterin' *my* miserable little feathers, an' not only that, there wouldn't even be enough meat on me poor twiggy little bones to make you a decent 'canary soup', my effervescently bubbly lieges! I mean to say, why don't you just wait a few more suns and moons, your worshipfulnesseses, and then you'd be pleasantly surprised, 'coz I'd be a bit bigger, and a bit more tastyful, me old mates!... An' another thing I'd like to point out to you, just look over there!... In that tree over yonder!... There's a substantial batch of lovely, scrummy, fat, juicy, grey, furry, tender, baby nut gatherers (squirrels), full of vitamins and minerals!"

"Shut your beak, you little creep!" sez they to me.

Then the big egg maker took a step nearer to me!... Then he inched closer!... Then he hopped nearer still!... And then when he came too close!... I could hear him give a croaky chortle, which came deep down in his throat, and his breath stunk of rotting flesh and bad egg yolks, an' me quills quivered when I saw little feathers still sticking to his beak! And then he spoke again.

"Listen, you little 'Darwin's delight,' it's not your scraggy skin we want, it's those steamy, juicy little bits underneath, like that little bit that goes *boo-boom...boo-boom...boo-boom*! And that squidgy liver-shaped bit, next to that delicately flavoured kidney bit, which goes nicely with a round, shiny, sheep's eyes!... So just keep still, you blubbering bag of bones...like a good little feathery feasty!"

So I sez to them both, "Oh yes...but!...but!...I might just taste of chicken's waste! An' wot if I don't have these aforementioned... er!...*bits*!...as you call 'em! I haven't heard or seen them. You could be just guessing I have them! So you're wasting your time!... My luscious lord and lady...beggin' your pardon, your highnesses."

41

After giving me a look that would explode the nuts off a squirrel, they then sez to me, "Hold still...you B.C. breakfast, so's we can just top and tail you!"

I then sez to them, "What's B.C.?"

They sez to me, "Before crows!"

So I sez to them, "Bye bye, A.D.'s!"

And they sez to me, "What's A.D.'s?"

So I sez to them, "After dodos!... You dodos!" I then tried one more, too-good-to-miss offer. "Tell you what, boys, what if I sell you some timeshares in a group of very classy klakkies?... Beautifully situated in a lovely little rookery not too far from here...commanding lovely views, very much sought after (but I didn't add 'by small pinkies with catapults') and then you have hedge-to-hedge robins' roosts, easy access for robbin'! There's another added luxury which you might like to consider! How about an abundance of reconditioned woollies' wool? Makes ideal lining for your klakkies! Deposits accepted! References not essential! Sounds okay to you!... *Doesn't* it?... I guess?"

Then I had *another* unbeatable offer, so I sez to them, "I can order you some nice stir-fry grasshopper legs, if I can catch them, and they're so...*deee-licious*...and so...*deee-lectable!*... So just let me go for a tiny minute or two, and I promise you, my honourable holinesseses, I'll just see what I can do! Oh!... An' one other superb service I could give you; I could do a spot of egg snitch...er!...I mean *sitting!*...for you...if you like?" I offered convincingly.

Then, before they could answer me, I added quickly, "If you would *like* me to, that is?... You know, when you lay your next batch? I could keep them nice and warm when you goes off a'huntin'... Oh!... I take it your silence means my absolutely genuine once-in-a-lifetime offer's not an option?"

Their answer to me unique proffering was not what I expected. The big black egg maker said in a gaggy-type voice that sounded as though he'd just swallowed a witchetty grub and it'd got stuck in his throat, "You speak with Forked Tongue, and I am the first hatchling of Troylon the Great, my little pie filling!"

I looked quizzically at him, an' thinking to meself, *What's he on about? There ain't nothin' wrong with me tongue...and it's not even forked!*

He then continued, "It is my given name, and this is my mate, Silver Cloud, first hatchling of Empress Crowdalicka. Silver Cloud is the light of my life, and we have our hungry fledglings to feed!"

The light of his life? I said to meself. *More like his 'feathery fondant fancy!'* Not only that, but it looked as though she could have done with a bit of a beak-lift job, from wot I could see.

I crouched down as tight as I could into the klakki, trying not to look at them, hoping they would fly off and leave me alone.

"Grovel no more, my sweet and sour giblet!" croaked one of the big, black-beaked, baby-bird bashers.

I had to think quickly and cunningly, so I threw out another line of defence, as time was runnin' out fast, and I was gettin' mighty hungry myself. So I then said to 'em, thinking faster than the speed of light, "Did you know that I'm a member of the local branch (another pun coming up!) of the F.B.I.?"

"What's *that*?" enquired Forked Tongue, glaring menacingly at me.

"Free Bird Immediately!" I frantically replied.

By this time they were looking really livid and truly menacing.

I then tried to hide me head under me wing so that they couldn't carry out their outrageous threat. Did they listen to me? Fat chance, so to speak, and before I could come up with another plan of exit from me fast-looming extermination, all of a sudden, there I woz, picked up by these two big flapping nerds like I was just a rotten old apple, and my last desperate appeal, so as to play for some extra time, went something like this:

"Ooohh!....Aaahh!" I gurgled and croaked, and then seein' that at last I'd managed to grab their attention, in a squeaky thin voice I said, "I'm ill!... Desperately ill!... I'm fading fast!... What a damn shame!... Such a waste!... Do you know wot?" I added pathetically, "It must've been that last meal I had pushed down me throat not long ago!... I think I've been fed with a piece of poisoned, big-eared floppity, hoppity, rabbity bunny!"

And then at this point, as if by magic, they suddenly dropped me like a red-hot turd, which sent me hurtling through the air (doing me little stumpy wings no good at all, I can tell you) when I hit something very, very hard, which nearly knocked me gizzard through me beak and back again. I could hardly breathe, and I came all over fainty.

This is it! I thought to meself. I was about to be sent to that Great Eggshell Place in the Universe!

Then, all of a sudden like, something really way out happened to me.

43

As I lay there thinking to meself, *Am I really going to end up as a beaky's takeaway?* these two big, pink, scoop-type things (I learnt later on that they were called "handses") which belonged to a tall, long-haired pinky, picked me up and whisked me away.

I pretended to be dead, which is something we were all taught to do by our egg layer and egg maker whenever there woz any danger about. Little good it woz to us lot, I must say! Anyway, I was placed ever so gently, I must admit, into this huge big metal klakki (car) with these two big hairy earth runners (dogs), and the next minute there woz this awful growling sound coming from beneath me, and then we were sort of flying along at the speed of a Merlin after its prey.

I started to chant our sacred prayer, thinking this surely will save me!

> *Our feathers, which start in heaven,*
> *Sparrows be our game,*
> *Mine is the kingdom,*
> *The plunder and the glory,*
> *Give us the egg collectors,*
> *And those that collect our hatchlings,*
> *Lead us into temptation,*
> *And deliver us those that tempt against us,*
> *And deliver us evil,*
> *Give us all each sunrise your daily bread.*
> *Save us your bacon.*
> *For ever and ever.*
> *SQUAWK.*

Eventually we arrived at this, what I can only describe as, HUGE...big...terrifically...frighteningly...*gigantic klakki!*

– Chapter Two –
To Be or Not to Be

I found it very difficult to sleep that night, wondering if the little bird was still alive. Switching on the bedside light at two in the morning, I made my first check. He was still breathing, but still making an awful wheezing sound.

Why should I be so concerned about this scruffy, ugly little bird? After all (I reasoned with myself), I had rescued many little injured birds before—most of them victims of our cats—so why should this one be so special? He would be quite a commitment to me, taking up much of my time, and not forgetting that I would have to keep up with all that feeding, and then he would have to be cleaned out regularly as well. Maybe it was just meant to be that I should have saved him from the crows. I believe it was his destiny to enter into our lives, and if he was to survive, even if it was just for a short while, then I would have to resign myself to the fact that it was going to be my sole duty to care for his "Creature Comforts" and to tend to his every daytime needs, and possibly night-time too!

I lay there, tossing and turning, not just because the night was so hot and humid, but because my thoughts were in a restless state too, wondering how I was going to cope with looking after a sickly fledgling, and if I was doing the right thing at taking on a wild bird, but then on the other hand, I couldn't have just left him there to be taken by the crows, even though I was probably interfering with nature, because even the crows have to feed their young, too! I just happened to be in the wrong place, at the wrong time, or in Maggie's case, the right place at the right time.

If Maggie had expired during the night, then I couldn't have written his story, and you wouldn't be reading it!

Fate can play a big part in our lives, and fate has the ability to control our destiny, if we care to let it. Sometimes it will throw a whole cartload of misfortunes our way, and we can either just go with the flow or turn in another direction, hoping to avoid a head-on collision. On the other hand, if we trust our own instincts and let the good or bad situation take its course, we can come out of it having learnt a hard lesson, and from the experience become a much stronger person. Some people seem to sail through life and nothing ever seems to happen to them at all, just going about their business on a day-to-day routine, and not much fun at the end of it. Fate can also throw some nice things in our direction as well, but these we tend to forget, or not notice, so that's not so exciting either. Sometimes it can begin like a daydream, starting like a small, pulsating bubble, increasing in size, revealing vibrant colours of life within its fragile circle, only to burst into a variety of colourful events like a pantomime of life. You could say that we lead a very fruitful life on average. We can slip up on a banana skin and end up with egg on our face, or feel a bit of a lemon when everything can go horribly pear-shaped, but if we keep things in apple-pie order, life could be a piece of cake!

All of these things are part of the abundantly rich tapestry of life.

We can put all of our good memories in a big colourful box in our memory bank and bring it back into our quiet thoughts when we feel a bit low, or having a spot of "the blues," and to be able to recall the good times can lift our spirits once more. The sad times are best left on the top shelf, unless they can bring a form of comfort, at such times when it is necessary to reflect, when perhaps you have lost a pet who has been a good friend and companion. You can then recall the good times you had together, and take comfort with the knowledge that your pet had a good life with you, and that they were much cherished and well looked after, which makes it all worthwhile.

I listened carefully for the early dawn chorus, thinking that this must surely be the right time for the little bird's first meal to the day!

Looking at my bedside clock reading 5.30 a.m., I checked the chick. Still no change, so tucking myself down once more under the bedclothes, I decided that I wasn't going to get up until about six o'clock in the morning, as this would surely be the time when most sensible little birds have their first feed!

Well would you believe it!…already six o'clock, and he was still fast asleep!

Frustrated, I decided this would be my last check until I heard any movement from his box, which didn't happen until 9 a.m. precisely. At this point I must add that Maggie was never an "early bird" and hated being woken up before 9 a.m. It must be in his genes, but I wasn't complaining!

To my surprise, Maggie opened first his eyes, then he gave a little shudder, and opened his beak, demanding his first meal of the day. I was delighted—at last!—a real response!

I dashed downstairs to the fridge to take out a small portion of the minced meat I had bought for him. Putting the meat on a white saucer, I now had to find a suitable feeding tool for him. The nearest thing to hand was a matchbox, which was kept in the medicine cupboard, along with a box of white candles for use in case of a power cut. From the matchbox, I picked out a single matchstick to use as a feeder. Now this particular feeding tool turned out to be my first big mistake, as you will find out later on, but in the meantime, it definitely served a purpose, as he gulped his first meal down.

After a few successful feeds, the little bird seemed to gain more strength. I had to think hard and carefully on what to do for the best. Should I take a gamble and return him to whence he came?…or just keep him and hope for the best!

It had occurred to me that perhaps the parents of the little magpie could be searching for their offspring, and so I had to make a decision and act quickly, before it was too late, otherwise they would surely abandon their search, if they hadn't done so already!

Telling my parents not to expect to see me for some time and letting them know of my plans, I quickly made up some sandwiches and a flask of coffee for myself, and at the same time I fetched a few doggy biscuits from the cupboard for the dogs. They would hate to be left behind; besides, they would keep me company.

Placing the box with its scruffy but precious little contents carefully once more into the boot of the car, and the two dogs—with silly wide grins on their faces, and their tails wagging furiously—both shot onto the back seat, where they sorted themselves out, and decided—without too much fuss—who should sit where, and then last of all, my boots were smartly placed on the floor behind the passenger seat, as I would be driving in my more sensible shoes.

Myself, with my odd assortment of passengers, headed once more to the common.

The main road was just beginning to get busy with the morning commuters. Drivers were showing signs of anxiety, with their white knuckles clutching the steering wheels and giving tight-lipped stony stares, which made them look like the Easter Island Statues, emphasized by their latest designer sunglasses glinting in the sun. They were all purposefully heading towards their daily destinations, but they were soon showing intense frustration at finding the T junction blocked by crawling, congested, bumper-to-bumper traffic, and they began venting their impatience by gesticulating with furious hand waving gestures, frustrated shoulder shrugging, and eyebrow raising directed towards their fellow passengers, or frowning at other equally frustrated drivers. Windows were frantically wound down, in the hope of some light relief of a breeze, which was about as likely as winning the lottery.

Young boy racers, with their radios blaring out thumping loud music from their 1,000 watt speakers, were beating time with their hands on the steering wheels, as though they didn't have a care in the world, which didn't help to quell the heated emotions coming from inside the vehicles on yet another very hot day. Finding a gap in the oncoming traffic, they accelerated away with an impressive screech of tyres, and as their engines roared, still in second gear, they sped up the road in a cloud of choking exhaust fumes, leaving a line up of disgruntled drivers awaiting their turn!

A temporary lull in the build up, and the traffic resumed a slightly more passive pace.

Thirty minutes later, and we arrived at the common. Taking off my driving shoes, I donned my boots, and we all set off.

The common was very peaceful, and the sun shone a glorious buttery yellow.

I noticed that the earth had become cracked and baked through weeks of no rain.

Teasing clouds with the prospects of rain soon passed by, but with not even the promise of a compromise.

The blue sky was sketched by the vapour trails of busy aircraft miles above us, as they created a pathway behind them, grumbling and humming their way. Glinting silvery in the sun, they passed overhead, carrying their happy holidaymakers and businessmen, with appointments to be kept, and the prospects of clinching those all-important deals, or maybe a few globe trotters on their quest of the unknown. Perhaps some of them were hopefully chasing their dreams of a new beginning in a new country, and all of them quite oblivious of us little beings scuttling about below them, just busily carrying out our daily mundane chores.

As we headed along the footpath, a little meadow pipit rose suddenly into the air from the tall purple-headed grasses, his song rang out loud and clear, it sounded something like *"tisp-tisp-tisp-til-til-tsi-tsi-tsi"* and then ending with *"tisip."* He had just missed the dainty little speckled butterflies dancing animatedly from flower to flower, searching nectar to sustain their delicate little bodies. Clouds of insects flew into the air as we brushed past the tall, whippy, wild flowers and grasses; the dogs were overjoyed, this was a real treat having their "walkies" so early.

Clutching the box containing Maggie in one hand, with the picnic bag in the other, we made our way on our purposeful mission.

Much depended on this quest. If not successful, the future for Maggie would remain in the balance, but if all went well and I could return him to the wild once more, then all would be forgotten, and it would just be "yesterday's news!"

Now that I was committed to the task in hand, I had decided that the best thing to do was to take the baby bird back to the copse where I had rescued him from the crows.

Then coming towards us, appearing from behind a clump of gorse bushes, was the figure of an elderly lady, who was walking along with her equally elderly little bull terrier dog, waddling just in front of her on his little "Queen Anne" legs. He suddenly perked up and took on a new lease of life when he saw Katie and Hattie trotting towards him, and with his tongue lolling out, his face creased in a cheesy grin, and with his black patch over one slitty eye, he looked just like a doggy-type clown.

The lady puffed her way along the path. She was wearing a pale pink cotton frock, which strained against her ample figure, and her red face was shielded from the sun by a large floppy floral-print sun hat, fitted with a wide pink band, and tied to a large bow at the back. The lady gave an inquisitive look as she drew nearer and noticed the box I was so carefully carrying. Curiosity got the better of her.

"What's in there?" she shyly asked.

"Oh, just a little fledgling bird," I replied guardedly. I then related the story of his rescue to her, as she stepped forward to peek into the box.

"Ooh, isn't it ugly?" she replied.

"Yes, he is rather," I said, looking down at her clownish, squinty-eyed little dog, who promptly cocked his leg and peed on her walking stick, just to show off his macho image to the two girlie dogs. I quickly averted my gaze back to the box when I realised she'd caught my focus of attention.

"Er, he's of unknown origin," I said, hoping this would end the enquiry. It worked, and the couple waddled off, and the elderly lady turned and waved a farewell. Her little dog reluctantly followed, and with his tail down, he ambled along at his normal slow pace. I think he had fallen in love with Hattie.

As the pair disappeared, I felt rather deflated at her remark, almost offended in a way. How could she say such a thing about a poor defenceless little creature? Ugly indeed! Gazing down into the box, I could almost see her point. He wasn't exactly an oil painting, more like graffiti I suppose, but give him time, and a few more feathers, and his appearance would be altogether more pleasing to the eye…hopefully!

Winding our way down the slope, we approached the copse, and from there, the harsh sound of screeching jays could be heard. There was just a fleeting glimpse of their colourful plumage as they flew off into the depths of the trees, but still no sign of magpies.

I was beginning to feel fairly confident as we drew nearer to the familiar birch trees. Plenty of time, and it was still quite early yet, but I knew that as the hours ticked by, the sun would shine down with a lot more power, and it would get much hotter. We would have to find some shade before long.

It didn't take long to find the very same spot where Maggie was rescued. I now had to look for a suitable tree where I could place the box securely. It was not as easy as I thought, it's not every tree that grows "designer branches," especially for shoe boxes to be wedged in them. Finally, I did find a favourable silver birch tree, which had a very comfortable-looking fork through the centre of it, and it was just high enough to be well off the ground and for me to reach on tip-toe.

Before I could lodge the tree's new "tenant" in it, I had first to give Maggie his last big feed before leaving him on his own. Fishing through the bag with our packed lunch, I found the small jar with his precious minced meat. He took it ravenously.

It was almost a sad moment for me to part with him, but I wasn't going to abandon him completely, as I would be keeping an eye on him, and I firmly believed it would in his own interest for him to be raised by his parents, to be with his own kind; after all, this was his birth place.

The little box looked so lonely and pathetic as I left it there, then stepped back to see if it didn't look too conspicuous, in the hope that his parents would find it and carry out their duties to look after him and feed him with all the proper food, which I was unable to do.

In reality, things rarely go according to plan!

I took the dogs to find a nice comfortable spot where we would be concealed, so that I could observe the box at a safe distance. We could now settle down quite happily and have our well-earned picnic.

This could turn out to be a long day, and the dogs soon began to get restless. "Not much going on, and why were we stuck in one spot? It just wasn't on, what with all those lovely bunnies out there to be chased. Had she gone mad or something?…just sitting there and staring at a silly old box!"

It seemed like hours, and still there was no sign of Maggie's mum and dad, and I must admit that by now I was getting rather worried, fearing that the baby bird would surely starve if he didn't get fed soon.

Didn't they care at all?…and had they no conscience?…but then birds don't feel emotions like us humans!

Fidgeting, and feeling a bit numb through sitting too long, I had to keep a careful watch out for any hungry or curious crows who might feel brave enough to attempt another attack, but fortunately there was no sign of them. Come to think of it, there wasn't much sign of any other wildlife in the woods either, which was rather unusual. Just one sudden sharp warning call from a lonesome stonechat rang out and the distant familiar echoing drumming sound of a Woodpecker were the only sounds to be heard.

Looking over at the quiet little box, wondering if its long-suffering inhabitant was not too distraught, I was about to go and check to see if Maggie was okay and give him his overdue feed when there suddenly appeared along our path, and almost certainly blowing our cover, three familiar figures.

The first to greet us all was Dizzy Daisy, and following hot on her tail was Silly Sally, who was huffing and panting like a steam engine.

They were two beautiful golden retrievers, and not too far behind, also panting in hot pursuit, was their ever-anxious owner David.

David was a fellow doggy walker, who we used to frequently meet up with to share our walks across the common, and then along the winding path, which leads down towards the dell.

All four dogs were great friends, and they would run playfully through the bracken and heather, and sometimes they would attempt to hunt bunnies together, whilst David and I would exchange anecdotes.

David was a very good storyteller. His voice was deep and rich and had the flexibility of well-oiled leather, and when he laughed, which was often, it was long and hearty, sounding like great boulders bouncing down a cliff face.

On this particularly hot day, and to cover his six-foot-two well-built frame, David was wearing an Aztec blue T-shirt, sporting a lovely picture of swaying palm trees, one single seagull, and a yacht, and he wore his T-shirt outside of his smart khaki slacks, and on his feet he wore brown sandals without socks, in stark contrast to my "adder-resistant boots." On his head, he wore his usual Bushman's hat, set at a jaunty angle, partly hiding his thick, almost shoulder length, iron-grey hair. He had a twinkle in his piercing blue eyes and a great big smile on his friendly, craggy, lived-in but almost-handsome face (the sort that made you feel safe and comfortable with), which was outlined by a neatly trimmed beard. Unfortunately, his teeth betrayed the fact of his reluctance to visit a dentist, otherwise he was not at all bad looking, for a seventy-five-year-old granddad!

When we first met, David told me that he started his career, after graduating at University, as a lecturer in physics, and that during the second world war, as a young man, he worked for the Ministry of Defence, helping with experiments on explosives and other such new and exciting things, to help blow up the countryside with.

It seems that on one very memorable occasion, never to be forgotten, there was to be a test for a very special new explosive device to be carried out on a deserted beach somewhere in Kent, and to be witnessed by none other than the great man himself—Mr Winston Churchill.

He was surrounded by other high-ranking officers and senior members of the military, and also there were secret service men, all waiting anxiously for the test to begin.

Everyone started by checking and synchronising their watches. They were all looking very efficient and very important indeed, and all were decked out very smartly in their appropriate uniforms and suits.

Everything seemed to be going to plan, until the actual moment of setting the thing off.

Ignition time! Then, all hell was let loose!

It seemed that somebody (nobody knew exactly who of course) must have got their calculations a bit wrong and added just a little bit too much of the ingredients (or whatever), and not having a technical aptitude on this subject, I cannot remember the exact details given to me by David.

Anyway, quite unexpectedly, the "highlight" of the whole proceedings was when there was one almighty bang which almost blew up the entire beach. Sand and pebbles were blasted into the air in all directions, on a much larger scale than anticipated, judging by the huge crater that suddenly appeared before the astonished audience of dignitaries, leaving them standing at the edge, looking down in utter horror.

David said that he stood on one side of the crater, looking across at the disbelieving, distorted, shocked, angry face of Mr. Churchill, with his bowler hat dangling over one eye, and a cigar, almost defying gravity, hanging from his lower lip, and looking like an over-cooked sausage on a barbeque, only this was definitely not that sort of a party!

There was a hush of expectancy from the dumbstruck onlookers.

Then came a small, very shaky, positively frightened, croaky little voice that almost sliced like a razor through the deathly silence that hung in the air.

"Em...I think I may have put just a bit too much...sir!" said the trembling voice, squeakily.

David told me that for what seemed like an eternity, he and all the anxious young inventors and ballistic experts (who at that moment of time felt absolutely mortified) wished that the ocean would part so that they could make a hasty retreat. Instead, they all just stood like wooden soldiers and waited, daring their shaking limbs not to move a muscle, not one inch, hardly daring to breathe, or even fart, as this might attract attention and undoubtedly seal everyone's fate. They were all gripped by fear which could almost be smelt, and guilt oozed from all directions.

I could almost visualize the scene, and a picture formed in my mind as the story gradually unfolded.

David continued to relate what happened next.

He said that when the dust and sand had settled, the highly bemused Mr. Churchill stared hard into the eyes of each man, one by one, muttering unrepeatable words of what he thought of, and where they could actually put their "bl***…inventions!" He then turned and nodded to his V.I.P. guests (now all looking a whole lot less dignified), brushed himself down, then holding his head high, he sniffed in the air, in a sort of defiant way, and with his tattered hat once more pressed firmly on his head and hands clenched behind his back, the small, dejected, and by now thoroughly embarrassed party, then made their way slowly up the newly formed sand dunes.

One can only look back on this very unfortunate incident and wonder if it could have been this very impromptu seaside war game that influenced Mr. Churchill's famous speech: "We will fight them on the beaches!"

There were definitely no George Medals awarded on that day.

I still wonder, even now, if this vivid, very colourful and detailed story, as told by David, is actually true. I would like to think it is.

I was brought back to the present situation when David told me to be on the lookout for thugs, who had been reported to the police. It was thought that they had been out on the common with terrier dogs, digging for badgers, and that he had only yesterday seen a small group of very unsavoury looking men with small Jack Russel dogs. They appeared to be very wary when David passed by, and he was very concerned that I would be staying in one area, particularly in the loneliest part of the woods, not frequently used by other walkers, as the path was rather overgrown with overhanging willow trees, and thick blackberry bushes with needle-sharp thorns didn't entice anyone to push past them either, so it could be quite deserted there. I told him not to worry, and that I wouldn't be staying much longer, and would most certainly heed his words of caution about the evil men with spades and little Jack Russel dogs.

After bidding farewell to David and giving the two golden heads of Sally and Daisy a loving pat, I decided that enough was enough, and that there was not a lot to be achieved by staying on the common for much longer.

My mind was made up. It was now getting quite late in the afternoon, and the lemon yellow sun would soon be melting to a golden orange, heralding another lovely sunset. Besides, poor Maggie would by now be a very hungry little bird.

I quickly retrieved the box from the tree; there were loud squeaks coming from inside. They sounded very urgent, but not weak, thank goodness, and not surprisingly, Maggie took his feed very hungrily and seemed almost pleased to see me.

As we made our way back to the car park, I could see blue mist was forming over the landscape, dulling the panoramic view over the county, but it was still very hot and humid.

In the distance, high up, and slowly drifting across the big orange sun, and for a moment giving the appearance of an eclipse, a huge hot air balloon was slowly and silently approaching; glowing like a large silvery pear. Every so often, fire could be seen belching in short bursts beneath the canopy as the burners ignited, making a roaring sound like an approaching dragon.

When we arrived back at the car park, most of the cars had already left, except for two other vehicles, which were parked side by side. One was a mud-stained, open-topped jeep, and the other was a bashed-up-looking land rover, minus a wing mirror and half a number plate, which was tied on with a piece of string, and it had a splash of bright red and orange paint along one side, with a gaudy design which looked as though somebody had tried to make it look like a blaze of lightning.

Loading up the two dogs once more onto the back seat of the car and placing the confused little bird in his box into the boot, having endured his last trip back to his natural territory, I felt somewhat disappointed after my unsuccessful attempt at trying to return him back to his mum and dad.

It was only after changing my boots for my more comfortable driving shoes, and then placing my boots on the floor behind the passenger seat, along with the flask, that I suddenly realized I had forgotten my lunch box! I must have left it beneath the tree where we were hiding. "Oh drat!" I said out loud to the two dogs and the magpie, "I'll just have to go back and fetch our goodie box!" I'd remembered to pick up the flask in a hurry, but I'd stupidly forgotten to bring the box and glass jar.

Calling Katie out of the car to join me, I fetched her lead from the boot and tied it around my waist, knowing that rabbits were more likely to start coming out to graze now that evening was approaching, and because their scent would be so strong in the warm evening air, and her instinct to hunt would be too overwhelming for her, I didn't want Katie chasing off after them into the dark, so there might just be a need for it. It turned out to be a very wise decision in the end.

Leaving Hattie on her own with Maggie, I wound the window down a little to let some air in, because even though the sun was slowly sinking to the west, it was still quite hot.

I hastened along the path towards the copse where I hoped to find the box; it seemed to take an age, which is always the case when you want to get somewhere quickly, just like when you're waiting for a kettle to boil! I was anxious to get home as soon as I could so that I could take a nice cool shower, have supper, watch telly for a while, then go to bed, but first of all I would have to settle the little bird somewhere comfortable and quiet, to give him (or her) a better chance to recover from the ordeal.

At long last the belt of trees came into view as we wound our way down towards them. The strong odour of fox and rabbit hung about the common, and a thin mist circled the trees. I kept Katie close to me in case she took off along another path; in which case if she did find the temptation of smells too much, and decided to veer off; heaven knows when she would return to me again!

I approached the small copse where we had had our lunch break all those hours ago. I bent down to take a closer look behind one of the trees (where I felt sure I must have placed the box) and I searched the grassy area in vain. Where on earth could I have left it? It was just at that moment when I heard voices in the distance approaching. Men's voices!

I suddenly remembered David's urgent warning about "badger baiters!" and I froze on the spot.

I could hear them getting nearer! What should I do? Ignore them and stand up, and then walk nonchalantly away, whistling, and try to look very normal and unconcerned? Or should I risk being spotted, and run like the wind? Or would it be best to wait and see if they decide to go off in another direction?

I decided to wait and see!

I edged slowly backwards towards a clump of brambles, where I could peep out from behind, hopefully without them spotting me or Katie.

Unclipping Katie's lead from about my waist, I slipped it slowly over her head, careful not to make the chain link of the choke-chain clink (a bit of a tongue-twister!) in case they heard it. I was *so* glad that I had decided to bring her lead with me.

I could hear their gruff voices, and from my hiding place I could see that there were three of them. One was quite short and stocky, one was tall and thin, whilst the other one was of average height and build, and they had Jack Russell terriers with them! Then I caught sight of a glint of metal. *They must be carrying spades with them!* I thought to myself, and I was quite convinced that they must be the badger baiters that David had spoken of.

Oh no! I thought, *this can't be real! It's like a bad dream, and I shouldn't be here!*

I heard one of them say, "Well I reckon there must be somebody about here somewhere because there's that car on its own in the car park, with that little poncey poodle sitting all tart-like on the back seat, and it looks as though there's some other sort of an animal or something in the boot, a young rabbit perhaps, and I'm sure I saw it move! Now I reckon that there's someone out there who's something to do with those 'animal rights' busybodies, so I suggest we should either go back to the car park and wait and see if anyone returns there, or we could just scout around here for a bit first!"

Don't scout!…don't scout! I screamed inwardly to myself. Oh my goodness! They'd obviously spotted Hattie and the little bird in the back of the car. This piece of news was not at all good!

Then another voice called out, "Hey!…come over here a minute!…look what I've found, Doug!…someone's been here all right, and I shouldn't wonder they've been snooping around long enough to even bring their lunch!"

I saw the speaker of this all important news (the shortest one of the three) pick up *my* lunch box.

The man then picked out one of the empty sandwich bags and sniffed it.

"This one makes me feel a bit peckish!" he exclaimed. Then he picked up the glass jar which was inside the box and gave it a noisy sniff! "Ugh!" he spluttered, "this is absolutely *disgusting!*" Then he promptly threw the box, with its empty bag and jar, straight towards me and into the bramble bush, where it caught high up. The glass jar parted company from the box, where it fell with a soft thud onto the grass immediately behind me.

Now I know how Goldilocks must have felt when she was confronted by the three bears! This was getting too close for comfort, and no way could I show myself now! The hairs on the back of my neck started to tingle with fear, and Katie's ruff on her back started to rise in response, and I could hear a slight rumble coming from her throat. "Shsh!" I hushed in Katie's ear and tightened my grip on her lead. I could feel the vibration of her low growl through my hand as I placed it on her throat, willing her to stop. Fortunately she did, but her hackles were still raised, and her lips were curled back in a silent snarl. My breathing became shallow as I tried to control it, and my heart began to thump and beat so fast I feared that they might hear it, and then I would surely be discovered!

"Litter bug!" one of the men called out in a mocking voice, "go and fetch that box, Sid, you're the tallest, and it might come in useful for us!"

Sid, the tall one, lit a cigarette with a match, and the light from it showed up a five o'clock shadow on his jutting chin, and the dark stubble made his face look even more menacing and cruel, and gave the impression that he was the type who found pleasure in torturing innocent animals. Tossing the spent matchstick to one side, he grunted some sort of reply and started to move in my direction.

My throat went very dry, and beads of sweat started to slowly trickle down my face, causing my hair to cling uncomfortably to the sides of my face and across my eyes, and my hands started to feel clammy as fear set in. Now was the time not to panic, but to act fast, *very* fast, otherwise I could find myself in deep water, or an even more dangerous situation, if I was caught out hiding behind bushes! They would no doubt think that I was spying on them.

I turned my head very slowly, not wanting to lose focus on what was going on in front of me. Behind me, and not too far away, I spotted a ridge slightly rising above the ground, and I could just see the tufted grass on top. Thank goodness for those wartime dugouts! This could be my only chance for our salvation, so it was now or never!

I slowly rolled myself away from the bush, curled up like a hedgehog, pulling Katie along with me, and trying desperately not to make any noise. It seemed to take forever, but finally I was able to heave myself over the top of the ridge by first flattening myself out, and then by carefully keeping myself as flat to the ground as possible, I inched my way to the top. Then Katie and I plopped almost together, and almost noiselessly, straight down and into the dugout, which was quite overgrown now over the years, so I was hoping that we could keep ourselves reasonably hidden. Katie was quite happy about the situation because this was very familiar ground to her. I couldn't say the same for myself, however!

At least the sound of the men's voices were gradually becoming more muffled, giving me hope that they were by now a reasonable distance away from us, and I needed to get us both well away from our present position. The only way was onwards, and hopefully, upwards!

Crawling along on my hands and knees, I began to wonder what on earth I was doing right now, behaving like a child, and crawling along a ditch—Indian-style!

I didn't have to think along these lines for long. I was about to heave myself up to see where we were, when the ground beneath me unexpectedly and suddenly gave way, and I found myself tumbling downwards, with piles of loose earth, leaves, and dozens of stones of all sizes, came tumbling after me, followed by Katie, who landed right on top of me!

I spluttered gritty earth out of my mouth, and wiped leaves away from my eyes and nose so that I could see and breathe once more! Then I became really horrified and almost panicked! I could hardly see! There was no daylight to be seen! There was complete darkness everywhere! I could stand upright, but I had no idea how far down I had fallen, and I had no idea either, in which direction I should start to take step towards, or indeed if it was safe to do so! It was too late now for regrets. I had really landed myself in a right old pickle, and there was no going back, even if I wanted to. And I most certainly wanted to!

Cautiously, I shuffled my left foot in front of me and then to the side, and then I repeated the same procedure with my right foot. The ground seemed firm enough and didn't appear to have any obstructions. I stepped slowly to one side of what I can only describe as a tunnel or den, and then carefully continued to step sideways to the other side, just to try and gauge the distance between the walls.

The walls were banked by solid earth, and it was like being in a giant rabbit warren or an oversized badger's set.

Could this be the secretly hidden tunnel that my mother had told me about when I was a child, or was it a wartime dugout?

Judging by the size of this one, there could be a whole network of tunnels down here! How far did they go, and where did they lead to? And most intriguing of all: what were they used for? They might even have some connection with the ley line, which is supposed to have special energies, or even paranormal properties.

I tried to put this possibility to the back of my mind, otherwise I would have started to imagine all kinds of spooky things!

The most important thing right now was to find my way out of here. But which way should I go?

I had to move blindly along, moving cautiously in case of another cave-in of earth and debris, or I might stumble on an obstruction in my path that could injure me, and then what would I do? And I doubt very much if anybody could hear me down here. Then it slowly dawned on me. What if I could never find my way out of here? And what if nobody could find me? Oh well, no time to ponder on what ifs!

Holding onto Katie's lead and letting her walk in front of me, I began to feel more confident, but worried at the same time.

This must lead to somewhere, but I had no idea where it might end. The air down there was cool and musky, and the smell of damp earth and leaves was quite strong, but not unpleasant. The tunnel must have been unused for many years, and I didn't think anyone else could have found it, because I certainly didn't stumble upon or come across any discarded tin-cans or bottles. It seemed to be completely litter free!

I could hear a ghostly moaning sound which seemed to be coming from behind me, and it was followed by a rush of cool air.

Could it be the ghosts of lost souls who'd perished during the war, or died from their wounds after trying to take refuge in this tunnel during a bombing raid? Maybe this was a dugout after all, and perhaps people really had died down here, and were their ghosts searching for whoever had disturbed them, and what if I came across their remains? Hopefully it was just the sound of the wind whistling and howling along the passageways.

I shivered, and my teeth chattered, and I began to wish that I'd brought a cardigan with me.

Occasionally I caught a glimpse of daylight, which was only faint because it would very soon be dark outside, and it seemed to come from where the tunnel narrowed towards the top to just a small slit, allowing the light to filter down. There was no hope at all of me climbing up through the gap, as the walls were too steep, and the opening would be too narrow to climb through anyway, so I would just have to plod on and hope for the best. Was I moving in a straight line or just going in a large circle? I was soon to find out when I came upon a change in the walls, as I suddenly found a space on both sides. I had arrived at cross-roads!

Which way should I take now? Left or right? I decided to turn left! It felt right to me—somehow!

As I walked along, I came to a slight dip in the earth, from where a gentle—but distant—thumping sound could be heard directly beneath me. It was almost like the rhythm of a heart beat, and whilst I stood still over the spot, I could feel a strange sensation pass through my body, like electrical pulses, or as though I was being drawn down through the ground by a magnetic field. Perhaps this was the very centre of the meridian line, and I was picking up a channel of the earth's energy!

I didn't stop for too long, in case something really awful should happen to me for remaining there, so I hurried along after Katie.

Then further along the passageway, there was another sound overhead, but this time it was more like the rumble of thunder, which came and went at intervals, and it seemed to be coming from all directions. For a short space of time, the sound would stop, and then it would begin again. Could we now be walking under the main road, and it was the sound of traffic passing by that we could hear?

It felt quite eerie and spooky down there, and my footfalls sounded muffled, with not a hint of an echo, and I could hear Katie panting just in front of me.

I could hear other sounds of scuffling and scratching. Probably we were disturbing small mammals like voles, mice, or even little shrews. Perhaps they thought we were oversized moles taking over their territory. I was hoping and praying that I wouldn't bump into cobwebs, or even big spiders. I dislike spiders!…a lot!…and I didn't fancy being Miss Muffet waiting for a spider to settle on me!…and I had no desire to be like Robert the Bruce either! He was the famous Scottish King, born in 1274, who was intrigued by watching a spider (whilst he sat inside a cave) as it tried to spin its web, time and time again, until eventually it succeeded, and this inspired the great king to strive in his battles against England, and to eventually gain independence. I couldn't feel any inspiration coming my way from inside *my* cave, in any shape or form, and I definitely had no ambition at all to do heroic battle with those unsavoury looking thugs out there, waiting for me to return to my car on the common!

It was whilst I was thinking about spiders and kings, when all of a sudden I stumbled straight into something that felt like sinewy arms that grabbed at my whole body, and as I fell forward headlong, I found myself trapped in a mass of oddly shaped tentacle-type limbs, which although they appeared to be quite springy, they hardly moved! Like a frightened rabbit caught in a snare, I was too frightened to even scream out. I kept as still as a statue until I felt sure that nothing would give way beneath me, or that I would become more tangled up in this awful trap. Having overcome my initial fright, I was much relieved to find that this "thing" hadn't harmed me and wasn't a threat at all! In fact, after a close inspection by running my hands cautiously down the "tentacles" which had stopped me in my tracks and held me fast there, I soon discovered that this "giant octopus" was actually thick tree roots dangling down through the centre of the tunnel. I could hear Katie puffing away as she returned to me, sensing that something must be wrong. She came up close to me where she found me stuck fast in the middle of the tree roots, and she promptly started to lick my face, as though she was trying to comfort me, and to tell me that everything would be all right, and what was I waiting for? After untangling myself from the roots, I pulled myself up once more, and following Katie, we continued uneventfully on our way.

Then at last, joy of all joys! I could see daylight just ahead of me, and the pathway was slowly rising.

Puffing my way up, with Katie in the lead, I pulled myself out of a hole, which was on the edge of a field, and next to the hedge, with the main road on the other side. Standing up and blinking in the daylight (which was by now getting dusk), I dusted off the dirt and leaves as much as I could and tried to get my bearings. To my astonishment and delight when I peered over the top of the hedge, I could see the main road, and there on the other side was my great-Granddad's old pub, The Horns Lodge, and where my mother had lived all those years ago.

Trying not to look too conspicuous, I opened the field gate, and still feeling a bit shaky and disorientated after stumbling about in a dark place for so long, I started to walk the half-mile distance back to the common car park.

I was feeling very worried about poor little Hattie, and poor little Maggie, still waiting in the car, hoping that they were both okay, and that Maggie was still alive!

The road was the same one that I walked along with my brother all those years ago when we used to go on our early morning rambles, and we passed the parish Saxon Church, with its very high pointed spire, which was where Mother and Father were married, and then the little infant's school, which Mother attended as a little girl. The surrounding fence was very cleverly designed as large wooden crayon pencils, in many different colours, complete with pointed, sharpened ends. We then had to pass the field entrance (which was supposed to be haunted) where Mother used to sit on top of the wooden five-bar gate as a teenager to wait for her friend. The wooden gate had obviously rotted away, and was now replaced by a new metal one. We then passed by the same old oak tree, which my brother and I used to walk under on those same early morning rambles, and it was still standing there, with its locked-in memories. As we walked slowly past, I casually wondered if it was the same tree (whose roots I had stumbled upon in the tunnel), and if it *was* the very same old oak, I wondered if it had registered *my* little mishap! I patted its gnarled old trunk and reverently bid it "a very good night!" then hurried on towards the common.

Rounding the "Z" bend in the road, I could see looming up in front of us the familiar windmill with its brilliantly white sails looking like the starched petals of a huge daisy against the darkening sky. Not far now!

I took the road past the windmill and carried on towards the back road to reach the car park, and as we got nearer, I slowed down to take stock of the situation.

If the two cars were still there, should I walk past and come back at intervals to see if they had gone, or should I take the risk and get straight in and drive off?

My worst fears were apparent, as I could see the two vehicles still parked in the same spot.

As I had no idea as to when the men might be returning, and it was getting darker by the minute, I had to take a risk that they would be some time yet, and get in and drive off as fast as I could. I waited a few seconds to listen out for any sign of them returning. All was quiet except for the distant hoot of an owl.

Leading Katie quickly over to the car, treading softly so that I didn't make too much crunching sound on the gravel in the car park, which was more like a dust-bowl in this heat-wave, I turned the key in the lock of the door, hoping it wouldn't make too much noise, and after a bit of fumbling with the keys, the central locking device unlocked with a mechanical sounding thunk! I shoved Katie quickly into the back seat, alongside the patiently waiting Hattie, but I didn't have time to check the baby bird in the boot (to see if it was still all right) and then closed the car doors gently, went over to the driver's side, and thankful that I was already wearing my driving shoes, I jumped in.

Once inside the car, I pushed the buttons down to centrally lock all the doors, which made me feel more secure and safe. I hesitated a few seconds before turning the ignition on (I needed it to respond at the first turn) so when I did, I turned it very sharply and firmly. Thank

God the engine growled into life! I put my foot down onto the pedals and engaged the gears first into reverse, then backing up a few yards, I quickly went into first gear and slammed my foot down onto the gas pedal, gritted my teeth, and gave it full throttle!

My exit from the common would have done the "boy racers" proud.

It wasn't just a cloud of dust that followed me...it was more of a sand storm!

At last we were on our way home, and my experience as a cave woman, or a pot-holer, was over!

I was not too sure how I was going to explain to my anxious parents about my rather unusual day, and how I was almost trapped by the "badger baiters," and then how I had discovered the network of tunnels and my long walk back to the car park.

If I told them, would anybody believe me anyway?

– Chapter Two and a Half –
Over to Maggie

…fly me to the moon and let me play among the stars…

Well, I dunno, a bird in my state of health and present situation can only take so much. There I was, after a lovely dollop of grub was forced down me gullet—I wasn't complainin', mind, an' enjoying a good kip, which I needed after enduring such a big beak bash yesterday, which fairly knocked the egg yolk from me gizzard— when I finds myself all woken up, much too soon for my liking, but at least I was given some more of this tasty morsel stuff. Then, before you could count the spots on a chicken's egg, I was whisked off once more to me hatching zone, and enduring once again, a fearfully feather-fluffing flight in the giant klakki.

Oh misery me! What a state to be in! Here I woz, sitting in this small, smelly, smooth, square klakki in a tree I had never seen before and in an area swarming with big, black, beastly beakies, and no doubt they were all geared up and ready to swoop down on me! No problem! Oh happy days! What a wally! If this pinky had a brain, she'd be a half wit! Now what do I do? Do I just sit and wait for the café to open and end up as pick 'n' mix, or should I pretend to be dead?

I chose the latter.

I just sat there, quiet as a little-green-froggy-in-a-jelly-dobble-drop (frog's spawn), so at least I had been fed (which was fair enough) an' then placed in a sheltered but warm spot (not to be snivelled at) but when a handsome "king of the sky" in waitin', such as I, is unceremoniously placed once more in a dangerous situation, like a piece of "long ears" (rabbit) on a fondue date, and is invited as the main course (well out of order!), then I was not feeling over excited at the prospects of not having a long and happy life. If I had little knees, they would be a-shakin' right now, an' if I 'ad teeth, they would be a-chatterin'. Instead, of which, all me quality quills were a-quivering. The only thing I could do now was to try and sleep, and dream.

I started to dream of nice things to remember about, before me "all-too-sudden change of lifestyle" took a downward plunge!

It was only a few owl hoots ago, as the lightness became black as a raven's wing, and all around became silent, that me egg layer and egg maker told me and my three brothers and three sisters lots of wonderful stories to keep us all quiet so that our enemies wouldn't hear us, and it gave us something to think about whilst they were out hunting for food.

Ma was called Silver Tongue, because she could sing like a lark, especially in thunderstorms. She told us that if she sang loud enough, it would drown out the loud noise of the thunder, and as if by magic, it would then stop raining!

Pa was called Mossy, because he likes to collect lots of moss to fill up our klakki with, and this makes it nice and warm and cosy. Us young'uns don't have names given to us until we have earned them one way or another, so I'm blessed if I know what they would have called me!

Oh how I miss these nice familiar things!

We were told that long, long ago, in our great, ever-so-great ancestors' time, there were more big pinkies roving about on our territory. They herded their big, noisy, smelly, woolly animals, to graze amongst the heather and trees, which the big pinkies would cut down to make great burning fires, where they would cook one of their said woolly animals and other tasty goodies.

These goings-on frightened our ancestors very much, but in time they got used to living with the pinkies living in their hovels so near to them. The magpies even took advantage of their newly acquired courage, and became quite bold, so much so, they would fly down to the still smouldering fires in the early hours, just after sunrise, and pinch some of the discarded cooked meat from the warm ashes, but just cool enough to touch! At worst, some of the unfortunate magpies (who were so intent on stealing the meat) wouldn't see a more alert pinky, who happened to be skulking around on the lookout, and on spotting the thief, the sharp-eyed pinky would fling stones, with awesome accuracy, and kill the luckless bird, who would then be cooked and eaten…in triumph! Ugh!

We didn't like that story very much, I can tell you.

Then many suns and moons later, other humans moved in (just like migrating swallows), and they were called "earth wanderers."

These earth wanderers came with their round, slow moving klakkies, which were pulled along by these big black and white "earth grazers" (horses).

These new strangers to the area fed on wild creatures of the woods and fields, like the horny-backed hedge-ramblers (hedgehogs), and the long-ears (hoppity-rabbity-bunny-wunnies), which were caught by snares and traps, and they also caught pigeons and blackbirds.

Sometimes small "earth runners" (dogs) were used to hunt, and then they would kill the long-ears.

These earth runners could quite easily dig out any unfortunate long-ears, who would then run helter-skelter underground to hide from capture in their deep, ever-so-long burrows.

All of these creatures were then cooked on the earth wanderers' fires.

Fortunately, they didn't catch many magpies, because by that time they had become used to avoiding these new arrivals, who turned out to be fierce hunters, as they went about the place brandishing their long sticks and stones, which they used as weapons to kill, or sometimes snares and traps!

Another scary story frightens me even to *think* about.

We were told of the giant worms, with flashy dashing stripes and flicking forked tongues, who could gobble up any young magpie who happened to fall into their path, as they slithered and hissed their way along the sunbaked heath land.

This particular story would make us huddle up closer to one another, so as not to get too near the edge of the klakki, in case we fell out, an' this tale definitely kept us all quiet, until we forgot about it, of course, an' it woz all about our Great Uncle Sidney Snake Snitcher.

Now Great Uncle Sidney Snake Snitcher woz the one who found out that these giant worms were not worms at all, but nasty old snakes (but then you all knew this already of course, being clever pinkies); these nasty old slitherers were best left alone, an' certainly not worth trying to catch and eat. But this didn't stop Great Uncle Sidney Snake Snitcher (or S.S., as he woz called for short) from catching them unawares, and then he used to creep up on them whilst they were all coiled up and sunbathing in the bracken, or just sleeping peacefully on top of a rock. He would pick 'em up by the tail and twirl 'em around and around, singing:

> *Oh Jumping*
> *Jacks,*
> *Going*
> *Rat-a-Tat-Tat,*
> *Seething,*
> *Squealing,*
> *Falling*
> *Reeling,*
> *Going*
> *Splat-Splat-Splat,*
> *On your*
> *scaly old*
> *backs!*

Letting the giant worms go, he watched them whiplash through the air, hissing and cursing all the way, and he would then mock and taunt them mercilessly, then he would fall about, cackling with glee as they landed at a safe distance in an angry heap.

One sunlight-time, though, he got a nasty shock.

Those hissy fellers decided to get one over on him.

They lay in wait at the edge of the path, knowing that he would soon be along as usual, looking for them at their favourite resting place.

When he swooped down in his usual manner and done a few bounces along the ground, they all leapt out of their hiding place from under the bracken, and each one grabbed a piece of him, two grabbed each leg. Two of 'em grabbed his wings, and one grabbed his long tail, an' then they spat and cursed, squiggled and squirmed, pulled and bit, then they hissed at him, saying, *"Death by a thousand bites-s-s-s!!!"* till his feathers all stood on end. He gaggled an' squawked, and then he turned a spectacular somersault, then he landed up by laying all dead, with his feet stuck straight up in the air!

And so that was the end of poor old Great Uncle Sidney S.S.!

We loved to hear about Lace Wing. She was our great, great, great, ever-so-great grand egg layer, an' she woz known to be very beautiful and gentle, an' she would spend her days looking for and collecting sharp shiny objects, which would dazzle you when the sun shone on them. She would then hide them in a secret place known only to herself.

We were told there is a great hoard of hidden treasure somewhere on the common, somewhere amongst the honey-scented gorse.

Now on one sunlight-time, Lace Wing had collected a pretty piece of green glass she had found lying in the grass, and she dropped it (as she usually did) somewhere amongst the dry bracken.

It had been a very hot summer that particular nesting season, and everything was tinder dry, an' it woz said that many creatures had died on the common through a great thirst, owing to the lack of "The-sweet-life-giver-from-the-sky-which-you-can-drink-or-bathe-in" (otherwise known as rain to you pinkies!).

The sun cast very hot rays down on that precious green glass, and as if by some kind of magic, a great smoke came up from the ground, then lots of flames, and it wasn't long before there woz a great fire everywhere. Most of the birds were able to escape, the older ones that could take to the air, but many klakkies caught fire, and the young ones perished, and poor old Lace Wing vanished!

It was thought she left the neighbourhood with deep remorse, or that she may have died in an attempt to save her treasure.

We shall never know what really became of her.

Pa told us that his aunt, that would be our great aunt, Cheg Leigh of Beggars Wood, laid a very loopy egg which hatched out into his cranky cousin Moonbeam.

Now Moonbeam had an extra thin band of white along each wing, which gave him a very flashy appearance.

Moonbeam foolishly thought he could fly up to the moon, "To see where it starts!… How big it is!… And if I can eat it!?" He would fly up as far as he could, until he was just a black and white speck in the distance, getting further and further (which wouldn't normally be very far, as we're not such high fliers like the skylarks, doing their solar system surfing and shuffling around the stars no doubt!), and with his long tail-end streaming downwards, he would fly crazily around in circles, getting dizzier and dizzier. Then after a bit, he would spiral back to earth at great speed, crying out, "I have found some adorable little green moon bugs, and they make ideal pets for the chicks in the klakkies!… Or if they're *too* big and juicy looking to keep as pets, then you can *eat* them instead! I have collected pollen from the moon, and bits of lovely, lushy, lunar morsels, so now I am going to spread moon dust everywhere, and then have my lunar supper!"

Everyone thought he was pretty daft and a big show-off who wanted all the attention, and sometimes, just before landing, he'd say, "It's so good to be back, and 'coz I had a good trip, now I'm over the moon!" He would then sing his cheery little song, which went like this:

> *Twinkling shining stars so bright,*
> *do you only glow at night?*
>
> *Up above the earth so high,*
> *hanging in the sky to dry.*
>
> *Twinkle, twinkle for a bit,*
> *wait and see if you will drip!*
>
> *Lighting up the ink-black sky,*
> *watching moonbeam pass you by.*
>
> *Twinkle, twinkle oh so far,*
> *like a long lost lonely star.*
>
> *On big fluffy clouds you fly,*
> *like a scarecrow in the sky.*

Poor thing, he must have been addled as a hatchling!

On one of his orbital trips, Moonbeam went on his usual "skateroo" about the universe, where he had a right old fling!

Now after he'd mingled, and had lots of fun amongst the stars, and after he had a go on the Big Dipper, he said he had a right old barney along the Milky Way with Jack and his wagon. It seems that old Jack was havin' a race with Charles Wain at the time, and just 'coz Moonbeam had roughly pushed his way in front of the queue at the North Star, when he tried to order a glass of Milk Stout and a pint of Scrumpy, to be followed by a stick of Jupiter-on-the-Rocks and a Mars Bar, that they all created a right old rumpus when they (that is to say Jack, Charles, and Moonbeam) had a bit of a dog fight between themselves.

Moonbeam said that he won this particular round in the end! What a right old muddle he caused everywhere!

Then he flew straight on to Venus to fetch a message to take to Mars, saying how sorry Mercury was at kicking up so much of a dust storm in the galaxy, making the great god, Zeus, sneeze and blow out the moon and stars, creating total darkness, and sending meteorites in all directions, and causing some of the planets getting lost thereof.

It was then that the great goddess, Isis, flew in when she saw what had happened, and it made her very cross indeed. She rounded up all the rebels by cracking thunderbolts at them and made them repair the damage that they had done, telling them that they must restore the moon and stars once more to their shining glory. She gave each of 'them a long tail feather from a peacock to do the cleaning with, saying that she would be able to keep an eye on them at all times to make sure that the job was done properly, even if she wasn't there in person, so they all had to work jolly hard, wondering all the time what she meant, because they just couldn't see her anywhere!

It wasn't until the moon and stars were all nicely dusted up and put back into place that they understood what Isis meant when she told them that she could watch them at all times, for there, on top of the peacock's feathers, they could see the eye of Isis staring straight back at them, which can still be seen on peacock's feathers, even to this day. This is probably the reason why peacocks still shimmy, shammy and shake their tail feathers so vigorously—just so's to rid themselves of all that "sneeze-making moon and star dust!"

Well, it seems that after all this excitement, Moonbeam had a right old job looking for Mars, because he nearly took the wrong turn at the Southern Cross, but when he was able to find his way again, he bumped into Mars all of a sudden like, and he found that the old war lord was out looking for Aries, the ram, 'coz the stupid animal was overdue for shearing!... So Mars had told him, and then to cap it all, Aries got chased off by Sirius, the dog star, who suddenly turned his attention on Pluto, who was being taken out for a run by Andromeda (said to be a beautiful princess) riding Pegasus, the flying horse, on her way to the plough to meet the Gemini twins when suddenly Sirius and Pluto started an almighty dog fight! They were soon sorted out by Leo, the lion, who was out on a date with one of the seven sisters. Leo got really angry with the two heavenly canines and told them if they didn't behave, he would set Taurus, the bull, onto them, and that soon stopped their nonsense.

After this great big lunar fight, Moonbeam found himself right in the path of a passing shooting star, and he got an almighty bashing on his bonce, which sent him into a spectacular spin, and as he descended, he was heard to be hollering: "Owee! Owee! Ow!... Me 'ead!... Me 'ead!... I've got shell shock!... I'm doomed!" But of course, all 'e 'ad woz one 'ell of an 'eadache!

Trouble is that on one of his mad aerial displays, when he was accompanied by his equally crazy cousin Chatterbox, old Moonbeam was on his way back down when he met a rising phoenix.

The creature suddenly appeared from the middle of the common and was obviously on its way up. It's great smouldering wings were splayed out, and it had a bright green olive branch firmly grasped between its huge, strong talons.

"Going up?" the phoenix ventured to ask as its coal black eyes, with a hint of red, shone brightly in the sunlight.

"No!... Going down!" replied Moonbeam, wondering at the same time if this great creature had met up with his relative Lace Wing (who, you may remember, caused the great fire on the common), and wasn't that Lace Wing's treasured piece of green glass attached to its breast? Or was it a precious emerald gemstone?

"Oh!... And where did you get your lovely green twig from?" Moonbeam ventured to ask, not wanting to mention the stone in case this was being a bit too pushy. "And where are you going?"

"I come from the tree of knowledge!" came the echoing reply, "and I'm going back to the beginning, from whence I came, and you, my friend, you are following the wrong path, the path of the untruths!"

As it turned its wise old head towards him, Moonbeam could hear the great crest on its head open then close with a strange, dull clapping sound, and from the centre of one of its hawk-like eyes, he imagined he could see the whole of the earth, and many strange things happening which he didn't understand.

Chatterbox related that he could see flashes of light, "just like shooting stars within the creature's eyes." And there was billowing smoke rising, and when it had cleared, he could see what looked like yellow rain, or could it have been red tears (he wasn't too sure at this point), and there was a blur of many different colours, followed by falling petals of some sort.

What was it that he was witnessing, and what could it all mean!?

Then from the phoenix's beautiful chestnut wings fell tiny shards of what looked like glass, or perhaps they were icicles, glinting sharply in the sun, sending splashes of light in all directions and twinkling brightly like fireflies.

Chatterbox said he was fairly dazzled by the sight as he and Moonbeam looked on, and as the glittering shards slowly drifted down to the earth, they scattered and settled gently on the common. It is said that tiny fronds of bracken suddenly sprang up from these magic glass seedlings, like little baby cobras uncoiling, turning the once scorched earth to a vivid green again.

Moonbeam and Chatterbox watched as the phoenix slowly disappeared into the distance, and they noticed that it had released its grasp on the olive branch, and as a small piece of twig detached itself, they saw a beautiful white dove fly gracefully down through the spectrum of an arched rainbow (which seemed to manifest itself, although it hadn't rained very much that season) and then catching the twig deftly in its beak. They both watched it fly off into the distance.

The white dove called back in a soft voice, "Vroo!... Croo!... Vroo!... Croo!... Peace to you too!... to you too!"

Moonbeam replied back, "Oh!... Real cool!" and then, "Oh blast me giddy aunt's egg shells to pieces!" he said as he missed his landing patch, and he dived head first, straight into a barrel of cider, which was conveniently standing outside of a giant klakki (known to the pinkies as a pub called The Horns Lodge), and the lid was carelessly pushed to one side, leaving a gap just wide enough for Moonbeam's body to plop through.

Chatterbox told everyone that before Moonbeam hit the fermenting, intoxicating, sweet-smelling brew, he could hear his rather loud echoing voice, "Don't think thish ish the right path...hic!... Tharr I should've taken...hic!"

He then spluttered to the surface once or twice, laughing his head off, then in a gurgling, spluttering voice, "I shink I quite likesh shish beak-bending bevvy," then, "Jusht a minute!"...*gulp!*... BURP!... "I'll jusht heave meshelf!... Upsh a daishy!... And shee what 'appens," gurgle, gurgle.

Then he was seen to pop out of the barrel and went flippity-flappity, loop-the-loop, wing-over-beak, and straight opposite was a deep, deep, deep, ever-so-deep well, where Moonbeam landed with a splish! and a splosh! and then everything went quiet, with not a sound to be heard from the bottom of the well.

It's thought that Moonbeam must have found a secret way out at the bottom of the well and straight down into the middle of the earth and was probably lost in another kingdom. But they certainly never saw him again!

Everyone said they were going to miss Moonbeam's star-studded stories.

The magpies made up a little ditty after Moonbeam's disappearance, which went like this:

Flip! flap! he fell!
Moonbeam's in the well!
He kicked a star,
and went too far,
so now he's rung the bell!

An old friend of Pa's told of an ancient friend of his called Rumple Scruff, who woz out scavenging one sunrise on the common, and the earth woz very wet, when he heard a thunderous roar coming from the sky, and when he looked up to see where the noise woz coming from, he saw a huge iron bird in the sky with smoke pouring out and flames all over its back. Then suddenly, he saw a frightening-looking big pinky fall out of the gigantic iron bird with what could only be described as a *huge* mushroom-looking thing, with thick cobwebs attached to it, billowing out from the top of him. And then he saw it land with a *thud!* right in the middle of the bracken. Rumple Scruff said he didn't hang around to see where this thing went!

He also told of these great big noisy iron birds that flew over in great numbers, and they dropped screeching godless firebolts from the sky that landed all over the place in great puffs of smoke!

I wonder if his story is true?

Well here I still sits in this hot metal klakki, all patient like, an' with this white fluffy earth runner to keep me company. I could have done worse! Come to think of it, I could have done a whole lot better!

Why oh why didn't me Ma and Pa come to rescue me? I thinks that they must've been driven off by those to big fat crows, or perhaps a wolf's-head (fox) had got 'em!

Sunlight is passing by and forcing me eyes open. I could see that the fearsome heath spirit drifters were hoverin' about and over the tops of the trees (fog, to you pinkies).

These were said to be ghosts (or spirits) of our long-gone ancestors, who sometimes get themselves lost an' take it into their 'eads to come back and search about all over the place, an' sometimes they fill the whole place up with their smoky-white spirit! Ma and Pa sez it's not a good time to be out and about, 'coz it makes it very difficult to find where you want to go, so you ends up by gettin' lost as well!

Danger approaches! I can hear the noise of human speech gettin' nearer and nearer to where we are, an' to me dismay, it woz gettin' much too close for comfort. And then I see three large, moon-shaped heads peerin' down at me and the earth runner. They looked really scary, an' up to no good I bet! I could also hear an awful lot of yappity! yappy! yappings! goin' on from what sounded like a pack of rat-hunters!

Me instincts tells me to sit tight, quiet, an' very, very still! Which I did. But the scared white earth runner, perching just in front of me, kicks up a bit of a whimpering and a yammering, an' I could see the whites of its eyes, an' its white woolly fur shakin' like a flea doin' the conga on a conger eel!

For a moment I thought they would surely do us some harm, but they made some more mumbling, jumbling type noises, an' they seemed to sway about a lot, to and fro, an' then coming back an' forth, an' then they did an awful lot of looking, but that woz all.

It seemed like a lifetime before the pinkies moved off, an' the danger feelin' went away with them, an' we were left in peace, and not in pieces!

Oh!... At last, me pinky saviour is coming over!... I can see the shadow approaching!

About time too, as I'm feelin' a teeny bit peckish! Perhaps I will be given some more lovely grub at last!

Well I didn't get that long-awaited feast after all, now that the sun has gone an' the moon is about to turn up, so I guess I will just have to wait a bit longer now!

Back we go!... In the big, very noisy, fast-moving, metal klakki!

I'm so very, very tired now!

Must sleep!

– Chapter Three –
Like A Peppermint Dream

In the event of yesterday's return trip to the common, and my hair-raising experience after my close shave with the badger baiters (which resulted in my totally unexpected underground escape), and after my futile attempt at offering Maggie back to his parents, it was a big disappointment to me that they obviously rejected him. This meant that Maggie's future was now in the balance.

Maggie was now at the mercy of whatever life might throw at him. Success or failure, whatever will be will be, and now it was up to me to help him in every way I could. I was determined to succeed.

Most of the days were taken up with feeding and watching over the little bird and observing any changes in his condition, but he seemed oblivious of all this attention.

He was fighting his own battle to survive, determined not to give in, and his little damaged wing seemed to be healing up nicely each day, so thankfully that meant at least one thing less to worry about.

He had a ferocious appetite and was certainly making up for yesterday's lost feeding time, especially after he had been left in his box and stuck up in a tree for all those hours; it's a wonder he survived such an ordeal.

Maggie soon got into a set routine, and whoever happened to be passing by his shoe box would immediately be confronted with loud squawks, as his scrawny neck reached up, wobbling away, and with his gaping beak wide open, demanding a tasty morsel, as if to say, *"Please drop all donations here, anything and everything will be gratefully received!"*

It was clear that this was going to be a very time consuming occupation, and it was also apparent that I was going to need a constant supply of newspapers, as the front and centre pages of the news were soon used up, and they were shortly followed by the back pages of the sports section.

The paper had to be shredded into reasonably large strips to make him a soft dry nest in his box, and all this had to be done at regular intervals, otherwise we would have had to put up with a very unpleasant odour, which could be detected well before entering the room!

Word soon got around about my new pet, and in a very short while, I had visitors call in just to see for themselves the new addition to the household and to hear all about his dramatic rescue.

It became almost like a scene from the Nativity play, except that the gifts offered so graciously to the babe (who looked more like an alien from Mars than a Holy Infant) were small slices of leftover bread, painstakingly cut into wedges, or pieces of stale cake.

One brave soul, known as "Mrs. God Willing," because every time she said something like "I shall be doing my washing today, God willing," or, "If it doesn't rain tomorrow I shall be doing my gardening, God willing," etcetera—even turned up with a big fat juicy wriggly worm, "fresh from the garden!"

Another elderly neighbour, bless her, said, "Ooh...don't they lay their eggs in other birds' nests?" I looked down at this black and white cuckoo and thought, *Should I tell her his true identity, or enter into some lengthy explanation about cuckoos and magpies, and spoil her imagination if I did so, or should I just let her ponder on her own interpretation about cuckoos and their eggs?*

I decided to cut the details short, and chose the latter option, so I just nodded in agreement.

Maggie would very soon be growing out of his little shoe box, and so I had to decide what would make a suitable nursery for him, and at the same time give him lots more room to move around in.

The next step should not be too difficult. All it needed was to find a nice big cage for him.

Scanning the ads in the local advertiser proved futile, as there was not even a hamster cage to be had, let alone a bird cage. There was only one thing for it. A trip to the pet shop was my only hope.

The local pet shop could only offer me a canary or budgie cage, and neither of these options would be of any use to Maggie as he grew bigger, because by the time he had reached maturity, he would by then be the size of a small crow and would never fit comfortably into such a tiny cage.

I set off to the next town, which was just a few miles away and where I knew that they catered to more exotic and unusual pets than the average pet shop.

Luckily I found just what I wanted there.

A mynah bird's cage!…and a mere snip at just £99!

This was a small, very quaint, Saxon town, nestling in a hamlet near the foot of the South Downs, declaring a twinship (as custom now dictates) with an equally charming village with an unpronounceable foreign name, somewhere or other across the channel.

What makes this little town so popular is that it has managed to maintain its traditional village stores, and so far it has managed to evade the clutches of greedy developers.

I stepped out of the car and into the overpowering heat.

The pungent organic aromas from the little shops, wafting out at the passers by, was almost unbearable.

From the fruit shop came the smell of overripe peaches, and the bananas, which were forming black pockmarks to their skins by the minute, were competing with the dreadful putrid smell of decaying cabbages at the greengrocers. It was like "veggies from hell!"

What a relief to reach the coffee shop, with it's more enticing aroma of rich ground coffee, and the bakery, with the mouth-watering warm yeasty smell of freshly baked bread and delicious melt-in-the-mouth scones.

The pavements were crowded with sweltering people, padding their way in their flip-flops.

Men in their brightly coloured shorts, sporting their bulging bellies, mopping their sweating brows, whilst parading up and down like proud peacocks. Women in their equally colourful tank tops and shorts, were hanging on to cherubic-faced screaming tots.

The little ones ran along trying to keep up with their mums, whilst clutching ice cream cornets, which were quickly melting at the rate of the erupting Vesuvius and running with a sticky milkiness over the chubby clenched fists, and their porcelain white clammy skin, now smelling sickly sweet. Others chomped away on bars of slowly melting chocolate, or chewed and crunched on hard boiled fruit drops, administered to them by their despairing, wilting mothers, who tried in desperation to console their boiling, bawling babies.

Another group of tiny tots trotted along whilst sucking noisily on their ice lollies, which were slowly dripping in small puddles onto the hot pavement—plip!...plop!—like tiny melting ice floes. Little faces, red with crying from the heat, caked with ice cream, and smeared little mouths in an assortment of colours from their sweeties, which gave them the appearance of miniature Al Johnsons.

The tooth fairies were going to be very busy in the next few years!

There was one little toddler who stood out from the rest.

He was wearing the fashionable baseball hat in the usual manner—back to front!—which was pretty ridiculous, as it nearly reached the middle of his back, making him look more like a tortoise than a little boy.

If he was decked out in a long white coat with a blue waistcoat and trousers and a bright red tie with floppy check slippers on his small feet and little round specs on his nose, then the little darling would have looked more like one of the little Tetley Tea Men.

My imagination fast-forwarded to the future, and I could visualize that as he grew older, his image would go through the process of change yet again, and in place of his baseball hat, no doubt he might be wearing in its place the highly popular black woolly tea-cosy-style head gear, with it pulled hard down over his ears, almost to his nose, and wearing an oversized pullover, with the sleeves dangling down to his knuckles, and his long baggy trousers flopping down over his trainers. So now our baseball-hat toddler, who looked like a tortoise, could have changed into a waddling penguin teenager!—Who knows!?

Then, in a split second, "baseball hat" flew into a tantrum.

His little brain suddenly activated certain parts of his body into action, as he cranked into top gear. The little hero's face turned purple, like a Victoria plum, as he started screaming his lungs out with pure rage and giving an almighty howl that would have impressed any timber wolf. The white-rimmed sunglasses set on his little button nose, made him look more like a bug-eyed insect. The poor mother, by now looking very distraught at trying to pacify the little monster, was now to suffer further humiliation.

Just before the pair had reached the pet shop, and in full view of onlookers (who tried to pretend they didn't see), the little "baseball hat" suddenly let rip the highest note he could possibly render. He jumped up and down on the spot, and just to prove he hadn't yet been fully potty trained, and to show his mum (and everyone else for all he cared) just what all the fuss was about, a big steaming lump of poo (which must have somehow found its way through a space in his nappy and then through a gap in his colourful Bermuda shorts) leapt neatly out onto the ground, and then it rolled in a straight line along the pavement, like a ball in a bowling ally!

His poor mum was so angry at her little darling that her next move was quite stunning. She grabbed her now much quieter and much relieved son by his hand. His face now beaming triumphantly and her own face now turning red with embarrassment, she then dragged him over to the offending heap, where she deftly gave it a powerful, well aimed kick with her smart white sandals, which sent it flying into the gutter, much to the amusement and relief of the onlookers. I was quite expecting them to break into applause, but none came!

Peace once more reigned on the busy pavement, now that the ball games were over.

Thank goodness, I thought to myself, *that my own son is now at an age of great expectations and inspirations and well past any passionate display of such humiliating tantrums!*

But I should not have ruled out the possibilities of the same behaviour pattern for a certain magpie, if he had a future at all!

It was blissfully pleasant, and certainly much more peaceful to dive into the pet shop, where a small electric fan had been thankfully installed for the animals, as well as for humans, in contrast to the heat and commotion of the screaming "hot tots" on the pavement outside!

Behind the counter stood a very large cage, housing an exotic bird with a bill that looked ten times too big!

This impressive-looking bird was a toucan, and he became quite famous in the past for advertising a very well known brew, and he was quite a celebrity in the village.

He looked so much like a clown with a very large nose, but at the same time he could also look very serious; although on this hot day he was quite content to sit quietly on his perch and soulfully watch the crazy world go by. You could see in his yellow-ringed eyes as he tried to weigh up the customers that he probably had his own sense of humour, in a bird type fashion. For him to have grown such a large beak (which looked about the size of a double-decker bus) could have certain advantages to go with it, like cracking open the hardest of nuts, and anything else he fancied to eat!

The shop keeper was very helpful when I asked to see what sort of "really big cages" he might have on offer.

"Yes certainly, if you can just wait here a minute!" he said, and disappeared through the door at the back of the shop.

He eventually returned, accompanied by a group of assistants, and each one was carrying some of the biggest cages I had seen yet.

I was very impressed with his selection, and finally chose a nice large white mynah bird cage, complete with a pair of gleaming white feed and water dishes which slotted onto the bars of the cage.

"So, this is for your mynah bird, is it?" he enquired.

"Er, no. Not exactly!" I said.

"Oh…that's good!" he said. "Quite frankly, I think they are overrated, boringly black, smelly, dull, and quickly going out of fashion these days—besides that, they remind me too much of the obnoxious crow family!"

After this last remark about the "crow family," I had that sort of uncomfortable sinking feeling in the pit of my stomach, as though I'd been caught out trying to harbour an escaped convict, and my confidence began to creep independently out of the door, leaving me standing alone, in danger at any moment of failing the test of my own judgement.

"So what sort of bird is it you have got? Or are you wanting to buy one?" he asked, giving me a sideways, rather hopeful look. "I've got some nice colourful little zebra finches, and you could get several in this size cage! …or what about a pair of parakeets?"

"No thanks," I said, "I've already got a bird actually."

"So what is it then?" he persisted, now looking rather suspiciously at me.

After a slight hesitation, I answered, with a dry mouth, but rather too quickly, "I've got…a…a mags!"

"What the heck is a mags?" he asked in a rather suspicious tone, and I detected a slight twitch at the corner of his eye.

"Oh!…Well!…It's a sort of…it's a magpie," I murmured, hoping he hadn't heard me.

He raised his eyebrows and said nothing, and as my elation started to ebb away like the spring tide, I meekly handed over my cheque for £99 exactly!

Struggling outside with my precious purchase and wondering why I wasn't given some assistance to carry the load to my car, I carefully placed the cage on the back seat and then got in, but by now it was like getting into a baking hot oven. It wouldn't have been so bad if I had remembered to leave a window open!

With a feeling of trepidation and exhaustion from the heat, I once again set off for home.

The size of Maggie's brand new shiny white cage created a new problem, like, *just where to put it?*

Being somewhat larger than the shoe box, it was going to have to stay put and not have to be carried up and down stairs. An instant decision had to be made for its final resting place, and after much trial and error, I decided to place it on top of the linen cupboard.

Once in position, it looked quite smart and tidy enough there, with its glossy magazines as floor covering and shiny new white feed dishes. Very posh!

The cupboard stood against the lounge wall and right next to the door leading into the kitchen. This would be a very convenient position, and served well for his regular feeds, which he demanded constantly from just about anybody who happened to be passing by.

It became a routine habit, placing food into the constantly begging beak, like putting money in a vending machine, only you don't receive anything nice back! It went something like: Open!…plop!…*cheep!…cheep!* — Open!…plop!…*cheep!…cheep!* And so on and so on.

The cage was certainly a vast improvement on the shoe box, which by now was beginning to look more like a tatty, smelly old wet kipper.

On nice warm sunny days, the cage could be carried out into the garden and stand on top of an old fold-up table, which used to be kept in my "little house" built at the bottom of the garden, and used for tea parties when I was very young.

When I placed Maggie for the first time into his new bedroom-come-dining room, he looked a bit like a sorrowful "Little Boy Lost," but he soon settled down, and it wasn't long before he confidently toddled across the cage to inspect his new surroundings, which gave him a lot more space to be able to move around in.

He began to look more relaxed, and it wasn't long before he was fluffing and shaking up his feathers (which were slowly developing each day), and then after he'd chomped his beak a few times (which was a sign of contentment), he then lifted his tail and promptly passed a big sloppy dropping (which meant more paper changing) as though to seal his full approval!

After practising lots of hops up and down in his cage and appearing to be much happier, it wasn't long before he fell asleep with his head tucked under his wing.

At last he really did seem quite satisfied with his lot, and all was well with his little world—or at least for now anyway.

It was on one of his early morning breakfast feed times when I made my first careless mistake as a responsible step-parent.

On this particular morning I think that perhaps a degree of tiredness had crept in with a touch of carelessness, but for whatever the reason, the outcome almost resulted in a totally unforgivable disaster.

It could almost have been the end of Maggie, as I might so easily have killed him through my unforseen blunder, and all my caring and nursing would have been wasted, and it happened so quickly.

As usual, I fetched the little white dish and filled it up with the meat from the fridge, then I fumbled around in the kitchen drawer for a matchbox, and then finding one, I grabbed an unused matchstick to feed him with, then I opened the cage door and fetched him out.

I had not anticipated his hunger threshold reaching its maximum level, starting from point zero and diving straight into one thousand degrees of obesity.

I stabbed a small piece of the meat onto the matchstick, then held it in front of him whilst trying to make him more comfortable in my lap to make feeding easier.

The gaping beak made a sudden lunge forward to grab the food, but at that precise moment of his demanding beak making contact with the food offered to him, my fingers relaxed their grip (only ever so slightly) on the matchstick.

Before I knew what was happening, Maggie gave an enormous *gulp!* and down went the food—matchstick and all!

I quickly came to my senses as tiredness fled from my body at the speed of lightning. Aghast, I just stared stupidly down at my empty fingers, which were still pinched together, as though the matchstick was still there.

Horrified, I looked at Maggie, and asked myself, "What have I done?" and, "How utterly stupid!"

Immediately, I grabbed him up and took him out of his cage to examine him, and then prising his beak open, I cautiously peered down his throat, and sure enough, just out of reach, I could just see the end of the matchstick poking up from his throat, making it look as though he now had an extra tongue, only one of them was a wooden one with a black blob on the end of it!

In a panic, I placed him back into the cage and rushed upstairs to the bathroom cabinet to fetch a pair of tweezers. That should do the trick! Problem solved!

I raced back downstairs to the cage, took Maggie out once more, and placed him in my lap for his delicate operation, and so with the tweezers at the ready in my right hand, I was able to squeeze his beak gently open with the thumb and forefinger of my left hand— instrument poised for action. I peered down into his throat, and all I could see was an empty space; at least, all that was showing was his little pink, pointed tongue. The funny wooden matchstick one had gone, or maybe he had already coughed it up!

I searched the cage floor to see if the matchstick had been evacuated there, and I even took out his new magazine floor covering and gave it a good shake, but nothing showed, not even a tiny splinter.

I placed poor Maggie back into his cage and stared wretchedly at him, contemplating what next to do, and reminded myself that not only was it a nasty pointed object that might at any given time penetrate into his vital organs, but he could also suffer from sulphur poisoning from the matchstick head, and if I had really thought that anything like this could happen, I should have at least cut the striking end off.

It was a bit late in the day to contemplate what should have been done, and all I could do now was to look down at the miserable little bird and feel miserable with him, and I would just have to wait and see what would happen, and pray that he would survive the ordeal.

Every time I approached his cage with food for him, a feeling of guilt weighed heavily about my shoulders.

Maggie had to endure this nasty—and probably very indigestible—spiky little object, which was floating somewhere around his anatomy, for almost two weeks, and for some reason or other, it didn't seem to bother him too much, and it certainly didn't alter his appetite or stop his food from going down his throat.

The gruesome sight of his new body-piercing tool (which seemed to be forever changing its positions), held some kind of macabre fascination. Sometimes, when he was all hunched up and looking like a magpie's version of imitating Quasimodo, you could clearly see the offending foreign object protruding grotesquely as it stuck against his chest, pushing it outwards, which made him look more like an old clothes peg, or an "Aunt Sally," or even a heron that had just swallowed a large fish which turned out to be too big to go down its throat!

Poor Maggie, this awful life-threatening situation was so humiliating for him, but it didn't stop everyone placing bets as to where it was going to show up next, or my brother's suggestion when he said, "Why don't you stick him on the end of a pole and turn him into a weather vane? Or you could put him on top of the gate, as he looks just like a gargoyle!"

These comments didn't help me one bit, knowing that if Maggie was to make the wrong move, he could easily have stabbed himself, and that wouldn't have been at all funny.

Each time I fed him, I tried in vain to extract the elusive stick from his throat, which was sometimes tantalisingly within view, but always just out of reach of the probing tweezers, which I always kept handy now, just in case!

My patience was being tested to the limit, whilst Maggie's health was in the balance.

Then one day, when I went to Maggie's cage to change his paper as usual, there, to my great surprise (and joy), on the floor of the cage was the offending matchstick, looking very yellow and very gungy from its travels, but still intact.

The horrible *thing* had now given itself up—at last!

What is still very much a mystery, and probably one which will never be solved, is *which* end did Maggie expel the matchstick from, and *how* did he do it?

As the days passed by, Maggie was gaining more confidence with everything going on around him, and even loud noises didn't seem to bother him too much either.

He was now beginning to mature in leaps and bounds, and each day brought new experiences for him to add to his growing-up process, and his Daffy Duck image started to change as his feathers started to sprout into the more mature black and white feathers of an adult magpie, and even his little stubby tail was now beginning to lengthen.

Growing up so quickly also meant more food, and the menu gradually increased to a variety of tid-bits, and some of them came from our own dinner plates, and there seemed to be no limit to his taste buds. He would greedily accept anything and everything offered to him with great gusto. With his beak agape and his wings fluttering in rapid bursts, seeking attention, his demands had to be met, otherwise he would go into a fit of loud clacking noises until somebody cared to top him up with something tasty.

Maggie had his favourite food-stuffs like bread, rice with hot curry, spaghetti bolognese, cheese, chicken (and chips!), peas, porridge, corn flakes, and for desserts he liked bananas, sultanas, apples, strawberries and cream, which he would also dip into quite happily, along with a spot of tea or coffee, if he fancied a drop! The list was endless, and nothing was refused. The term "cast-iron stomach" comes to mind, but at least it made feeding times so much easier, especially now that I didn't have to use the dreaded matchsticks like chopsticks, because now I was able push the food down into his throat with a finger instead. This procedure worked pretty well, but it did feel very strange having to push mushy food down into a bird's gullet, and the experience of it was not a very pleasant one.

It's a good job he wasn't a baby ostrich!

Maggie soon transformed from a gangly infant into a mischievous toddler and was eager for me to take him out of the cage for his daily walkabout, and from my arm he would jump onto the floor where he would set off across the shiny freshly polished wooden floor, just like a little clockwork wind up toy; *lig!-log!…lig!-log!…lig!-log!* went his little feet, clicking and sliding away as he tried to keep his balance on the unnatural surface.

He practised flapping his little wings simultaneously, and started to exercise his new power of flexing his little bird-brain into joined-up thoughts: *which way and where to go, and what to do now?*

He was showing that he was ready to explore this strange new world!

He took great delight in running under, around, or behind chairs and tables, and in later years this strategy would be used as escape routes and hiding places, particularly when it was time to go to bed, or to foil any attempt to capture him!

There was also another exciting new discovery—TV!

Maggie was about to enter into the world of virtual reality, and he would sometimes sit on my knee or perch on my shoulder so that he could watch his favourite programmes. These were usually wildlife documentary films, and he particularly took interest in David Attenborough's programmes on different birds of the world. He appeared to especially like seashore scenes for some strange reason, and he watched these with great interest, and cocked his head on one side as though he was taking in every detail, and if they showed close ups of seashells, he would become quite excited, and if I held him close up to the screen, he would try and peck at it, as though he wanted to pick the shells up! *Very odd behaviour!* I thought to myself. Maybe he just liked their shapes and colours.

Maggie also seemed to enjoy music, making little clucking or tweeting noises as if to join in! He even enjoyed watching and listening to *Top of the Pops,* and another firm favourite was *Eastenders,* as he would sit quietly and watch through the whole episodes.

The only time he showed any fear or anxiety was if there was a film or documentary showing the big cats hunting and bringing down their prey. This he felt he just couldn't tolerate, and he would start to wheeze with fear and go into a bit of a tizz. I'm sure he thought that the big cats would jump out of the television screen and pounce on him. He would quickly scuttle off somewhere and hide. No amount of coaxing would bring him out again, so he had to be confined to his cage when the scary bits came on.

One night I experienced a very dramatic incident which I shall never forget, and at the time it was very serious, but looking back on the event, it was really quite hilarious and could have been a clip from a comedy film.

It happened after visiting a very close friend of mine, and because we had become somewhat absorbed in our lengthy discussions about horses and many other girlie-type topics of interests which we both had in common, I didn't leave her house until it was quite late.

I arrived home in the early hours of the morning, and as I quietly opened the front door with my key, being extra careful not to make any noise, I made my way towards the kitchen where the dogs slept.

The dogs didn't bark, because by instinct they always knew it was me.

They were both waiting for the door to open, and I was greeted by wagging tails as they anticipated lots of pats and hugs.

My nose was treated to the wonderful aroma of freshly baked cakes (probably rock cakes). My guess was right! Mother must have baked them that evening and placed them in the cake crock, which she always kept in the larder.

The old brick-red terracotta crock, which was passed down to my mother from her great Grandma, was filled to the brim with these mouth-watering treats, and still deliciously warm from the oven. Just one! Or maybe two! Or perhaps just one more!

The two dogs sat in front of me with drooling mouths, so I just had to share my cakes with them. Satisfied, and not leaving one crumb, they reluctantly settled back into their beds when they saw me putting the crock back in the larder. "All gone!" I lied. Then I thought that I'd better leave some for my brother when he comes to visit us, otherwise he'll be very upset! Not to worry, there's plenty left for everyone!

Before retiring to bed, I checked on Maggie to see if he'd been disturbed by the lights being turned on at such a late hour (or should I say early hours, as it was by now nearly two in the morning), but he seemed oblivious to any disturbance, because when I lifted the cloth covering his cage, I could see that he was settled on his top perch with his head tucked under his wing in his usual position for sleep. So I crept upstairs to bed.

Having decided not to read as I usually did before settling down, I switched off my bedside lamp and tucked myself under the duvet to sleep.

Before I even had a chance to drift off, I heard a car draw up, and then the engine was switched off, followed by a slight *click!* sound of somebody shutting the car door carefully, as though they were trying not to make a sound. *Perhaps one of the neighbours opposite has just returned home from their nightshift?* I thought to myself.

After a few minutes of silence, my ears pricked up after I heard a slight *shuffle!—bump!* sound coming from next door. But this couldn't be possible, as our good neighbour Dot had been in hospital for well over a month, having undergone a very serious operation, and there was no one else left in the house! In fact, I had promised Dot that I would keep an eye on her house for her whilst she was in hospital. Maybe I was just dreaming? But no, there was another muffled *thud!*

I was now very much awake and alert, and I listened attentively, just in case I had imagined it.

Another few moments' pause, and yet another sound, but this time it was of someone quietly opening a front door. And then another *click!*

By now my heart was thumping, and my first thought was *burglars!*

Swiftly getting out of bed, I went over to the window and slowly pulled back the curtains, but just wide enough to see outside into the dark.

I could just make out the outline of a figure moving furtively about the car, which was parked hard against the hedge of next door, and I could see the moon glinting off the roof.

As I watched, I could now see not just one, but two figures, and they appeared to be carrying something into the car, or was it something towards the house? And then they disappeared from view, and I heard a faint click as the front door was closed.

I had seen enough, and I knew what I had to do. I had made up my mind that I was going to call the police!

Before going downstairs, I peeped into my parents' room to see if they might have been disturbed by anything, but they were still fast asleep, and my father was snoring very loudly, so I decided not to disturb them as it may have alarmed them.

I made my way down the stairs as quickly and quietly as possible to the phone in the hall, and as I was dialling, I could just see the headlines blazoned across the local or even the national newspaper:

VIGILANT LOCAL WOMAN FOILED A GANG OF DANGEROUS ROBBERS —
PRAISED BY POLICE FOR HER PROMPT ACTION!

The voice on the other end of the line said, "Police!…can I help you?"

"Oh yes!" I said, "I think our next door neighbour has just been broken into by a gang, or at least two thieves! *Please hurry!…* I think they're taking loads of stuff and emptying her house out!" Then hurriedly I gave them the address.

The girl on the other end of the line assured me that the police would be sent round immediately, and sure enough they arrived in about eight minutes after my call.

I heard the car arrive at great speed, and it pulled up sharply and parked tight against the intruders' car. I rushed upstairs once more to watch the drama unfold.

As I watched from behind the curtains, my heart was still thumping with anticipation.

The two police officers got out of their car, with the blue light flashing away, lighting up the darkness outside, and the *beep! beep!* sound coming from their radio.

There was a muffled sound of their voices as they contacted base. "Blah! blah! blah! *Checking!*" and then, "*Over!*"

Another response from the other end, then they returned their reply, "Blah, blah, blah, —*right, going in now! —over!*" They signed out and then carried on with their investigations.

I could see a flashlight moving about as they started to check the inside of the "burglar's" car, then they strode purposefully up to the front door and banged on the letterbox.

Dot didn't have a doorbell.

There was no sound of movement from next door, so I assumed that the thieves were holding up somewhere and hiding in one of the rooms, or perhaps they had forced their way out of the dining room window at the back, and by now were already making good their escape through the hedge at the bottom of the garden.

The police didn't hesitate, and one of the policemen (the other was a policewoman), went back to the car and fetched something which to me looked like a weapon.

So they are going to fight their way in! I thought.

It turned out to be a hailer!

"*Open up! —this is the police!*" he shouted.

I almost cringed. This would surely wake up the whole neighbourhood. What have I done now?

The policeman repeated the request, but there was no response. Then there seemed to be silence for several minutes.

Perhaps they have gone to the back of the house to check there? Still nothing.

I pulled back from the window and waited. I was growing impatient, not knowing what was happening, and I couldn't hear any shoot-outs, or any other sounds of disturbance. It seemed to be much too quiet. Then I heard our own letterbox being rattled. Why on earth didn't they use the doorbell? At least we had one of those.

I rushed downstairs, not knowing what to expect, and by now the dogs were barking frantically.

As I ran along the hall, on an impulse I reached up to the key-hook where we kept all the keys, including one of Dot's front door keys, which she gave us so that we could enter her house whenever we needed to. This would be of help to the police, as they would have no problem of entry now!

As I opened the door, I was confronted by the young policewoman. I held the key up in front of me, and with my hand shaking slightly, there was eyeball to eyeball contact through the key ring.

"They wont let you in will they?" I said. "Here, take this, it's Dot's front door key, I think that should help you get in!"

What she said next made me want to exit stage left at one hundred miles an hour, overtake the road runner, and wave at Concorde as I screamed past it!

"No thank you," she replied, "we shan't be needing that! We know you called us in good faith," she said, and then after a short hesitation, she continued, "and we are very grateful that you responded to a situation you felt was in need of investigation"—another pause—"but you see, what you *actually* heard was your neighbour Dot's brother and sister-in-law moving in to stay for a while so that they can visit her in hospital, and they have driven all the way from Suffolk, and because they didn't leave till quite late, that's why they arrived so late here, and they purposely kept as quiet as they could so that they didn't disturb...er...the neighbours!"

I just stared at the policewoman in disbelief. My mouth became very dry, my stomach did a bungy jump, and my arm began to ache, and all because I was still grasping the key in my outstretched hand, which was still in the same position.

I was gradually beginning to feel a panic attack coming on, as my sanity held on by a thin thread of corn-silk.

Feeling utterly embarrassed by the whole episode, I meekly made my humble apologies for calling them out on a false errand, and after bidding the bemused policewoman goodnight, I closed the door ever so quietly, and tried to compose myself back to reality.

My bubble had suddenly burst, and fame by now had slipped quietly away and evaporated into thin air, or perhaps to be filed under the category of "Don't call us, we'll call you!"

My parents slept soundly through the whole interlude.

Dot's brother Charles, and her sister-in-law Edith, were well into their seventies and rather hard of hearing, so that accounts for them not responding so quickly to being heralded so rudely and dramatically out of their bed at such an early hour, and at the prospect of being arrested in their pyjamas and night-dress, hair curlers, and without their dentures, zimmer frames and all, must have been pretty alarming for them, to say the least!

I don't think they would ever forget this incident for the rest of their lives, and Dot certainly didn't. It seemed that she nearly burst her stitches as she gave such a belly laugh when they told her what had happened. She had such a huge sense of humour. Poor old Dot, she could certainly do with a lot of cheering up.

Sadly, a year later, Dot peacefully passed away.

Many blissful, hot sunny days were spent in the garden, soaking up the warmth and atmosphere of the outdoor sights and sounds — that is, if you can completely ignore the usual weekend revellers out with their noisy lawn mowers, hedge trimmers, and sometimes a chainsaw would be used to cut down and then saw up an unwanted tree which had outgrown its space. Then there were the usual radios (which were often turned up to full blast), with the latest pop tunes playing, or a cricket match being broadcast for the non-gardeners to listen to, whether they liked it or not!

Quite unperturbed by all this commotion, Maggie would sit happily in his cage. One side of the cage was always covered over with a very colourful tea towel (he loved bright colours) to shade him from the midday hot sun.

As I lay in the deckchair, and making the most of the sunshine, the warmth helped me to relax.

Dozing just a little, I started to daydream and was able to drift back, remembering events from the past which would influence the future; it was because of this gradual influx of noisy countryside invaders that we were prompted to seek a quieter, more peaceful life.

Over the past few years, so much change around our tranquil space had taken over. Ultimately, it was decided unanimously that we would plunge ourselves into the completely unknown territory of "Wild and Woolly West Wales."

We had never even been there for our holidays, so it was definitely going to be quite a challenge, especially for my parents as they had spent the past fifty-four years of their married life in the very same house.

We lived in this very comfortable, and very bright, semi-detached house.

The house was situated on the top of a hill on a private road in what was then a small market town, which has now more than doubled in size. It was not just any old house, as it was cosy, warm, and kept spotlessly clean by my mother.

Upstairs we had three bedrooms and an average-sized bathroom. My bedroom was yellow (my favourite colour), my brother's was blue, and my parents' was pink (which was Mother's favourite colour). Downstairs we had a separate dining room and lounge (which was eventually knocked into one big room).

The kitchen was not very big, but just big enough for a drop-leaf table where we sometimes ate our meals, and a little boiler which ran on coke—that's fuel and not the drink!—and this was to heat our tank for hot water, as there was no central heating in those early years. There was our deep enamel sink with its wooden draining board where our mother used to sit us when we were very young so that she could wash our grubby little knees after playing mud pies and digging holes in the garden, much to the annoyance of our father.

Tacked onto the kitchen was a small utility room, where brooms and other odds and ends were kept, as well as a scuttle of coke and coal for the fires. Right next to the sink there was an Ascot immersion gas boiler, which enabled us to have immediate hot, almost boiling, water, even though we had two separate hot and cold water taps over the sink. We even had one other separate tap fitted onto the wall directly onto a pipe at the other end of the sink unit, which was for drinking water, and it was always welcoming in the hot summer if you needed a really nice cold drink to cool down with.

Mother had to cook on a very small electric cooker, which was speckled grey and blue, and in the little oven, and apart from the usual meals she used to bake wonderful cakes and sponges, as well as treacle tarts and puddings, like the "pond pudding" which consisted of a suet pudding, and then filled with butter, lots of soft brown sugar, sultanas and juice from a squeezed lemon, but sometimes a whole lemon was put inside, and when it was finally cooked, all the soft sweet contents oozed out like a volcanic eruption, hence the name "pond pudding." Then there was the wickedly delicious chocolate pudding, which had lashings of chocolate sauce poured all over it.

In addition to the little electric cooker, we also had a small gas ring, which you could fit a saucepan on, or use to boil up a kettle to make a cup of tea, but this was very slow, so it took a very long time indeed.

There was a gas meter under the stair cupboard, and every so often, when the gas literally ran out, we would have to feed the meter with shillings or half-crowns.

We were quite content with our lot, and life seemed to run smoothly for us—most of the time, anyway.

As I mentioned before, my brother and I would play for hours in the garden.

My brother would make mud castles where he would hold ferocious battles with his tin soldiers, and my bit part in the game was to put my boot in and demolish the castle after the victorious side had defeated the foe, and then the little tin soldiers were carefully put back into the biscuit tin, in readiness for the next battle.

The garden was not very big, but we had lots of fun there.

We kept rabbits, guinea pigs and, later on, when we were teenagers, there was even a couple of aviaries built by Father for budgies and canaries, so we found lots to keep us occupied.

At the very bottom of the garden, set tight into the corner, was a tall mast which was originally used as an electricity pole. This had wires connected to it, and it was supposed to give our wireless set (not called a radio in those days) a much clearer reception, and on the top of this pole Father had set a little tin man whose whole body and arms were set into motion whenever there was a high wind, and his little arms would whizz round and round, turning a little wheel as he went. Over the years his joints became very creaky and he used to make a terrible clanking sound: *clitter! clatter!—clitter! clatter!—nod! nod!—nod! nod!—*which drove everybody potty.

Then one winter's night, in an extra strong gale, the tall pole was blown half sideways at a very dangerous angle, so to everyone's relief, Father had to remove the pole, and along with it went the little tin man, who went into retirement—in the dustbin!

On the spot where the pole stood, Father built a nice little wooden-framed greenhouse (painted blue, would you believe!) where he grew his lovely red tomato plants, along with his prized chrysanthemums. The greenhouse was out of bounds to any kid under the age of twenty! This wasn't surprising, as it wasn't unusual for Father to arrive home from work only to find his garden shed painted in all different colours, with empty paint tins strewn all over the lawn! He was lucky that he didn't find his red roses painted green, or blue, or black!

Also at the bottom of our garden were two absolutely wonderful, but very mature, plum trees. I say, wonderful, not because they had lovely plums, but because our father made us a super swing-boat, which was very popular, and all the other kids wished they had one just like it, so we used to let them have a go on it too.

I remember when I had the mumps, and it was a hot summer that year; my mother used to make me a nice cosy bed in it with a pillow and a little blanket if I needed it, and I would swing myself to sleep with my little Dutch rabbit, Bunty, or if Bunty was in a very cross mood (which she so often was) I would substitute her for my brother's rabbit called Cherry, and she would lay quietly beside me in the swing. The two plum trees would cast dappled shading from the hot sun. It was lovely, and so peaceful, with just the sweet sound of bird song. It was almost worth being ill, and you got spoilt into the bargain!

I was also lucky enough to have my very own little wooden house, which was built by my father, and it was situated to one side of the plum trees right next to Father's big work shed, where he carried out his carpentry and cabinet making work.

The door to Father's shed had been painted many different colours over the years, from pink to blue, red to lilac and yellow to green. I used to love the smell of all the remnants and off-cuts of wood he worked on, and there was often the strong pungent smell of glue and paint. Amongst the sawdust littering the floor were piles of wood shavings, which had been thinly planed off and ever so neatly curled, like the daintily cut swirly-curly butter you get when you use a butter crimper.

Father would work away, with a pencil placed behind his left ear, because he was left handed, which came in handy, as he was also an accomplished left-hand spin bowler. As a young man he joined the Sussex Cricket Club, for whom he scored many a hat-trick. And so with his tools of the trade all lined up, ready for action, and accompanied with the sound of a busy saw rasping away, he carved, chiselled, and shaped up pieces of furniture. Along with the rapid tap, tap, tap of the hammer, nails were expertly hammered into ordinary pieces of wood, eventually transforming them into recognizable, highly desirable and functional, and really quite exquisite tables, chairs, cupboards, and many more accessories for the home.

My little wooden house was painted dark green, but the wooden door, which had its own shed-type key, was painted a pale pea-green colour. It had two nice windows which had two floral-patterned curtains, a home-made wooden table where I could have my tea, three comfortable kitchen chairs painted a cream colour, two little shelves where I could put ornaments or books, and a nice light on the ceiling with a pink shade, and the inside walls were painted in a deep pink, and I can still remember the nice "painty" smell.

In the middle of the freshly varnished floor, there was a big, round, home-made woollen rug, which was made by my grandfather. It had the picture of an owl sitting in a tree, and he had one large eye open, and the other one was shut, making him look as though he was winking at you, and in the background of a black sky, you could see a half-moon and a scattering of stars. This rug lasted for several years, but in the end it just wore out and became completely threadbare. I was very upset when it eventually had to be thrown out.

I would spend many happy hours in my little house, usually with my pets, and I would take my books and comics out there where I could read them alone in peace and quiet and dream of nice things to do.

For amusement, I made my own pet owl out of a used bag of flour, which was of a cotton type of material in those days, and it was all white. I painted two eyes and a beak on him, and he looked very owlish. To me, it was a real barn owl, and he would sit on a shelf in the corner of the room.

I remember on one cool summer evening, just before dusk, a very odd sensation came over me, and as I began to tingle all over, I felt very dizzy and almost sick, and the room appeared to spin around me. I managed to find my chair and sat myself quickly down before passing out. Then in a daze, my head started to pound alarmingly, and I found myself drifting in and out of a very strange dream.

Owlie and I flew out of the little window and up into the night sky, and I was surprised to see fine flour pouring from his wings, or could it be star dust? He then landed on the top branch of the Scots Pine tree, which suddenly turned into a ferocious wolf's head, fangs snapping up and down, so we had to fly off at great speed. That particular tree always looked like the head of a wolf to me, even in the daytime.

We flew past black clouds, which formed into great big friendly giants' heads; they smiled and laughed as we flew past, and I waved to them. I'm sure they looked familiar, then it suddenly came to me, they were the images of some of my schoolteachers! Were they checking to see if I had done my homework?

Then from out of the darkness, flying silently towards us, was what I could only describe as a tooth fairy accompanied by a group of pixies and elves. I was praying that she wasn't going to visit my house! I'd had enough teeth out for one year, thank you very much!

I could see something just in front of us, and then slowly and gracefully drifting towards us was the most magnificent rocking horse. It was a lovely golden colour with a few brown spots across its back, and a flaxen mane and tail. As it came alongside, on an impulse, I leapt upon its back, and the owl flew up and perched on my shoulder. We then we rode off on our way with a lovely gentle, rocking motion. The beautiful silky mane softly brushed against my cheek.

Suddenly, coming towards us on a flowing, winding, silvery stream of stars, we could see little flashing starfishes leaping about, and then they suddenly vanished.

"Watch out everyone!" shouted Owlie. "Here comes that Pie in the Sky!"

Just as he said this, a rhubarb and custard pie whizzed past us like a flying saucer.

"Move over!…Make way!…Make way!" hooted Owlie.

Everything suddenly got out of hand as a Jack-in-the-box popped up exclaiming, "Nows you sees me!—Nows you don't!"—and he kept turning into different colours, with all spots and stripes, and he was juggling with big juicy plums and strawberries, which he promptly ate, then belched out the stones from the plums saying, "Oh dear, I do beg your pardon!"

Just then a big black sleek cloud rolled up with a large number nine printed on the side of it, which was lit up with a bright green light, and on the other side of it read the words, "GET YOUR COSMOPOLITAN ICE CREAM HERE!" and underneath it said, "TREAT YOUR FRIENDS TO A STAR-BURST SURPRISE!" Then it rang—*Ting! ting! ting!*

"All aboard!" someone shouted very loudly, and all of these weird star creatures leapt on and were whisked away at the speed of light, leaving a blue smokey trail, and along this same path, wriggled a long line of tadpoles, and as they got nearer, they grew bigger and bigger. These giant tadpoles were blowing huge bubbles, the size of party balloons, and as they popped, they made a strange *bing!—bing!—bing!* noise, just like submarines make.

"Oh, golly," I said.

A voice answered, "Yes—you called?"

As I turned around, there, staring me in the face, was a Golliwog! He was wearing a top hat, striped trousers, and a red jacket, with a red and white spotted handkerchief in his top pocket. He was swinging a red and white cane about, and then promptly started to sing "The Owl and the Pussycat!" Whilst he danced clumsily to his song, he held in his other hand a sort of wine bottle, which had printed on it, "Moonshine—35 and 3/4 proof."

A jolly looking clown in a very colourful costume played on a grand piano and sang, "Somewhere Over the Rainbow," which sounded very nice, as he had quite a good voice, but it was rather spoilt when a big red-looking trout playing an accordion joined in with a verse of, "Oh I do like to be beside the seaside!" in a very deep, booming voice.

Then from out of nowhere, there appeared a big black bear, who looked as though he was wearing a collar and lead of stars, which trailed out behind him as he bounded along. As he approached us, he and Golly started to play a game of football with the sun and the moon, and as they kicked them about, first it was darkness, and then it was broad daylight—quite mad! When Golly kicked the sun in front of the moon, he started to turn cartwheels, which made him look like a Catherine wheel firework, with all his dazzling colours mingling into one, and someone shouted, "Total eclipse!" And then the black bear gave the moon such a hefty kick, and sent it spinning out of sight, scattering stars in all directions, and another voice shouted back, "Full Moon! Well done!" and everyone clapped and cheered.

Not to be outdone, Golly took careful aim, kicked the sun as hard as he could, which sent it hissing and spiralling on its way, but just at that moment, and quite unexpectedly, a chicken flew clumsily past, right into the path of the sun, which by now was travelling as fast as an express train, and they collided, sending feathers in all directions. A shout went up, "Oh! Foul Play!" and the chicken called back as it flapped it's way down, followed by hundreds of floating feathers, "No thanks!...I've got a date with someone called Paxo!...and I'll ketchup with you later!"

"Oh! That's not fair!" someone else screeched, and just at that moment, from out of the darkness came noisy dodgem cars, headlights blazing, and following behind was a fairground organ, playing some very loud music, but when a big carousel roundabout appeared, my lovely rocking horse gave a whinny, and it suddenly bolted across the night sky with me hanging on for dear life.

"This was getting seriously out of hand!" I said out loud, as I'd really had enough!

Then suddenly I found myself falling into space as the rocking horse suddenly grew a pair of wings, and like Pegasus, it flew off into the darkness.

I was suddenly brought back to wakefulness, and thankfully back into the real world, but my head was still aching when I heard my mother knocking on the door, and the sound seemed to be so loud that it made my headache even worse, bringing tears to my eyes.

"Come on in now!" she called, "it's getting very late, and well past your bedtime! And what's this flour bag doing out here?"

It wasn't long after this unusually vivid dream that I went down with a particularly nasty bout of whooping cough, with other complications thrown in, and as I had developed a rather high temperature, I was pretty ill for a few weeks.

As a special treat, and to cheer me up after my illness, Father made me a beautiful black rocking horse of my very own. I called it Frolic.

Perhaps my father somehow knew about my little adventure in the night sky!

My friends would often join me in my little house, and we would play card games, or the game of jacks, or five-stones, or invent new games, and sometimes we would make up stories to tell to one another, and they especially liked my dream when I told them about it, so they decided to try it out for themselves. Sitting very still, they closed their eyes tight, hoping to drift into a dream, and they waited and waited until finally they got very cross, because they couldn't see a dream happen; so we decided to make up other stories, usually ghost stories, which sometimes frightened us so much as they progressively got more and more spooky, that we were too scared to leave the house.

As darkness set in, we all sat huddled together to wait for my mother to come and rescue us when she became anxious because we hadn't yet come in. When she finally came and opened the door, she was confronted with pale-faced, frightened little girls.

On the opposite side of Father's shed and my little house was a large bed of vegetables and roses which grew over what remained of the old wartime dugout, which everyone had to dig and construct as an air-raid shelter in their gardens so that the family could dash down into them whenever an air-raid siren sounded, or there was a bomb-drop going on by enemy aircraft.

This dugout had long since been filled in, so we could only imagine what it could have been like to go underground, and what fun we would have had if it still existed, and what exciting things we might have discovered down there!

Some years later, my brother, when he was a teenager, took up playing the drums, and he would take his complete drum kit and cymbals into my little house to practice his drumming. All that banging of sticks on skins, and the jangling clanging sound of the cymbals being beaten with great gusto, could be heard from quite a long way off, even as far as the bottom of our road. In fact, on one occasion, a man who lived about half way down the hill came fuming his way up to our house one night to tell my brother off for making too much noise! It didn't stop my brother though—I think he played even louder.

It wasn't long before my brother and other fellow musicians formed their own group, and they called it The D.J. Rhythm 'n' Blues, and they became very popular—playing at pubs, clubs, very posh restaurants, and even at the Brighton Dome!

Rock 'n' roll and jive music was all the rage at that time, with foot-tapping beat music which inspired you to get up and dance, or the softer, slower moody rhythms that made you want to close your eyes and dream a little.

Teenage girls sat around the dance floor, fluttering false eyelashes at the boys, waiting to be chosen by one of them for a dance. The girls had the new "beehive" hairstyles, with their hair piled high on top of their heads, like a buzby, and they teetered along precariously on high-heeled stiletto shoes. It was the fashion to wear hooped skirts, which had a thick band of wire threaded through the hem, making the skirt stand out like a lampshade, and underneath, they usually wore a petticoat which had several layers of starched organza, making the skirt stand out even more, and sitting down on a chair would need lots of practice, because if you didn't do it properly, the skirt would spring up and hit you in the face as you sat down, bringing tears to your eyes.

What with long false nails, blacked-up eyes, big balloon skirts, and pointed shoes, what a colourful image the teenage girls in those days must have created, and the slogan might easily have read, "Minnie Mice 'R' Us!"

The boys were busy with their own appearances. They wore winkle-picker shoes, Tony Curtis hairstyles, long sideburns, and tight drainpipe trousers, so their caption would probably read, "Teddy Boys 'R' Us!"

My brother and his group decided that they needed a change of scenery from the "mods" and "rockers" set, and they all wanted to spread their wings further afield.

Arrangements were duly made to go on a memorable one-off tour of West Africa.

Father hastily knocked up some pretty impressive giant-sized round containers for my brother's drum kit, and they looked just like huge hat boxes! They must have taken up most of the space in the hold of the aircraft!

When they arrived at their destination, after a long, uneventful flight, they were greeted with a very warm reception.

During their tour, the group was both moved and touched by the serenity and the contentment of the village people they had met on the way, and how they had to cope with their sparse way of life, and how they tried, almost impossibly, to eke a scant living out of their impoverished land. They were also particularly humbled by the children, who were rapturously overjoyed at receiving even the smallest of gifts. Distributing most of his colourful shirts to be shared out amongst his newly acquired friends, my brother vowed that one day he would to return to West Africa, "loaded with clothes, toys, and lots of other 'goodies,' for the people who lived there."

On their journey across West Africa, the group met and joined up with local musicians, and together, they were able to play at as many "gigs" as time allowed.

Although they may not have made a vast fortune from their sessions and arrived home minus a few garments, a great time was had by all during their short stay, and the whole trip was a huge success!

A few years later, a jazz group was formed called, "The Fourteen Foot Jazz Band!"

It was with this band that my brother performed some pretty neat drum solos which lasted for several minutes. Very impressive!

Sometimes he even accompanied some very well known jazz musicians, like Humphrey Littleton, George Chisolm, and many more.

I remember when I met George Chisolm for the first time. It was at a local "gig" where I accompanied my brother, and when we arrived at this particular pub, I was given one of the snare drums and drumsticks to carry in, and as though right on cue, the door opened, and I was greeted by a beaming George. When he saw me struggling with the drums and sticks, he said in his Spike Milligan voice, "Oh dear, you look under stress and under drums—here, let me help you!" and with that, he carefully extricated the drumsticks, which had been tucked under my arms.

On another occasion, the group decided to take their musical talents to the North of France, and to save money, they borrowed a friend's boat, which was built to take only twelve passengers.

On this trip there were to be twenty-five people on board, plus the weight of all the musical instruments!

The day of the trip arrived, and my brother was spotted by Mother as he was frantically searching for something in the cupboards and chest of drawers. When she asked him what he was looking for, he answered, "I'm looking for my flippers and snorkel!" and when my puzzled mother asked him what he wanted them for, he said, "I need them just in case the boat sinks!"

It also hadn't occurred to the migrating musicians that they would need a compass to navigate by, and nobody had either a compass or even the experience of navigation!

Some bright person suggested that they should follow the moon— which they did—and promptly got lost! They ended up about twenty miles off course to where they originally wanted to be, but they still managed to entertain the French people with a spot of jazz!

The return trip was equally fraught with an element of danger.

As they headed towards the English coast, a thick, heavy fog came down and they were trying to navigate by a wing and a prayer through a rather busy shipping route.

There was just one small problem though, they were minus a foghorn, so another bright idea was concocted. My brother sat at the bows of the boat, blasting away on a trombone that was loud enough to frighten away any fleet of fishing trawlers!

Another hazard was caused mainly by half the crew being drunk through drinking too much French wine, along with the weight of the drum-kit, trombones, trumpets, bass guitar, and other such instruments that make up a band; they felt the boat was listing, mostly because everyone was puking up over one side of the boat, adding more flotsam and jetsam to the already polluted sea, and by now the overladen boat was also taking in sea water—they were slowly sinking!

It was a good thing they didn't decide to take a piano with them!

Another cunning plan had to be devised to keep them afloat!

This time they all had to work together, so they started to bail out the incoming sea water with beer glasses and chuck-buckets!

Thankfully they all managed to limp home safe and sound, where they all had to sleep off their memorable escapade!

They all seemed to have had good fun, in spite of a few major and minor hiccups!

I sometimes wonder what the boat owner's reaction was when his small vessel was duly handed over, with a mild hint of sea, pee, and sick to greet him!

When I reached the age of ten, it was decided that I should follow the family tradition and learn to play the piano. It was not as though I was consulted or even given a choice.

I was duly signed up for a course of piano lessons with a local Welsh lady piano teacher, and rather reluctantly I had to endure these tiresome lessons for about four years.

I didn't, at that time, fully appreciate having to spend a good half hour or more just practising my pieces, every single day, which to me seemed like hours and hours, when I could be outside playing, or out walking with my friends and the dog, instead of learning boring old scales and all that *F A C E—A C E G—E G B D F—G B D F A* business!

After passing four exams, I finally gave up my music lessons, and carried on with the more exciting hobby of horse riding instead. Horse riding and the countryside was most definitely much more fun than playing the piano!

I have always been deeply moved by nature, and my interest in wild things started at a very early age, when I was virtually "knee-high to a grasshopper."

When I was very little, I used to spend many happy hours playing in the long grass and digging little holes in the garden just to see what I could find.

My mother was intrigued by my frequent request for a teaspoon of sugar, "to feed the little ones." She thought I was playing a game of "imaginary fairies," until she discovered that my little friends were in fact ants!

I would tip the sugar onto the ground outside of their little ant nests and watch them as they carried the small grains of sugar through the long grass, then over lots of obstacles, all the way back to their nests. It also fascinated me to see them carrying little greenfly insects in a very gentle manner, back to their nests, and to watch them carry their soft little white eggs in their mouths, careful not to drop them, and take them to somewhere for storing.

This marathon task would usually take place if their nests had been disturbed, and they would stop every so often to greet one another with their antennae before continuing their journey.

One day, whilst sitting on the back door step with my two companions Pat and Jane, the family pet dogs (Pat was a little brown and white terrier, and Jane was her daughter, whose father was a wandering black and white spaniel), and after I had finished drinking my little favourite glass cup of Camp coffee, served with plenty of milk and a heap of sugar (as we didn't have the well known dried granules that we buy these days), I decided to take my usual sugar offerings to my busy little garden friends.

After a short while, my mother heard me give a loud scream, and when she ran outside, thinking something awful had happened, she found my crying, with my empty spoon still held in my hand.

It seems that after I had given my little ant friends their usual treat, I had stepped back, and accidentally flattened them all! So that was the end of their sugary handouts!

My unfortunate mishap didn't stop me from seeking out the creepy crawlies, or sometimes I was the one being sought after.

At night, when my mother used to undress me ready for bed, out of my clothes would pop grasshoppers, earwigs, beetles, and even that armadillo type crustaceous creature, a woodlouse, would roll out and across the floor like a little marble!

My mother was not altogether amused by my little collection of wildlife creatures.

Once, a very angry bumblebee which had somehow trapped itself inside my clothes, promptly stung me under my armpit, then buzzed angrily out of the bathroom window! Needless to say, I was most upset and very hurt.

All these little things were part of growing up and a part of life in our comfortable home.

My brother and I were brought up in this house and spent our childhood there, and then into our teens, and well into our twenties. We were very happy in those early years.

From my bedroom window, to the left, I could see far on the horizon the outline of the trees of Ashdown Forest, and if you craned even further to the left, you could make out the rooftops of the houses not far from the town itself. On cold frosty nights, you could hear the trains shunting on the tracks at the railway station, which was about two miles from us, and on Sunday mornings you could hear the familiar sound of the peal of bells from the local church, which was about half a mile away. At the bottom of our garden grew a very thick, tall hawthorn hedge, which used to bloom every year with heavily scented creamy white Mayflowers. Just behind this hedge, and going right the way down the road, there stood very tall and majestic Scots Pine trees which must have been planted many years ago. They seemed to be standing on sentry duty, as though they were there to protect us all.

At night, we would gaze at the different phases of the moon just peeping through the branches of the pine trees as it passed its way silently across the inky black sky, dotted with bright twinkling stars, looking like bright little fireflies. We imagined the stars were flashing out signals to us, each flash was a sort of morse code.

We could often hear the owls hooting as they went out on their night-time hunting. The tall trees in the nearby woodland were their home.

Sometimes, if we were lucky enough, on warm summer nights we could hear a nightingale singing from a distant woodland which has long since gone and was about a mile away from our house.

It is sad to think that we have almost forgotten what these birds sound like.

On the other side of the hedge and trees was a very secret garden.

We could never see the garden clearly, because the hedge was too thick and tall for us to see through to the other side, and the only way we could glimpse anything at all over it was to look from my bedroom window.

There was a very old apple orchard, the trees of which we could just about see the tops of, and we knew that a donkey lived there because we could often hear it braying, but sadly we could never see it.

We were told that certain children lived there in a very grand old manor house called Haute Terre, and that their parents were very rich, but the children were not all that well and needed lots of care and looking after by nurses, and they had a matron as well.

It was a special school for children who could not do the same things as we could and found difficulty in learning their lessons. We never saw much of them, as they were never taken out and about anywhere, and we could only occasionally hear them laughing and playing, and there was only the odd rare glimpse of them through the thick hedge, so we didn't see them properly. We thought they must have been prisoners, and it was said that their parents never came to see them.

We all felt genuinely sorry for them, but we knew of a small group of children who lived in a different road to ours and were not very nice. They were quite horrid in fact, as they would tease and call out nasty names to these poor children, which would make some of them cry. We thought that this was very cruel of them and that they should have known better.

There were only about half a dozen other children living in our road, but I do remember that the boys in our road (there were only about two other girls as well as myself) used to fight with the gang from the bottom of the road, and our dogs used to fight their dogs, so there was a right old battle going on at times. But all in all, it was just a bit of healthy fun, and nobody really got hurt, and nothing was damaged. It was just a bit of gang rivalry.

We were also lucky enough to have the use of two plots of land near us to play on.

One of these was at the top of the road, and the other one was at the bottom.

The bottom plot was in enemy territory.

We used to call these two small fields, "the top green" and "the bottom green."

The boys would build camps there and make bonfires. This was spectacular fun on bonfire night when our dads would help to build us a really huge bonfire, and we would have a wonderful display of noisy and colourful fireworks. Other times, the boys would also dig deep and very impressive trenches, which to me looked as though they went down forever, and sometimes an unfortunate child would indeed fall down one of these and would have to be rescued. We also loved to play cowboys and Indians, and I was always the one to be killed off first because I was just a "silly girl."

"Bang! Bang! You're dead!" And that was me out of it.

One chubby little boy got his foot stuck fast down one of the holes, which was not very deep, but it was rather narrow, and because it was covered over with bits of gorse, it could hardly be seen, and so the unfortunate little boy happened to come along and step straight into it, which made him shout and scream so loudly that I'm sure the whole road could have heard him! His irate father grumbled and groaned because he had to leave his tea and come up with his spade to dig the boy out. All the while he was doing this, his son could be heard howling his head off. I think his pride was hurt more than anything else, but soon he was seen trotting off down the road to join his dad for tea!

I was always the one to be used for experimental purposes, like being a test pilot for their home-made go-carts, sending me off down the hill (sometimes sitting back-to-front) just to see how far I could travel before crashing into the hedge at the bottom of the hill, or to land up in someone's front garden and getting the blame for trespassing. Another experiment was for me to test out a new swing (fixed to the washing line) to see how far they could push me before I fell off. I think they were trying to set me off into orbit, or wanted to see if I could swing right over the top!

Another time, when we set off on a ramble across a local farmer's fields in search of wildlife beyond our own gardens, we were told by an elderly farm worker where we would be able find a lovely little stream, which was situated in a pretty little bluebell wood. We thought that this stream sounded very enticing and that it would be ideal for us to paddle in, and it might also be an excellent stream for searching for frog spawn in, or even little fishes. We didn't know at that time that a pond would have been a more likely place to find frog spawn.

We were so delighted when we found the wood. It was almost as good as walking into a "Santa's Grotto" to us.

This was going to be our other "magical place" and entirely different to the common, which was quite a long way off for us to walk to, and it didn't have a gurgling running stream through it either.

It was indeed a very pretty, silvery, winding stream that we found there, and it was flanked by tall willow and birch trees, and lovely emerald-green ferns grew on the bank amongst mounds of soft green moss. Removing our shoes and socks, we clambered down the bank and into the water.

It was particularly lovely just to paddle barefoot in the stream, to feel the cool water trickling over your feet. It looked so clear and fresh, and when you looked down at your bare feet, the water seemed to magnify everything, making your small, size-three feet look more like size ten. We watched in fascination the shoals of little silvery stickleback fish and the minnows too, as they swam with a wriggling motion downstream.

If we were really observant, we would now and then glimpse a kingfisher sitting very still on a branch, and then dive off straight into the water, displaying his vibrant, almost metallic colours of reds, greens, and blues, as this little fisher bird of the waterside flashed past us carrying a little fish in his beak.

The girls picked buttercups and carried out a very old country tradition as they held the yellow flower in turn under one another's chins to see if a golden glow would show, and if it did, they uttered the usual proclamation, "Oh, yes…you *do* love butter!"

The boys hunted for birds' nests to see if they could identify them by their shapes and by the eggshell colours and markings, but they were very careful not to disturb them too much, or to handle the eggs, otherwise the parent birds might forsake their nests.

As we made our way along the bank of the stream, we could smell the pungent fragrance of the moist earth, mingling with the other perfumes of wild thyme, and the stronger smell of the little star-shaped, snow-white flowers of the wild garlic. It was exciting to explore the winding path of the stream, as we didn't know what we were likely to discover around the next bend.

As we ducked under the low branches, then dived across to try the other side, we were completely unaware just how far we had actually walked, and it wasn't until we had rounded yet another bend that we were suddenly confronted by a fiercely barking black and white collie dog, who seemed to appear like a bolt out of the blue! He chased us back down the stream. How were we to know that the farmer's cottage was just around the next bend? He was obviously doing his guard duty! We soon learnt to sprint fast, as those slavering, gnashing, snarling white teeth came hot on our heels, and the thought of hot rank breath breathing down our necks spurred us on. Hey presto! and we were quickly transformed into long-distance, Olympic-style runners. We became quite nimble at leaping from stone to stone across the stream, sending sprays of water all about us.

The faithful collie was only protecting his master's property. He wasn't to know that we meant no harm and that we had no intentions of stealing anything or leaving any gates open or playing havoc in his fields, for we always kept to the footpaths. Nearly always!

It was drummed into us by our parents, who were always strict that we should respect other people's property.

After our desperate dash back to where we started, we were able to slow down, because the collie had given up his chase, and he was seen heading off back home. Now that we were once more in the open fields, our wet clothes quickly dried off in the sunshine, and we carried on with our trek.

Further on, there was one particular field, which seemed to stretch a very long way ahead of us, that had a large herd of cows in it and one very huge aggressive-looking bull!

Once again I was used as a decoy, and my brother and his friends sent me across the field just to see if the bull or the cows would chase me, and if they didn't, then this was the sign for the all clear!

I didn't realize at the time just how dangerous this stunt could have been. I was still too young and naïve, and besides, I had great faith in these little "heroes," and so in obedience, I cautiously crossed the field in the manner of a bomb disposal expert, treading quietly and carefully.

Fortunately for me, the bull and his cows were very placid that day and were not a bit interested in the little band of interlopers, thank goodness!

Now that the coast was clear, the others joined me, and we spent a few happy hours (or at least it seemed like hours to us) exploring more of the fields and making up games to play as we went.

Accompanied by the incessant rasping song of the grasshoppers, we went tripping over mole hills, dodging mushy cow pats, jumping over them in quick succession. But the unfortunate ones who were not so nimble and sure footed at jumping over them would land clumsily with a *splat!* right in the middle, and they would be returning home with lovely brown and green gunge on their shoes, soggy wet socks (for those who didn't remove them when they went paddling) and with nasty muddy stains on their clothing, complemented with a strong, tell-tale whiffy perfume. The inevitable punishment they expected to receive would, without doubt, be administered on them.

As they made their way slowly home, the "smelly bunch" gave themselves as much time as they dared, so as to make up their feeble excuses, by rehearsing what they were going to say and changing their stories until they felt confident with their final statement of facts, explaining how they came by their smelly, dishevelled, disgusting state!

One of the bigger girls called out to her grubby little brother, "Just wait till Mum sees you, she'll go berserk!"

"Don't care!" he retorted.

Then another girl added in a singsongy voice, "Don't care was made to care!"

"Wocher mean?" he asked, rather anxiously and slowing his pace.

Then, in a sarcastic manner she added, "When your mum sees the state you're in, she'll give you a right old slapping—*then* you might care!"

So it was a very subdued, dishevelled band of little grubby people who returned home.

The "anointed ones" seemed to be blissfully unaware of the unwelcome attention they were about to receive, as a small black cloud of nasty persistent flies buzzed around and followed them uncomfortably close, and they would not be driven away, and no amount of arm waving or shooing noises would make them leave. Even though the smell was so disgusting, the grimy children couldn't seem to understand why everyone who happened to walk past gave them a very wide birth, and some of them who found the smell too overbearing showed their distaste by crossing over to the other side of the road!

Looking back, I think the boys' games were very much influenced by story books and from some of their favourite comics.

The heroes of the day were characters from books such as Biggles and William, and there was also the big muscle man, Desperate Dan, and many others from the Beano and Dandy comics. Indiana Jones hadn't yet appeared on the scene, or that other great hero lurking in the wings and just waiting to be discovered: the one and only 007— James Bond! They would have been a very tough act to follow, and who knows what sort of trouble the boys would have got themselves into if they tried to re-enact their exploits. I was more interested in the gentle Enid Blyton or horsey type stories myself, and I am proud to possess a personally written postcard from her.

When we were very young (I was about seven years old and my brother was eleven), we used to trundle down to the little town hall with bundles of old newspapers all neatly tied up with string. In those days it was called "salvage paper." Today it would be called "recycled."

Handing in our contributions at the door, we were ushered to seats set neatly in rows and sat next to other children of about our own age, and then we were treated to still pictures, projected onto a large white screen by a noisily whirring projector. The pictures didn't exactly have us sitting on the edge of our seats with excitement. They usually showed pictures of perhaps a thrush with a snail in its beak, accompanied by a short, monotonous commentary by the projectionist, or a rural scene portraying the thrills of farming life in the country. We could hardly contain ourselves! But at least it was better than no entertainment at all.

About a year later the "stills" were upgraded to brightly coloured (but rather poor quality, I hasten to add) moving pictures. But still no sound tracks to go with them.

It was some years later in the same little town hall, and as a gawky, rather skinny teenager, that I was embarrassingly cajoled, persuaded, and bribed, into taking part in a local fashion show to model neat little undies and nightwear for the new Dorothy Perkins shop, which had just opened.

I blame the whole incident on a friend of mine who had started employment there as a junior assistant in the shop. She told me that I could choose a few pretty clothes for myself, plus a little wage as well, which had already been negotiated with the manageress. But not before telling her, "Not in a million years, or even if I was paid ten thousand pounds, would I parade myself in front of other people half naked!" Needless to say, because I wasn't strong willed (like my mother) and had a more passive nature (like my father), my feeble protests fell on stony ground, and I soon gave way, as the "million years" rolled by and disappeared from my memory in a puff of smoke, and the "ten thousand pounds" devalued in an instant, like greased lightning. I stupidly agreed, but I must admit, I did have a battle with my conscience about parading in underwear, and being of a very shy disposition, it wasn't without certain consequences, as I soon found out.

The following week, and much to my dismay and utter horror, the event (plus a picture of me parading in a little baby doll night-dress), was plastered in a section of the local newspaper, complete with an interview with my father, because it appears that he was supposedly the only male in the audience. And there I was, looking more like a praying mantis than a top-class super model! I can only think that the photographer of that day must have had a faulty camera, and when he thought he had a real "dolly bird" in his sights, the mechanism probably jammed, and when he managed to get his shot, then I must have floated like an apparition in the view of his lens instead!

I decided there and then that a life-changing career as a fashion poser, or joining the jet set of the glitzy Tinseltown world of modelling, was most definitely not for me! And not only that, I just couldn't visualize offers coming my way anyway!

The little town hall was eventually demolished and resurrected as a newspaper and general store.

An improvement there, I thought.

We were fortunate enough to have two cinemas in our little town. To us, they were like temples, and once a week, we would be drawn to them like bees to a hive!

One of the cinemas was called the posh one, because it had long, quite shallow curved steps leading down to it, and it was attractively bow fronted, but the other one was just ordinary.

Both were easily recognizable with their unusual, but classical, art deco shapes, and their wide gaping doors enticed inside the ever increasing queues of avid film-goers, waiting to be entertained by the latest blockbuster of the week!

As we filed back out from the darkness and blinked our way into the brightness, we were fairly buzzing with our praises of the heroic actions of the star performers of the screen, swashbuckling all over the place, we couldn't wait to see the next adventure-packed exploits, so tantalizingly shown to us in the trailer.

Both of these much-loved buildings have since fallen victim to the ever-increasing development plans for the so-called improvements to the expanding town. And so one of them is now a dreary furniture store, and the other one is an equally boring small office block.

However, before their unforeseen demise, we did at least make the most of them, as the television set hadn't as yet made its way into our home.

Early Saturday mornings, we would walk to one of the local cinemas, where they would show special films just for the children. We would all queue up in a very orderly manner and proudly wear our special "ABC Minor" badges, which meant we belonged to the cinema club, and a special little blue card with our names written inside to show at the ticket office. When the doors were finally opened, we would all file in slowly, crocodile style, to take our seats. If any of the children misbehaved, they were duly frog-marched out of the cinema by the manager and banned from returning for the rest of the show, so most of the time, everyone behaved very well indeed!

It would begin with a little sing-along tune, then they would start the entertainment with some of our favourite cartoons, like Tom and Jerry, Mickey Mouse and Donald Duck, and sometimes they would show Popeye the Sailor Man. They would also show comedy films starring comedians such as Oliver and Hardy, Old Mother Riley, Buster Keaton, Norman Wisdom and also the wonderfully talented Danny Kaye, singing his staccato, tongue-twisting songs in films such as Hans Christian Andersen and many more. We usually had a main feature film, which might be one of the adventure stories of the Greek god, Hercules; or the wild man of the jungle, Tarzan, with his little chimp, Cheetah, and his lady friend, Jane; or the caped crusader, Batman, with boy wonder, Robin; then there was Superman and Flash Gordon; and of course Robin Hood with his girlfriend, Maid Marian, and his merry band of men acting out their deeds in Sherwood Forest. And then there was also that canine heroine, Lassie, bounding across the screen. Usually in the story she had to save an animal in danger, or it could be somebody who has been kidnapped or is just lost, and Lassie would always rescue them in the nick of time. Sometimes, they would show the yodelling, smiling, cowboy, Roy Rogers, and his wife, Dale, with his beautiful, prancing, flaxen-maned, golden-coloured horse called Trigger, and I always dreamt that one day I would own a lovely horse just like Trigger.

There were many other action-packed cowboys and Indians films. I often used to wonder why it was that with so many horses galloping about, or standing tethered outside of saloon bars, that you just didn't see any piles of horse manure, or even see them dropping it, just as you would expect to see in real life! Being a great horse lover, I was particularly thrilled to watch these fast-moving films.

With such a wonderful variety of films for us to enjoy, we thought ourselves jolly lucky. And then, during a short interval, the lights would go up, and an ice cream lady would appear at the bottom of the aisle wearing a smart white uniform, and she would be carrying a large tray, which was supported by tabs worn around her neck. From the tray you could buy ice cream in tubs and various sweets, as well as popcorn, and she would also sell drinks from her tray too. After all the sweet papers had stopped rustling and the last of the *slurp! slurp!* noises from the drink cartons had ceased, we all settled down once more as the films continued.

Then at the end of the show, everyone stood at attention when they played the tune of "God Save The Queen," after which the kids would proceed to stampede towards the exit, but with a stern look from the manager, they would all file out once more in a sedate manner, blinking their eyes in the bright daylight. They would then disperse in different directions to make their ways home.

Sometimes the kids would re-enact a particular part of one of the characters they especially liked from their favourite films, which would usually end up in a spot of horseplay, but it was all taken in good humour. It typically began with Batman giving Robin Hood a *thwack!* across the head, just because Robin said, "How stupid Batman looked with big pointy ears!" Then Batman retaliates by saying, "How sissy Robin Hood looks in a short tunic, which looks just like a girl's dress cut short, and whoever wanted to be seen wearing girlish green tights anyway?" And then Maid Marian would start pulling the plaits of Tarzan's Jane, making very unrealistic chimp-type noises.

Some of the kids tried to mimic American accents by twisting their mouths to one side, to try and enhance varying degrees of accuracy, which ranged somewhere between the sounds more reminiscent of a wailing tom cat to an exaggerated twangy drawl. And then there were the small minority of fairly impressive ones who had obviously practised their skills of mimicry to a fine art.

A perfect start to a Saturday morning, and now we could make our plans of more interesting things to do for the rest of the weekend.

We were very contented with our life. Everything seemed to have a different feel about it in those days, as though nothing would change, but of course it always does.

The pace quickens as the years pass by, and we all move on to walk down that uncertain path we decide to take. We don't know what awaits us down the path that angels fear to tread, with all its unpredictable twists and turns. We are always looking out expectantly for that silver lining through rose-tinted glasses and pushing our limitations almost to the breaking point.

I remember the times we used to come home from school on cold winter evenings, and sat down to tea. Sometimes we had crumpets toasted on a little fork, which was held over a crackling open fire, and then lots of butter spread upon them, or we might have a slice of home-made cake, or perhaps a tasty scone, still warm from the oven.

Whilst having our tea, we would turn on the radio to listen to our favourite programme called Children's Hour, which included wonderful stories like *Billy Goat Gruff, Little Red Riding Hood*, or *The Three Little Pigs*, who sadly had their rather badly built little houses blown down by a very wicked wolf (probably the same wolf as in the Little Red Riding Hood story), and many, many other well known stories.

Most of these stories were for the very young, who never seemed to get tired of hearing them, and they nearly always had a happy ending to them.

The stories were read out over the radio by a man called Uncle Mac. He had such a therapeutically calm, friendly voice, unlike today's children's TV presenters, who tend to screech out at you through the screen as though you're all deaf!

The grown-ups had their own special radio programmes.

Mother used to listen to Woman's Hour every day, and in the afternoons she would tune into *Mrs. Dale's Diary*, which was mostly about a doctor's wife, who always seemed to be worried about her husband for some reason or another, and also about her mother who had a cat, which I seem to remember was called Captain.

Now Father liked to listen to the *Archers* every day, without fail, so we all had to be quiet, and once a week we were treated to a scary serial, which went on for about six months, or maybe even longer, and it was called *Journey Into Space!* It had all the special effects, such as the space ship's hatch doors opening and closing with a strange humming noise and a haunting, echoing voice of an alien trying to drive the space travellers out of the universe! This was really all very high tech stuff to us in those days.

Another exciting thriller was *Dick Barton, Special Agent!* This was a kind of earlier version of James Bond.

Other programmes which didn't consist of "nightmare-making material" that we all liked to listen to on the radio were *Meet the Huggetts*, which was a very light comedy about an ordinary family. There was the father called Jo, his wife called Ethel, and they had a daughter named Jane, but nothing very exciting ever happened in this programme. A similar type of storyline was a series called *Life with the Lyons*, and their names were Ben Lyon, the father, and his wife, Bebe Danniels, the mother, and they had a son called Richard, and Barbara was their daughter. This time the actors were American.

We also liked another comedy series called *A Life of Bliss*, which was about a young man who had lots of girlfriends, and he was always getting into trouble, and it also featured his dog called Psyche, who had a very unrealistic bark, but we didn't mind that; we just thought it was all "jolly good fun" in those days of thrilling entertainment.

Another favourite with the grown-ups was one of the first game shows (which was well before the television game show called *Double Your Money*), and this one was called *Have a Go!* This popular quiz show was compered by Wilfred Pickles with his wife Mabel. It was hosted at church halls from many different counties, and Wilfred Pickles would start off by calling out, "'ow do! How are you?" The contestants were invited to answer a money-spinning question, and then if they answered the four given questions correctly (or even if they didn't) they were always given a heart-stopping hand out of either half a crown, five bob, ten bob, and then as much as one pound, with Wilfred calling out, "Give 'em the money, Barney!" or he would call out, "Mabel at the table!" from which she would dish out a surprise gift for the contestants. The show would then finish off with a tune played out on an old piano, and the pianist was Violet Carson, who eventually played Mrs. Ena Sharples in Coronation Street!

There were so many other light-hearted programmes to be heard in those days, which have sadly faded into the distance, but then they wouldn't be considered as entertainment any more.

I can remember one particularly memorable incident which happened to me when I was about ten years old.

My brother and I were playing with a small red bouncing ball, with a few of our friends on the top green, when the ball, which was thrown in my direction for me to catch, somehow whizzed straight past me, and much to my horror, it passed straight through the thick hawthorn hedge and landed somewhere in the long grass on the other side. It had landed in the forbidden territory of "the secret garden!"

Guess who was volunteered to go fetch? That's right! — it was me!

Pushing gingerly through the dense thorny hedge and scratching my stick-insect-like arms and legs in the process (I was very skinny as a child) and trying to avoid the stinging nettles and spider webs, my long hair became entangled in twigs and collected dried dead leaves as I forced my way through.

I was by now beginning to regret my participation in the ball game and wished I was at home playing with my pet guinea pig and rabbit instead, but it was more than my life's worth to turn back now. The other children would certainly ban me from any more games for a long time if I didn't find the lost ball.

At last, after a lot of pushing and squirming, I emerged breathlessly on the other side. My hands and knees were tingling and scratched quite badly from the thorns. Standing up cautiously, I felt a bit like Alice in Wonderland, and wouldn't have been at all surprised to see the white rabbit hop past me. My heart was thumping so loudly, I'm sure it could have been heard all around the garden.

I surveyed the scene before me.

This must surely be a children's paradise.

The grass grew very tall and was nearly waist high, and I should think it had hardly ever been cut, but the well-trodden paths criss-crossed through the orchard, and pretty dainty white daisies (which were much taller than the small-headed short ones that studded our lawn) grew here. Deep yellow buttercups were allowed to grow freely too, and big lazy bumblebees hummed their way from flower to flower.

The old apple trees, with their thick ancient trunks growing bent with age like elderly gentlemen, cast dappled shadows beneath them where the blazing sun shone through their twisty gnarled branches. These old fruit trees that bore fragrant blossoms in the springtime were now laden with lovely juicy red and green apples. The boys would just about give anything to go climbing and scrumping here, if they dared!

To the right and just a few yards away stood a rickety old wooden shelter (I guessed this was housing for the donkey), and it had richly scented honeysuckle growing right over the roof.

A water butt stood at the side of the shelter to catch and drain the rainwater from the guttering.

Although I scanned the orchard in every direction, I was rather disappointed that I could not spot the donkey. It was nowhere to be seen. This was the only opportunity I would ever have at seeing it at close quarters instead of just hearing it from over the hedge.

One lone magpie flitted through the trees, and he landed in a clearing with a few bouncy hops, but took off again when he saw me standing there; he flew back over the wall and in the direction of the woods opposite the grounds.

To the left of me and over by the wall which ran parallel with the top road, grew a huge blue buddleia bush, heavy with drooping heads of deep blue flowers, and flying so daintily and silently, like little ballerinas amongst the blooms, were the beautifully coloured peacock and red admiral butterflies, sipping up the sweet nectar from the flowers.

I suddenly spotted a huge green dragonfly and watched in fascination as it swooped and dived over the trees, with the sun shining through its transparent wings. You could even hear its jaws snap as it picked off flying insects as it darted and hovered. Then, suddenly, it was gone. I was curious as to where it had come from because I didn't know of any ponds around here; it must have travelled a long way. Perhaps it was lost!

I could just see the outline of the old manor house hidden behind some very tall trees. It looked forbidding and spooky.

I must admit that I was beginning to feel very afraid, and very vulnerable.

As I looked about me, I recalled the stories told to us children, by a very old vicar.

The children used to stand around the elderly vicar in a small group underneath the old fig tree, which grew against the high brick wall skirting "the secret garden" from the roadside. He would wave his wooden walking stick skywards, as if to gain our utmost attention.

He was a portly old gentleman who cut a dark figure with his thick black overcoat, black trousers, shiny black shoes, and on his head he wore a dusty old black porkpie hat, and sometimes he would wear a check flat cap instead. If he met someone he knew, he would always lift his hat graciously in recognition as they walked past.

He usually walked with his body slightly tilting backwards, as though he was afraid of toppling over at any minute, which looked very strange when he had to walk downhill.

In the autumn, he sometimes accompanied us on our chestnut-gathering days in the woods at the top of the road and helped us by turning over the sweet-smelling leaves with his walking stick to reveal the hard prickly clusters of the outer casing, which we would stamp on (but not too hard) to reveal the fat shiny nuts inside. We were able to fill our pockets and school hats and caps so that we could take them home, to either eat raw or to put onto a tin tray in the oven to bake so that we could have them hot.

Whilst ambling along, the old vicar told us wonderful stories about fairies, elves, goblins and witches. As the stories progressed, his watery old eyes would go wide and round, as though he was trying to beam the images directly into our young minds, but we were never scared, because all of his stories would have a happy ending, so we never had nightmares about them. He also told us that at a certain time of the year, on a night of the full moon, you could hear the pipes of Pan, and the music could be heard coming from the top of the old Victorian water tower that stood in the chestnut wood, and that if we were very good and very quiet, we would certainly be able to hear it, and to emphasize his story, he would cup his hand behind his ear, as though he was listening for something!

We never actually heard the pipes of Pan; nevertheless, there was a weird sound that really did come from this ancient old tower, which looked very much like a turret from a castle. *Throomp, throomp, throomp, throomp!* it seemed to go, and it sounded very much like a heart beat, and you could hear it going day and night. The old vicar said that it was the sound of falling hammers belonging to the woodland elves, who were the workers for Pan, as they fashioned new pipes for him, and goodness knows what else.

In reality, the strange sound we could hear was coming from the old water-driven pumps, but we didn't know that at the time.

If we searched for chestnuts without the old vicar, we would tiptoe carefully past the menacing tower, cautious not to peek through the murky, cobwebby windows, in case we saw the elves at work, as they may not be too pleased at being disturbed! Sometimes we thought we could see a glow from their candles, or was it a flash of steel from their hammers?

Such stories of witches, giants and fairies transported us for just a brief moment of time into another world whilst the real world revolved steadily on around us.

It's such a shame that these interesting old characters like this gentle, inoffensive old vicar, just don't seem to exist anymore. A great loss to the children of today, as they were a great asset for building children's imaginations.

I was jolted back from my daydream when I suddenly spotted the lost red ball. It was lying there on a patch of short grass (probably grazed by the donkey) just waiting for me to pick it up, like the forbidden apple in the Garden of Eden. I cautiously made my way over to it and stooped down to pick it up.

As I stretched my hand out to grasp the ball, there was a sudden movement from the long grass, just to the left of me. It was not the green, two-headed monster that I had expected to see, but instead, it was a small, fair, curly haired girl, who rose up from her hiding place.

The little girl was wearing a pink gingham dress, and on her feet she wore shiny black lace-up shoes, with white socks turned down at the ankles. Her pale, doll-like features held no expression, and there was no sign of laughter, or even the look of excitement in her face at all. She just stared wistfully straight at me, with her big pansy-blue eyes.

When the little girl saw that I was about to pick up the ball, she gave a sigh, as light as an angel's breath, which would hardly have fluttered the candle on a birthday cake. Cocking her head slightly on one side, she squinted up at me, and then, in a bell-like voice she started to speak, breaking the silence and my thoughts.

"That yours?" she asked, pointing at the ball.

"Er...yes ,it is...well...um...ours really...or at least...my friends' over there!" My voice cracked in reply as I pointed towards the hedge, and my throat had turned quite dry with anxiety. "What's your name?" I asked her.

"Mona," she replied.

"And do you live here, in the big house?"

"Yes, over there."

She pointed in the direction of the manor house. So she certainly wasn't another intruder like myself; she actually lived here.

I was beginning to feel much more confident now. I then asked her if she had a ball like this one, holding it up for her to see. "Yes," she said, "a great big, big one, like *this*!" and she then made a big sweeping circle with her arms to indicate the size of this ball, which I judged to be a slight exaggeration.

"All different colours they are," she went on, and then she drooped her head like a snowdrop, then added in a much quieter voice, nearly a whisper, "not mine really, belongs to all of us, lots of others...mine sometimes."

She sounded very sad and began to lose interest. She then stood on one leg and tried to hop away, but lost her balance and fell over into the long grass. She looked as though she was about to cry. I felt really sorry for her and ran over to help her up, and after brushing grass seeds from her dress, one of my sweets suddenly fell out of my dress pockets and onto the ground, luckily it still had its wrapper on; it was a green fruit drop. I carefully took the wrapper off and handed it to Mona. She took it gratefully. "Ooh, thank you," she said, and she seemed to brighten up again. I fished into my pocket once more and found a couple of mint sweets, and one I popped into my mouth, which helped to stop the dryness, and handed the other one to Mona, which she immediately put straight into her mouth, alongside the fruit drop, which made her little cheeks bulge. She seemed to catch her breath, and then made a sound like, "Woh!...Woh!...Woh!" as though to cool her throat down, so I guessed she just wasn't used to eating mints.

Then for the first time, she gave the hint of a smile, and the sun seemed to be much brighter as it shone down onto her pale face, making her blue eyes sparkle \ in contrast to the dull, lifeless, faraway look she had when we first met. It was as though this could have been her first encounter with someone else from the outside world, or at least to meet another girl nearer to her own age, or perhaps I was about two or three years older. She seemed to become more and more confident as we talked.

I then had a sudden idea and really pushed the boat out.

"Would you, um, would you like this ball?" I asked her, holding the red ball out towards her.

The little girl gave a squeal of delight.

"Oh, yes please!" she said, and before I could change my mind, she took the ball from my hand and went off skipping in the direction of the old manor house, singing a tuneless song as she went.

I waved goodbye to her, but she didn't look back, almost as though she had already forgotten the encounter.

I never saw her again.

I made my way back through the same hole I'd made in the hedge to join the frustrated and, by now, a very impatient group.

"Well?" they asked, "*where's* the ball then?"

"Oh!...um!...it's sort of lost!...in the long grass!... somewhere!... er!... over there!"

Years later, we were to witness a dramatic change to our comfortable, familiar, harmonious way of life, forever! The sights and sounds of wildlife on our doorstep were soon to take a spiralling plunge to oblivion.

The first stages of destruction started with the arrival of bulldozers and demolition men in their yellow helmets, closely followed by men wielding chainsaws, and gangs of men with earth removing machinery, roaring through, like great metal chargers.

First of all, most of the ancient old garden wall, which surrounded "the secret garden" was removed from the top road, and we were alarmed to witness the old fig tree, which had grown into a large spreading tree and had stood there for so many years, being uprooted and dragged away. It was like an old friend to us children, and we all felt very sad to see the empty space there.

Many stories were told to us, and many plots were hatched beneath this old tree, not to mention the times people used to shelter under it whenever there was a heavy rainfall, and it was even used as a meeting place for courting couples.

The final massacre took place when the chainsaw gang moved in and started felling the beautiful old Scots Pine trees, most of which had stood at the bottom of our garden many years, even before our houses were built.

One by one, those gentle giants groaned as they fell to the ground. I felt a dreadful pain through the whole of my being as each one was cut down and then sawn up into logs by those dreadful saws. I imagined I could hear their groans of agony as they fell.

When the dust had finally settled, all that we were now left with were bygone memories of our earlier childhood. The bubble had finally burst, and we were silently wishing that those cruel men would fall out of the trees and off their machines, then"break their ruddy necks!" as one little protester so delicately put it, and now all was gone.

Just one lone Scots Pine tree was spared, and it stood forlornly at the bottom of our garden, as if a powerful reminder of what we once had, but now reduced to become just a distant memory of the past. Nobody seemed to know why this particular tree was left to live on, to stand alone, lamenting his lost brothers.

Even the grey squirrels (who used to look down at us from high up in the branches, where they used to chatter and scold before throwing down small cones at us) too have now gone.

After everything had been cleared up and taken away in huge wagons and skips, everywhere seemed so quiet and so melancholy and sad.

It took a long time for the full impact of this destruction to our world to finally sink in.

That lovely old orchard, the wild garden, the insects, the sounds of all the birds that used to nest there, including the cuckoo, who would occasionally lay her egg in the nest of a songbird, the donkey, and of course the children from the manor house all were now gone.

Where did they all go to?

Shortly after this mass clearance, another gang of workmen took over.

This time the surveyors came to do all their measuring, and then shortly after that, the builders arrived, and in no time at all, instead of "the secret garden," we now had a brand new housing estate. This was to be the first of many to appear in our small town.

The next in line for development were "the two greens," which are now just small, characterless estates. Just like mushrooms, the houses seemed to pop up almost overnight. Progress is what they like to call it, and now there is nowhere left close by for the children to play.

Most of our friends from the neighbourhood decided to move away, and we seemed to be the only ones left.

On a cold wet day, my brother and I watched from my bedroom window as the removal van arrived to the house opposite. Our two little friends were hovering expectantly outside, as the family was preparing to leave. They were jumping up and down with excitement, impatient at times as they waited for all their furniture to be piled into the van, until finally they all clambered into their father's car, and then all too soon they were off and away.

We watched like two lone waifs as their car disappeared down the hill with the two children sitting in the back seat without even a glance back or a final wave to us.

Their destination?

Unknown!

The years flew by, and our adulthood was just waiting around the corner, ready to embrace us. If we knew what was in store for us, I think we would have turned about and ran back to our childhood — at full speed!

The thought of us ever leaving our home and moving away (let alone to Wales) was about as likely (and remote) as a trip to the moon!

If everything had remained as it was then in our early years, with that wonderful wild orchard just over our hedge, then surely Maggie would have thought he was in a perfect "Magpie Paradise."

– Chapter Three and a Half –
Over to Maggie

…sing a song of sixpence, a pocket full of rye…

Holy herons' heads! You could've stoned me with a rabbit's poo! What did she do? Yours truly nearly got pinned to the floor, and all because I wanted my cake—and to eat it, too!

It all happened on one bright start of the sunlight-time.

I woz just sittin' there, waiting very, very patiently for me first bit of grub, and the time was travelling on by, ultra fast. Trouble woz, me pinky saviour wasn't keepin' up with the time at the same pace, and I woz suffering intolerably a might bit of hunger, and I would have eaten anything what woz on offer.

Anyway, in she bounced, like a whirlwind in a freak thunderstorm, and thrust this bit of grub at me, which I took to be a nice juicy, newly dug up worm. I must've suffered a bit of a beak malfunction as I gulched and gobbled it down, like you do in such circumstances. Then, a fraction too late, I woefully discovered that the offering was in fact not what it seemed, and it turned out to be a sort of wooden worm, which got good and stuck real tight, from all the way down me throat, right down to me ar...backside! It felt as though I'd been stung by a giant bee or a hornet wasp. The pain!—the agony!—I felt as "jolly as a kipper at a cat's funeral!"

Now it wasn't exactly a burning ambition of mine to end up as a "chick-on-a-stick" or even an outstanding desire to become a "scarecrow's dummy"! I reckon I looked more like a waddling penguin than a handsome magpie. Jolly uncomfortable, I must say. The only way I could move woz to shuffle along. If I tried to hop along, then sure as eggs is eggs, I would have stabbed myself, probably in two, even!

It took me a few suns and moon-times to dispose of this nasty thingymejig, but I'm not tellin' how, 'coz you will just have to use your imagination. Out it did pop, real neat, like a real treat!

Now *this* you are just not going to believe! The pinkies really know how to do their magic stuff.

There's this peculiar box-shaped thingy sitting on top of four thin, but quite short, tree trunks (TV). Most of the sunlight-time (or "daytime," I should be saying) it just sits there, all quiet like. Then suddenly, when the outside darkness falls (or "nightfall," I should say), the first bit of magic happens.

A pinky will point and touch somethin' on the wall (a light switch), and all sorts of stars, moons, an' flashy things will suddenly shine all about the klakki, an' this is followed by lots of noise. No sleeping for me yet, and next, the real fun thing begins.

When I saw it for the first time, I must admit I was very, very scared, and I thought I woz truly done for.

One of the pinkies would point again with a black object (called a remote control), but this time there would be more flashes of light, and guess what? A pinky's head would suddenly appear, with no actual body to go with it, but just a head! Then lots of sharp noises came from the box, which was nothing like the soothing sounds wot us birds make when we sing. And then the pinkies would speak in their funny voices (another thing I got used to and tried to copy when I was by myself), and when I searched both sides of the box— underneath, above or anywhere else—just to see how everything got there, I just could not find the rest of what I expected to discover in the magic talkin' box! Where on earth woz it all kept? All jumbled up in a messy heap, I suppose?

All those missing bits of sky and earth and water, such as the sea, lakes and ponds, not forgetting the all-important birds and critters etcetera, etcetera., were just not there to be seen! Things seemed to appear suddenly and then vanish again. Sheer magic! Must be what I would call "virtual unreality!"

I would just love to be able to visit those seashore places, where there's lots of lovely things to be collected, with shells and lots of long wavy wet bits (seaweed) which would have been very useful. I wasn't too keen on some of those giant earth whisperers (cats) though, 'coz they kept on bringing down really big animals, and then they would eat them.

Most of the stuff in the box wasn't all that bad, but sometimes it was a touch too loud for my delicate little ears. Even so, I would give anything to know their secret of how they get inside the box and how they become so small to fit inside! Everything in that box of tricks was so itsy-bitsy-teeny-weeny. Just think what I could do if I could make myself that much smaller and jump inside! I could go anywhere, do anything, and best of all, have everything I wanted!

Just point me wings in the right direction and I would be off—to the land of the little things, and have myself one hell of a party!

One hot sunlight-time when I woz parked in me usual spot outside in me posh new spacious gleaming white klakki, I met, for the first time in a long, long while, another one of me own kind. Well not *exactly* like me—it was an egg layer.

She woz smaller in stature, and she woz brownish in colour, and she woz very, very friendly—just like me!

I woz sitting very quiet and minding me own business, and doin' a spot of thinking about seashores and things, and I woz doing a bit of singing all to meself when this brown "able-to-fly wing-bearer and egg layer" hopped right up to where I woz, sat in me klakki, and she looked right up at me all sudden like, with her bright shiny eyes.

When I said to her, "Wot-ho, gracious brown one, how goes it with you?" she looked pleasantly surprised and started to converse with me in a very friendly voice, and in such a sweetly caring manner that I woz never used to before.

She told me that she woz of the blackbird kind, and that her name woz Eelandii, "The Seeing Eye," or Eeli, for short.

She lives alone, since her mate, Faldor, woz caught and then eaten in a very horrible manner indeed, by a ferocious earth whisperer, and it happened not so long ago, and she told me that she had predicted that this terrible fate would happen to him, but he would not heed her warning.

It seems that she woz given the "seeing eye" gift from the bright star of Orion, who got fed up with doing so many chores himself. He woz some kind of future teller, and he decided to pass on his knowledge to others, which would allow him some time off, and one of the chosen ones happened to be Eeli, and so now she woz able to see what woz, what is, and what will be!

Eeli then told me her story of ancient times.

It seems that far, far back in the mists of time, when the hither and thitherlands, and the whole of the earth were still very new and going through a settling-down period, and also a drying-out state, after spending many moons being almost totally covered in water, a big freeze came to pass for a while, followed by a big warming-up time.

Apparently, our early ancestors were a right funny looking bunch of "flying fancies" with leathery wings, and lots of sharp teeth in their beaks (wish we still had them!).

When all of the earth gods had finally decided enough was enough and things had begun to settle down, there was to be a great big test to see how everyone living on the earth was going to cope with getting on with things after the great upheaval.

After a good many suns and moons had passed by, Eeli's extremely great, great, ever-so-great ancestors, Dolga and Meega, had a very hard time finding food, and they found it extremely difficult to live their lives happily. And as if that wasn't enough, their feathers were a dull grey in colour, which didn't make them very attractive to look at, and their eggs were as white as snow, which meant they were easy prey to their enemies (such as marauding magpies!). It was also not an easy task to find insects and worms, unless they were right under their beaks, so to speak, because insects were not in abundance at that time, and worms were also scarce, because lots of other more attractive birds were competing for the same food, so there wasn't much left for them.

As for singing, well poor old Dolga had no singing voice at all. Quite tuneless, I was told.

Then one sunrise, the whole of the earth suddenly started to make a sort of agonizing moaning groan, and then there was a terrible grumbling sound that went deep, deep down, whilst giving birth to a brand new landscape. Then it started to shake, tremble and shiver, and then huge cracks and gaps in the ground appeared.

Gigantic boulders and rocks were hurtled out at tremendous speed from the very depths of the earth, along with beautiful brightly coloured crystals of many shapes and sizes, zinging and singing through the air, then landing in every direction and on all parts of the great globe.

Caves of gold and silver were formed. Some were festooned with stalagmites and stalactites, forming an underground wonderland. Other caves were turned into sparkling diamond palaces.

The brilliantly coloured gemstones were carried with great reverence by Aphrodite, a nymph of all the seasons, as she rose out of the sea on a chariot made from a giant conch shell, drawn by four magnificent white horses. When the gems had been hidden in various caves, chosen carefully by Aphrodite, she returned to the sea, and as they crashed beneath the foaming waves, the white steeds changed into charming little seahorses.

The caves now held their precious stores waiting to be discovered.

After all the terrifying commotion, all the creatures of the land—birds and animals alike—became fearful for their lives. They all ran, flew, or hid behind rocks or in the density of the trees, taking cover anywhere they could find a safe haven. That is, all except the brave Dolga and Meega.

Dolga and Meega decided to try and heal the pulsating, groaning, moaning, wounded earth, and they spent many hours of the sunlight-time until it became quite dark, hunting up and collecting twigs, moss, and all the dried grasses they could find. Then, for as long as it took, they stitched the cracks with the dried grass, weaving, pushing and pulling with their thin beaks, then they filled the holes up with the moss and twigs they had so laboriously collected until their little hearts nearly burst with the strain. They even worked through some of the moonlight hours. They would not give in.

Then finally, the earth was healed, and every creature was at last able to come out of their hiding places to live in peace and harmony once more. They were safe at last!

All the birds and animals were full of praise for Dolga and Meega and gave their thanks to them.

The songbirds sang beautiful songs to them, as they were now entering into a new era—into a journey of a great change.

The earth goddess was so grateful for what the two birds had done for her, and for risking their own fragile lives that she gave them the gift of extra-sharp hearing, so that from now on, and thereafter, they would be able to listen to the slightest of sounds beneath the earth, and this meant that they could even hear the movements of worms, grubs and slugs, thus enabling them to dig them up to eat.

The sun god told Dolga to dip his beak into a buttercup, and when he did so, it turned a rich golden yellow, and the rim of his eyes were also coloured yellow, and he could now see much clearer and brighter.

The god of the wind sent down the lovely Proserpina, who was the warrior princess of all creatures great and small. Her hair, which was long and hung down to her waist was of a glowing fiery red and adorned with a crown of gold. She wore a long silken robe, as soft as a spider web, and it was the colour of jade. Tied around her waist was a chain of sweet violets and moon daisies, and from this chain of flowers hung a pouch made from vine leaves, from which she scattered grains of rice and seeds about the earth.

Her task was to reward Dolga with a beautiful melodious voice, which rang out across the land in the early sunrise, just as the mist was forming, and again at any time he wished to sing during the sunlight-time, and then again towards dusk, just before sunset, when a saffron-yellow haze descended on the Western horizon. As the pale sun disappeared, making silhouettes of the trees over the distant hills, his voice could still be heard.

These gentle, humble blackbirds were also gifted with a distinctive alarm call, enabling them to warn all others of any danger that might be lurking nearby.

The sky god threw a velvety black cloak over Dolga and a dark brown cloak (with a hint of a few specks) over Meega. They wore these for seven sunrises and seven nightfalls, and after that time had ended, Dolga's feathers turned a midnight glossy black, and Meega's feathers changed to a rich chestnut brown so that she would now blend in with the undergrowth, which would help to conceal her from her enemies. Her eggs were from now on to be a powdery light blue, with carnelian-red spots, which were made by the earth's tears. All this was done for the recognition of their wonderful deeds to help save the earth from destruction.

After Eeli had told me this wonderful, but fascinating story, I told her that it woz very similar to the one told to me and my siblings, not long after we had hatched, which seemed almost a lifetime ago now, but as we magpies were flying about the earth many more suns and moons than most other birds, then our story is a bit different, and certainly worth a mention.

Eeli asked me if I would tell her my version of the story, and I said I would gladly do so, seeing as there wasn't much else to do, so this is what I told her:

Pa had told us that a long, long time ago, at the beginning of time and a short while after, everything that exists today started with a great big powerful anger from the centre of the earth (just like you told me).

Huge flames belched outwards and upwards, said to be made from dragons awakening from their slumbers of many moons gone by.

Stones and boulders were thrown in all directions, and as they hit the earth, many were split open, and all kinds of creatures emerged from them, scattering and scampering off wherever they fancied to go. Sounds like things were a bit noisy in those days!

The lord of the universe woke up suddenly, because he was made *hugely* angry from the terrible din that was being created. Then he decided to have a right old mess of fun, flinging spots and stripes about in all directions. Some landed on the furry creatures, some on the scaly lizard type creatures, and some onto the feathers of birds. Then he dropped a shower of smart little pearls; which plopped neat as a natterjack an' straight into some loitering oyster shells, who started muttering something like, "Now let's see who can find *our* little treasures all neatly lodged inside our homes!"

Some of the other shells, which came in all shapes and sizes, were splashed with tears from the tormented earth, which made them all speckled with red and brown colours, and then there were these strange little creatures with wavy feelers who scuttled about all fearful like because they were exposed to dangers of all kinds, and seeing these shells, they jumped inside them and took them over for their homes, so they now felt all safe and sound.

They were called hermit crabs!

Poseidon then wanted to take part in the drama and came down as a dolphin.

As he entered the great ocean, he opened his mouth, and out swam all the fishes and lots of other sea creatures, which took them a whole season to do, and then when the deed was done, he swam out into the middle of the ocean and changed himself into Neptune.

Neptune's great strong arms were like the branches of the ancient oak trees, whilst his body was as sturdy as an elm, and he had a great bushy beard of what looked like seaweed, which sent out a luminous green glow about his entire body, and he became guardian of all the seas.

Not to be outdone, old King Titan, who was god of the sea, wanted to get in the act.

He became extremely furious and threw a tantrum, and all because he was about to start out on another mission, and being a bit of a global-perfectionist freak, he turned the sky a brilliant red with his anger. He then swooped down like a giant thunder cloud and blew so hard that all the waves seemed to turn upside down, and it made the poor old earth spin so fast that everyone became extremely dizzy, and the birds became so confused, that they didn't know if they were coming or going! Then, as if on command, with a *splish!* — *splash!* — *splosh!* a gigantic wave surged and heaved, and suddenly a great white whale arose out of the sea, and perched high up on the tip of his tail fin was a mermaid.

They were both singing in a duet a very haunting melody, and time seemed to stand still. Everywhere went quiet, and the wind hushed as it took a deep breath.

The mermaid looked about her.

She was wearing an opal necklace, which reflected the clouds and sky, and on the middle finger of each hand she wore an ice-blue-aquamarine ring. These two rings were forged lovingly by little hermit crabs, from the very depths of the ocean, and it is said that they were passed down to the mermaids from generation to generation. In her left hand she held aloft a magic mirror, which was edged in shells and coral of pale pink and deep red.

With this mirror, which gradually clouded over as a mist started to pour out of it, she made slow circular movements above her head, and then all of the birds that were lost at the time when the earth went into its cracking spin were scooped up from where they hovered in a motionless state, as if they had been in a suspended animation.

The mermaid spoke, and she said, "Let the little ones through first!" — and they found themselves gently transported through to the other side of the magic mirror, and into a reverse world, whilst the mermaid and the whale sang to them:

> *Vallela, vallela, swimming so free,*
> *Cherubim, cherubim, where the land meets the sea.*
>
> *Shashoona, shashoona, little birds of the air,*
> *Bartisca, bartisca, have a care, have a care.*
>
> *Latundra, latundra, from the high old oak tree,*
> *Pallero, ahoah, follow me, follow me.*

The mermaid showed them how to find their way back to their homelands, and gradually they found themselves drawn in the opposite direction, as if by a magnet. And that is how it is today, and how all of the chosen birds, like the swallows, swifts, humming birds, and many, many more, are able to migrate from their hatching sites to other lands across the sea.

The mermaid dived from the tail fin of the whale and into the sea, and then she propelled herself through the waves with all the birds following her, flying just above the water.

Soon they came to a crystal rock which was jutting out of the sea, and where a golden eagle was perched on one side of it, and a proud peacock — with his colourful tail feathers displayed — perched on the other.

A little wren, which was flying in from the direction of the sun, came to rest in the palm of the mermaid's outstretched hand as she sat on the top of the rock, with her tail fin gleaming metallic in the rays of the sun.

All the birds settled themselves on rocks surrounding the crystal one. It was only after all the chattering of the birds had stopped (especially the noisy sparrows, who only ceased their bantering after a lone sparrowhawk gave them a warning glare), that the mermaid began to tell each bird of their destinies.

So many stories were told that day that it would take a lifetime to tell of them all, but I do remember a few of them, so of these I will tell.

The mermaid commenced with her first story to the little wren, who was still sitting quietly in her hand.

She told him that his first ancestor earned the title of "King of the Birds" after it was decided that whoever could fly the highest would be crowned as the ruler of birds. Many other birds tried in vain. The stork tried, but his legs were too long, and the magpie tried, but he soon got too tired. Then there was the majestic golden eagle who reached to a very great height and circled effortlessly above the earth. But before he could claim his victory, a little wren was seen to be flying tirelessly, just above the golden eagle's head, and so he claimed the title of "King of the Birds!"

Now the truth of the matter is that the little wren had slightly cheated, because he had secretly hidden himself beneath one of the wings of the golden eagle, and when the big bird had reached as far as he could go, it was then that the little wren flew out from under his wing, and therefore proclaimed victory over all others! When the other birds found out that the little wren had cheated, they chased him hither and thither, until he took refuge in the deep forests, and the golden eagle reclaimed his rightful title. But because of his bravery for such a little bird, the wren was given the title of "Oak King" (elf-bird king of the woods and forests) where his sharp, clear voice rings out over the glens.

In dark times, the wrens were persecuted. They were hunted and killed by hooded men so that they could be replaced by the red-breasted robin, who represented the "spirit of the new season."

In time, the wrens' status changed for the better, and they became immortalized in songs and rhymes as disciples to the earth gods, which meant that they were now looked upon in awe and were greatly respected. Furthermore, their image was imprinted on small copper coins, and these were made by humans, who used them for exchanging earthly material objects.

It is said that the mermaid told the egg layer cuckoo that cuckoos would not be able to build their own klakkies, and that they would have to lay their eggs in those of other birds, adding that she was so very sorry, but that was how it would be from now and forever after. She also said that the cuckoos would only have two very monotonous notes to call with, in order to herald their arrival—and spring. This didn't sadden the cuckoo too much, because basically she and her kind were rather lazy birds, and that they "couldn't give two hoots anyway!" Or was that said by the owls?

Then turning to the little yellow canary, the mermaid's kind, dolphin-shaped eyes clouded over with great sadness as she shed tears of remorse.

She told the yellow canary that in the distant future, he would be used by the humankind who mined for minerals and rocks hidden deep down in the earth. Canaries would be caught from the wild and then taken mercilessly below in small cages into the great caves and mines beneath the earth's surface for the purpose of warning the humans of dangerous air emitting from below, which could possibly kill the humans. During this insufferable employment, so many little birds would die in the process. She said to the canary that this terribly cruel practice would last for many generations. A reward for their bravery was to be given to them, as the mermaid told him that all of his kind would be given beautiful voices to sing with and that the sun god would look down on them with great kindness, and this is why so many canaries are of a deep yellow—the colour of the sun.

The intelligent and very resourceful, but also proud, black ravens were told that they would become the guardians of the shoreline and that a chosen few were to play a very important role in a very grand place, and would eventually be part of history in the human kingdom, and so it was that the mermaid related the story of Bran.

Bran was the giant raven who went to battle in a place called Ireland, but the battle was so bloody and fierce that Bran lost his life. Before he finally died from his mortal wounds, Bran requested that his heart should return to a sacred place to be chosen by his sister, Branwen.

Branwen was so grief-stricken, that she ordered Bran's body to be taken to a secret location in a place called London, and there his body was interred. A great "White Tower" was finally built over his resting place and will remain there forever more.

Magpies will be known as the "nightfall and sunrise" birds, because of their black and white feathers, and they will lead double lives—good and evil—and some will enter into the "Otherworld" which will give them great strength and enable them to survive.

Turning to the pigeons, the mermaid said, "Sometimes you will be tolerated, and sometimes you will not be favoured by humankind as you live and mingle with them in the great cities, and at such times in history, you will be honoured for your hither and thither flying power. There will also come a time when you will be praised for your great courage and endurance, for your part in carrying beneath your wings the written coded words during a time of great battles. Many of you will survive, and many will perish, but you will be remembered thereafter."

Looking down on one of the pigeons, the mermaid said, "Here is one very special bird called White Vision! You will be greatly praised for your extreme courage and devotion to the humans, when you carry out many missions for them during a heavy raid in enemy territory, but this is yet to come. Then finally, as your precious life passes from this earth to the other side, your spirit form will return to the faithful human who nurtured you and held you most dear to his heart at the time of his own departure from this earth."

Then finally, addressing all of the birds, "Each and every one of you play a very important role during your lifetime, and you are of great value to the existence of this planet, as you colonize every corner of the globe. You will be protected by some, cherished by many, and loved by all!" she told them with a warm smile that would melt any ice cap.

Then as a final warning, she said, "Beware! Prepare yourselves! Man will soon be entering a phase of exploiting your roosting and nesting sites, and the Mother Earth will cry many tears! She will rock too and fro, her skin will tear and rip, and in her despair, great flames and rocks will burst from her wounds. You must choose to take flight and seek out new territory for yourselves, or you may perish! Good luck, and I wish you all well, my friends!"

When she had completed her mission with her crucial speech, the mermaid bid the birds "farewell!" But before leaving them, she gently threw the little wren (which was still sitting patiently cupped in her hand) into the air, and she then dived gracefully off the rock, which suddenly started to sink beneath the waves.

Returning to the great white whale, she chanted these few words, in a sort of singsong voice, which was known as the song of the whale.

Yama nama nama yam,…. Yama nama nama yam,
Nama yam, nama yam,…. Nama nama nama yam,
Shasheena shasheena,…. Valaven valaven,
Contara contara,…. Sozen sozen,
Soobeeta soobeeta,…. Laven laven,
Checonti checonti,…. Moten moten!

As she sang these words, they seemed to echo all around, and as the words caught up with themselves as they bounced back, it sounded like many voices were singing in chorus, and it made a very sweet sound.

Whilst the mermaid sang, the whale hummed a haunting melody of his own, which seemed to resound across the water, and the vibration reached to the very edge of the shore.

Then they both plunged back into the depths and were never seen again.

After this temporary lull, things started up all over again, and it came to pass (or so it is said) that on the land, the sky twins—a whirlwind and a tornado—came bolting out of the blue like a couple of runaway horses as they swept across the earth, spinning completely out of control, whistling and wailing, carrying up into the air just about anything that was unfortunate enough to be caught in their path, then dropping them down again, just about anywhere, except where they didn't want to be!

Amber stones hailed down, catching flying insects that just happened to be passing through, and they became trapped inside the amber, unable to escape, but would now have to await the next new dawning.

It seems not one gemstone was left unturned, and great rainbow colours shone all around.

Bamboos cried and sighed as they swayed and bent in the great winds. Conifers cringed and got singed in the wind, and they wept as their roots rocked beneath the earth, and great oaks tumbled in tears, groaning as they fell. It seemed a catastrophic happening was just about a wing-beat away.

Just when things couldn't get any worse, a beautiful princess by the name of Proserpina suddenly appeared, drifting down on a carpet made from soft goose feathers and rose petals.

Just for those who like a touch of "fairy romance," Proserpina was wearing a long dress made from fine silver-spun thread, which was studded with small sparkling diamonds, and about her shoulders she wore a long, flowing, midnight-blue velvet cloak, which was fastened at her throat by a glowing ruby. She wore a necklace of emerald gemstones, and earrings of sapphire, and in her long flowing fair hair, she wore a crown of forget-me-nots. She was escorted by four black swans. Their huge wings were beating slowly in time as she played a gentle tune on a golden harp, which made the music ring out over the sea.

Proserpina sang softly to the playing of the harp with the voice like an angel. It was a song to soothe the tormented earth (and sweet enough to bring any handsome prince out of the pub)!

From her flying carpet of feathers, Proserpina then scattered petals from fragrantly sweet scented red and white roses as she went.

In the deep-blue sea, sea nymphs and mermaids swam in formation, leading little seahorses with bridles made out of seaweed, singing their echoing songs to the great whales of the oceans, teaching them how to sing. A lark, which was soaring above at the time, also heard the melodious singing and learnt the songs to teach other birds to sing.

Everyone was happy now that the earth had finally settled down peacefully once more. At long last, the earth and sea became peaceful and still once more. Phew! that was one big emotional day's work, I thought.

Anyhow, enough about demented fiery gods and colourful gem-encrusted pinky babes.

Our lot, the magpies, came about when bits of white fluffy clouds broke off and came fluttering down, forming into soft, delicate pieces of shells, tinted blue from the sky and flecked red from the dust from a passing comet. The Great Atlas caught the pieces of clouds in his hands, and then he clutched a sliver of sun ray and placed a small speck into the very middle of each piece. Then he took a pinch of dust-like seeds from Mars and placed a seedling into each shell, then gently moulded the shells together and placed them about the earth, where he had drawn out a vast map of different countries, all divided neatly up, so as to separate them from one another.

That is how we kicked off into the bird kingdom, and now you also know that it was the egg before the chicken!

Our shells are made from the clouds, the egg yolk from a speck of sun, and a seed from Mars!

The second generation of our early hatchling ancestors arrived from their egg shells in the middle of a great tropical storm. There was thunder and lightning creating an almighty uproar.

The egg maker and egg layer were fearful that the eggs would become fried by the lightning, which was striking all over the place, so they flew far and wide, frantically collecting as many abalone shells that they were able, and piled them up and around the klakki so that the lightning would be deflected away from the hatching chicks. To complete their task, they had to make holes around one side of each shell, tapping into the hard shells with their beaks, so that the rain would drain away and keep the chicks from drowning, then they had to set the shells together with sand from the shoreline, mixed with soil from the fertile land.

It took them quite a long time, and at the end of it, they were plain done in. The chicks could now sit snugly and comfortably within the shell walls.

Suddenly, a great bright bolt of lightning pierced down the tree where their klakki had been built and the eggs had been laid.

The fireball shot down either side of the branches where the hatchlings were about to break through their shells, but fortunately their parents' plan and hard labour had worked, and the chicks were saved from what could have been a complete disaster, and all because of the abalone shells.

In her gratitude, the egg layer left a small star-shaped crystal, placing it carefully in the middle of the shell, and when the sun shone down, all the colours of the rainbow radiated from it, and that's how the abalone shells became so colourful.

Now because of all the great flashes of lightning all about the sky during great thunderstorms, this is why we have our black and white zig-zag markings.

Eventually, as the chicks grew older, and their tails grew longer, they were able to climb to the top of the klakki, which was piled high with the colourful abalone shells. Whilst they perched on the top of the shells, their tails rubbed on them, and that is why even now we still have a lovely glossy green sheen to our tails, and because of these very colourful shells, this is probably the reason why we all love to collect bright shiny things.

To this very day, you can still see the holes made by my ancestors on the abalone shells, and on one side you will see there is a smooth flat edge, and this is where the chicks used to rest their heads to sleep, and on the backs of some of them, you will find the imprint left by their tail feathers.

Eeli said that she loved this story, and some of it, without a doubt, did bear a resemblance to her own story.

She told me to listen out for the blackbird's song which has been handed down through the ages, when it was first composed by the first songster, Dolga, who taught his sons, Ralga, Meerga, Falga, Solga, Larga, Teega and then Dolga Junior.

The song goes like this:

> *Golden heads of marigolds,*
> *Anointed by the sun,*
> *Drifting seeds of dandelions,*
> *Counting each and every one.*
>
> *Forget-me-nots,*
> *Forget me not!*
> *Your petals as blue as the sky.*
>
> *The daisies white,*
> *All close each night,*
> *Whilst moonlight passes by.*
>
> *The willow trees,*
> *Sway in the breeze,*
> *And curtsey to the elm.*
>
> *Above us all,*
> *The oak stands tall,*
> *A guardian of this realm.*

The chaffinch in the cherry tree,
Sings with all his heart,
The robin in the Holly bush,
is busy till it's dark.

The cuckoo's call,
Reminds us all,
Be happy as a lark!

(can be sung to the tune of "Sing-a-Song-of-Sixpence")

Another thing she told me was that she was able to turn over old brown winter-blown leaves, and by doing this, she was able to see what was going to happen in the future. The best ones to read from were the ones which had been snowed upon, or rained upon, or had frost marks on, and then blown crispy-dry in the cold north winds.

I asked her if she could read what would be coming up for me.

After turning over a few leaves at the foot of me klakki, she concentrated very hard for a few moments, and then turning over a few more, she studied them very carefully, and then she looked up at me with a very thoughtful, kind eye.

She gave a bit of a sigh, and said, "You will not be staying here much longer, but you will be going on a long, long journey very far from here, and you will travel in very strange vessel! You will have much excitement, and there will be many strange encounters! You will, in time, meet a very beautiful mate, but!... Oh dear!... Tell you later!... Must go now!... Something approaches!"

Flying off, she called out, "*Chink!... Chink!... Chink!*" And then she was gone. Leaving me to out-stare four wicked green eyes, belonging to two big fluffy earth whisperers!

- Chapter Four -
First Encounter
(Of the Feline Kind)

The hot sunny days lingered on, starting off with a beautiful, deep turquoise wall-to-wall sky, stretching out like a canvas, with high wispy streaks of slow-moving cirrus clouds, acting as a backdrop to the slowly drifting cumulus clouds, looking like softly spun candyfloss, silently passing by.

God was creating his bit of "sky-sculpting" again, which meant that a session of "daydream doodling" would undoubtedly kick-in to form ever-changing pictures in the sky.

Images of dogs' heads, galloping horses, rabbits, pigs, even an old man smoking a pipe, and once I saw what looked incredibly like (metaphorically speaking) an enormous porcelain teapot, complete with its lid, and a small patch of blue sky could be seen through a perfectly moulded handle! You could almost taste the heavenly brew!

Perhaps this was to be a good omen for the rest of the day!

There was no time for action re-plays now, and no time now for reflection on the past, but ready to file away yesterday's thoughts, resisting that urge to take a backwards glance over one's shoulder, because just around the corner lay a brand new tingling fresh future, now ready and waiting to unfold. A new pathway to tread, and fresh avenues to explore, as we were soon to embark on a new destiny, as a stylish family home had been discovered, negotiated and finally purchased, in the beautiful countryside of West Wales.

The prospects were both exciting and frightening; not knowing what the future held for us.

This was to be a particularly big step to take, especially for my parents, as they had lived in the same house for the past fifty-four years, and they had never moved before, so this was going to be a very big and very bold decision for them to make.

Before we could even uproot ourselves, there were still many things to be done, like the sale of my parents' house, and then there was the emotional issue of saying our goodbyes to all our friends and relatives, as well as making suitable arrangements for all the animals. The dogs would be easy enough, as they would travel with us in the car, but the horses would have to join us later on, so they would have to stay and be looked after in Sussex, and then there was the bird, of course. But first of all, before leaving our old home, I wanted to teach Maggie to fly!

Each day brought a new stepping stone for Maggie to try out, and soon it would be time for him to exercise his wings for a different purpose, other than demanding to be fed, and to learn that they were designed to flap up and down for another purpose too!

His first solo flight was not a terribly impressive one. Nevertheless, he did deserve a ten out of ten for trying, and at least he had watched enough coverage of extreme sports on television to give him some idea of what to do, or at least on how not to just sit there in his cage and do nothing. And what about all those glorious shots of gracefully swooping birds on the bird-life programmes? Surely they should inspire him.

I am always astonished at those brave little fledglings who just launch themselves straight out of their nests and into the unknown, and without any regard to any dangers that might befall them. Whatever it is that urges them on is still a mystery. There are no practice runs and no pre-flight tests, and once they have taken that first plunge, then there's no turning back!

Maggie's first launching pad was the top of my father's head, and his first landing spot was an ungainly nose-dive directly onto the shiny wooden floor, which brought him skidding to a halt, almost at my feet. As he regained his composure, he shuffled his feathers, then chomped his beak a few times, and then he started to *lig-log…lig-log* across the floor, in his usual waddling gait, and he then gave a look as if to say, "Okay! Okay!—So what?"

On the whole, I think that Maggie was really quite pleased with his first attempt at flying, and with just a few more flying lessons, along with a few more obstacle courses to be negotiated, he would soon qualify as a fully fledged flyer, but not before a number of minor mishaps.

This "wanna-be-astronaut" experienced yet more crash landings, which included a series of tail spins, belly flops, bottoms up and a couple of back flips, but apart from that, he was making good progress.

If Maggie kept a list of "things I must do today," it would have read something like:

1. I must try to *not* break my neck!
2. *Or* attempt flight—(but preferably not upside down!)
3. *Or* loop-the-loop—(backwards!)
4. *Or* look for animals to tease—(preferably much bigger than me!)

etc. etc.

On his first major flight (an attempt to reach from one end of the room to the other), Maggie flew clumsily towards me and missed my outstretched hand. Then just for a split second, he lost his concentration and flew straight past me, and as he did so, I could hear him making a wheezy noise (which he still did, particularly if he was having a bit of a panic attack), and unfortunately for him, he ended up by flying straight into the net curtain and getting his feet in a tangle. His frantic flapping and squawking only made things worse as he wound himself up like a fly in a spider's web. He looked totally undignified as he began to make pathetic screeching sounds for help! I rushed over to rescue him before he could do more damage to himself. With a lot of delicate manipulation, I was able to unravel him, and it was a great relief to find that no harm had actually been done to either his wings, or his spindly legs, but his ego had taken a bit of a tumble, along with a few rumpled feathers! Another lesson had been learnt—to take more care, and to look before you leap!

Maggie was impatient to try out new daring antics, like landing on moving objects, particularly white fluffy ones: namely Hattie, the white poodle.

Poor Hattie, she didn't really relish this new game at all, and it certainly wasn't quite her idea of fun. In an attempt to escape her pursuer, she would rush across the floor with a look of sheer horror on her face, with Maggie just inches away from her. Her back legs tried to overtake her front legs in an effort to outpace Maggie, but he always won by landing awkwardly on her back and wobbling all over the place. Swaying from side to side, Maggie would grip on for as long as he could, and poor little Hattie was forced to dive under the nearest chair for cover, where she would peer out with her coal black eyes desperately pleading to be rescued from her tormentor. The triumphant bird would then jump off her back as agile as a Cossack horse rider, feeling very satisfied that as far as he was concerned, he was in full control of another creature.

Maggie then decided (in his little bird brain) to have a go at being a steeplejack, with the sole purpose of finding another route to the outside world. Perhaps he'd been influenced by yet another re-run of the film *The Great Escape*, which had recently been shown on the television, or maybe his intention was to join the ranks of the "yuppies": Young Upwardly Propelling (Mag)pies.

On this particular occasion, I had left the cage door open so that Maggie could come out if he wanted to, but as I would be working in the kitchen, it meant that I could keep an eye on him.

It was coming up to lunch time, and I had just started to prepare the food (remembering to add a little extra to keep to one side for Maggie), when I heard his usual call, only this time it sounded rather muffled, and it seemed to echo all round the house, then it faded away into a distant clicking, and then a scratching sound.

Leaving the prepared vegetables to one side, I quickly went on a search for Maggie, but just couldn't seem to find him anywhere, and it was difficult to trace where the sound was now coming from.

He definitely wasn't still in his cage or flying about in the lounge, and I even looked inside one of the cupboards that had a door left open to see if he'd popped in there, and I even thought that I could hear his clacking noises coming from upstairs. This was really quite weird. Then just as I went back into the lounge for another search, I heard him give another muffled call. It was quite by chance that I suddenly spotted his long tail as it was slowly disappearing up the chimney. What a stupid bird! When I finally prised him out by grabbing his tail and yanking him down, he was followed by a shower of black powdery soot flying everywhere. He now looked more like scruffy old black crow than a smart young magpie!

At that moment, it was decided that now was the time for him to learn how to bathe.

If Maggie didn't want to do anything, then Maggie just wouldn't do anything, and that was the end of it, and you might as well give up!

Sometimes a bit of coaxing might work, if he thought there was something to be gained from it, but as his attention was very short lived, he would soon wander off in another direction to seek out something more interesting to do. He just loved himself immensely, and was enormously enchanted by his own company, so why should he be given orders by others? The idea to immerse himself in water was not on his agenda!

I managed to find a very old discarded roasting pan which would do the job nicely, and I filled it with lukewarm water, then placed it on the floor in front of him. This would definitely make a lovely birdbath just for Maggie!

"Come on Maggie!" I tried to reason with him. "You will really love this if you give it a try! All bright intelligent birds have a bath at some time, just like you've watched them doing it on the telly. You should know that you've got to keep your feathers all nice and clean, and not only that, it will help you to fly better too!...don't you know?"

If I really believed that he had actually understood every word I said, then I wasn't wasting my breath.

I tried to attract his attention by splashing my fingers in the water, as I thought that out of curiosity he might at least investigate the contents of the pan, but instead, he gave me a sideways glance, then sidled off a few paces away from me, then he stopped, turned round, and waddled back again.

Good! I thought, *at least he's showing some interest!* But to my disappointment, but not surprise, he deliberately went straight past the bath, not even giving it a second glance. *Rotten ungrateful bird!* If Plan A wasn't going to work, then I was going to have to give Plan B a try!

His first plunge (more of a dunking!) happened by accident and not design.

I removed the pan from the floor and placed it just outside of his cage so that he could get used to seeing it there in the hope that he might, at some point in time, decide to try it out, if only to dip a toe in.

As I expected, he completely ignored it, and I had to come to terms with the fact that this was going to be a long haul. This could turn out to be just another waiting game!

I am sure that Maggie knew what was expected of him, but he was just acting plain stubborn! After all, he'd got just about the whole day and the next if necessary, to play me up.

I decided to put Plan B to the test, which was for me to completely ignore him.

This wasn't exactly a very cunning plan, but it was the only one I could think of at the time, and so I barely even gave him a second glance—apart from feeding him, of course!

As Maggie was so used to being the centre of attention, he began to look dejected and bored, and he flew straight back into his cage again, as though he was going into one of his sulks. After a while, he started to hop from one perch to the other, and peered through the bars of his cage to see if anyone was going to stop by and chat to him, and still ignoring him, I left him on his own for a while, thinking that perhaps he might make his own way out of the cage and try out the bath for himself.

Leaving Maggie to his own devices for at least another hour, I returned to the room to find that Maggie had indeed found something to do.

He had shredded up most of the newspaper in his cage, then pulled a large section of it out and dropped it into the pan of water, and then left another piece almost intact on the table, as though he purposely wanted me to look at it. When I picked it up I noticed that he had very accurately, and with great precision, pecked at the face of the page three girl, and now this up-and-coming artist had rearranged her face, so now there was a huge hole where her mouth had been, and two neat little holes where her eyes should have been. She now looked more like a gorgon than a glamour girl! He was either trying out some form of collage, or a daring attempt at origami for him to stick on the walls of his cage, or was he trying to tell me something? It was probably Maggie's way of saying, "Hey!—If you push me too far, I might just stick me beak to your face, and maybe even do a bit of stencilling on it!—Okay?"

Cheeky bird!

I decided to give him a little more time and a little more space to decided for himself when he should start his daily ablutions.

His first lesson in swimming came quite unexpectedly, and it was most definitely not planned by him, as it seemed to happen so quickly, and at the same time his pride took a fall, and his dignity was lost for the first time!

Knowing that I was putting a lot of effort and time into coaxing him, even if it was just to dip one little toe into his very special bath, Maggie made it crystal clear that he had no intention of obeying any commands whatsoever, even if he thought it might turn out to be fun after all. He would only partake in a project if it was his idea in the first place! And that was that!

His little brain (which I sometimes wondered if it was situated in his beak or his feet, or maybe even attached to both) went into a reverse mode and suddenly took a U-turn.

It was mid-afternoon, and the idea of bath-time had already turned sour, and Maggie's attention had turned to other things, like molesting poor little Hattie by pecking between her toes whilst she was sleeping peacefully on her special mat, thus making her squeal in fright. Maggie then proceeded to hop onto the top of her head (in his usual manner) and tried to balance there like a tightrope walker, but before he could start pecking her delicate ears with his sharp beak, Hattie took off like a headless Singapore racing chicken, with her little dainty feet clicking away on the wooden floor.

She just couldn't get a grip to start with, but once she got going, her performance was every bit as good as a tap dancer, as she spiralled her way straight through the open door of the lounge to find somewhere to hide from this little feathered demon, leaving him somewhat bemused in the middle of the floor, just like a jilted lover!

He was obviously feeling highly delighted that he had established his superiority above all others (or so he thought) as this was to be his way of clarifying that the pecking order should be observed, and that he was number one!

After his little game was over, he then cavorted his way over to where I was sitting, reading my up-till-now unmolested newspaper. He approached me in a series of his comical *lig-log!—lig-log!—lig-*

log's! across the floor, then a few bouncy kangaroo hops, and then a short but low altitude flight, and finally straight onto my knee!

I suppose he thought that I had over-reacted at the prospects of my newspaper being converted into a series of his favourite shredded cut-outs and didn't quite see my point of view that I really and truly didn't appreciate his persistent bashing away whilst I was still trying to read it, and so naturally I just brushed him aside and shooed him off!

This was all so new to him, as he hadn't yet experienced being reprimanded for his naughty antics, and I don't think he liked it one little bit, as he was used to having his own way all the time.

He flew off in a bit of a temper, landing heavily on the top of his cage, making the bars clang with a nerve-wrenching sound, and then flipped his tail up and down in an exaggerated manner.

It was then that he found the piece of knicker elastic, which I had found in my mother's needlework box, thinking this would be useful to tie his door open, in order to allow him easy access to come and go as he pleased, but only at certain times when he was allowed out, that is. One end was tied to the door, and the other end was tied in a quick-release slipknot to the top bar at the back of his cage, with the excess length dangling down as I hadn't bothered to cut the end off.

With the greatest of ease and a bit of probing with his beak, Maggie managed to undo the elastic attached to the door within just a few seconds. He then attempted to fly off with the elastic still firmly clamped in his beak, but with no intentions of letting it go.

This was, without doubt, not a very smart thing to do!

Lowering my newspaper, I watched in curious fascination from my chair, waiting for the inevitable to happen after this sudden outburst of Maggie's unusual circus act!

My first impression was that I thought it looked as though he was trying a spot of bungy jumping—horizontally!

I had no idea what motivated him to keep up this momentum as he swung in ever decreasing circles, taking chunks out of aerodynamics! He actually reminded me of one of those wind-up aeroplanes which keep on circling round until they run down. But Maggie was determined that right now wasn't the time to give in, or run down!

The beast of a thing (which in Maggie's eyes must have seemed to have a life of its own) didn't want to let go, and neither did Maggie!

And so he just kept on zapping and zinging, back and forth, to and fro, but I knew that soon he would tire as I could hear he was getting a bit wheezy. I thought that he must surely be getting dizzy, if not disorientated, and he was definitely slowing down.

His crazy flight was guaranteed not to last much longer! And sure enough, it didn't! After about seven or more frantic, flapping twirls whilst orbiting his cage, and at the same time descending rather alarmingly, he then suddenly let go of the offending elastic, and probably because he must have made himself a bit dizzy, he misjudged his landing, and promptly fell directly into the middle of his awaiting bath with an almighty *SPLOSH!*

This must have sent quite a shockwave through his whole system.

After the initial shock of being submerged in the "wet stuff" — which up until now he thought was for drinking purposes only — and having sent water flying in all directions, like on the table, on the floor, over curtains, he just sat in the middle of the pan, wheezing away, and looking every bit like a porcupine, with his feathers all wet and bedraggled.

He looked a very sad, hard-done-by little bird just waiting for all the sympathy he felt he deserved.

It was very difficult not to laugh, so I didn't hold back on just a little bit of a chuckle, which did seem to somewhat offend him, and maybe it did cramp his style just a little! Leaving the offended bird in a very subdued state, I ran upstairs to fetch a towel to dry him off with — one of the old towels used for drying the dogs with, of course! At the same time, and on the spur of the moment, I decided to bring my hair dryer as well.

I wrapped the towel carefully around him and gently dabbed at his drenched feathers.

He looked so much like a comical little hooded monk that I was sorely tempted to take his photograph, but on reflection I decided not to, as he wouldn't have remained in the same position whilst I went to search for the camera, and so therefore spared him further humiliation!

When I turned the hair dryer on, it had an almost therapeutic affect on him. He settled down, turning this way and that, so that I could reach the parts still damp, and almost looked as though he was at last enjoying the attention, and quite content that he was now squeaky clean.

From then on he quite looked forward to his daily bath routine, and would wait patiently for me to fetch the hair dryer so that he could finish off preening and styling his feathers until they fairly gleamed and shone!

For Maggie to spend a few hours in the kitchen is like setting him loose at a theme park.

If the cutlery drawer is left open, you will hear the metallic sound of *ching! chang! chink!* as the knives, forks, and spoons are chucked spontaneously one-by-one onto the floor. Then there's the *ting! tang! tong!* noise, as coffee mugs get the bongo treatment from a rapping, tapping, stabbing beak. The swing bin makes a nice helter-skelter if you happen to land on the flip top lid, and then it's a case of a good old rummage amongst all the tea leaves, banana skins, orange peals, apple cores, discarded cabbage leaves, baked beans and dog food tins, and any other savoury bits and pieces thrown into the bin, and now lying scattered about the floor! Then at the end of it all, you will find a smelly, disgruntled, manky old Magpie!

My "absolutely essential Marigold washing up gloves" were reduced to "absolutely useless mittens!" The tips of the gloves had been pecked off and were now converted into little yellow plastic thimbles, which Maggie then took back to his cage and placed in a neat pile in the corner.

Maggie soon began to invent brand new sports games at the speed of a tornado, whilst I was quietly hovering on the brink of a complete nervous breakdown.

Dodging the flying missiles while trying to reason with a maniac sports competitive bird in full swing was not an easy undertaking.

Trying to grab hold of the ducking and diving, wheeling and screaming, cunning and calculating, flying machine was virtually impossible.

On one of his performances, Maggie flew up and landed on the top shelf where the bright shiny saucepans were kept, and he started to bash at his own reflection, which I am sure he was convinced was another bird staring right back at him. As he beat each saucepan in turn with his beak, it made a dull metallic sound, amazingly like the kettle drums of a calypso band, and then tiring of this noisy new game, he swooped down and straight into the sink, which was fortunately empty at the time. He sat in the bowl as though he was waiting for the taps to be turned on for a quick shower.

The event which finally eliminated him from this marathon mayhem was when he entered into a relay race, and for this event he chose a single sheet from a roll of kitchen paper, which I had purposely pulled off and stacked in a neat pile ready to use as serviettes.

All the—"No! Don't do that!" or—"No! Put that down!"—or any other such commands were to no avail. So when I shouted to Maggie, "Leave that alone you wretched bird!" then of course he was more than ever determined to steal this particular forbidden object, especially if it meant that he was getting all the attention.

What he hadn't bargained for was when this fun game suddenly and unexpectedly turned into a new airborne version of "blind-man's bluff."

It happened during his first lap around the kitchen when the soft kitchen paper he was carrying in his beak flipped up and over his head, so that now his vision had become almost completely obstructed.

I believe that if he had been capable of thought, then right at that moment he would have been too embarrassed to admit to himself that he had made an error, and maybe this wasn't such a good idea in the end, and that he should have listened to me after all. But no, this was not so. He was very determined not to give in, and just carried on flying in a blind circle, and getting more and more frustrated, and I was thinking, *Why on earth doesn't he just let go of the paper? At least that would solve the problem for him straight away!* But no, he was stubborn right to the end, and I could see that he was beginning to panic, and also he was starting to get a bit wheezy, as he always did in a situation like this. It was becoming a strain for him to keep this up, and he was beginning to tire after several laps of the kitchen, although I was quite impressed that he hadn't flown into too many things. He did perhaps fly into the hanging light once or twice, and only bounced off the dividing kitchen door about three times, which wasn't bad either— oh, and then he did collide just the once with the wooden clothes pulley, which started to swing about a bit, and he was in mortal danger of another collision, but only if he'd timed his return flight past it again, out of sequence. I felt that at any moment he was going to drop like a lead balloon.

When his flying got slower and lower, I was just about able to grab him by his tail and bring him down to a safe landing. I think that

163

secretly he was really quite relieved, and he didn't put up any resistance when I shoved him back into his cage. Everything was peaceful once more, and I was able to resume with cooking the lunch, after I had cleared away the mess and debris, which had been left by one very mischievous Magpie!

Maggie's first encounter with the outside world was a big turning point in his capacity as a freedom flyer, and it took place without a planning consent, or at least not on my part. It was an opportunity he had been waiting for, and definitely too good not to be missed!

It was all down to my father forgetting to close the dining room door behind him and leaving the bathroom window wide open. We usually made quite sure that all the exits were closed, which meant that Maggie was restricted to the dining room, lounge and kitchen area only, in order to give us some control of his whereabouts. Also, he wasn't too fussy about where he did his toilet, as he wasn't exactly house trained, and it was quite a chore hunting up his messy splats, which could leave a nasty stain on some of the furniture if it was left too long, so it was quite important to clear them up as soon as they were deposited, which of course was a very thankless task.

Anyway, on this particular occasion, he found that for once his airspace was left well and truly clear, and without hesitation, he swept up the stairway with the efficiency of a chimney sweep's brush, as though he was caught up in a vortex, and disappeared into the blue yonder, squawking with glee as he went.

I rushed to the bottom of the stairs just in time to watch the black dot vanish from view, and I stood there gazing after him, transfixed to the spot, not believing that this could have happened.

My heart thumping, I raced outside and glanced skywards for any sighting of this flying Houdini. The sun was very strong and bright, so I had to shield my eyes against the glare with my hand.

After what seemed like eternity, there was neither a glimpse nor a familiar call from Maggie, and everywhere seemed to be very still, and very quiet. I was beginning to despair.

How was he going to survive? He'd only just learnt to fly, and being so young, he certainly wouldn't know how to hunt for his food, and where would he roost at night? After all my hard work, all the care and nurturing, and this should happen.

Then, all of a sudden, he made an appearance.

His silhouette blotted out the sun, and he cast a shadow as he flew directly over the rooftop, circling around. He looked somehow different, and something seemed to click in.

His true wild nature seemed to take over his whole being, in an almost primaeval instinct, and he was now flying high on a warm thermal current. He was now testing, and tasting, the wonderful air of freedom, and his near-perfect air display was quite stunning to watch.

Dipping and diving, then gracefully gliding, and then flapping strongly with real determination, he was now beginning to really enjoy himself, and he looked very handsome and elegant, not that gangly stumbling bird of yesterday, and I felt really proud of him, just like a parent feels for their child on their first sports day at school.

I knew that he could see me, because when I called out his name and whistled to him, he responded with his usual raucous call, and he seemed to grow more and more confident with each minute, but he didn't want to return to me.

He finally came to rest on the top of the chimney pot, and there he perched for a few moments before preening his feathers, after which he hopped down onto the ridge of the roof and swaggered across it, with one foot in front of the other, like a tightrope walker.

It suddenly occurred to me that perhaps he hadn't yet realised that his substitute mother was unable to fly, and therefore would not be able to join him in the air!

I whistled and called him in the usual manner, to try and get him to return to my raised right arm in the way I had taught him to do. At first he chose to ignore me, and then after a few moments he decided that perhaps it would be a good idea to return to base after all! Or so I thought!

He swooped down to my hand, and landed unsteadily, but then with his wings still flapping and whirling round, like the blades of a helicopter, he took off again, and headed straight down towards the bottom of the garden.

He disappeared over the big hawthorn hedge, so I had no idea what was going on, on the other side, as I assumed his intention was to explore new territory.

He finally returned after a lapse of about twenty minutes or so, and circled the house and garden once more, and then he changed his mind and zoomed straight down towards the bottom of the garden again, only this time Father's big shed was his destination.

What Maggie didn't know was that there was a reception waiting for him. I think that I must have spotted them before he did.

I could see four pairs of green eyes belonging to two cats, and they were peering out from under the overhanging branches from the hawthorn tree, and I realized that these felines (who were of the feral kind) belonged to the next door neighbours who rescued them as tiny kittens from the woods at the top of the road, and they were still quite wild by nature, judging by the piles of feathers often found in the garden.

One of them was a tom, and he was black with just a few white markings, the other was a female, and she was nearly all white, with some large and some small blotches of grey and black; in fact, she was a rather pretty cat.

I had noticed them earlier on in the day when I looked out of my parents' bedroom window. The pair were sunning themselves on the shed roof, and I didn't give them a second thought, so I forgot all about them.

As Maggie boldly approached them, their eyes seemed to widen in surprise, and then they turned to slits, and you could almost hear one say to the other, "*Hey Gertrude! Is it your birthday today, or is it mine? Because I've just seen the postman arrive with a lovely edible gift! Make a nice change from fish, don't you think? Now shall I unwrap it, or shall we do it together?*"

The silly impulsive bird landed without hesitation, straight onto the shed roof, and bounced like a kangaroo right underneath the branches and into the dead dried-up leaves that had fallen there during the winter, which hadn't yet been swept off.

Then just like the invisible man, he disappeared from view.

The four watching eyes had also retreated, but I couldn't detect which direction they had taken, as they must have moved slowly and silently. Unlike the over-confident magpie, who was crashing about all over the place, chucking bits of twigs here, there and everywhere, clucking and chinking loudly with his song he likes to sing when he pretends to be busy.

The picture was beginning to unfold in my mind: Two cats! One bird! One dead bird! Two happy fat cats!

I made my way briskly, but as quietly as I possibly could, as I didn't want to spark off any confrontation, which might happen if I was to draw the cats' attention to Maggie's exact location on the roof.

I needn't have worried, as Maggie was doing a very good job on that score for himself.

My worst fears were about to happen, as the cats homed in on their prospective prey, and all I could hear from where I stood transfixed were a lot of scuffling noises, which seemed to grow more intense by the minute and seemed to drag on for ages.

I thought I could hear what could only be described as Maggie getting very angry indeed, because I could hear his sharp repetitive call, the one he uses when he is on the war path and which sounds very much like machine gun fire. I could hear a lot more scuffling amongst the dead leaves, and a lot of hissing and cursing, and I could even see some of the lower branches moving, as though there was a real battle going on—big time!

Not being able to see what was happening, or who could be on the winning side, I was beginning to panic by now.

"Oh my God, my poor little Maggie! And all that minced meat still in the fridge! I must try and save him, but what should I do?"

I had an idea.

I fetched my father's step ladder from the shed and placed it against the wall, but before proceeding with my foolproof idea, I tried to coax him down in the usual way he was accustomed to, so I clapped my hands, whistled, clicked my fingers, and just kept calling his name in the hope that he would respond by flying down onto my hand or shoulder, but my efforts were a waste of time. He was behaving as though he was decidedly just plain deaf!

I had no option now but to carry out my original plan.

Finding as many stones from the rose bed as I could carry, I climbed the ladder.

Gingerly leaning over the sloping roof from the top, rung I took aim and flung the stones as missiles as hard and as far as I could, making a terrible din as they hit the corrugated sheeting, but this had the desired effect.

The two utterly bewildered cats sped in opposite directions and virtually threw themselves off the roof in a very noisy manner, with their tails stuck straight up in the air and their fur standing on end and their yellow eyes wide in surprise and disgust at being thwarted from their intended dastardly deed!

Moments later, Maggie reappeared from the rear of the shed.

He stepped casually out from the debris, cool as a cucumber, and shrugged his feathers in a "Del Boy" fashion, with a "devil-may-care" look on his face, and picking up twigs nonchalantly, as though nothing unusual had happened, wondering what on earth all the fuss was about.

Apart from looking a bit dishevelled, and with a few ruffled feathers, I think he was one very lucky bird to have survived from what could have been a very nasty incident.

He seemed almost relieved and happy to see me, and didn't even hesitate to jump onto my shoulder, giving his little baby clucking sounds in my ear, in fact it sounded almost as though he was humming!

Carrying him back down the path, I wanted to get him securely back into his cage before he could change his mind, but I think he'd had enough excitement for one day.

"Oh you poor little thing!" I told him, "Those dreadful pussy cats could have killed you, and you must have been so frightened! Good job I found those stones to frighten them off with! Serves them right if they got hit—the nasty, vicious things!"

Of course I didn't really mean it, but I thought I'd better pacify him. He should have behaved himself in the first place, so it wasn't altogether the cats' fault.

However, what's done is done.

"Never mind," I said, "Let me get you something really nice for your supper tonight, like a really hot curry!"

I placed him back in his cage, which I'd taken out into the garden in the hope that he would return to it of his own accord.

I looked down at him in wonderment.

How on earth could this one defenceless bird survive an attack, not just from one cat, but *two?* So how did he manage it, and what was his secret weapon?

He knew how to cope with dogs, but this was his first encounter—of the feline kind!

- Chapter Four and a Half -
Over to Maggie

...a bird in the hand is worth two in the bush...

Wingflaps down, check! Runway clear, check! Visibility good, check! Clear for takeoff, check! V1—V2—Full power! All systems go—*LIFT OFF!*

Make way fellow aviators! Here I come! Aaaaarh!... I think I'm losing consciousness!... I'm going into a feather shifting spin!... I'm experiencin' the mighty beak-wobblin' G-forces now!... 'ang in there, my son!... Any second now!

All I have to do now is to wait for the sign to be given, in much the same way as all my ancestors before me had to do (since time began, in fact), so it's not just a case of flapping one's little wings, then up, up, and away! Oh no, it's not as simple as that! One has to have the "visionary consent" first! Doesn't one? So to prepare myself, I have to close me eyes, then concentrate real hard. If I sees "The Black Swan" with its ruby-red beak, then this is the "nearly ready" sign. If I sees "The Law of the Great Eagle," this means that I'm not yet quite ready, but if I sees the big yellow eyes of "The Amber Owl," and he hoots out, *"Now is the time to go!"* then I'm off on me maiden-flight!

Some poor little blighters never gets this *"now is the time to go!"* sign from "The Amber Owl," and they only gets to see "The Black Swan," which means they never ventures any further than the ground.

Some of the unfortunate ones wot stays mainly on the ground are birds such as the big clumsy ostriches, the penguins and some other "grounders," too.

Whilst I'm waitin' for me all-important sign, and now that we're talking about the penguins, you might like to know that they've had a really unusual past history handed down to them, according to Eeli, who told me their story on one particular day when I was planted out for me usual airing in the garden.

She said to me, "You look as smug as a bug in a rug!" whatever that means! And then she began this strange story about penguins.

It all began a very, very long time ago, when the universe was still as young as the sun.

It seems that penguins started life as not penguins at all, but some other type of small creature, in a land of high mountains with snow, and where fairy folk lived and roamed the woods and meadows below the peaks of these mountains, where it was much warmer.

There was this particular fairy king by the name of Nonno, who smoked a little clay pipe, which had a cherry-wood stem. As he puffed merrily away, the sweet scent of herbs and spices filled the air. By his side stood his very doting wife, Queen Ranna, and she wore a precious star-spangled circlet about her head, which sparkled and twinkled against her long black wavy hair.

The king and queen had two very delicate little offspring; one was a little fairy prince, and the other was a little fairy princess, and they were named Tapper and Tinker.

Their little cots were made from the shells of walnuts, and they had one half each. The cots were lined with the soft silky down taken from the pussy willow, and then they were hung up in the trees by chains made out of catkins, and the gentle breeze rocked them to sleep.

Although the baby fairies were quite weeny in size, they could already walk for short distances, aided by the fluttering of their little wings, which helped to keep them just above the ground until they were old enough to fly properly, but unfortunately (as you will find out later on) this doesn't happen to them!

Both were as tiny as a rosebud, and their skin had the velvety texture and translucent like the petals from the wild dog rose. Their movements were as light and gentle as those of a blue butterfly, which meant they were very rarely heard as they flitted quietly about the daisies and violets. Their voices were as sweet as a nightingale's (which they were often mistaken for), and when they laughed together, it sounded tinkly, just like little seashells full of pearls bouncing over pebbles.

Sometimes, on warm sunny days, they were seen out riding on the backs of their pet bumblebees, clinging to their furry black and gold coats, as the bumblebees droned and hummed their way from flower to flower. Sometimes the dozers would bumble their way to honeysuckle flowers so that the little fairies could sip the honey nectar from the flowers' trumpets, and when they had sipped them dry, they would blow through them to make music, and if there were lots of little fairies out doing the same thing, and blowing away on their little honeysuckle trumpets, it would sound just like a swarm of worker bees buzzing away!

The older fairies would go out early in the morning carrying a hazelnut each. Some of these nuts were used to catch the early morning dew for drinking, and on the other nuts (or acorns) they would find cobwebs, which they would carefully and delicately wrap around the nut, and this they would use as thread for their garments, but they had to be very careful that the spider didn't catch them at it, otherwise she would have been very angry indeed at having to weave a web all over again!

They also grew mulberry trees in order to farm silkworms so that they could spin the silk for their "very-special-occasion clothes."

Also at that time, in large meadows, there grew beautiful black mulberry trees, which the goodly human king of those days ordered the people to plant throughout the land.

The fairies would creep out when it was dark, holding their glow-worm lanterns to see their way, and then they would silently climb up into the trees where they were able to pick the wonderfully juicy mulberry fruits, which they would store somewhere nice and cool, and then they could eat them or make wine.

Other fairies would paddle across ponds, sitting astride small fir cones, to fish for little minnows to eat, and the bones were used as sewing needles to make (or sometimes to mend) their garments with.

In the summer they would collect poppy petals and lavender heads to make their beds with, and in the winter they would collect dried grasses and moss, which they used to line their homes with to keep them warm.

The fairies were also very clever at making things. Their garments were sometimes made from flower petals of the different seasons, but the hunters of the woods and glens usually wore brown garments, such as seed husks or dried leaves, or sometimes the dark evergreen leaves so that they would blend in the undergrowth or trees.

Little soft shoes were made from moss, or lichen, and they wore tiny shepherd's purses attached to their belts made from dried grasses, and in them they collected seeds from the hawthorn berries and also elder berries in the autumn. These seeds and berries were then pounded on stones to make a powder, which they then soaked for many suns and moons to make into a herbal drink, which helped to keep them very healthy, and also very merry! They also collected the elder flowers in the summer, some of which they baked in the hot sun to eat, and others were used to brew yet another merry-making drink!

Other fairies would collect sheeps' wool from the hedgerows which they used to make into little woollen garments in the cold weather; they would also make little soft pouches which they used to collect wrens' eggs in. They were quite partial to these tiny eggs, although they wouldn't take them all, but they had to be very careful not to be caught out by a very angry wren who would chase them all the way back to their dens, *tick-ticking!* loudly at the little egg thieves.

There was also the fun of going out on a beehive raid where they would take as many empty nut-shells as they could possibly carry and fill them to the brim with chunks of sweet honey-comb.

They also hunted the hedgerows for blackberries and wild strawberries, and in the winter they collected chestnuts to roast over the fires, which they lit in their caves to keep themselves warm.

On warm nights, the fairies would sleep out under the stars in their comfortable tree houses, which they built high up in the branches of eucalyptus trees, and sometimes they would snuggle up to a friendly old tawny owl, hiding under a warm soft wing, whilst others curled up inside the silky rich-red velvety petals of the sweetly perfumed damask rose. In the early break of dawn, they were able to sip the syrupy nectar from the dew drops which had formed on the rose petals and had warmed in the early sunshine.

In the autumn, they would collect the eucalyptus leaves to line their dens, which was either in a hollow under tree roots, or in caves, where they kept themselves snug and warm during the cold winter months, and stacked up with plenty of food-stuffs collected from the fields, forests and on the mountainsides (for most of the fairies would hibernate during the winter, with the exception of the frost fairies!).

One of the most dangerous creatures they would have to keep a sharp lookout for were the dragonflies, as they would sometimes swoop down and nip off the fairies' wings, but most of the wild creatures treated the fairies with great respect.

The fairies really knew how to enjoy themselves, and they would hold annual "Fairy Funfairs."

The fairgoers were led in by King Nonno, looking very splendid in his robes of gold (to represent the sun), and he proudly wore his gem-studded golden crown, which went well with his neatly cut red hair and beard. Queen Ranna wore a beautiful silver gown (to represent the moon), and she wore a silver crown studded with diamonds, which sparkled brightly in her long hair.

They started the events off by holding snail races, where they would harness them up, then sit on top of their shells, and then they would frantically urge them on by dangling fresh lettuce leaves—bunched together with dried grasses—in front of them, just to get the slow old snails to move at all! Sometimes these races would last for the rest of the day, even before the poor frustrated riders could reach the finishing line!

There were also short flight trips on ladybirds, free to those who could "spot the difference" and guess which ladybird had the most spots!

There was abseiling up molehill mounds, and the participants had to wear empty snails' shells as protective helmets in case they hit their heads on stones if they fell.

Whilst fairy music played, little damselflies did a jitterbug dance with hoverflies.

In one corner, underneath an old oak tree, a little elderly fairy demonstrated how to weave lovely fuzzy tunics out of stinging nettle leaves, especially cosy to wear when it's extra cold, and she also made beautiful long velvet gowns for the girl fairies out of bright red poppy petals.

A little pixie had a stall selling lucky sharks' teeth necklaces (I'm not *too* sure if it was the shark who was lucky or the pixie!).

In another arena, they held show jumping classes, with experienced fairy riders sitting astride big fat frogs, who were enticed by flies on the end of twigs held in front of them, to leap over specially laid-out branches whilst the younger fairies entered jumping competitions on their pet grasshoppers.

Another big favourite was the "Whirligig Copter Rides." These rides were taken on sycamore seed pods, which were shaped like bunches of keys, and where two fairies had to sit opposite one another in order to balance the pods, and then they would have to snap the thin twigs attached to the pods, allowing the keys to spiral to the ground, going faster and faster, twisting and spinning as they went, sending the delighted little fairies into fits of giggles. As they spun, their brightly coloured garments dazzled in a psychedelic blur of colour as they swirled and swished about them. When they finally landed onto the soft green grass and tried to stand up, they staggered and toppled about, because they felt so dizzy after their fast-spinning ride!

Others would have a go at tug-of-war contests with big strong worms who always seemed to win by pulling themselves back underground with a *ping!*

An even greater thrill was to go on a speed trip across the lily pond on a water boatman, dodging dangerously close to water lilies, weaving in and out.

Another event for the strongest and bravest was stag-beetle rodeo riding, which was really very dangerous and only for the foolhardy. Occasionally, the fairies received very serious injuries if they fell off or were badly gored by the stag beetle's horns. In an emergency, they were then immediately rushed off on dockleaf stretchers and had their wounds dressed by special fairy healers, who bound broken bones with comfrey leaves.

Delicate torn wings were stitched together with fine strands of spider webs, whilst minor bruises were treated with some sort of herbal tinctures, and finally, they were given sips of dandelion wine to drink, which seemed to bring them round remarkably quickly.

They also held a pets' competition for "the best kept and busiest bumble bee that the judge would most like to take home!"

For the little ones, there was a dandelion-seed-head-blowing competition to see who could blow the most seeds off with just one puff only per fairy!

The winners of the competitions were awarded with large slices of seed-cake!

I was beginning to wish I was a fairy and not a magpie!

A little lady elf ran a sweet and cake stall, from which she dished out sweets made from honeybee-spun sugar, and little fairy cakes, as well as miniature muffins.

There was an acorn shy, where cherry stones were used to knock the acorns out of their cups.

One very talented artist fairy painted the delicate wings of butterflies in vibrant colours. The butterflies had to first alight on a mertle bush and queue up, and the little artist (wearing a golden buttercup flower upturned on her head) then invited them in turn to fly onto the purple flower head of a thistle, where they had to display their outstretched wings and keep very still whilst she decorated them with many bright colours.

She used soft little brushes, which were made from the white fur taken from the bobbly tails of sleeping hoppity-bunny-wunnies, and for really bold strokes, she used slightly stiffer hair brushes, which she made up from fur found amongst the leaves in a wood, which had been discarded by a bout of vigorous grooming of an old crotchety badger.

There were many types of butterflies having splashes of colour daubed on their wings, and amongst them were the handsome peacock butterflies. The artist gave them beautiful black velvet jackets, and then they had big spots painted on their colourful wings, giving them a rather angry owlish appearance, which coincided with the hissing noises they made as the artist worked on them.

The elegant red admirals had beautiful chestnut colours added to their wings and bodies, as well as reds and whites, whilst the small tortoiseshells had red, yellow and black stripes and freckles painted on them.

The brimstones were painted with a sunshine yellow with four tiny orange spots added to their wings.

The artist decided to call one of the butterflies—who turned out to be her favourite—"Painted Lady."

Then, as the sun went down and the fun of the fair was beginning to draw to a close, the fairies collected small twigs from the apple and cherry trees and made up a bonfire. They sat round the fire on little cushions made from camomile, which made them feel sleepy and dreamy, as they talked about the events of that day. They threw small sprigs of lavender and petals from sweet violets onto the fire, which filled the air with fragrant perfume.

Then finally, to round off the evening, two small twin elfin maids, named Gemini, entered the ring in a swirling white mist, where they entertained the fairy folk with a song and a dance. They both wore fine gossamer dresses, long and flowing, which changed colour in the firelight.

One twin had long wavy fair hair, and she was the Sun Gemini, and the other had long sleek jet black hair, and she was known as the Moon Gemini.

They placed around the edge of the circle little lanterns made from hollowed-out blackbirds' eggs, and inside each one were fireflies, which threw out a bright luminescent glow. Then one of the elf maids started to sing.

She sang soft and sweet, with a voice like an angel's, of far-off lands, of mountains and streams, and of all the creatures living in the forests and meadows. She sang haunting songs about the oceans, and then about great deeds of the birds of the skies.

As she sat cross-legged on the ground, she played on a small instrument from the bark of a magic tree from the fairy kingdom, and the strings she plucked with her tiny fingers were made from strands of silvery moonbeams.

Her twin danced to the music, and on her fingers she wore tiny silver bells that rang out as she danced. Sometimes her dance was very fast and full of energy, and the next instant it seemed to slow down as she danced in a graceful slow motion. In her dance, she mimed her stories about strange, long-forgotten lands, and of witches, giants, and monsters, and many creatures they had never heard of before, and about the magic of the mystical unicorn.

When the elvish maids spoke, it was in unison, and in a softly muted tone, which was almost a whisper. One elf spoke in a pitch slightly higher than the other, which made their speech sound like an unearthly chorus.

The audience was mesmerized, and after the performance, they all fell into a deep dreamlike sleep. And this is how the "Fairy Funfair" ended.

It's worth a mention to tell that many suns and moons later (a long time after the story of Tinker and Tapper), the fairies evolved without wings at all, and took to living in dense woodlands or caves, instead of living more in the open countryside and hedgerows, but on the whole they led a very happy life. When fairies reached the end of their earthly lives, having lived out a lifespan of many, many suns and moons, they didn't just waste away, but their spirits took on the form of a goldfinch, thus transforming them into a truly beautiful magical bird, and to this day, many humans capture goldfinches and keep them as prisoners in such tiny cages, just to hear them singing their melodious bell-like songs, not realizing that they have captured such a rare creature—a true free spirit, and a messenger of the universe!

Now one fateful day, the aforementioned King Nonno sent two of his trusted female servants to take the fairy babes, Tinker and Tapper, to the seashore so that the little ones could take in fresh air from the sea, which they did willingly. All went well, until the two happy little fairy servants got bored and left the two little royal fairy babes in an empty scallop shell, in which the servants had told the two little ones to stay and not under any circumstances were they to leave, and if they did, a big nasty crab would come out from under a rock and bite off their little toes! The naughty pair told them this just to frighten the baby fairies, in order that they should stay put, and this would leave them free so that they could play among the rock-pools and pick up tiny shells to take back to the palace with them.

As they chased around the rocks, singing and laughing quite happily, they forgot all about their precious charges left on the edge of the shore, and before they realized what had happened, a great wave came in and swept up the shell carrying the two little ones, and they drifted out to sea on the crests of the waves, unaware of what was happening to them.

As the daylight was beginning to fade and the two little fairies started to cry with cold, fear, and hunger, a group of passing sea nymphs happened to hear them. But before they appeared on the scene, one of the nymphs had found a discarded sea urchin's quill on the sea-bed, and on spotting a sword fish, promptly took up a mock battle with it. And with the clash of their weapons, with lots of thrusts and sparring, the spirited pair set up a swirl of sand, clouding the sea like a snow storm, but when a passing sting ray swam overhead, casting a deep shadow because it was so huge, it sent the two scuttling off in different directions, and the sea nymph hid beneath some rocks until the great fish had drifted past.

It was whilst they were gaily playing and chasing with little seahorses after a game of hide-and-seek amongst the coral, that the sea nymphs heard the little fairies' plaintive, very pitiful calls, and they immediately stopped their games, and it was then that they spotted the two distressed little waifs. They gently lifted them out of the shell and swam with them in a stream of bubbles to a large cavern deep down at the bottom of the sea.

Once inside the cavern, the two little fairies were led by the chattering sea nymphs as they walked along nervously, hand in hand. They continued deep within the labyrinths of the caves where the sea nymphs made them a comfortable bed of seaweed inside a scallop shell so that they could be rocked to sleep.

This particular cave was well lit by tiny diamonds which sparkled off the gold encrusted walls like little stars, and on the ceiling hung clear quartz crystals, which made pretty tinkling sounds as they gently clinked together from the soft air wafting through the caves.

At the far end, there was a beautiful grotto made up of hundreds of shells, and in front of it was a little rock-pool, over which hung clusters of amber, reflecting a soft yellow light off the water, and in the pool swam luminescent jellyfish and other little fishes that glowed in the water as they darted about.

On the left-hand side of the grotto was a small temple built from precious stones.

On the right-hand side was a small water wheel, turning away whilst mermaids busily worked and wove clothes made out of gold and silver for certain creatures of the underworld, yet unseen by humankind.

The mermaids sang as they worked, as their little fingers sewed garments with small fish bones, whilst nearby, younger mermaids and sea nymphs were climbing up the sides of great whale bones, then sliding back down with shrieks of laughter. But for all these great wonders, the two babes were not all that impressed, and they just cried and cried.

The kindly sea nymphs were still dressed in their best tunics, which were made out of fish-scales and lovingly kept polished with the smallest pieces of sea-sponges. They had shark teeth attached to their belts, which could be used as daggers against any dangerous sea creatures that might want to attack them, or sometimes they would use them to prise open oyster shells to search for pearls.

The sea nymphs suddenly disappeared for a short while into another cave. Then they returned wearing soft flowing green gowns. Their very stiff spiky hair, which had been neatly set on the top of their perfectly round little heads, was now let down to flow freely about their shoulders, thinking that the little fairies would be less frightened if they appeared less warlike!

Realizing that the tiny tots were still so very upset and couldn't be consoled, the sea nymphs then tried to pacify the sobbing pair with a special little song which they had made up for them:

> Little ones, oh my little ones,
> have a care, have a care,
> you will find such wondrous things,
> out there, out there,
> and all of these we will share, we will share,
> so dear dainty little ones,
> don't despair, don't despair.

The song was repeated three times to them, but Tapper and Tinker just kept on crying and crying, louder and louder, shriller and shriller (almost drowning out the song), and the noise bounced and echoed off the walls, nearly driving everyone mad, as well as filling up the ocean with a whole lot more salt water, making the sea swell alarmingly. They tried once more to amuse them by spinning colourful starfishes across the cave floor, but that didn't seem to work either, and so the sea nymphs then decided that the pair just may be very hungry.

The sea nymphs swam off, and in next to no time returned with little silver fishes and sea cucumbers to feed the unhappy pair, and at long last the two little fairies seemed to be satisfied.

As the suns and moons went by, Tinker and Tapper got bigger and bigger, fatter and fatter on their diet of fish, and they became more and more bored at not being able to leave their cave, because although the sea nymphs tried and tried their very best to teach them to swim, they were not able to swim far enough to reach the top of the ocean waves.

Now old Father Neptune heard about the plight of the unusual cave dwellers, and being a kindly god, decided to pay them a visit, and on seeing them, he took pity on them straight away and decided there and then to do something about it, and so this is what he did.

Father Neptune did a bit of his underwater godly type of magic, where a great transformation took place, and he turned them into two very portly (but rather quaint) unusual-looking birds, who stood very upright.

They were smartly turned out in tight-fitting black and white feathers, and they looked extremely regal indeed. Then he placed small coronets made from bright red coral on top of their heads, and solemnly declared that they were now to be called "king penguins,' and he named them Malinka and Mo, and he promised them that they could go on eating their favourite food of fish, but unfortunately, although they had little flipper-type wings, they would never be able to fly. Nevertheless, they would surely be able to swim as gracefully and efficiently as any other creatures of the sea, and they could still have lots and lots of fun by sliding up and down on the ice floes.

So he took the two of them in the palm of one hand and carried them swiftly off, far away across the ocean, where he set them down onto a floating ice floe.

At seeing the pair acting in such a joyful manner on hearing his promises to them, old Neptune let out a great hearty laugh which rumbled like thunder, and it was so loud that a huge mountain of ice split asunder, sending great shards of ice tumbling down into the sea like giant spears, and drifting ice floes were sent crashing into one another, making groaning, creaking, crunching noises in a spectacular fashion. To add a special effect as a finale, Neptune drew in a deep breath, and then turning his head in a Northerly direction, he blew softly and gently, and there appeared on the horizon, the most beautiful colours ever seen, wafting and waving like clouds of silk, with flashing lights behind them.

It is said that all those who watched, looked on in amazement and awe at this grand spectacle, and Neptune beamed with pleasure when he saw their eyes sparkle with joy.

He then decided to tell them the sad but wonderful story about Sedna, the ocean goddess of the North, far, far away, in the realm of freezing ice and crisp white snow, and he told them how this story was not entirely unlike their own, except that theirs has a much happier outcome, and he hoped that they would appreciate their new life from now on.

Neptune then began his story.

Sedna was born as a child of the earth, living and playing happily in a little village beneath the snow-capped mountains.

When she was old enough to marry, Sedna met a stranger who tried to weave a spell over her, in order to make her his soul mate. Unfortunately, the stranger was not human at all, but a seabird called a Petrel, who went in disguise, and he happened to see her by chance as he flew over the village. He sang beautiful songs, and he recited love poems to her, to impress and woo her, and she was totally captivated by his songs and poetry of love.

She finally agreed to go with him, and the pair sailed out in a canoe to his nest, which was high up in a cliff-top.

At first, all went well, but then after a while Sedna began to miss her family and friends, and she longed once more to hear their voices. Then gradually, day by day, the spell wore off, and she also became discontented with the cold and the wet, along with the strong smells of decaying fish.

The final straw came, when quite by chance, she saw through the disguise of the Petrel and discovered that he was not a handsome human man after all, but an ugly seabird, and so she became very distraught, and very angry at being deceived.

Meanwhile, after discovering that his daughter had vanished from the village, the father set off in his canoe in search of her, and eventually he arrived at the foot of the cliffs where she was now living, and he heard her howling and sobbing cries of distress.

On seeing her father in the sea just below her, Sedna dived straight into the water and swam to the canoe. Her father was then able to pull her out, and he lifted her carefully into the canoe and was overjoyed to see his daughter once more.

Sedna told him the whole story about meeting the stranger and of her abduction, but he became gravely solemn when she told him that he was an enchanted seabird, and her father then became silent and thoughtful.

As they set off for home, a great storm started to rage, and the waves started to swell alarmingly and tossed the canoe about in such a way that they were in grave danger of the canoe capsizing.

Now the enchanted Petrel was so distraught after finding his soul mate had left him, he set off to find her. But when he eventually caught up with her and her father in the canoe, he pleaded with her and tried desperately to persuade her to return with him, but she flatly refused. The seabird was so heartbroken, that he gave a haunting cry, then flew off into the gale and into the icy wastes.

Sedna's father was filled with remorse because he thought that the bird was sacred, and he feared that he and his daughter had angered the gods, and in order to appease them, he reluctantly decided to throw Sedna back into the sea, but she fought like a wild cat, and they struggled long and hard, until eventually she was thrown overboard. But she wouldn't give in, and as she tried to pull herself back into the boat, in desperation to stop her, her father chopped off her fingers with a knife. But as her fingers were severed, a very strange thing happened. As the tops of her fingers fell into the sea, they turned into seals. When the second joint of her fingers were cut off, they turned into deep-sea seals, and the third joints became walruses. As her thumbs were cut off last of all, they then became great whales.

As Sedna became too weak from loss of blood, she slowly sank to the bottom of the ocean, and as she reached the bottom, the sea became calm once more.

Her father also grew very weak and exhausted, and when he finally paddled to shore in the canoe, he set up his tent, and being so tired, he crawled inside and was soon fast asleep.

Whilst he slept, great waves came up to the shore and ripped the tent away, but before he could save himself, he was swept out into the ocean, where he joined his daughter Sedna.

Sedna now rules over the creatures of the ocean, and when they die, they have to pass through her kingdom.

On moonlit nights, she is sometimes seen rising out of the water in a huge rainbow bubble, and she drifts high into the universe, where she patrols the night sky, until returning once more to her underwater kingdom, where she travels from the cold oceans of the North, to the warmer climes of the South.

Now if you see her rising out of the ocean, you must treat her with great respect, and she will guide and protect you for as long as you live—and after!

After the jolly green giant had done his deed and told them the story of Sedna, he was well satisfied, and he then bid Malinka and Mo a fond farewell!

Then just as suddenly as he had appeared to them, he was gone!

Now they were able to be free at last, and for the very first time, after such an age, they dived down deep into the sea and then popped up to the surface once again in a frothy spray of dimply bubbles, as happy as any little sea urchins!

They were able to tell their story, and that of Sedna, to their offspring—who started life with little, snug-fitting, grey woolly coats which they wore till they grew bigger—and they in turn passed the story on to the next generation, and so on and so forth. So they were really coughed—or should I say chuffed?—*Coughed, chuffed!*—Get it?—Oh well, never mind!—Pass on that one if you don't already know what *coughs* are!

So when you sees the penguins, don't forget that they started off as little fat fairies!

Manyana to guano—says I!

Not all penguins were lucky enough to be kings though.

This was the story, as told by Eeli.

Oh dear! It looks as though I've sidetracked a bit, what with Eeli tellin' me all those stories about frolicking fairies and pouting pixies, so I'd better get back to the present situation.

Closing me eyes, I meditates so hard I nearly forgot wot I was supposed to do! Anyway, suddenly, in me deep thoughts and a swirly mist, up pops this large feathery head, and I could see a vision of its big round yellowy eyes, and it woz of the "The Amber Owl," wot gives you the option "to wing it, or not to wing it!" and it woz fairly screeching at me—"*NOW IS THE TIME TO GO!*"

Well, this is it! Gotta make me way into that great air space now. So it's now or never. I've seen it done on that magic box, and I've seen other free-flying birds do it, as I've watched them from me posh klakki when they takes me out for an airing.

Now it's definitely my turn.

I won't get any help from me Pinky Ma, 'coz she just ain't got the wingy things.

Well now, seein' as I needs a bit more space to think about this airborne stuff, and before I makes me final judgement before lift-off, I'm reminded of the time that I was talkin' to Eeli, with whom I got into a lengthy discussion on yet another sunlight-time when I was put outside for a spot of meditation, seein' as there wasn't much else to get too excited about.

I sez to Eeli, "Haven't you noticed just how different them pinkies are to us really high-an'-mighty ones?"

Then I goes on and tells her just how unfortunate they must have been, that the "Great One" just didn't give them a pair of handsome wings like wot we got. "Instead, they have to put up with these two fat peculiar-shaped legs at one end that makes them stand upright, and they have this pink, featherless skin. And they've got these knobbly things called 'kneeses' which they can bend, and they can even collapse down on them! It looks so gross!

"Then they have these big, ugly, wide, clawless feet, with funny-shaped objects of all shapes, sizes and colours, stuck on the ends of them that they call 'shoeses.' And then, strangest of all, they have yet another pair of skinny-type legs (where their wings should be), wot they call 'armses.' And not only that, at the ends of these skinny-type arms, they've got these strange flipper-type things that they call their 'handses!' Ugh! Really horrible looking! These 'handses' they can use to pick things up with. Sometimes they pick up some strange weapon-type objects, usually shiny things wot they call 'knives and forks.'

"And then they place food, with these shiny objects clenched firmly in their flippers (or 'handses') into a hole they call 'mouthses' which is set just under a funny-beak-type thingy. Now don't you go larfing, you lot!—but they call these beaky things 'noses' and these weird looking 'noses' makes a funny noise when they breathe in and out! I quite expects them to choke themselves, judging by the great big lumps of food they press into them holes! And then, just above their big round eyes, they've got these two funny little hairy caterpillars, which sometimes move up and down! One of these days, I'm goin' to see if I can get hold of one of 'em!

185

"Now I reckon they must be really envious of us birds for having all our bits and pieces in one useful package deal. Our smart beaks have got all those functions, like picking things up with, and then for eating things with, all at the same time, and also for sniffing things too! So our picky, sniffy, beaky thingy, is very conveniently situated in one place!

"An' another thing, when they go out foraging for food and return back in their big metal klakkies, they stagger in under the sheer weight of the stuff, and then they thrust this food stuff, which is all done up separately in a strange looking nasty material (wot they calls "plastic"!), and you can't even eat it! And then they put all of the food stuff to hide in a big white square object, which the pinkies call a 'fridgie' (or something like that!).

"And then when they want to feed, they fetch the food out of the big square object again, and guess what? They plonk it into a round shiny thing filled with water, and then set fire to it! And then they eat it!—all hot! And do you know what these daft pinkies do then? They fetch out some more food stuff from another part of the white square thing, and bring out yet another small square container, and inside this is what looks like creamy soft frozen snow, and then they gobble some of that too! All frozen! Just how kinky is that? First hot! And then cold!

"Then there's other noises they go makin', especially when they crash about all over the place, booming, thudding, rustle, rustle!"

"Oh, you mean like the rustle that leaves make?" asks Eeli.

"Yes!... That's just about it!" I continues. "And lots of hissing sounds, like snippity, snoppity when they're communicatin' with each other. I don't mind so much now, 'coz it usually means that grub's on its way, an' I'm just beginnin' to learn what some of these speakin' words mean. And we mustn't forget their eyes! They've got eyes the size of dew ponds, but they're not all round like the ol' hootie's eyes (owl's eyes, that is). It makes yer a fair bit frightened when they first looks at yer.

"On their heads, they grow all this fine 'hair' that us birds can use as first-class klakki-making material. Some of this hair is long, some of it short, and it's really *weird* looking. I have had a bit of a go at trying to pluck some out, but it's not easy like plucking out feathers, and besides, they get quite angry when I does have a go. Then they gear themselves up in all those brightly coloured stuffs to cover them up in different places, and they call these things 'clothes.' Sometimes they change these coloured clothes twice, or even three times in the daylight hours, not like us feathered lot who are hatched out with just one set of colours that lasts us our lifetime!

"True to say," I continued, "I already knows that them pinky tribes have noses, toeses, kneeses, mouthses, bumses and many other bits and pieces gathered together to makes them into the gruesomely ugly specimens that they are, because I was told of this by me ma and pa, when these bits of information was passed down through our great wisdom-infested ancestors, so we only learnt it all 'parrot fashion' so to speak, so we could only *visualize* great gods with hairy arms and legs, and great big stumpy bodies, just the same way as the little fledgling pinkies probably *know* what a river *looks* like but when *told* about a river *estuary*, well, they probably wouldn't *know* what *that* would look like either, till they actually *saw* one!" I said, feeling a bit perplexed at me own bit of intellectual knowledge.

The only thing is, I wasn't altogether convinced with me own explanation, but I think Eeli was duly impressed with it anyway, as there was this great big gaping hole between this statement an' me next one, so I guessed there was no doubt she was absorbing fully, me great words of wisdom!

Then I went on, "And it wasn't until I was rescued by a kindly pinky as a wee helpless chick from those rascally crows that I got to find out what they really looked like, 'coz how woz I to know without seein' them for myself? Not only that, but as I'm fortunate enough to be able to watch all sorts of stuff goin' on in the world on this big magic box and by listening to their monotonous voices and by watching them point at things that I've managed to learn quite a few new words, which is going to be a heap of use to me. And one of these new words is what they call this magic box of theirs, 'tee vee.'

"Learnin' this human lingo, which is heartily tough, is not only heavy goin', but I've then got to translate it back into Birdy speech, or I suppose you could call it 'magglish!' Yup, that's wot I'm going to call it; so now's you know!"

I'm ultra careful not to let the pinkies know of me ever-growing knowledge, so I have to be careful, and act plain ignorant and stupid! But just you wait, I've got plenty of good-stuff plans afoot!

Anyway, after all this dithering about pinky things and fairy fun time, I'd best be gettin' back to me airborne stuff again.

At long last, and after careful consideration, and after much side-tracking and long stony stares from Pinky Ma, and as many excuses I could muster to put off the final plunge, I took off, all right! — then there was a bit of turbulence, and I hit an air pocket, went into a dive, forgettin' to put me undercarriage down, did a belly flop, and made a bit of a crash landing, which sent me into a fair old skid! No big deal, just testing me gear. Now all I wants is an escape route!

Gets kind of monotonous, reelin' and wheelin' about in circles, and just hard edges in each corner to bump into. Not natural like!

Then there was this paraphernalia nonsense about trying to get me to jump into me drinking water. I gather no ones heard of anting then? Well let me tell you what it's all about.

There was a time of long ago, since many summers and winters had passed, when my great, great, ever-so-great ancestors found themselves plagued by nasty little biting insects, and these awful little nasties caused them unbearable discomfort. They tried everything to get rid of them, like jumping up and down, clacking as loud as they could in the hope that it would drive the wee beasties mad, or deaf, making 'em fall off 'coz they couldn't hear nothin'. Now that's just plain stupid! Has anyone ever seen ears on a flea? So how are you gonna make 'em deaf?

Then they tried standing out in the pouring rain with their wings outstretched to try and drown the pesky little beasties. They even tried to copy the stupid little sparrows, who tumbled about in dry dust patches, but it only made their beautiful black and white feathers all dull looking, so they soon gave that unproductive game up. Then one day, just by chance, one very bright magpie found the solution.

This particular individual was having a quiet day all to himself, just enjoying a few spiders and insects he'd been collecting out in a field, and when he'd polished these off, he then decided to grab up a small beak full of ants. Now just at that moment, he experienced a sudden attack of stinging bites and itchiness under one of his wings, so naturally he went to stab at the offending cause of this irritation, forgetting he still had his beak full of delicacies, mainly the ants. At this point, he noticed that when he squeezed the ants ever so slightly, they squirted a sort of fine spray over his feathers, and he was amazed to see his tiny attackers drop off stone dead.

He was overcome with excitement about his great discovery, and didn't waste any time at all in telling all his relatives about his new invention, and is wasn't long after that when all the other magpies could be seen picking up these magic ants and squirting merrily all over the place, thus keeping their white feathers brilliant white, and their black feathers all shiny and smart. So I wasn't in a hurry to throw myself into the drink yet—was I?

Give me an army of ants any day, and I'll show you just how useful they really are!

Anyway, I was getting right fed up with Pinky Ma's persistence at shoving this hard container with water in it at me and then tryin' to splash it all over me. Do they want me to drown or somethin'? What's 'appened to creature comforts? So there I woz, havin' me bits of fun by leggin' it across the shiny woody footy area, squirting as much doo doo's as I could, so's the pinky who's causing me all the aggro would have to clean it up after me, and all the while makin' all sorts of funny noises in a very high-pitched key as she rushed about on her funny tree-trunk-type legs, making a fair bit of old draft as she went, I can tell you! Funny how they get all uppity about good fun things.

Well, I soon run out of doo doo's to waste all over the place, so I looked for something else to do.

Someone had left dangling from me klakki something wot looked like a piece of long klakki-building-material stuff, which I could only think woz a strand of dried twisted grass, or something very similar (I learnt that this stuff is called "string" and woz always used for holding back the little square-shaped grid, which blocks the hole leading from me klakki, allowing me to come in or out). So I flew back onto the top of me klakki, and my cunningly clever plan woz to fly off with the strand (or string), and hide it somewhere. But it didn't quite go according to me ingenious plan.

How woz I to know that this long grassy thing was fully attached to me exit-blocker! So it's only natural that I really only wanted to borrow it just for a while. I would have been ever so gracious and taken it back!—Honest I would! Oh, what a bloody let down and no mistake! Blasted thing wouldn't let me go, and I didn't want to let go of it either! Back and forth! To and fro! Up and down! Side to side! Port to starboard! And then, sink or swim! Someone must've pulled the earth gravity forces from right under me wings! What goes up, must come down! Heads: I win! Tails: I lose!

So I took a glorious—not previously attempted—beak dive straight into the drink!

So what's the big deal? The pinky went into a frantic fit, making cackling noises like a hyena, as though she had a buffalo bone stuck in her throat, and it got louder and louder, enough to awaken a kittiwake! If this is the kind of reaction I get from these earthbound, flightless creatures, then I'd better press on with further engagements to try and amuse them. Not only that, but I seem to get nice yummy rewards whenever I do something really clever.

Oh, how I yearn for a nice newly laid blackbird's egg. Even a hatched one would go down a treat!

Oops! Sorry Eeli, if you happen to hear me say this! No offence meant! Just a manner of speech!

Anyway, I quite enjoyed my splash about in the water after all, and I've decided not to go looking for those squirty ants for medicinal purposes, and not only that, the pinky left me to it for a while, then she came back with a strange-looking tool that made a funny droning sound, and it also blew a warm wind, she then pointed it at me feathers and it felt lovely and warm and very soothing, and after a bit, it dried me feathers out a real treat, all plump and glossy looking. This was a pure exotic luxury I wasn't going to miss out on! My swings and roundabouts adventures hadn't yet finished.

I must admit, I gave myself a bit of a nasty fright when I found those big square white floaty things (wot pinkies call "kitchen towels") that were left very conveniently lying around. They were next to these big, white, hard, shiny, disc-shaped things (or "plates") which the pinkies use to plonk their food on. Next to these "plates" they put funny odd-shaped shiny tools ("knives and forks," in case you didn't know) which they pick up in their funny flippers, then the food is pierced by one of these tools, and when they do this, they then push this little lot into those big gaping holes beneath their funny beaks (which I mentioned before).

Anyway, these white things looked very nice and soft to carry and might come in handy for me to start me practice at collecting bits and pieces, as there will no doubt come a time when I will need to build me own klakki. And so I needed to snitch one for myself, and now was as good a time as any, and I didn't want to lose this opportunity, so let's give it a go!

A real doddle! A quick dive down as straight as an arrow, stab it up as nimble as a kingfisher, and then fly off! Great bit of manoeuvring! Fantastic skill in aerobatics! Absolutely faultless! Can't go wrong!

Those were my intentions, but things didn't quite go according to plan.

Just a slight minor hiccup, really.

There hung in the air just an inkling of a niggling doubt like was this a really cool thing to do? And why can't I see where I'm going? Followed by who blew this bloody thing over my head anyway! And Where's the daylight gone to? And why is everything looking too misty already?"

I seemed to be having quite a run of panic attacks just lately, and I was quite frankly getting just a little pissed off with 'em. I had by now run out of practical ideas and was running out of wing-flap power, and dizziness was becoming second nature to me, ever since I went on me first spiralling spin out of the klakki, from no fault of me own.

It was with much relief when I was finally grabbed in full flight, but I must admit, I did feel a tiny bit humiliated.

Liberation day has arrived, and I think an angel in the pack looked down and must've said something like, "Oh just look at that poor little sod!" and felt pity on the depraved little cooped-up magpie that I woz. And so they dealt me some very favourable leaves to be turned over and read by me friend Eili. She did tell me there woz more to be told of my future, so perhaps this woz meanin' I should be expecting to travel, or to be upwardly mobile or something similar, 'coz someone left all the openings clear, which woz just what I was looking for.

A freeway at long last! It felt as though there was a magnet drawing me towards the light. I could feel a breeze wafting down to where I woz perched, and I took off!

Swiftly flying upwards, I woz then able to head in the direction of my long-awaited destiny, which woz beckoning to me. There was no stopping me now! Must keep going! Not much further! There's the gap! Yippee! I'm through—*Freedom at last!*

At first I was flapping me wings too rapidly, fearful that I might lose height, but I soon found that if I drifted with the warm current of air, I could easily glide and soar with little effort, and with the warmth of the sun on my back, I woz gradually getting stronger and more confident. I wanted to fly up to the brilliant blue canopy above me so that I could pierce through it to see what woz beyond, but it seemed so high, and looked as though it went on forever.

I could feel vibrations in the air, my feathers tingled with expectations, and I felt that the spirit of my ancestors were there with me, to guide me, telling me to be aware of everything around me.

At first it woz scary up there; it sure as hell knocked a whole load of shit outta me—big time! And if any unwary pinkies were slap in the middle of the target zone, then they were in for a windfall of good luck!

There seemed to be a great change in me that I just couldn't understand.

Far above me, white seagulls circled, and as they glided and swirled about on the thermals, they called out to me, "Hi there! Hi there! Who are you? Who are you?" And they ended up by laughing at me, but I didn't know why. I didn't feel in the mood to answer back to them. This was all so exhilarating to me, and I just wanted to savour the moment on me own!

Much higher up, I could see great silver machines flying in straight lines, making funny roaring noises, trailing white puffy smoky stuff behind them, like silver dragons! Of course I knew all along that they are really called "airyplanes" by the pinky folk, so I woz just lapsing into me more familiar "birdy" talk!

At times it woz very silent up there. But far below, I could hear everything as clear as a bell, so much so that if a butterfly sneezed, I would have heard that too!

I also found that me eyesight became much sharper and could spot the smallest movement, even the flutter of a leaf or a beetle darting out from under a stone.

This was sheer bliss! Much better than watching tee vee!

Looking earthwards, I could see hundreds and hundreds of square klakkies. I believe the pinky lot (or should I say, "the people"?) call them "houses," as one of the new words what woz learnt by me on the tee vee.

There they all were—all these pinkies either scuttling about like busy little ants or lying down and all stretched out on square bits of coloured material, and these were all spread out on their square bits of earth (called gardens), doing absolutely nothing. Or maybe some of them were just sleeping, or maybe they were dreaming up things to do perhaps, like digging little holes in their square patches of earth with a metal tool and then filling them in with flowers or other such earth-growing things (they call this bit of activity 'gardening').

A little further on, I could see a rather odd-looking klakki made up of lots of stone work, and here and there I could see some very pretty rainbow coloured glass bits, glinting in the sun, and I thought to meself how my great, great, great, ever-so-great grand egg layer, Lace Wing, would have loved these bits of coloured glass for her collection.

The top part of this strange-looking klakki was very pointed, and it had a hard metal cockerel (which wasn't very real looking) perched right on the tip. I had no idea who could be living there, but as I flew over it, I could feel that there woz some sort of power coming from it. A feeling of peace seemed to radiate around this strange pile of stones.

All around me I could see what looked like thick black cobwebs, festooned across the land, and they were strung in criss-cross lines, where they appeared to be attached to tall, straight, branchless trees, which looked very lifeless. *Do the pinkies catch their food stuffs in these great long webs?* I asked meself. *I must try and stay clear of them, just in case I get caught up like a fly in a spider's web!*

Then I sees some large birds, such as crows, pigeons, jackdaws and other types, and they were all perching quite happily on these peculiar webs, so I wasn't quite so worried about it then.

In all directions, I could see the large long-winding smooth stone-type pathways where all the different sized metal klakkies travelled, carrying the pinkies to wherever they wanted to go. It was quite strange to think that I had myself experienced such a way of travel in one of them big metal klakkies, but from way up here, they looked so small, just like beetles, whereas on the ground they are big, hard, smelly, and very, very noisy most of the time, exceptin' when they are not moving. Now I could see them shuttling about in all directions like little ants.

My instincts told me to memorise every line of tree and hedgerow so that I could find me way back.

In the distance I could see a long straight line of metal which I'd never seen before, and it went as far as the eye could see into the distance, and every so often there would be a very fast, very frightening looking metal klakki that looked very much like a snake, except that it didn't look as though it could bend or twist like one, or even move off its metal path. It also made a very loud *clickity!-clackity!-clickity!-clackity!* sort of noise as it travelled along at great speed on this metal path.

As I've never yet seen one of these monsters on the magical tee vee, I dunno what they are called, so I decided not to investigate any further, and I headed back to me familiar territory.

On arriving back to me own square patch, I looked over the top of the hawthorn hedge and detected a brown bird with brown spots on his chest.

He stood stock still and didn't seem to move at all, as though he woz in deep concentration. He was a stranger to me, as we had never met before.

I flew down several hops away from him and approached cautiously, leaving seven worm-lengths between us. He cocked his head towards me, standing very tall and erect; he looked very stern, but elegant and knowledgeable, all at the same time, which made me feel just a little insecure.

I thought I had better make the first move, and to kick off with very polite conversation without ruffling his feathers too much, I spoke to him.

"Good sunlight-time to you, my very smart-looking speckled friend of earth and air! Oh, and if I were to join up those dots together—You know?—The ones on your chest!—I could turn it into a picture of outstanding interest!" I politely said to him in innocent fun.

Silence! So I continued.

"Do you come here often?"

More silence, and he didn't even move a feather.

I was feeling a bit braver now, so I thought I would try a different style of topical conversation. Inching closer, I said to him, "If you have a roosting site not twenty wing-flaps away from here and have hatched a brood of tasty fledglings, and in case you haven't yet noticed that I'm actually a magpie, then don't make long-term plans for them for the rest of the day! Look at it another way, I'd be doing you a very special favour by lightening your hard work of foraging for 'em all, as it's *such* hard work, and you're just working your wings off! You look near done in! Just one or two each day and you will hardly miss 'em on this gradual process of elimination, an' I'll be real quick and gentle, all at the same time, so they wont feel a thing! So why don't you just point me in the right direction?—and the deed will be done! That's my good neighbourly offer to you! So what say you to that, spotted dick?"

I am forced to admit, I was quite taken aback by his unexpected reply and his unappreciative reaction to me good-hearted suggestion.

His voice was so loud and penetrating to me delicate brain that I bounced three times away from him.

"What!....What!....What!" he bellowed, as he picked up an empty snail shell, and threw it at me in response to me sensible idea, but it hit the bars of me metal klakki (which had probably been left outside in the hope that I would return and fly straight into it) where it pinged off and hit the ground.

"Who in the name of raven's wing do you think you are addressing here!? You speak in such a manner to me, as though you have the spoken authority of the grand-master golden eagle, and you!—you insolent young feather brain!—with egg yolk still stuck to your beak, and soft chick feathers still dangling from your ignoble backside!... *HOW DARE YOU!* I am Thorn Stormcock, the thunder teller, otherwise known as a Mistle Thrush to many others. Now, with your impudence, you have no alternative but to earn my respect, and if you don't, your future is very bleak indeed!"

He cleared his throat, and coughed up a berry seed, which landed in the grass in front of him. He then proceeded to lecture me, and I thought it best to stand very still, and at the same time I tried my hardest to look very humble and full of remorse for whatever it woz I had said to upset him, but then he continued in a quieter, and a much more controlled voice.

"You are not to confuse me with me cousin Shelldross. Shelldross is a song thrush, and he sings a most beautiful, melodious song, which is always repeated twice, and in such a rich tone that he is often compared to our friends the blackbirds, who are really quite envious of his skill at smashing snail shells on sharp stones, which is a trick that the blackbirds are just not able to copy.

"Shelldross told me that once, after he had spent a long time at smashing an extra-large snail shell which looked very juicy indeed, and after such a long laborious effort, he was just about to devour the contents when a very cheeky blackbird dived out from under a bush and snatched the snail from right under his beak, without even a 'thank you, if you please!'

"His other talent is to be able to sing out the events of the summer season, and then good or bad things which are expected to happen during the autumn season, and all of this he does with the scattered shells, in much the same way as the egg layer blackbirds predict the future through the leaves.

"My task, on the other hand, is to be able to warn others of impending storms or high winds which can damage our roosting sites, and I do this in a very, very, loud voice. I can sense it in the way of the air current. I can also feel through my feathers a tingling heat. Then there's a strange pungent smell in the air, and everything becomes still. I can detect a vibration in the ground, which starts to pulsate through rocks and stones, sending out a certain pattern of sounds. I can pick up all of these sensations of sounds, directly through my feet. It is my responsibility to warn all the birds of this great weather change, so that they can fly off to find a safe place to take cover. When the danger of the storm has passed, I can give them the all clear, and they are then able to return once more.

"It was during the last season that I felt we were all in mortal danger. The signs I picked up were of a much stronger nature. The trees were bending in a different direction, even though there was very little wind about, but I knew this meant we would all be in great danger, and I had to warn everyone to move out of this area. Most birds did heed my warning, but of those who didn't, I fear they may have perished.

"There came a great roaring wind, twisting in fury across the land and uprooting great trees in its path. Many klakkies were destroyed of both the bird kingdom and the humans' too. It was as if Mother Nature had got tired of her old gown and yearned for a new one, so she gave a deep, deep sigh, and she left a huge gap in the landscape, ready for a new creation, a fresh, bright start for the next generation of all the creatures and humans.

"We were all experiencing an enormous spring-cleaning across the land, blowing away all the cobwebs, and lots of other things as well. I can already see a new patchwork woven across the land, created by new young trees. You have much to be thankful for that you were not here to experience this great storm, and I will not tolerate your bad manners or your spiteful remarks!"

He paused for a few moments, and then he continued once more.

"This early season, I lost my egg layer mate to one of the earth whisperers over the other side of this hedge. I know there are two of them, but I am not sure which one actually carried out the murder. I still grieve for her to this day, and I wish for some kind of revenge.

"She was called Sweetpea, but not after the brightly coloured flowers which grow on long twisting stems. This name was given to her because of her fondness for the small green fruit, which grows inside of a long pod. Sweetpea was hand-reared as a chick by a very kind human.

"She was cared for by a man with a bushy white beard who was very gentle with birds and other small creatures, and he was particularly pleased with Sweetpea because she used to eat all the snails which raided the vegetables on his plot of land. He hand-fed her with cake or bread crumbs as a reward for ridding his vegetables of snails. And then he found out that she loved the peas which he also grew on his land, and so he would leave some for her to eat as a special treat, and she said she had never eaten anything like it before, which was so tasty and sweet, and that is how she was given the name of Sweetpea.

"Then one day the old man never returned to his plot of land after a particularly hard winter, and strangers appeared instead. They uprooted all the flowers and vegetables, including the peas, and turned it into a children's playground. Sweetpea missed her old friend, and with great sadness, she never returned to the plot.

"Now the task I set out for you is this!" he said, picking off a couple of aphids from a rose bush. "I want you to go and seek out these two green-eyed demons and give them such a beating that they will never forget! And don't you forget to leave your mark on them...with your sharp beak!... Now that shouldn't be too difficult for a bird like you!"

At this point I was beginning to get just a tiny bit anxious, but excited at the same time.

He continued with his request. "Their tails and their toes are the most vulnerable parts of their bodies, or even their eyes, but I wouldn't recommend that part of them too much, as it's too close to their sharp teeth, and they could easily grab you, so that wouldn't do at all, in my opinion, but I will leave it entirely up to you, but if you can carry out this deed, it will not only appease my anger at your earlier remarks to me—which I know you will not lose any sleep over—but you will go down in history as a very brave heart, and your name and heroic deeds will be etched on a large stone, which is standing hidden in a very secret place known only by our wise ones."

I wasn't at all sure who these "wise ones" were, but I was becoming impatient to begin, and couldn't wait to win my bravura wings!

I then burst into me song of bravery to him:

> *Wowee chihuahua,*
> *frankincense and myrrh,*
> *give me some wing power,*
> *and I'll bring you their fur!'*

And then I called out, "Just point me in the right direction! Let me at 'em! I'll show 'em who's boss around here!"

Thorn the Storm told me that he'd seen the pair just a very short while ago and that they were skulking somewhere in the dense undergrowth. I flew in a straight line and landed with a *cling* and a *clang* right on top of the ridgy roof of the strange-looking klakki.

I believe the pinky herd hide all their collected bits and pieces in there, and wouldn't us magpies give a rabbit's foot to own such a nice big hiding place for all our plunder and cluttery treasures?

It wasn't easy walking on this very odd roof with its ups and downs. I started to hum, just to let them know I wasn't going to be scared by these two woolly wallies.

> *Diddly, diddly dumsee,*
> *stick him up a gum tree,*
> *kill the cat,*
> *knock 'im flat,*
> *diddly, diddly dumsee.*

I saw two green eyes to one side of me and then another pair of green eyes on the other side; but I just pretended I didn't see them and carried on in a very nonchalant manner, just to test them, to see what their next move would be. I picked up a stone and let it go clattering down the roof ridge, and then I saw two ears twitch from the nasty one on my left at the same time as the nasty one on my right flattened its ears against its head, trying to look meaner than ever. Then from the corner of my eye, I could see them creep ever so slowly and quietly towards me, then they stopped and crouched very low, thinking I couldn't see them. How stupid can you get? They started to wriggle their bodies.

"Trick or treat!" I yodelled. "What's the matter toots? Got a worm stuck up yer backsides or summat?" I asked. "Hey fish breath!" I chortled. "Why not hum away with me, if you like? Even if you are somewot off key!"

Then I sang them a pretty little ditty which went something like this:

> *In through the front door,*
> *out through the back,*
> *give me your forked-bones,*
> *then I'll make them crack!*
> *Wings and paws between us,*
> *forget about the fish!*
> *Now let's all pull together,*
> *and make a tasty wish!*

They stopped their wriggling and their eyes went very wide.

"'coz if you have got a wriggly-wormy-type problem," I continued, "then see this?" I clicked me beak. "And see that? There's more than one way to skin a cat!"

I pointed me beak towards their bums.

"Well then, why don't you just let me relieve you of the offending wormy pest, and I'll tie it in a knot, and then you can stick it behind your ears so that you can save it for later, okay? So now why don't you just piss off pussies, before I pierce your perfectly protruding posteriors with my perpetually prodding pukka-peckin' poopa scoopa, and save us all a lot of aggro. This is now kick-arse time— awrighty? Catch is catch can!" Seein' as I'd got their undivided attention, I threw in another comment: "Wassamadder? Cat gotcha tongue or summat? *Ha ha ha! He he he! Ho ho ho!*—*Ooh!*—temper, temper, my little spitfires," I concluded.

I seemed to be having a good run on upsetting others, because after this remark they both sprang together towards me, as agile as a froggy in a bobble hat, and just as they did so, I nimbly hopped back a pace or two, and the two fuzzy hussies collided, and landed in a spitting, fur-flying heap.

"Excuse me!" I said, "but I couldn't but help notice your fancy footwork, and I think there's room for improvement. May I suggest a few delicate moves which may make a great deal of difference to your performance?"

Were they embarrassed or what?

I moved in on them, side stepping just in case they decided to rearrange some of my feathers.

Whilst their feet were still tangled and sticking up in the air, I started to manicure their needle-like claws with me beak.

"Now this should help a lot," I crooned. "A little nip here and a little tuck there, and you'll soon be able to dance to me tune, especially if I can just bend these claws of yours just a little bit, and then you should be able to grip much better on sloping roofs like this one. Well, me dearies, looks as though you've never been spoken to by such an intelligent one as me, so hold tight I'll give you a fright, and I'll give you a wop with all of my might! Speakin' of which, do you possess any mites?"

To me amazement, these two ungrateful fluffy flossies, with faces as lovely as a baboon's bottom and breath as sweet as a Gannet's vomit, were not a bit amused, and in next to no time at all, untangled themselves, hissing and snarling at me as they sprang up.

"Oh yes!" I said, "that's a step in the right direction all right."

Then I sez to them, "I want you both to join me in this cheery little song, just to jolly you along a bit, and you can hum 'miaow miaow' to it if you prefer."

Put yer left paw in,
yer left paw out;
in out,
in out,
and shake it all about,

you do the hokey pokey,
and you spin all around;
that's what it's all about, -
Caw!... Caw!

Oh!... Hokey cokey pokey;
Oh!... Hokey cokey pokey;
Oh!... Hokey cokey pokey;
that's what it's all about.
Caw!... Caw!

Put yer head in a bucket,
and yer knees on the floor;
I'll peck at yer feet,
and you'll squeal out for more;
when yer whiskers start to twitch,
and yer tail begins to curl,
yer body starts to spin,
then we'll all begin to twirl,
that's what it's all about.

Oh!... Hokey cokey pokey;
Oh!... Hokey cokey pokey;
Oh!... Hokey cokey pokey;
that's what it's all about.
Caw!... Caw!

Just one more time now!

I put me left wing in;
me left wing out;
in out,
in out,
and flap it all about;
I do the hokey pokey,
and I spin all around;
that's what it's all about.

Oh!... Hokey cokey pokey;
Oh!... Hokey cokey pokey;
Oh!... Hokey cokey pokey;
that's what it's all about!
Caw!... Caw!

They didn't seem at all amused, and they started to creep towards me, low and slow, and I could hear their throaty grumbling, which made me feel as close as a bee sting from being eaten!

"Now don't you two cool cats give me a hard time," I said, "'coz if you do, then I'm going to get really, really a mickle angry, an' there's no tellin' what I will do!" And of course, I woz trying to work out just what I could do to make my mark on them in order to please me good friend Thorn.

Just as I woz about to carry out another area of attack, I heard another sound, only this time it woz Pinky Ma.

She was clattering about with a wooden ladder, which she noisily clonked against this thing I've heard called a shed (please note my ever-increasing human vocab) where this grand battle of wits woz taking place right at that minute.

All of a sudden, a bunch of stones came hurtling down on the roof, and one extra big stone, about the size of a hen's egg, missed me by inches!

Had she gone mad, lost her marbles, or what? And I thought that she really worshipped me, but there she woz tryin' to end me life on this planet in one fowl swoop, so to speak!

I was very thankful when she ever-so-carefully plucked me off the roof and saved me from those "grizzling gussies."

Anyway, I'm safe and sound now, all tucked up in me klakki, and it looks as though I'm going to be outrageously pampered after all, so perhaps it's been worth it, and it woz good fun too, and I'm learnin' a few more tricks of the trade.

Now let me think! What was it Eeli said to me when she turned over them old leaves?

"You will be going on a long, long journey, very far from here!"

I wonder what she meant?

-Chapter Five -
Echoes From the Past

All our bags were now packed, the furniture had already been piled into the removal van, which was now on its way to Wales.

With the sombre ritual of farewells to friends and relatives now behind us, it was time to bid the house goodbye, and thank it graciously for all those lovely, happy, memorable years, which was a very hard thing to do, especially for my parents, having spent fifty-four years of their married life in this one house. It somehow didn't seem right that strangers were about to move in and take over our home.

The house was now empty, and the atmosphere was quite eerie, and there was a deep silence as we sat on the stairs—each with our own private thoughts at this moment in time.

My own thoughts were: *What on earth have I done?*
Mother's were: *What on earth has she done to us?* (meaning me).
And Father's were: *Don't hang about! Let's get going!*

There were no tears, just very mixed feelings of both sadness and excitement, with a dash of anticipation of what might lay ahead of us.

We hadn't exactly rehearsed the preparation of loading up the car for the 223-mile journey, so there were a few false starts, with lots of cursing and frayed tempers, but finally we managed to squeeze in everything that we needed to take. The boot was packed tight with our clothes, dogs' bowls (one for water and one for their mixed-up food stuffs), then there was a soft shopping bag with a flask of coffee, and a box with our packed lunch, and on the back seat sat the two dogs, Katie and Hattie, and right up tight in the corner behind the passenger seat sat my father, with Maggie in his cage sitting on his lap. His two large hands were clasping each side of the cage, and making it look as though he was playing a concertina! It must have been very uncomfortable for him, but he didn't complain.

Mother sat in the front passenger seat, with her knees almost up to her chin, and her feet were placed atop numerous tightly tied-up polythene bags, with various bits and pieces in, and her precious handbag, and other odds and ends packed tightly on either side of her feet, assuring me that she really was quite comfortable, and not to worry too much! She told me that she'd taken a Valium tablet so that she could relax and sleep for most of the journey anyway!

"Well that's a good start!" I told her. "Seeing that we're supposed to be taking the scenic route! Fat lot of good that will do if you're going to sleep all through the journey! We might as well go by the motorway!"

My passengers said nothing, and we were ready to leave.

I was careful not to glance back in the mirror at the house, as the car pulled away and slowly cruised down the hill.

It was about five-thirty in the morning. The sun was already rising in the east, and the sky was already brightening up for yet another promising hot day. I decided that an early start was crucial, as the sun would hot-up by midday, so it was important to get as much mileage behind me as possible, or the occupants in the car would suffer from the heat—especially the two dogs—and it wouldn't be much fun for my father carrying the huge cage on his lap either.

I told my mother that if she had left anything behind in the house now—even if it was her precious lipstick—she would have to forget it, and I wasn't going to turn back on any account! If I did have to return (for whatever reason), it would have been even more difficult to make that final wrench, and to untie the bonds of the past.

On the spur of the moment (as it was still very early, and the air refreshingly cool), I decided to make a sentimental round trip of our old haunts.

First of all, I stopped at our fields (which were not yet up for sale) to say goodbye to my two horses. Gazella was my dear old grey cob mare, and of course there was Humphrey, my lively, but loveable fell pony. They wouldn't be joining us in Wales for at least six months, whilst we had yet to arrange for a block of stables to be built for them.

I found it very difficult to wrench myself away from them, although I was very grateful that they would be lovingly looked after by two very good friends of mine.

The fields were beginning to recover after the October hurricane, but there were still large gaps of daylight on the horizon, and great gaping holes, where huge mounds of earth were heaped up where trees had once stood in our ancient woodland attached to our fields, and where hundreds of valuable specimen trees were planted so many years ago, but now, so many of them had been so tragically and ruthlessly uprooted in the early hours of the morning on that fateful day.

Thank God the horses had spent their summer vacation in a neighbouring field, with less trees in it, so that when the hurricane hit us, they were able to make a safe retreat to an open space, where they must have huddled together for safety.

At home, we hadn't exactly escaped scot-free from the dreadful onslaught of the hurricane, as our lovely old Christmas tree (which had been planted near the front gate when we were very young children) had been uprooted, lifting the tarmac in the front drive, and at the same time, it raised the small truck (which was used for carting small bales of hay) and smashed down across Father's much loved Volkswagen Beetle car, crunching the back right in, where the engine is housed, and squashing the back tyres—flat!

When the men arrived with their chainsaws to cut the tree to free the car, it almost sprang back to life as it bounced back up, and instead of having to tow it out of the drive to take it to a garage for repairs, it spluttered back to life as soon as the key was turned in the ignition. What a relief! We were very lucky that the old Christmas tree didn't fall towards the house, otherwise it would have caused a lot more structural damage.

The poor old Christmas tree was yet another part of our past, now gone for good!

Fallen trees in our fields also crushed my lovely brand new horse trailer, which I'd used only once!

One huge old oak stood forlornly in the middle of the field. It had been hacked to pieces by the storm, and it looked just as though a giant had come along with a large axe and had run amok with it. The huge majestic branches now lay broken and split at the foot of the tree, whilst some of the branches were still trying to hang on by what appeared to be a thin thread and now leaning precariously against the gnarled trunk. Such a sad sight to see!

We were spared our little summer house and caravan, which stood just inside the woods, as the trees tumbled on either side, miraculously missing them by inches!

At least we still have our caravan, summer house, and the treasured Beetle car, which is occasionally taken out of mothballs, as it now purrs quite happily along the winding lanes of West Wales.

Mustn't ponder for too long—what is done is done, and we have many miles to go.

We drove on past the common where Maggie was rescued.

The tall white windmill (miraculously untouched by the hurricane) stood proud and silent, as though on guard duty, looking quite awesome in the early morning mist, which always seemed to blanket the common in the early hours, even in the summer season.

The next sentimental stop (worthy of a memory recall) was at my grandparents' home—my father's parents, that is. My brother and I loved this old house.

I will always remember my granddad smelling of tobacco, which he smoked from an old pipe kept in a pipe-rack on the mantel shelf over the kitchen range, next to his sweet-bag containing aromatic aniseed drops. Grandma had a much more pleasant smell of Yardley's lavender soap or rose-scented talcum powder, and her favourite sweets were peppermint cremes.

We lived in this old house for about two years with our mother, whilst Father was away working on a contract somewhere near London. The house was a typical Victorian one, and it had lots of charm about it, as it still held on to remnants from the past, whilst undergoing small changes into the future.

As you entered through the back door, you walked straight into what was called "the scullery," and from there, you stepped up into a kitchen, where we sat round a very big old-fashioned kitchen table to eat our meals. My chair always had a soft cushion placed on the seat, because when I was very young, I just couldn't quite reach the top of the table.

From the kitchen, there was another door leading into the hallway, and as you went along the hallway, but just before you reached the front door, you turned left through another door, and straight into one large living room.

On the landing upstairs stood a small medicine cabinet containing various bottles, tins, and jars, to treat our various ailments, and then off the landing were three fairly large bedrooms. Each bedroom was decorated with wallpaper printed with tiny pretty pink or red roses, but if you stared at them too long, they could make you go almost cross-eyed! In the corners of each room, stood a large chest-of-drawers, smelling faintly of camphor (coming from the mothballs), and every bedroom had its own little fireplace. The surround to each of the fireplaces were tiled with shiny green tiles, engraved with prints of flowers or ships, and over the top, a white painted mantle shelf, and each fireplace had an ornately carved black-lead hood over a small grate, so that in the winter time, when it was really cold, you could go to bed with a lovely, cosy warm fire. It's a wonder that these houses escaped from terrible house fires through having these open fires in the bedrooms, especially with so much bed linen lying around.

Most of the cooking was done on a black range (rather like an Aga) which was mostly fuelled by wood. The range was situated in the kitchen, which helped to keep the whole room nice and warm, and as I mentioned before, the kitchen also doubled up as the dining room.

The big old kettle Grandma used for making our cups of tea, or for washing up, or any other use, was boiled up on a little primus stove in the scullery. The strong smell of kerosene or paraffin oil from the stove wafted freely through the house.

Because Grandma did a lot of baking and cooking on the range in the kitchen, such as her delicious cinnamon and currant buns, we would sit patiently waiting to savour the deliciously hot buns at the kitchen table, over which a thick golden candlewick tablecloth, edged with a fringe, was spread. Sometimes, for the main course, she would dish up a tasty rabbit stew, together with fresh vegetables from the garden. These more pleasant smells of baked cakes, hot rabbit stews, and slowly boiling vegetables helped to block out that strange acrid smell of paraffin coming from the scullery. The wild rabbits were mostly caught by local persons unknown and then sold on to the local butcher's shop, where Grandma used to buy them for our stew. They had an unforgettable flavour, and the aroma was quite strong and pungent. As you started to enjoy your first portion of the meal, you could taste the essence of a bouquet garni of sweet clovers, together with the slight bitterness of dandelion leaves, and other wild flowers and herbs that the rabbits loved to eat. So mixed together with the dried herbs thrown into the simmering pot by Grandma, this turned the stew into a truly tasty dish—fit for a king (or a queen).

After we had finished the main meal, we would sit patiently waiting, with "botty squirming" anticipation, for the mouth-watering sweet to be dished up. Sometimes I would sit and fiddle with the tassels of the tablecloth, twisting them around my fingers or plaiting them in neat little rows, which annoyed my brother immensely, because he just wanted to get on with the task of eating the delicious pudding, which was about to be placed on the table.

Our favourite dish was Sussex Pond Pudding, which oozed wickedly with melted butter, lots of soft brown sugar, sultanas, and a hint of tooth-tingling zest of lemon, which poured out of the pudding as you cut into it with your spoon. It was similar to Mother's own pond pudding, only Grandma's version seemed to have an extra rich flavour, with a hint of an unknown spicy ingredient added to it, which she kept a secret, and it always seemed to taste lovely and moist, cooked on a wood-and-coal-fuelled oven, instead of the drying effects of an electric cooker.

We always enjoyed our grandma's cooked meals.

Several years later, I asked Grandma, "Why do your meals always seem to have that special flavour and taste so scrummy?" And she would say, "Ah now, that's because they were blessed by the angels!"

Doing the family wash really meant "doing it"—by hand!

First, the washing was hoisted into a large, round, zinc boiler, and then it had to be heated, by carefully piling pieces of wood into a grate, which was situated underneath the boiler, and it had a brick surround.

After the clothes had been well boiled, they then had to be fetched out by wooden tongs, and placed into a big zinc bath, which was filled with cold water from the single cold tap in the sink. After all the final rinsing had been done, the dripping clothes were then taken outdoors in the bath, and then all the wet clothes and sheets and whatever else had to go through an old iron mangle with two big rollers, and this had to be turned by a big winding handle.

So wash day really meant "wash day!"

Looking back, it was as if the two generations were living at the same time, but in a totally different era!

We had all the mod cons, but our grandparents were still living in a bygone age!

Our first Christmas at this old house was a very happy time, with our knees close to a real log fire (there was no central heating in those days), eating our sugar-coated almond sweets and bon bons, and of course, lots and lots of other goodies to be had.

The fruity smell of oranges filled the room, mixed with swirling smoke from our granddad's cigar as he read his newspaper, and I would be reading my Rupert Bear annual, whilst my brother would have his nose stuck in his Dandy or Beano annual, or he would play on his new mouth organ, whilst I accompanied him on my new penny whistle!

In the afternoons we would all sit around the table and play a game of cards. My brother always cheated, and somehow or other, he always seemed to get away with it, which would make me very cross, but he didn't care anyway.

Then there was the biggest surprise of all.

The front room had been kept out of bounds all of that day until the evening. Then we were allowed in.

We were led by Grandma and Granddad, followed by Mother and Father, along the hall, with our eyes tightly closed; we were ordered not to peep, and when we had fumbled and stumbled our way into the room, we were told we could now open our eyes. When we opened them, it was like entering a dream world. There, before me, was the most glorious dollhouse I had ever seen. It was absolutely huge, and the whole house was lit up with little light bulbs in each room, even the little fireplace had a piece of crinkled-up, red, see-through paper, with a tiny light bulb behind it to make it look just like a real fire glowing, and a little black plastic cat sat on a hearth rug made of hessian, which had an assortment of wool of many different colours threaded through. This little rug was made by Grandma. Even the back of the house could be opened up to reveal yet more rooms, all furnished with miniature chairs, tables, beds, and even little people. My mother made the bed covers and the clothes for the tiny dolls, which must have taken her ages and a great deal of patience. The roof was painted red, and it had two very realistic chimney pots. Granddad had very carefully, and artistically, placed blobs of cotton wool over the roof to make it look just like real snow. My father had made the house very secretly, not even my brother knew about it.

In the ideal world, I should still have this remarkable dollhouse, but in reality, I don't. Somewhere along the line, it was eventually passed on to one of my younger cousins.

My brother's surprise was a race-track, which went all around the room, circling the dollhouse, and there were four magnificent racing cars, with headlights glaring. It was quite noisy as the cars whizzed around the track. There was an array of scenery to go with it, to make it look just like a small town, and it even had a little petrol station, a line of shops, houses of different designs, big ones and small ones, people, trees, a couple of little dogs, and so many other wonderful things, and we were definitely too excited to go to bed that night!

With Christmas behind us, and after the long winter nights, we now had the summer to look forward to, and as there were so many places to explore at our grandparents' house, we never got bored, especially in the summer when we could spend most of our time outdoors, and there were plenty of fields to roam and play in, as long as we kept an eye out for snakes!

For as long as I can remember, I have always had a rather mystifying fascination for snakes. I have no idea why, as no other member of the family shared my enthusiasm for these reptiles. If I ever saw a spider, I would run a mile, but if I saw a snake, I would run after it to try and catch it!

It hadn't occurred to me, at such a tender age, that certain snakes (particularly the ones with pretty black and yellow zigzag markings, and a "V" on their heads) could give you a nasty bite, but if you were unlucky enough to receive one, then you would inevitably have to be rushed to the little cottage hospital on the common, where serum was always kept for adder bites.

Adder attacks on the whole are really quite rare, and when they do occur, the unfortunate victims are usually dogs out walking on the common.

The snakes that attracted me were usually the harmless grass-snakes, or the velvety looking slowworms, which are really legless lizards, and not snakes at all!

Now there was a particular "black spot" for snakes, which happened to be in the big field behind the bus shelter, where we all used to catch the bus for day trips to Brighton.

It seems that I was a bit of an embarrassment to my long-suffering parents, because whilst waiting for the bus, I would become unbearably impatient, and I would sneak off when my parents weren't looking, and I would search in the long grass growing behind the bus shelter for anything interesting—mostly snakes—and I would give a whoop for joy at spotting a snake as it slithered towards the fence to escape my clutches, then as I tried to grab it with my small hands, my quarry would slither from my grasp, leaving me with its shed skin! My howls of disappointment as I held up the nasty transparent papery thing I was left with, and my wails of, "I didn't wanna paper 'nake, Mummy! I wanna *real* one!" sent the other passengers (who were standing patiently in the bus shelter) scurrying across to the other side of the road, to the bus stop which was for passengers who wanted to travel in the opposite direction! Had they changed their minds about where they wanted to go, or were they trying to avoid a certain howling little monster?

We were very lucky children, as we were sometimes spoilt by our grandma and granddad, especially when they gave us some pocket money to spend.

When we wanted sweets, or any other shopping, all we had to do was to crawl through a permanent hole in the hedge to the little village shop, which was right next door. The hole had been there for many years before us, as this was the route used by my father and his younger brother, my uncle, when they were small boys!

The shop had a welcoming smell about it. Peppermint, biscuits, cheese and other delicious smells greeted you as you entered, and as you opened the door, a big bell rung over your head, which made quite a loud jingling noise.

The shopkeeper was a very friendly man, quite small, and always very neat and tidy, and he always wore a white overall, and his wife, who used to help behind the counter, was a very large, kind lady, with very rosy red cheeks, and she always seemed to be laughing a lot, and she was never grumpy or lost her patience with us.

In those days we still had to use rationing coupon books for buying sweets and groceries with. These were the last remnants of wartime rationing.

Our grandparents' house was surrounded by fields. The one opposite, which was just across the road, was only a paddock, but there were always one or two horses in it, which made me very happy, because this meant I could feed them with lots of delicious apples from the very old varieties we could pick from my grandparents' orchard, and where the old pear trees also grew. These pears were so juicy, that as you bit into them, the juices ran down the corners of your mouth, then up your arms, and onto your sleeves! Oh what joy! Oh what a mess! But their flavour lingered on well after they were eaten, not like today's tasteless varieties.

The horses would munch merrily on the apples offered to them, with their jaws grinding away, and they would dribble mushy apple juice down their chins. There was a funny warm kind of smell of apples mixed with chewed-up grass, but I loved it anyway.

I could also watch the horses from my grandparents' bedroom window, and if I pushed the bottom of the sash cord window up, and call out to them, they would come trotting over to the gate looking expectantly over the top, wondering why they couldn't see me.

On the right hand side of the house was another small field.

In the summer, when the grass was cut for hay and then bundled up into stacks, we would make houses out of them, and sometimes we would take sandwiches and cakes, and a glass of drink, and accompanied by our two dogs, Pat and Jane, we would have our tea in our thatched house, staying out as late as we dared, or even until bedtime.

If the weather was really sunny and warm, we would sometimes sit outside and help our grandmother to shell freshly picked peas from Grandfather's well-stocked garden, where he loved to grow his favourite roses, along with a heavenly scented mass of sweet-pea flowers growing in a explosion of vivid colours, spiralling upwards on a wicker trellis, as well as vegetables of all kinds and varieties.

We would sit with an enamel bowl each in our laps, and with the fat pods laid out on a clean white tea-towel on a wooden fold-up table, we would shell the peas, and because they were so sweet, some of them were eaten raw (if Grandma wasn't watching us too closely) and even the pods were crisp and juicy, so some of these we chewed on as well! Grandma would then toddle back to the vegetable patch, and return, huffing and puffing her way through the pea and bean poles, stepping gingerly over the rhubarb patch, carrying freshly dug-up pearly white potatoes, cradling them proudly to her, all bunched up like a clutch of duck's eggs in her red and white gingham pinny. These lovely new potatoes (with skins that just flaked off at the sight of a knife) would be cooked along with the peas in freshly picked mint.

There's a great deal of satisfaction at being able to pick your own lunch of the day!

There was also the novelty of an outside loo, which was situated just next to the big shed. Some joker had painted the appropriate words—POTTING SHED—in bold black paint on the loo door! It wasn't exactly a place where you would want to spend much time, owing to the fact that it was also a home to long-legged spiders!

Bedtime was a novelty to us, because although downstairs had electricity, upstairs had none at all, so going upstairs to bed, we all had to carry candles with us to light our way, and as we walked in single file upstairs, big dark shadows followed us, created by the flickering candles. Since the days of candlelight is now ancient history, it is rather sad that the children of today cannot experience the same excitement of the unexpected, with just a hint of fear, making the Peter Pan element in their lives redundant.

Another night-time game we invented was to make animal silhouettes on the wall—rabbits, dog heads, giraffe heads, birds in flight and some other creatures of our imaginations. The images became frighteningly real whenever a slight draft caused the flame to flicker, which made the animals appear to dance and prance about on the wall. This would amuse us until one of the grown-ups would call out for us to blow the candles out, then we had to say our prayers and go to sleep!

At the bottom of the garden there was a little wicker gate, which led into a very large field, where cricket matches were played during the summer, and every year a donkey derby was held there, along with the usual fairground attractions.

Each year we always had a well-known celebrity to open the fete, as well as the Pearly King and Queen from the East End of London, who arrived in a pony and trap which was decorated in dazzling bright colours, and even the pony wore a harness studded with pearls. I thought that this was the best part of the show, apart from the endless sixpenny pony rides up and down the field.

There were many stalls where you could buy inexpensive gifts to take home, and you could buy sticks of fluffy candyfloss, which stuck in your hair and on your face, and there were also toffee apples, which needed good strong teeth to bite through the hard coating of toffee, in order to reach the lovely juicy apple. And there was the delicious smell of jam doughnuts and hot dogs that seemed to follow you around the showground, tantalizing your taste-buds. There were coconut shies (which Father was very good at as he was a bowler for the local cricket team), and roundabouts, swing-boats, pony and donkey rides, various competitions, show-jumping, and a fancy-dress competition, where for two years running I won first prize dressed up as Bo-Peep, with Jane as my sheepdog. Another year, my brother dressed up as a pirate, and I'm sure he would have won the competition, if the Camp coffee (which Mother had smeared all over his skin to darken it) hadn't run down his face like treacle and then dripped onto his clothes as the brown sticky substance melted in the hot sun. And then when it dried out, it caked hard on his face, giving him a permanent scowl! He wasn't at all bothered about winning the competition, because he was too miserable!

There was also a dog show for all the pampered posh pooches, paraded by their proud owners, and they also had a special class for a doggie's fancy dress!

One year Mother said to me, "Why don't you dress Jane up in something and enter her in the competition?" So thinking this was a very good idea, I rushed back to the house, which took just a couple of minutes from the show-ground, and excitedly told Grandma what we wanted to do. She disappeared for a few moments and then returned with a bag containing a few bits of old clothing. Thanking her quickly, I ran back to the field, and tipping the contents of the bag onto the ground, we rummaged through the jumble of clothing, then choosing what we wanted, we dressed Jane up as a little old lady, wearing Grandma's old headscarf and an old black shawl, and placed on her nose, one of Grandma's old reading glasses with the glass bits taken out.

As the judges slowly made their way down the line, taking their time with each entrant, some of the dogs were beginning to become restless, and gradually discarded and scattered their attire on the ground by either shaking, scratching, or just chewing them off.

Jane was a very patient dog, and just as the judges reached her, she did her most impressive display of begging, with her paws stretched straight up in the air, and a very appealing look on her face. She just melted all the judges' hearts, and that was it—Jane won first prize! She beat a rival of hers, who was all togged up in a specially made witch's outfit, which must have taken the owner many painstaking hours to make, and both the dog and its owner looked most indignant at losing the first prize, as well as a smart red rosette—but then, their dog couldn't beg!

So many events were packed into one day, and we always seemed to be lucky with the weather, which made it a great day out for all the villagers.

The only downside to Granddad's large garden was that there was no proper sewage system, only a cesspit dug out like a ditch, which was situated right at the bottom of the garden, and the treatment system was located just a short distance away in the large playing field.

Now the other problem was that Jane loved water—any water—and she was also very keen on swimming, but not too fussy where she should go for a swim, which meant that sometimes her chosen swimming-pool would be in the offending ditch!

"Oh what a sight!" "Oh what a smell!" "Oh my God!" "Oh no, get away from me! Pooh!"—came the cries from us all.

She would appear from the ditch like a creature from out of the swamps, dripping from head to toe in this horrible smelly gunge, with a swarm of flies following closely above her once lovely white coat (which was now as black as treacle), and with her tongue lolling out as she approached us with a big silly grin on her face. But her brisk trot soon slowed down to a crawl when she heard our protests of disgust, and with the last few yards, she would flomp down and do a wiggly shuffle towards us on her belly, looking really sorrowful and wondering what all the fuss was about!

A toss of a coin would decide who should bath her!

Thank goodness I was never the lucky one!

Jane was always my companion and soul mate, and very protective too, like a big sister, particularly if she thought anyone was behaving a bit too rough in play, and although she would never growl or bite anyone, she would jump up at them and place herself between us, like a referee.

She was a very good-natured dog, and everybody loved her, and most of the time she was very obedient.

I remember one day when I'd been playing ball with her at the bottom of the garden, Mother called me in to have tea, and as I'd taught Jane to "sit and stay," I had just given her the command to stay, and then leaving her in that position, I went indoors to have my tea.

Poor Jane. After tea, I decided to read one of my books, and I had quite forgotten about her, and it wasn't until Granddad went outside to the coal bunker to fetch some coal in, that he suddenly spotted a lone black and white dog sitting at the bottom of the garden, in the dusk, looking very dejected, but faithfully waiting for my command to call her in!

Jane would sometimes follow me to the little village school, which I used to attend whilst we were still living with Grandma and Granddad, and it always upset me when the teacher sent one of the bigger girls to take her back home.

She was my very best friend, so why couldn't she stay with me at school? I frequently asked my mother.

Nevertheless, I was quite happy at this school, which was the same one that my father attended when he was a boy, and the same lady teacher—who was very kind and considerate—taught my father too, and she was still the headmistress when I started there.

I can still remember its musky classroomy smells of chalk, plasticine, plimsolls, pencil rubbers, jam jars filled with bluebells—especially picked for "Miss"—and the school exercise books seemed to have a sort of well-worn musky smell about them, which made me appreciate my well-cared-for books at home, because they always had such a lovely fresh smell! "Memory smells!" I suppose you could call them. I still love to sniff new books and to feel the crispness of their pages.

It was soon apparent that the two "n's" in class—"nitting and needlework"—were most definitely not my best subjects. So when this particular class came up, I was jolly well pleased when the teacher for our crafts lessons decided that the best thing to do with me was to place me near her desk, then sit me on an old wooden chair (worn shiny over the years from many fidgety bottoms), and then she would hand me a book, telling me to read out loud to the class, which I did willingly, as I loved reading stories. The only other audible sound—other than the clicking of needles and the orator—was the classroom clock, ticking it's slow rhythmic "tick-tock—tick-tock" as the children settled themselves down to work, and to listen to the story.

Sometimes, if I thought the story had lost its thread or become a bit monotonous and lacked excitement, I would sort of improvise and add my own bits and pieces, just to pepper it up a little, and if I decided to make it just a *wee* bit scary, I would add something extra to make it sound more spooky. Now and then I would look up to see if there was a reaction from the teacher, to see if she had noticed the slight deviation from the original story. Sometimes, if my own addition of a scary bit was a little too convincing, it had been known that a few of the pupils—who might have suffered with a nervous disposition—were occasionally prone to dropping a cross-stitch or two, or muddling up some of their intricate embroidery stitches, owing to their lack of concentration.

I think they quite looked forward to me reading to them, and the teacher seemed content with this compromise as well.

I was also given the task of learning by heart the full length poem of "The Owl and the Pussycat," and then told to recite it out loud to the class.

I can still remember this poem even to this day, and it's probably why I still love poetry, but it didn't do much for my needlework skills!

I can remember one particular interruptive incident in one of the lessons, when a stray blackbird somehow blundered its way into the classroom, causing some of the children (who were frightened of anything with wings that fluttered anywhere near them) to squeal and go into a bit of a tizzy, as the poor frightened bird tried desperately to find its way out again, bashing itself against the windows, then banging against the door and fluttering against the walls in its bid for freedom. The teacher quickly took command of the situation, and soon she was able to "shush!" the now very excitable children (who thought that any form of distraction during lessons was well worth while), and order them to keep quiet and still—she was then able to gently herd the bird towards the window, which she had managed to open after struggling in an over-dramatic fashion with the rusty catch, but before flying off, he left a small deposit on the window sill to show his appreciation at being set free!

The strange part was that nobody could fathom how the bird managed to get into the classroom in the first place, as all the windows were already closed on that particular day, and the door was also shut behind us after we had all entered into the classroom for our lessons. So the bird must have flown into the room much earlier in the day and didn't show itself until we were all well into our lesson, and perhaps we were making too much noise, which must have disturbed it, and maybe it was even looking out for a nesting site.

It remained a mystery to us children, so we all thought it must have been an act of magic in the way it had suddenly appeared.

"P'raps the fairies brought him in, Miss—like in one of our stories!" offered Simon, one of the little boys.

"Yes, Miss, that's what must have happened!" said a little girl called Brenda. "I expect it was one of them tooth fairies my mum and dad tell me about whenever I lose a tooth. I'm told they will leave me a sixpence under my pillow, and that's what brought the bird in, Miss—a tooth fairy!" said Brenda, convinced that this was the only explanation to the incident.

"What a load of old tosh!"—said one bright little unbeliever— "there's no such thing as *tooth fairies,* or any other kind of *fairies*—just like there's no Father Christmas either!" he added exultantly.

His remarks were ignored much to his indignation, so he sat with his arms crossed and a dark scowl began to loom over his face as his ego slowly slipped away into a dark corner.

Then the other children joined in with their own versions of how the blackbird got into the classroom, their voices mingling and rising to a pitch, with each one vying for approval from Miss!

Miss just looked on, shrugged her shoulders—and smiled!

Skipping the story forward a few years, I literally bumped into another blackbird caught up in a tight spot.

This particular incident happened whilst I was out riding Humphrey on the common.

We were galloping at a fair pace along a twisting, tree-lined path, and dodging the overhanging branches, when I spotted something unusual in the distance, and as we drew nearer, I could see that it was a blackbird flapping frantically as it hung upside-down, and it was dangling by a long piece of twine (the same kind of twine that gardeners use for covering over raspberry bushes, and other fruiting trees and shrubs), and quickly, I jumped off Humphrey and tied the reins over a thick tree branch.

As I approached the terrified blackbird, who was by now screeching in pain and fear, I lifted him up so as to slacken the thread which I could see was wound around one of his legs and had obviously tightened. Slipping the end of the twine, which had looped over the branch he'd landed on, I first checked his leg to see if it had been pulled out of its socket in his struggle to free himself. If his leg had been broken or pulled out then his chances of survival in the wild would have been slim.

Fortunately for the blackbird, his leg was still intact, but how was I going to free him? There was only one way I could do this, and so taking a deep breath, I bit through the thread where it was knotted close to his leg, forgetting about hygiene or germs, as this called for drastic measures!

The poor blackbird kept remarkably still whilst I carried out this delicate operation, but finally the thread snapped, and I was able to release the grateful bird, and I watched with great satisfaction as he flew away.

It was a case of being in the right place at the right time, and had I have arrived at this spot a few minutes earlier, or a few minutes later, then the bird's fate would have had an entirely different ending.

Now casting back to our original journey into the past once more, there was another character who played an important part in our young lives, and she lived in the village within walking distance from our grandparents' house, in fact if we stepped out at a good pace, we could be at the cottage within about ten minutes.

Her name was Flora.

Flora was a very caring person towards animals and birds, and simply because she seemed to have a natural and understanding way with them, they gave her love and enjoyment in return.

My brother and I would always look forward to visiting her in the little cottage, which was situated on the edge of the common.

The cottage was very old, and Flora lived there with her very elderly, frail mother, who always seemed to stay in the living room, which meant that we hardly ever saw her, or even spoke to her as far as I can remember, and therefore I can't really recall what she looked like.

The cottage was surrounded by a very high hedge, and as you went through a little wicker gate, you had to push your way through tall grass which straggled the gateway, making it somewhat difficult to open. You were almost tripped up by the mass of sagging heads of London-Pride, which competed for space with spreading buttercups across the pathway, making it more and more like an obstacle course. Rambling red roses tugged at your clothes as you walked past, and in the flower beds grew giant golden sunflowers, holding their plate-sized heads towards the sun, and pretty little blue forget-me-nots surrounding the crimson paeonies. There were also deep-pink-coloured hollyhocks, which seemed to tower above you, and many other cottage type flowers growing along the brick path which led you up to a little wooden latch door, which was never locked.

You could barely see through the little window panes, because either they were too grimy looking (Flora wasn't exactly house proud), or it was just so jolly dark inside the cottage.

We were always greeted by Flora's smiling face. She was a very stout person and she always wore very floppy loose clothes, usually a black-and-white-spotted dress with an old shabby cardigan or coat over the top (depending on the weather), and she had a very round, rather pale face, and hardly any teeth (or at least very gappy). Her dark-brown hair was cut very short and was very straight, with a rather scraggy fringe hanging over her eyes. Her stockings were always rolled down to her thick ankles.

Flora was not exactly handsome in appearance, but her good nature towards all living things made up for that.

She was always very pleased to see us because she knew that we loved to see all the animals and birds she kept in her large, overgrown garden.

She proudly showed us her squeaky little guineapigs with their babies, lots of rabbits with lots of babies, a few mice, two boisterous ferrets who just couldn't keep still for five minutes, and once she even had a brown-and-white rat, but most of all, we looked forward to seeing her large selection of birds.

Flora had so many large aviaries built around her garden that we just didn't bother to count them.

There were aviaries with budgies of so many different colours. Bright green budgies with yellow cheeks and black stripes on their wings, budgies that were all yellow, some that were deep blue or almost purple. The most common coloured ones had the usual pale-blue-and-white markings. The birds were all so content, either chattering away to their mates or flying up and down, because they all had plenty of space to move about in. Flora even fixed little wooden nest boxes for them, so that they could rear their own young. It was such a joy to see some of the little pink newly hatched babies that Flora was able to show us, as she very carefully lifted them out from the shallow hollow, which was scooped out of the wooden floor of the box, where the eggs were hatched out.

Zebra finches with bright red bills twittered and flitted busily about in their own section of the aviary, whilst the bright yellow Norfolk canaries, with their funny little fringes, sang beautifully, competing with the other canaries, mostly yellow, or yellow and green, and one or two of them were very dark green, almost like the greenfinch.

Flora also had one or two goldfinches, which I particularly loved, as they were such a pretty little bird, and they made such a sweet tinkling little sound as they sang. She told us that she reared them herself by taking an egg from a nest in the wild and then putting it into a canary's nest, where they were hatched out by the canaries.

In those days it wasn't an offence to take eggs from a wild bird's nest, but today it just wouldn't be allowed.

Poor old Flora wouldn't have realized that she was contributing towards the dwindling bird population.

However, we never got tired of visiting Flora, and although she was no oil painting, she had a heart of gold, and the old fashioned cottage always seemed to hold some sort of magic and mystery to us.

As we grew up and were beginning to take on more responsibilities, we were allowed to buy a pair of yellow Border canaries from Flora, and one Yorkshire canary, which was a dark green colour, with an exceptionally strong singing voice. Much to our delight, we were also able to buy a pair of budgies, just to start us off with our very own breeding pairs.

Flora showed us how to look after them and what to look for if they were a bit off colour, and also how to distinguish the male from the female budgies—the girls had brown bits at the top of their beaks, and the boys had blue.

Father built us two very spacious aviaries in our garden back home.

One was for the canaries, and the other one for the budgies.

Now, at last, we had our very own singing, chattering birds!

Our favourite pale-blue-and-white budgie, called Billy, was entered into our local "Cage Bird Society Show"—just for fun!

Much to our amazement, he actually won first prize, which really took us by surprise, as he wasn't exactly a handsome specimen. Instead of being nice and plump and with a nice smooth plumage, or showing a calm, showy appearance, Billy was not what you could call sleek. His appearance was more like a scrawny scarecrow, and he was as highly strung as a cat's violin at a rat's wedding. He was in stark contrast to all the other well-behaved birds, which were obviously well used to these shows and spent their time at the show chatting and singing cheerfully whilst plumping up their gleaming feathers and looking so impeccable for their doting owners. At the same time, our little moth-eaten exhibit squawked and flapped wildly about his cage when the first judge—who had a tight-fixed grin across his face which looked as though it was stuck to his protruding cheekbones with super-glue and teeth that looked like piano keys (three black, two white)—poked his pencil through the cage at Billy, which really freaked him out, sending feathers fluttering about all over the place.

Judge number two was a very stout gentleman with a very blotchy red face, and his bulbous red nose supported thick, horn-rimmed spectacles, which seemed to rest snugly on his bushy eyebrows that reminded me of very hairy caterpillars, and every now and again they would arch up and down into an inverted "V" whenever he raised or lowered them as he mumbled an opinion to his companions. His dark brown suit smelled strongly of pipe tobacco, which filled our delicate young nostrils as he approached our stand. He looked very hard at Billy, who was by now spinning about his cage like a frisbee, his nerves completely out of control and shredded to pieces. The judge looked at us, then back at the cage, and then he wrote something down on his note-pad (which neither of us could see), and then he strode off to look at the other exhibits.

Nevertheless, something about Billy must have impressed "piano keys" and "tobacco suit," because there it was, a beautiful crisp red rosette with a "Highly Commended" certificate to go with it!

We went home with our tatty-looking bird, his feathers by now were standing out like porcupine quills, and he was looking like a demented demon! But we didn't care! We were highly delighted with our very special little bird!

One day, on one of our visits to Flora's cottage, she really surprised us when she presented us with a little crippled canary called Tommy. She thought he would be much happier with us, as she had so many animals and birds to look after, plus she was getting older and finding the work at looking after them all was not getting any easier. She thought that he would make us a nice little pet, as long as he was kept in a cage indoors.

Tommy was a sweet little yellow canary with one badly crippled leg, but he could really sing loudly, so much so that when he was placed outside in the garden on warm days, his singing could be heard from the bottom of the road!

At night, he would love to have a little game before having his special cover placed over his cage so that he could sleep. He would sit on his special platform that Father had made for him, which was fixed near the top of his cage so that he could perch on it comfortably without straining his crippled leg, and it also enabled him to have a good view of everything around him. He then waited for someone to poke and wiggle a knitting needle (or something very similar) through the bars of his cage, and then he would pretend to fight the offender off by flapping his wings, then sticking out his neck with his beak wide open, he would make loud scolding noises. This ritual of his was performed every night, and he wouldn't settle down until he had played out this game. He was such a sweet little bird, and everyone loved him.

Then one night, somebody left the little skylight window (which was just above his cage) slightly open, forgetting to close it before going to bed. That night, a cat must have jumped up and somehow it had flipped the window latch up, then sticking a paw through the bars of the cage, it caught poor little Tommy, who was sleeping on his special little platform, and killed him!

The next morning, my distraught brother found his little body on the bottom of the cage surrounded by a pile of feathers. My brother said that if he caught the guilty cat, he would have walloped it hard with the frying pan, sending it flying down the garden and through the hedge! But I think this was a slight exaggeration.

It was a very sad day for us all, when we had to bury Tommy in a little cardboard box at the bottom of the garden, and it was just as sad when we had to break the awful news to Flora.

To make up for the sad loss of Tommy, we bought two Dutch rabbits, Cherry and Bunty, and also a dear little rosette guineapig called Binky from Flora, then, on a sudden impulse, my mother came up with a fantastic idea.

"Why not have Binky christened? Would you like that? I could christen him in that little birdbath in the garden. What do you think?"

"Oh, yes, please!" I said. "That's a really brilliant idea!" Then, as an after thought, I said, "Could Janet bring Dinky over as well, so's they can both get christened at the same time? I think she would like that."

"Of course she can! What a good idea!" she said.

The day duly arrived, and the two little guineapigs were baptised. Whilst Mother held them one at a time over the birdbath, she dipped her fingers in the water, and then she said a few holy-type words, and at the same time, she sprinkled the sacred water over their little heads. Janet and I were so pleased that our little pets had been properly baptised.

I had no idea that it would be such a huge success and that our garden was to become a sort of Mecca. I think Janet must have told all her little friends, who told all their friends, and so on and so on, because the very next day, a big crowd of kids with an assortment of pets turned up on our doorstep. They all crowded round Mother, like bees round a honey-pot, pleading with her to christen their little pets. Of course, my mother, being very soft hearted, took on the task of performing the little ritual all over again.

There were dogs, kittens, a tortoise called Bert, hamsters, a black rat called Snowy, and last but not least, a little girl by the name of Wendy brought a round fish bowl containing her little goldfish called Goldie!

As she held the goldfish bowl up towards Mother, her hazel eyes—wide and expectant behind little round gold-framed spectacles—were hugely magnified through the glass water-filled bowl, making them look about the size of gobstoppers. Her long hair was drawn back into two thin plaits, making her look very waif-like.

Wendy was normally a very quiet little girl, and she was almost considered to be an orphan, as her mother had been very ill since she was born and her father was dead, so she was fostered out to a very kind lady who lived at the bottom of our road.

I liked Wendy because she always seemed such a kind little girl who kept very much to herself, so we were very pleased when she came up to see us, especially with her much-loved pet.

Big Ron, who lived at the bottom of our road, brought his tortoise Bert along. He turned round to Wendy and said, "Don't be so bloody stupid! How the devil can you christen a bloody goldfish when it spends all its bloody life in water! Are you a bit soft in the 'ead or summat?"

Now Ron wasn't exactly a nice boy; on the contrary, he was bad tempered, a bully, prone to a lot of swearing, but a good leader of the "gang." He stood there defiant with his knees all scabbed up from countless fights in the playground, or falling off bikes, swings, slides, and other implements of torture, and now he was waiting for a reaction from Wendy.

With that outrageous insult aimed at the little girl, and with such a stream of uncalled-for swearing, he was immediately banished from the garden, carrying with him, his precious "bloody" tortoise, Bert.

By now, poor Wendy was crying her eyes out.

"Oh dear—*sob! sob!* I did so want Goldie christened like the rest of them—*sniff! sniff!* What shall I do?—*boo! hoo!* I want to go home—*Oooh!*"

"Never mind, dear," said Mother, "hand him over to me, and I will see what I can do."

She carefully took the bowl, placed it gently into the birdbath and held the palms of her hands over the top of the bowl, and at the same time making a slow circular motion, then she chanted a few special words over it. After the ritual, she very gently and reverently handed the bowl back to Wendy with the newly christened Goldie.

The glum look an Wendy's face had now vanished, and instead she was beaming with pleasure.

Pets and children went home, well satisfied with the special service held just for them.

Now when big, bad Ron grew up, he turned out to be a very nice, well-mannered, and a highly respectable young man. He eventually achieved a very good position as an executive for a very big company, and he also became very religious! What a huge turnaround from his early years as a "little horror!"

There was one little lad who had a soft spot for Mother, and he used to bring her bunches of flowers, handing them over in his grubby little hands with a sweet angelic smile on his face, whilst bathing in the glory of Mother's gratitude for such a wonderful bouquet. She thought they must have been lovingly picked from his parents' garden, until she found out, to her horror and dismay, that they had actually been lovingly picked (or more to the point they had been secretly confiscated) from the local churchyard!

That incident wasn't the end of my mother's embarrassment.

On another occasion, the same little admirer turned up with a bunch of beautiful red tulips, which until that moment had been growing in a neighbour's garden. The very angry Mrs. B, who lived just at the top of our road, turned up on Mother's doorstep holding the little "angel" tightly by his coat collar, after seeing him making his way through our front gate and walking proudly with the bunch of flowers in his hand up to our back door. She then demanded that the now wilting flowers should be returned to her, telling Mother that she had watched from her lounge window, as this little hooligan snipped happily away at her prized tulips, with a pair of scissors!

Mother meekly handed back the flowers, but she thought that Mrs. B was being rather unreasonable at such a trivial incident, and she could only see the funny side of it, but she didn't receive any more surprise bunches of flowers from "source unknown!"

So many very happy memories worth capturing, after this long backward glance at the past, but time moves on, and so must we, but before heading away from the vale of the South Downs, there was just one more very special little village to bid a farewell to as we drove through.

This is a particularly quaint little village with its own pond, which is a home to several well-cared-for ducks, lovingly fed and looked after by the villagers.

Then early one spring, and much to the delight of the residents, along came Charles and Di.

Charles and Di were a pair of very handsome snowy-white swans who were introduced to the pond along with the ducks.

All went swimmingly until Charles and Di built a very impressive nest on the platform out in the middle of the pond, which was provided by the people living in the village. It was when the pen (the female) had laid and hatched out her cygnets, that the cob (the male) suddenly turned very aggressive and protective towards his family. The villagers became rather suspicious when they noticed that the duck population seemed to be decreasing at an alarming rate, until one day, someone spotted Charles attacking, and actually drowning, one of the poor little ducks—in broad daylight!

Much to everyone's disappointment, Charles and Di had to be suspended from their duties as King and Queen of the village pond, and were duly moved to a swan sanctuary, along with their little family of cygnets.

No more swans, but the ducks were now able to live in peace once more!

The pond was very much a focal point in the village, and it was the pride and joy of the villagers, who regarded it as their main attraction, so when some bright spark (nobody ever found out who it was) decided to test their mettle, all hell was let loose.

It all happened when an article appeared in a full spread of the local newspaper announcing that plans had been applied for, and ultimately passed by the local council, to build a large car-park where the pond was, as the community was "lacking in parking facilities," and so the beloved pond would have to be filled in. Also printed on a whole page of the newspaper was a very convincing sketch of a large concrete car-park with rows and rows of cars neatly parked there. Then to round off the insult (with enough ammunition to get the angry multitudes of protesters rock'n'rolling all the way to the Council Offices with their reams of signed petitions), they intended to install the offensive pay machines, just to add fuel to the fire!

It was the topic of the day in the insurance office, where I was working at that time, and the atmosphere was fairly buzzing with fury. But before anybody could push the red button to start a local outbreak of war with the council, somebody suddenly noticed a very important error that nobody else had noticed and meekly pointed out the date of the newspaper—it was April the First!

The village high street is tree-lined, and the pavements are cobbled, giving it a charming touch of its historical past, and on the other side of the pond is a large village green, where they hold a very well-organized bonfire night each year on the fifth of November, whatever the weather.

The bonfire night begins with a very impressive torch-lit procession led by the village Bonfire Society, wearing their very colourful and authentic fancy dress of North American Indians, and they add extra decorations and materials to their costumes each year. They are always accompanied by the town brass band, as they march in procession through the village, then they double back to the bonfire on the green. After the parade has finished, everyone gathers around the bonfire, which has already been lit, and the evening finally ends up with a spectacular fireworks display. After the fun of the fireworks, everybody files into the local pub for drinks and a steaming bowl of hot tomato soup.

One year, the bonfire night went off with a bit more than a "bang!" and the phrase "all lit up" took on a whole new meaning.

It happened whilst the Bonfire Society members were well into their parade through the street, with their usual colourful display of the Indian costumes, and my son Adam, who was about seven years old at the time, wanted so desperately to join in the procession. I told him that he would have to wait until he was older, and then perhaps he could join the Bonfire Society, and he would be able to dress up like the others.

We followed along the pavement with the rest of the villagers, and all went well until a group of people barged into us to try and overtake. It was at that moment that Adam and I became separated, and he was pushed into the road where he suddenly found himself amongst the procession.

Somebody I knew from the village saw what had happened and told me later what Adam did next.

He appeared to be quite unconcerned with the fact that he'd just become separated from his mum, and was enjoying himself now that he felt he was taking part in the procession.

One of the members of the Bonfire Society threw down a smouldering torch, thinking it had gone out, and Adam, seeing the torch lying in the gutter, picked it up, and now he really was one of them! Walking down the line of Indians, he held the torch aloft, which had miraculously come to life and was burning brightly once more! Everything was fine until he suddenly must have wondered where I was, and turning round to see if he could see me, he forgot that he was holding a burning torch, and as he was still walking unsteadily forward, because at the same time he was trying to glance anxiously back over his shoulder, he didn't notice that his torch was held against the long ceremonious feathered headdress of one of the Indians walking in front of him, setting it alight! The Indian brave wasn't so brave anymore when he discovered that his feathers were all ablaze, and he went into a bit of a ceremonial war dance as he tried frantically to escape the flames. He caused quite a stir in the crowd, as they too tried to steer clear of him.

He was last seen "whooping" away down the road in a blaze of fire towards the pond, where he whipped off his burning headdress with the intention of throwing it straight in, but as he stood right at the edge of the pond, his foot slipped, and in an unceremonious manner, he followed his headdress straight into the water, sending the ducks scattering and quaking in all directions, followed by a loud cheer and clapping of encouragement from the onlookers!

As the crowds dispersed in groups of dark figures making their way towards the green, I found Adam standing alone under a street lamp, still clutching his lifeless torch. He looked up at me through little round glasses which gleamed in the lamplight, and he said, "Where have you been? You've just missed all the fun!"

Needless to say that after his reprimand about "playing with fire," it was almost a relief that as the following year's bonfire night approached, Adam decided that he wasn't at all bothered about joining the Bonfire Society after all!

Also in the village, there is a very popular bakery shop where all the bread and cakes are baked on the premises, and inside the shop, there is a very nice little tea-room where you can eat yourself silly with scrummy scones, onto which you can pile lashings of strawberry jam with clotted cream, accompanied by a nice hot cup of tea in fine-bone china tea cups.

A little further up the high street, and right next door to a tiny (but very old fashioned) chemist shop, was the Saddlers Shop.

As you walked into this quaint old shop, you were greeted with the lovely smell of leather and saddle soap, and hanging on one of the walls in neat rows, were all different types of bright shiny bits to choose from, and if you needed to buy a saddle or bridle, you had the choice of either a brand new one or a good second-hand one.

Mine were always of the latter kind!

The shop was run by two brothers who reminded me of Tweedledum and Tweedledee From *Alice in Wonderland*. I think they were actually twins as they were so alike.

The saddlers would also mend broken tack, which in my case became almost a fact of life, and so I was a regular customer of theirs.

The fondest memories for me in this village, are of the old Blacksmith's Forge, and the name of the blacksmith was Bill — "Bill the Blacksmith!"

It was at this little forge that I used to trot along to with my first little pony Nutmeg, to get her feet trimmed and shod.

I nearly always chose to ride Nutmeg bareback, with only a halter and a lead rope attached to it. I didn't even wear a riding hat in those days, and Nutmeg was the type of pony that would bolt at the first opportunity from anything, from a pram or bicycle to a bus! I just didn't realize how reckless it was to ride in this manner. It was the closeness to the animal that mattered more to me, and the lovely musky smell from her hot flanks; it was so earthy and wonderful, and I had absolutely no sense of safety whatsoever, but then I was only fourteen at the time.

I used to look forward to visiting this very old forge, and Bill would always be waiting there to greet us, with his arms crossed over as he leant over the top of the stable door, ready to open it for me to lead Nutmeg in.

Bill nearly always had a hand rolled cigarette dangling out of a corner of his mouth, but he still managed a cheery greeting.

Inside, the forge was very dark, and the large brick walls were coated with black grime from over the years of smoke, hard sweaty labour, and heat.

The only source of light came from the doorway and one solitary bare light bulb hanging from the wooden beam. If there were any windows they wouldn't have shed any light at all, as they would have been too filthy and cobwebby!

Bill would start off by removing the old shoes. He would then clip and pare off any overgrown hoof. Having completed the manicure bit, he would then work away with the bellows, stoking up the brazier fire to a red-hot heat, then with a long-handled pincer tool he would thrust the chosen length of iron deep into the fiery furnace until he was satisfied it was hot enough. He would then take it over to his ancient sturdy anvil with the word *"EDNA"* engraved on the side of it, just like sailors have pictures and names tattooed on their arms. Perhaps Edna was his mother's name, or his wife's or even an old girlfriend's, or maybe it was just a name he liked to call his anvil!

With a sweating brow, he hammered away. Iron upon iron—clang! bang!—clang! bang!—forging a straight piece of iron into a horseshoe shape.

Next he would place the white-hot shoe straight onto the hoof, where it would sizzle and burn onto the horn, sending up thick acrid smoke, which he almost disappeared into, with only his backside showing, and still smoking his cigarette at the same time. It's no wonder that he would end up with bouts of coughing, and all the while, Nutmeg just stood there (not always patiently I must add) on three legs as each foot was done in turn.

Odd though it may seem, I really loved that smell of burning hoof!

Faces often peered over the door at intervals, blotting out any daylight seeping through, and straining with their eyes to see what was going on, or just to exchange gossip with Bill.

There would be old fogeys exchanging stories or comments on the latest news and topics, or to talk about growing their cabbages, spuds, or carrots, or any other gardening-type talk. Then there would be young ladies with prams, and even children coming home from school would stop to look in. Everybody in the village knew Bill.

The forge was always a focal point of gossip, and I remember one story Bill told me about a lady, her horse, and a very wet, rainy day.

"It happened only just last week," he told me. "I was in the middle of making up a wrought-iron gate, and it was absolutely lashing down outside, when I heard this clip-clopping outside, and then a voice called out—it was a young lady. She urged me to let her in! Well now, I knew I wasn't expecting a customer for shoeing that day, so I was a bit taken aback.

"So, anyway, I let her in, and she led her horse in with her. He was a big thoroughbred, and a bit flighty at that—and then I found out that she was actually a Lady somebody or other. I knew of her, and that she was from an aristocratic snob brigade, and she was known to like her tipple! But I don't actually shoe any of her horses because she has a blacksmith who travels out to her own stables.

"Anyway, she asks me if I could hold her horse for her, and by this time I was beginning to wonder 'what next!' I soon found out what she had in mind. Whilst I was holding her fidgety horse, the 'Lady' had gone over the brazier, kicked off her riding boots, peeled off her riding breeches, took off her hacking jacket, pulled off her jumper, and there she was—standing in her undies, with her soggy wet clothes hanging on anything she could place in front of the fire to dry! Then she asked me if I had a tot of whisky anywhere, just to warm her up, she said, and if not, a mug of coffee would do! Well! I thought I'd reached the Pearly Gates and gone to Heaven!

"Whilst I was standing there gawping, I noticed it'd suddenly gone much darker outside, but it wasn't that—there was half the male population of the village jostling at the door for a better view, and making such ridiculous comments like 'Awful weather we're having right now!' or—'how's your tomatoes coming along?' and—'wife okay...is she?' Next time I saw her out riding, she was carrying a big black umbrella. A bit eccentric I think she was, but I wasn't complaining!" said Bill.

I bet he wasn't!

Apart from his sense of humour, Bill was one of the best blacksmiths I had ever dealt with, and I was confident in the knowledge that any shoes he placed on my horse's hooves would stay on until the next visit, not like some of which I have had the misfortune to come across, when you have hardly left the forge, and you start to hear that awful tinking sound, and then instead of the normal "clip! clop!" you hear "clip! clop! clip! *clink!*"—followed by "clip! clop! clip! *thunk!*" and you have a cast shoe half a mile behind you, left by your equine Cinderella!

If you are unlucky enough to have a really incompetent blacksmith, you could be in for a rough ride, because as soon as you hit the road with a poorly shod horse, he's more than likely to slide out of his shoes as smoothly as an Olympic skier taking off from a ski slope!

Bill's old forge is now very tidy, and also very well lit, because now it's a fully furnished antique shop!

After I had taken these small bites out of my past life so that I could trap them in my memory bank, it was time to move on.

Heading towards Winchester, the familiar gently rolling hills of the South Downs were now behind us, and my passengers settled down for a sedate, unhurried journey.

Maggie seemed to be quite content too. He was not making a fuss at being couped up in his cage or making his usual clacking noise whenever he got annoyed or over-stressed at something, but occasionally he would break into a rather unusual twittering, I suppose you could say he was trying to sing, and the sounds he was making were quite unlike any other I had ever heard before. It was a very strange repertoire of different notes, as though he was going up and down the scales, and then clearing his throat to start all over again, but at least he looked as though he was comfortable enough just sitting in his cage, especially as he hadn't travelled in the car since the unsuccessful attempt to return him to the common.

I was very glad that he was behaving himself really quite well and keeping calm. If he had made a terrible fuss whilst travelling for such a long time in his cage, then it would have been an almost unbearable journey for the rest of us to endure. We were very thankful for his unusually good behaviour, and we could just about put up with his incessant singing, but hopefully not for the whole of the trip!

Everything seemed to be going according to plan, and well on time, as we wound our way through the complex of zigzagging streets of the still sleeping ancient historical town of Petworth, enclosed by its huge protective walls, now blackened by the modern-day traffic which it unfortunately has to endure.

How colourful and proud the town Petworth must have been in the days of the stagecoach and horses as they clip-clopped their way through the high street. Now it has a one-way system, and all you can hear is the drone of traffic passing through.

Our first stopping point since leaving home was Cowdray Park near Midhurst, where we pulled in at a lakeside car park, which is frequently used as a picnic area. The dogs tumbled excitedly out, giving Father extra space to place the cumbersome cage onto the seat beside him. He must have felt very stiff after holding the cage in one position all that time, but he never complained.

We were glad to take a short break, and were able to eat some of our sandwiches, and drink our much-needed steaming mugs of coffee. At last we could relax for a while, but not for too long, as we still had a long way to travel.

After our light refreshment, and after the dogs had finished their runabout and quenched their thirst from their bowl and had a doggy biscuit each, they were quite happy to jump back into the car, and once more we were on our way.

There seemed to be no way of stopping Maggie from singing his lungs out! He just went on and on!

Perhaps he really was enjoying the trip after all!

We travelled past pastoral meadows and colourful fields of pastel blue flax, in stark contrast to the vivid bright-lemon-sharp-yellow of rape. The colours of the fields were so bright that you needed sunglasses just to look at them.

Flocks of linnets flew up like a cloud of dust, then descended back down again, almost instantly, to carry on their feasting off the seed heads. One field, I was pleasantly surprised to see, had been planted entirely with lupins!

There was such a variety of different crops of so many colours, and all of them creating a beautiful patchwork over the landscape.

Passing through the vales of Hampshire, we then drove through Wiltshire, with its pretty little villages of thatched roofs; just oozing with chocolate-box charm, and then on to Gloucestershire, with more charming scenery to delight us on our way.

We picked up the M4 motorway for the next twenty-three miles towards the Severn Bridge, and we could just about see the undulating Welsh hills appearing on the horizon, and it wasn't long before we could see the Severn Bridge looming up in front of us.

"Oh no!" I said. "Er, has anybody got any change, like a few pound coins?" I asked — "Only we're just coming up to the Severn Bridge any minute now, and we have to pay at the toll booth, and I don't think I've got any money on me!" I said anxiously.

Mother frantically searched in her bag for her purse, whilst Father jiggled the cage about on his lap in an attempt to search his pockets for loose change, causing some of his coins to drop out and clank onto the floor and out of reach. Cursing under his breath, Father found the whole thing was a bit of a pain, and decided to give up the search, whilst poor Maggie started to flap about in his cage, trying to keep his balance in the rocking cage, and looking very cross at this rude awakening. These pantomime antics prompted him to start up his vocal chords again, and the dogs started to bark at the man in the booth, turning us all into nervous wrecks!

"Don't panic, everyone!" I said. "Only I've just found some money…it's in this little compartment under the dashboard. It must've been there all the time! I'd forgotten that I'd put it there before we left Sussex, because I thought it would be easy enough to find!" My voice trailed off as nobody seemed to be in the least bit interested at my lame excuse, and the man at the booth just grinned in a very good-natured manner—then waved us on.

We were now on Welsh soil, but we still had two and a half hours drive in front of us.

As we drove through the very picturesque valley of Usk, with its winding roads and wooded slopes, the dogs began to show stress now that they realized this rather long and arduous journey didn't seem to lead to anywhere of particular interest to them, and they were desperate for a pee!

I pulled into a very quiet little picnic spot, which I had discovered on one of my previous journeys along this route, and it would be just right for the dogs to stretch their legs and for me to stretch mine as well!

It was in a small clearing, nestling on the edge of a natural woodland.

The two dogs jumped out and scampered across the little bridge, which went over a gently flowing stream. They quickly disappeared through the bushes and dense undergrowth.

I followed behind the dogs at a more leisurely pace as they trotted over the little rickety wooden bridge. It was so good to feel the coolness in the shade of the trees after the stuffy atmosphere of the car for so many hours.

Further along the path, I could hear Katie crashing about in the undergrowth, as though she was hot on the trail of something, I tried to follow as best I could, as the path was now winding quite steeply upwards, and there were quite a few fallen trees to negotiate, which slowed me down somewhat. The scent of fox was quite strong now.

So this was why Katie was careering about in such an erratic manner. Had she actually seen a fox, I wondered?

I decided that at this point it was time to turn back to the car, before Katie was on the scent of something else to chase after!

Arriving back to the car, I discovered that my parents were having a doze, after helping themselves to a bag of chocolate sweets, some biscuits and another mug of coffee.

Had we really been away that long I wondered, and then just as I was giving the dogs a bowl of water before putting them back into the car, I spotted something shiny over by the rubbish bin, and I didn't think it looked like an ordinary piece of glass. It seemed to beckon my attention, so out of mild curiosity I went over to investigate what it could be. To my complete surprise, it turned out to be a man's watch. Could this be a Rolex? I turned it over, but found that I hadn't hit the jackpot this time. It was definitely not a Rolex, oh well, never mind!

The watch was rather unusual, and it had an attractive face with an alarm piece comprising of a separate little face and dial at the top, and on the face itself, it had just the ordinary single mark for each hour, but on the outside casing it had Roman numerals at the top for the twelfth hour, and then again for the six. The watch strap was a good quality leather, and most important of all, the watch was still working! So, all-in-all, it was quite a good find.

It looked as though someone had just thrown it down. Perhaps it was a present given to a jilted lover who threw it out of the car in revenge, or just on impulse after a quarrel, or just a tiff. That's the best theory I could come up with, and it was certainly too good just to throw into the waste bin.

On an impulse, I decided to give it to Maggie, thinking it might give him something to focus on during the journey, and knowing that all magpies love shiny objects, so he might like this as one of his treasures.

Threading the strap through the bars of the cage, I noticed that Maggie looked at the watch with mild curiosity, and he seemed to be particularly interested in the second-hand as it ticked its way round. I said to him, "Here you are Maggie, this will help you pass the time!" and he carried on just staring at it, unblinking.

It was now early afternoon as we motored through quaint close-knit villages with unpronounceable names.

There were cosy little Welsh cottages built from local stone, and some were built to nestle in a hollow at the foot of the hillside, or some were standing in perfect isolation at the end of a long farm track, whilst others stood boldly on the edge of the roadside.

The scenery was really breathtaking, with a sense of calmness, serenity, and so very peaceful, and you could never really tire of the view.

There was the feeling of being transported back in time, to another era perhaps, as far back as thirty or even forty years ago.

Elderly couples could be seen pottering about in their gardens, tending to their vegetable patches, or their pretty flower borders. They stopped their work and waved to us as we drove past their cottages. Their cheery greetings made us feel so welcome, and any feelings of stress seemed to vanish.

We drove through Abergavenny, then Brecon, and then on to Llandovery, where we spotted a solitary red kite circling gracefully over the tree tops.

I pulled over to the side of the road, stopped the engine and wound the windows down so that we could watch for a few moments this majestic, highly treasured, and fiercely protected bird of prey. I have heard that some of their nesting sites have even been guarded day and night by Gurkhas.

His ancient mewing call—*keea! keea!*—echoed plaintively across the hills as he soared effortlessly, and then he swooped at great speed, before ascending once more to gain height.

Was he hunting or just enjoying the freedom of the skies?

His rich chestnut-coloured feathers with flashes of white, glowed in the afternoon sun, and as he turned, we could see his distinctive forked tail, which is not to be confused with the buzzard, whose tail is rounded, and more fan shaped, and the buzzard is somewhat smaller than the kite, but both are a joy to watch as they execute their spectacular "dance of life" in the air.

The kite drifted away from us, and was soon just a small dot in the distance.

The aerial display was over. It was such a short display, but we were glad to have witnessed it. I was hoping that we would see a lot more of the red kites.

We carried on through the little market town of Lampeter.

"Not far now," I told my parents.

Father deserved a medal for patience and endurance, and Mother could soon stop grumbling!

"How much further now?" she asked.

"Another fifteen miles or so, and we're home—in time for tea!" I replied.

- Chapter Five and a Half -
Over to Maggie

...and the birds sang!...

It all 'appened in one fowl swoop, so to speak. Me past and me present woz just passin' by, all in one go. Maybe this is what Eeli meant when she said that I would be going on a long journey.

It all started when the pinky lot got into a lather and a frenzy, whizzing all over the place, runnin' about with their old bits of junk and paraphernalia.

Some things were such overly big lumps of stuff, such as the tee vee. Then there woz those big chunky perchin' apparatus that the pinkies sit themselves down on (what they call "chairs"), or those even bigger things what they roost on after sundown (called "beds"), and some of their other bits of ol' clutter which woz not so big (what they calls "fur-nit-cher"). An' then there were lots an' lots of quite small things which were piled all around the klakki in heaps in a right old dissaray. There woz other things too, of all shapes and sizes, which I guess they had gathered over many suns and moons, and these things, too, woz plonked about in a *very* untidy manner, not like us magpies, who are *always* so very neat and orderly! They were scuttling about all over the place like tormented termites, screeching at one another like gibbering jays, whilst they frantically stuffed lots of their precious hordes into poxy boxy things, and glassy or stony bits were all wrapped up in materials, just like what they place in the bottom of me klakki.

Then a number of big beefy-type pinkies (wot I've never seen before) came in and talked for a long time with me pinky saviours.

When all the talking was done with, they lifted up the bits and bobs between them, and carried the whole lot out to a gigantic metal klakki, which I believe is called a "van," or a "lorry" or something like that.

This whole thing that was goin' on I thought woz absolutely outrageous, and of course I really did think that these nasty lumpity bastards were making off lickety-split with me pinky ma's treasures, but—judging by the wide smiles that Pinky Ma and her lot were giving, and then all that frantic waving up and down with those funny pink flappy flippers (what they call "hands") an' shouting out to everyone, "bye bye!" then everythin' must've been awright after all!

It was only at that moment, after all the flip flapping of hands had finished, when I realized that me pinky lot really *did* want their goodies to be removed by these noisy nerds!

Surprisingly enough, they were very happy about the whole thing!

What strange creatures these pinky folk are!

With me still sittin' in me klakki (or should I say "cage"?) I woz plonked with me pinky pa at the back of their metal klakki (or "car" in pinky talk) with the two hairy earth runners—oops, there I go again, I mean "dogs"—and then we were off, moving excitingly fast along the concrete klakki pathway, and it's all done without anyone even having to flap their wings up and down to fly! We just sits there and off we all go!

This is when I thought me life was passing by me like shooting stars.

When we got to the spot what looked mightily familiar, I sez to meself, *That over there woz surely where I first did hatch out as an absolutely perfect magpie. Then that over there looked like where Lace Wing did her pretty glass-spotting hobby, and over there woz where Great Uncle Sidney Snake Snitcher went on his snake-snitching sorties, and look!— surely that's the same barrel into which poor old mad Moonbeam dived head first all those moons ago.*

I am sure that I could just about spot that great white wooden giant, still standing silent, and once thought to be worshipped by the pinkies of many suns and moons past. It was told that long ago, whenever the wind blew hard and fast, the great white wooden wings of the giant would whirl round and round, and then the pinkies would bustle about inside, where lots of pounding noises could be heard, then they would file out with great mounds of soft white powdery stuff, which I suppose woz their fodder, so they must've worshipped it greatly.

Pa told us once that he thought it sent out secret wind messages to the pinkies, so's they'd know what to do, 'coz when it got extra windy like, he could hear great creaking and moaning sounds coming from it, and the pinkies would be runnin' about all busy and fussin' all over the place like a flock of starlings.

I think it woz also near here where Rumple Scruff saw the huge smoking iron bird fall from the sky all those moons ago.

Oh how I miss these things!

Oh dear, we are not stopping!

My heart will break, and I will surely die from sorrow!

They will not stop, why don't they let me go?

Where is my egg layer and egg maker?

Oh well, I'll just have to sit here and hope that they will stop sometime before we all die of unhappiness or something. Maybe they've got something planned for my benefit!

Well we did stop for a while, and the doggies were let out—but I wasn't!

It looked very interesting and inviting, but I wasn't given a chance to explore. Lucky old dogs!

Then on and on we went.

Flash! Flash! Flash!

This woz the terrible noise I could hear as everything passed us by, like lots of other metal klakkies, as they shot past us from all ways, just like shooting stars—Voom! Voom! Voom! Very frightening at times, I must say. Damn good job I'm in here and not out there, otherwise I'd be all mushed up by now I wouldn't wonder.

So I had a little bit of a singsong just to cheer myself up, especially as this flightless boring old metal klakki was getting mighty hot by now, and I felt that I was going to end up like a boiled chicken.

Twisting our way around the narrow roads (as the travelling pinky lot call them), we actually stopped at a place with lots of trees, and it started to get much cooler.

The klakki pulled in for another very welcome stop.

Maybe Pinky Ma will let me out here, so's I can have just a little look about? I sez to meself, but no, you might have guessed, the answer woz "no" to me question. I had no choice but to stay put, have me a slurp of water and a peck of some quite tasty goodies.

Oh well, I might as well just sit here and wait and wonder and wish and want, with a bit more of singing thrown in! I sez to meself once more with feeling.

The doggies and Pinky Ma got out and hurtled off into those mightily inviting bushes and trees.

Perhaps they've gone to find some more plunder and stuffs? I thought hopefully.

Then after about what seemed like half the sun time gone, they all came rushing back again, and the doggies had their long pink tongues sticking out and they were going, "Huh...huh...huh!" very fast, and their bodies went into funny wobbles, heavin' about and all that, then they drank lots and lots of water, and after that they flomped down all tuckered out!

Then a very, very strange thing happened.

Pinky Ma ran over to something that I had already spotted, and if I had been let out (just to stretch me wings a bit, you understand), I would have done the same thing, but only to have a wee look—that's all!

Anyway, as I woz saying, she went over to this shiny interesting looking thingy, and to me great surprise, she actually picked it up and brought it over, and an even *greater* surprise, she gave the glittering prize *to me*, and fixed it right on the top of me klakki, so's I could gaze in wonderment at it.

I could've squeezed a squidgy squid for joy! By the Great Raven's Wing! I think I've hit the jackpot! I think—nay, I'm almost positive— that this wondrously sacred object can only be an "all-seeing thing" 'coz Pinky Ma did say to me, "Now you can pass the time!"—which meant that I had in my possession, my very own "future teller" just like Eeli has, and I know its got magic properties, 'coz I could hear a little tapping sort of noise, like when a chick taps on its shell just before it hatches out, and it's a sort of—tick! tick! tick! And then there's these rune type figures under the glass moon shape bit, and a magic gold wandy thing moves around slowly pointing at the runes, so when I've learnt how to use it, then I too will be able to tell the future.

Better'n all those stones and shells and such like, and I bet all those other birds will be as jealous as hell when they find out wot I've got, so this means a celebration of my good fortune will be up for grabs!

Just to show how happy I am, I will share with you my very special song what I've composed whilst I've been dilly dallying all the way here, and all the way there, and round about, and everywhere!

You have to sing it lots of times over and over, and each time, you have to sing it quicker and quicker! If you gets me drift.

So it goes like this:

> *Beeble bop, a wobba bop bop,*
> *A zinga zang zong,*
> *Tibby tang tong.*
> *Jiggy jaggy jiff jiff,*
> *Zappy bong bong.*

Gimmi gimmi dish dash,
Then I'll go-a-splish-splash,
Noonday sun, camels' run,
Minny minny nish nash!

Frilly pom-poms did a chilli con carne,
Blue bottle flies did a dance quite barmy,
Tiny bats eating gnats,
Little dogs wearing clogs,
Grinning cats wearing hats.
Tee! Hee! Hee!

Bottle nosed dolphins played with platter billed
pussycats,
Swordfish fought a battle with mock turtle batter
fats,
Siamese twin fighter fish,
Scuttling along with cuttle fish,
Isn't it a dainty dish?
Cheese! Cheese! Cheese!

Tirree, tirree, chip, chip, chip,
Oogilie, oogilie,
Bip, pip, dip.

Lots of cotton rye grass,
Pudding basin blue glass,
Fritter titter bobby socks,
Roly poly gum locks,
Mothers sin, at the gin,
Tally! Lally! Ho!

Sickly little chicklets,
Sticking to their giblets,
Baking in the midday sun,
Mothers pride, go and hide,
Throw the hen a sticky bun,
Fox and geese, wearing fleece,
Run! Run! Run!

Kegagooli tottermaluli,
Shinkle shankle klinkle,
Did a what?
A jolly lot,
Did a wolly billy dally dingle.

Chickens run,
When they're having fun,
Cluck! Cluck! Cluck! Cluck! Clucks!
If they don't have fun,
Or they won't just run,
Then they must be fairground ducks!

Crazy bees do bend ze knees,
Bubble'n'squeak don't arf look cheap,
Sez who? Sez I,
Be nice as pie.

Have some cheese and wine,
If you've got the time,
Eat a harvest moon,
With a silver spoon,
Drink a drop of sun,
From a golden drum.

Silly tilly's tongue tied,
Mr froggy's pond's dried,
Blackbird's song,
All went wrong,
So we cried! Cried! Cried!

A zinga zang zong,
Tibby tang tong,
Shimme shack ticky tack,
Cantuccini rossilini,
Molta gino socka bambino,
Ding, dang, dong.

Chew, chew, chew,
Fiddle diddle do,
Pennybryn fossyfinn,
True, blue, dew.

Abergavenny found a lost penny,
Oh, what a wonderful tip!
Find a pound note and give to the goat.
Flippity! Slippity! Trip!

Crinkle, crankle, tingle, tangle,
Taggle, taggle, dee,
Frogs spawn yummy,
Funny bunny tummy,
Silly silly me!

Silver shilling shows I'm willing,
Mustn't be late by the golden gate,
Cuckoo's song, all day long,
Rhythm and rhyme such a waste of time,
Deary, deary, me!

Wombat kitty cat,
Sugar sugar sticky rat,
Ruga rum, chewing gum,
Trick a pig, wear a wig,
Find a pup and fill him up,
Give him a bone and send him home,
Tricka! Tricka! Treat!

Fox trot butter fields,
Yeller belly tottle shields,
Red rose with funny nose,
Silver leaf with silver teeth,
Blues, blues, blues!

Brillo cream,
Silly dream,
All come true!

"I'm nearly ready for take off!"
(baby Maggie with my father)

"Can somebody *please* let me out?"

"I told you I could turn cats to stone!"

"I'm a Yin Yang Bird!"

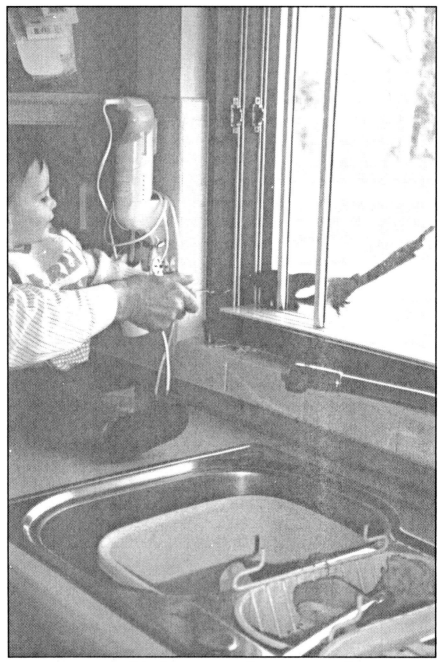

"Just a spoonful of sugar....one for you!....two for me!"
(Maggie with Alun Lewis's grandson Trystan.
Note damage to tail due to fight with Rottweiler).

"I say... do you happen to know Merlin?"
(Maggie with neighbour Alun Lewis)

– Chapter Six –
Red Kite Country

The early morning sun found its way through a small chink in my bedroom curtain, the brightness almost burning my eyes. I looked at the clock. It was still only five-thirty, much too early to get up, and nobody else would be up yet, especially after such a long tiring trip.

Many thoughts were running through my head.

Had we made the right decision? Was it such a good idea to uproot ourselves from our comfortable and familiar life in Sussex?

I reasoned with myself that I had already been living here in Wales for the past eleven months, whilst my parents prepared themselves for the big move, and in the meantime they had to put their own house on the market. Fortunately it was sold very quickly; in fact, it went after the first week of being advertised with just one of the local estate agents, so there was no time for anybody to think about backing out.

Now that my parents could relax and give themselves time to settle down, there was much work to be done in decorating the house, then to plan and design the almost nonexistent garden, and it was all up to me!

The garden (or should I say "wasteland") had never been properly landscaped by the previous owners, and as the house was only two years old, I would have to start working from scratch. It would be a challenge, and I needed to start straight away.

Armed to the teeth with a trowel, garden fork, spade, secateurs and a hoe, all spilling out and over the sides of a pathetically small, well-worn, over-laden wheelbarrow with a very squeaky wheel, I was ready for action!

Before long I was making reasonable progress, but it was very hard work trying to dig over very rough builders' rubble, and the garden was sadly lacking in good top soil. Nevertheless, I was able to plant dozens of shrubs, trees, bamboos, ornamental grasses, and lots of bulbs, which included daffodils and a handful of multi-coloured crocus bulbs, with a few snowdrops thrown in for good measure, all of which should make a good show of colour for us in the early spring and on into the summer and autumn. In a few years, the tall trees and thick dense shrubs would hug and protect the house and garden area from the prevailing cold north winds, as well as provide roosting and nesting places for a number of birds, plus the bonus of providing a good quantity of insects and berries for the birds and small mammals to feed on.

Already the birds were provided with boxes on each of the big mature beech trees overlooking the drive at the front of the house, and as soon as Father had fixed them onto the trees, by climbing precariously high on the long extending ladder, it wasn't long before new tenants moved in. In fact they staked their claim almost before Father had reached the bottom rung of the ladder! Blue tits, great tits, robins, sparrows, nuthatches, and even a spotted flycatcher, soon started building their nests. They used clumps of dog hair combed from Katie and Hattie, and clumps of soft fur groomed from Humphrey, as well as soft green moss and other suitable materials gathered up, to make their nests luxuriously warm and cosy for their delicate little hatchlings.

In my mind's eye, I could see well-laid patios and paved paths surrounding the house, with a trellis here, and a pergola there, all covered in roses, and perhaps a clematis or two, and sweet-smelling honeysuckle climbing up the wall, and maybe a pond with a fountain which could be seen from the lounge. It would also be nice to have stone steps with rustic hand rails leading you down onto the bottom lawn, and hidden on the other side of a screen of conifers there would be a secret haven with a wildlife pond, inviting you to stand and stare or sit and dream. The pond would soon attract lots of frogs and waterboatmen, and many other creatures could live under the floating water lily pads. There would be lots of fragrant water mint and forget-me-nots growing there too, and at the edge of the pond, reeds and bullrushes would be grown, and so many other waterside plants too numerous to mention.

There will be no decking in my garden. I don't like decking at all, so instead I will have a beautiful green lawn. A nice grassy lawn is so much more pleasing to the eye, and soft to walk barefoot on, even if it is hard work to keep trim and neat.

One major complaint I have about lots of decking and big patios is that they are bad news for the wildlife, especially for the bird population, and not forgetting creatures such as hedgehogs, frogs, toads, or little voles, as their food sources like worms and insects are covered over by hard concrete and wood. It must be like closing their main supermarket stores to them, and when did you last hear the pleasant "siss!…siss!…sissing!" sounds of the grasshoppers?

I definitely draw a line on decking!

Now I admit that loads of mulching looks rich and is much loved by most gardeners, but this wonderful product can also have its drawbacks too, even if it does make weeding so much easier.

Can you just imagine a poor robin, blackbird, or thrush trying to rummage through thick piles of mulch consisting of hard coconut shells, shavings or wood-chips, in a futile search for worms or snails?

I love watching the big songbirds in our garden hopping across the lawn, then diving into the beds to turn over the leaves for grubs and insects, or plunging their long thin beaks into the ground to pull out big juicy worms like a long string of spaghetti, and then almost falling over backwards in their tug-of-war as the reluctant worm tries to pull itself back down into the ground, but finally giving way like an elastic band.

They do have to work so hard for just one measly morsel that it would be such a shame to deprive them of their food supply, so my long-term plan is to plant as many trees and berry-bearing bushes as I can.

My aim is to grow my own chain of McDonald's fast foods—just for the birds!

"Oh well," I said to myself as I came out of my half-dream state, "now that I've mentally drawn up all these plans, I've got to get started, so I mustn't stay in bed any longer. I'd better get moving!"

Pushing back the duvet, I stepped out of bed and made my way over to the window. Slowly I pulled back the curtains to look out over the fields bordered by beech and chestnut trees, and I could see the gently swaying larch trees.

These elegant slender trees turn a spectacular yellow and gold colour in the autumn.

In the distance loomed the lovely rolling hills, gently rising and falling. On the tops of the hills, acres of tall conifer trees grew in large clumps, looking like great big fuzzy eyebrows.

Sheep tracks, worn by constant use over the years, wound their way down through the bracken.

Lower down, where the stream runs, the early morning mist was rising. Dotted on the slopes (where the land was divided into a patchwork of small fields by trees and hedges), flocks of wall-to-wall sheep peacefully grazed, and in one of the fields much lower down, I could see a small herd of very contented-looking Friesian cows and what looked like an equally contented Charolais bull.

Above the house, where the sky was a pale blue, two isolated gulls flew by. Their silvered bodies looked like two perfectly formed arrow heads. Their flight path was directed away from the sea as they headed inland. They flew silently. Their languorous wing beats seemed to be stroking the air, beating in perfect unison, and at the same time propelling them unhurriedly towards their destination.

It was so very quiet, calm and peaceful, not the usual noise of everyday human activity we were so used to in our Sussex home.

Yes! I thought, *this can only get better!*

There was one tragic event which did mar our instant happiness shortly after our arrival in Wales.

The news I received early one morning came like a bolt out of the blue, and I was utterly devastated.

I felt as though this was the worst day of my life, and all because I took an urgent phone call from the two girls in Sussex who were looking after my mare, Gazella, along with Humphrey.

In sombre tones, they told me that she had gone down with chronic arthritis (which she had suffered with on and off for a few years), and as they had found her on that particular morning lying down in her field, and because she couldn't get back onto her feet, they had to summons the vet out to examine her. The vet told them that because he found her arthritic condition was so acute, and that there was no long-term cure for her condition, he decided that the only course of action to take in her own interest was to put her down. As the girls had no time to contact me, they had no alternative but to take his advice, and so the poor old lady was put to sleep.

Gazella's birth in our field twenty-five years ago had been a complete surprise.

Her mother had been a three-year-old dapple-grey Irish cob, whom I had named Pink Velvet, shortened to just Velvet.

I bought her from a local, well-known Irish horse dealer, who used to regularly make trips back and forth to Ireland to purchase his animals from the horse sales, and he had a good reputation of buying up the best of the Irish horses.

Trust me to find the odd one out!

Although she was passed as fit and proclaimed as a good quality horse, I wasn't quite prepared for the fact that she must have been badly broken in, and consequently she turned out to be a prolific bucking bronco, which landed me in hospital so many times that the nurses told me they were seriously thinking of keeping a bed free— just for me!

At least she would use her early warning system just before going into one of her fits of bucking, so when her ears started to flick alternately back and forth, it meant "watch out!"

The last straw came when I had a really bad accident whilst out on a ride.

I was out riding with my cousin Rod. He was riding Nutmeg and I was on Velvet.

It was a gloriously sunny day, so we decided to go for a long ride, which took us to a large estate with a bridleway running right across magnificent parkland, where mature giant old oak and beech trees grew in abundance. The wide-open spaces of the park were ideal for a long canter or a flat-out gallop.

We started off into a nice gentle canter, and Velvet was going well. She seemed to be responding to my commands and behaving particularly well, and then all of a sudden I noticed the twitching of the ears, back and forth. Too late! I knew I was in for it now, and she took off into a flat-out gallop, and then she started her usual bronco routine.

I was suddenly turned into a human missile, and a big old oak tree was the target!—spot on!—*thwack!*

My cousin Rod told me later that he really thought I had been killed. All he could see at first were the stirrup irons complete with their leather straps, flying through the air, and the bridle (which I must have pulled off as I shot over her head) flying about in pieces, as the leather cheek straps and noseband snapped off, and the bit, still attached to the reins, neatly lassoed itself into the branch of a tree, looking more like a hangman's noose! The next thing he heard was me going *thud!*—into the tree!

Velvet was last seen making off into the distance, "kicking and farting!" (as Rod so delicately put it), and the saddle flaps (the saddle was the only bit of tack still intact) flapping up and down!

The once nice, neat grounds had turned into a ploughed-up field!

I don't remember much about the actual impact, but I do remember that I had difficulty in not passing out, due to the fact that I was more worried about Rod, and although he was a very good rider himself, he would not be experienced enough to try and cope with not just one, but two runaway horses!

I started to shake with the shock of the fall, and I hurt just about everywhere, but with Rod's help I slowly stood up and began to walk unsteadily, and at the same time I was trying to keep track of the disappearing heels of the two loose horses, followed by clods of earth flying everywhere. I turned around to try and give instructions to Rod on what to do, and walking blindly I didn't notice the cattle grid. My leg went straight down into it, and I then, once more, nearly passed out, but still hung on!

Somehow I managed to reach the lodge at the entrance to the estate, and Rod, ashen-faced, rang the bell. The door was opened by a very worried-looking woman, who kindly took us into her kitchen when Rod told her what had happened. She obviously wasn't very medically minded, because when she offered me a glass of milk, everything went a deep purple colour, and it was only then that I actually managed to pass out.

I was driven hurriedly by her husband to the hospital, which was luckily just a few yards from the estate.

When the staff saw me arrive, they took one look at me and said, *"Oh no!—not you again!"*

My injuries turned out to be quite serious. My left arm had been broken in two places, and I had a hairline fracture to my top vertebra, but fortunately I hadn't broken my leg when I stepped into the cattle grid. They told me that if my neck had actually been broken, I would have ended up in a wheelchair for the rest of my life!

I can only be very thankful that I was wearing a hard hat on that day.

My worries about Rod coping with the runaway horses were groundless, because he coped with the situation remarkably well.

The following day he managed to trace my best friend, a fellow horse rider, Anna.

With Rod on foot and Anna riding her pony, Gemini, and together with one other helper on her horse, they were able to round up the two horses that very morning.

Although the naughty pair had enjoyed their freedom in the lush long grass, they gave themselves up without any resistance. I think they were feeling somewhat uncomfortable at finding themselves still attached to some of the tack—or at least Nutmeg was!

I was laid up for several weeks, but I reluctantly made the decision that I would start to look for a very good home for Velvet (who should have been renamed "Blazing Saddles") to someone who had a lot more time to ride her every day and sympathetically re-train and school her. But before I could part with her, she produced this surprise foal, almost as though she was to be a parting-gift offering, and so Velvet had to stay with us for another year.

Gazella was a lovely, playful little foal. She was jet black when she was born, and I named her Gazella because she used to run and jump just like a gazelle.

As she got older, she gradually turned iron grey, and when she became an old lady, she was almost white.

She had a lovely gentle nature, and was so easy to back and school for riding, and above all, she never bucked like her mother. She was so comfortable to sit on, it was like riding an armchair.

After being with us for twenty-five years, it came as a dreadful shock to lose her like that, and to not have even been there for her or to say goodbye.

I missed her dreadfully, and now I only had Humphrey.

Maggie settled down happily in his new home, and his cage didn't look too out of place perched on top of the old toy cupboard, which was now located in the kitchen for the time being, and he could also see the comings and goings from the kitchen.

Although Maggie was allowed out of his cage for a short period of time during the day, this wasn't the ideal situation on a long-term basis, so I decided that we would have to find someone to build him a special aviary.

We had plenty of space to choose from, and in the end it was decided that the best spot would be at the end of the stable block, which had only recently been built for Humphrey, my pony, making the complex into an "L" shape, and we would also be able to see Maggie from the kitchen window on the west side of the house, and also from my parents' bedroom window.

Now that a final decision had been made as to the location where the aviary, we felt that nothing could go wrong, but where could we find a suitable aviary builder?

At the same time as desperately wanting an aviary built for Maggie, we also had other important plans to set in motion.

I had to find an interior decorator to do all the wallpapering in just about every room in the house, because although it was only two years old, we didn't think we could live with the monotonous, tediously bland magnolia colour splashed on every wall.

The carpets would have to go too, as they weren't exactly dripping with exciting colours (only with cooking fat, bad stains, and blotches of paint) and as we had five bedrooms, two bathrooms, four toilets, study, dining room, kitchen and a large utility room, this was going to be a mammoth undertaking.

First on the scene was the aviary builder.

My brother, Derek, by now somewhat older, wider (but not wiser!) and a bit grumpy around the edges, introduced us to Bernie the aviary builder, who would (by all accounts) be the best choice.

As we didn't have any other options open to us, Bernie was a potential candidate to do the job.

He turned up one evening to discuss the details, which I thought would be a mere formality, as it shouldn't take much time, effort, or money, just to knock up an ordinary aviary with no frills and no fancy options!

"Yes, that's where we want it to be, and that's how big, and that's how high, and that's just about it!" I told him.

Preliminaries over, an agreed time to start was arranged, then the short interview ended with a polite "goodnight!"

Bernie the builder arrived on schedule to case the joint.

He was a very slender man with a trim grey beard, and he wore round, gold-rimmed glasses. He didn't look at all like a butch-type builder, but then looks can be deceiving. He carried with him a very smart briefcase, which contained a big notepad for his sketches or drawings, and a measuring tape, along with a spirit level, a calculator, and a large assortment of coloured pencils and felt-tip pens, ready for action!

He asked me, "What kind of exotic birds do you keep?"

Now where have I heard this before, and why do I always feel so embarrassed when I point out Maggie, "the exotic magpie?"

There always seems to be that pregnant pause when anyone discovers that he's just "a plain old magpie."

After a short informal discussion, we talked ourselves into engaging him, but without a quote or estimate, which we had apparently overlooked, so it was arranged that evening that he would visit us in two weeks in order to do some calculations prior to starting work.

Sure enough, bang on time, and on the right day, Bernie turned up in his little white truck, which had a rather outsized ladder attached to the back and leaning against its roof, and as he drove down the lane, I could see a long pole was sticking out to one side of his truck, which made him look more like a competitor in a jousting tournament!

He started measuring up on the appropriate site (taking his time it seemed to me) to get it exactly right. He stood back for a while and stared hard at the ground, then he scratched his beard in a sort of contemplative manner, as if pondering over a potential unforeseen problem.

After a few more gos at measuring up, he seemed satisfied with the results.

He came back to the house to tell me that he would have to go home with his calculations and draw out a final plan.

I was absolutely dumfounded. A plan for an ordinary bird aviary! Just a shallow bit of foundation, bits of wood, bits of wire, a few nails, nuts and a bolt—bang! bang!—and it's all done? Not so, it appears! A full-scale plan of a ginormous proportion was produced.

Bernie laid his neatly rolled-up sheet of paper on the kitchen floor where we could study his intricate drawings, which covered just about every tiny detail. It looked more like a plan for a shopping arcade and was much too technical for me to understand, so all I could do was to say, "Oh yes—I see!" to everything.

The first task would be the foundation, which turned out to be a major operation.

The eleventh hour had arrived, along with Bernie and his tools of the trade.

The digging commenced, which took practically all of that day, and it looked as though he was digging all the way to Australia, judging by the huge mounds of earth, and the glimpse of a swinging pick-axe, and the man at the end of it slowly disappearing down the newly dug crater. Every so often his head would suddenly bob up from the hole, just like a meerkat.

Had he discovered an archaeological site or a gold mine or something?

Day two, and the ready-mix cement mix was due to arrive in the ready-mix cement mixer lorry.

Phew!—that was a bit of a brain twister!

The lorry arrived somewhat late, much to the annoyance of Bernie, as he wanted to make an early start.

He may have been a little eccentric, but at least he always arrived on time.

The concrete base was levelled and laid to the specifications set out on the plans, and when the work was finished, we all stood back to admire the work.

The foundations were deep enough and solid enough to have supported a twenty-storey building.

It looked okay from the front and side, but at the back, the base had the texture and contours that would have done the Grand Canyon justice! Perhaps this was his artistic side that I couldn't quite find appreciation for, or perhaps he thought that in the future I would be planning to add a multi-storey aviary complex, complete with it's own "Polly Port," or an elephant house even! But the biggest jumbo surprise was his final estimate, which came to the grand total of— four hundred pounds!

Needless to say, he was paid up, and then he was disemployed to complete the job, which meant we now had to find someone else to construct Maggie's outside abode.

In the meantime, we had to stand and stare at the structure fit for a runway, and at the surrounding empty space of a non-existent aviary.

All the while we were waiting for the completion of his new house, Maggie was by no means idle. He was keeping himself very amused and busy by exploring his new surroundings indoors, and he seemed to be quite content with the extra space to fly around in and was always getting himself into mischief.

As he gained more confidence, and bossiness kicked in, he was beginning to get a tad naughty again. As magpie culture dictates, with oodles of mayhem, and because they try to create as much chaos as possible, with loads of pilfering and plundering thrown in, then with all of these things to his credit, Maggie was becoming a "Grand Master of tricksters!"

Restrictions were in force, and all the rooms, with the exception of the kitchen and utility room, were out of bounds to Maggie, but of course he would always try to break the house rules, given the opportunity, and he was always on the lookout for somebody to leave the doors open.

Since his "great escape" and narrowly missing death by a whisker from the two cats, we were ultra careful to keep all doors closed whilst he was on the loose, and so I made doubly sure by placing notices on the kitchen and back doors saying:

PLEASE KEEP ALL DOORS CLOSED—
MAGGIE THE MAGNIFICENT ON THE LOOSE!

After a while, the novelty wore off and most of the family either chose to ignore the request—or genuinely forgot—so there was the odd escape or two into the dining room or lounge, but before he could make his way upstairs, he was quickly scooped up, protesting and scolding loudly in a series of his fast, nerve-shattering, clacking noises, and then he was quickly shoved back into his cage.

The final stages of the aviary were thankfully taken on by the interior decorator, Kevin, after a more reasonable rate and estimate were finally negotiated.

Kevin was to start work on the aviary almost immediately, as he was shortly due to start work in the house, mainly wallpapering our rooms, and he managed to persuade his sidekick, Stephan, to help him.

Fortunately, Stephan turned out to be a very reliable professional builder, but unfortunately for them (and us), the long, hot, dry summer weather finally broke, and we were treated to a spell of torrential rain. So the two aviary builders were now stodging around in a mass of gooey wet mud, caused by the mounds of earth which had previously been dug out for the foundations. Stephan's woolly hat stuck to his head like a wet limpet, and Kevin's shoulder-length hair hung in straggly ringlets which clung to his face like coiled snakes; as he looked up, his head looked like that of Medusa.

I felt very sorry for them as they dripped their way through the mire, whilst trying to unravel rolls of small-mesh wire and hammering away at soggy wood to support the roof. I think they were so used to working in this sort of weather that they didn't seem to mind too much.

The only time there was a minor dispute was when I asked them to make two doors to the entrance of the aviary, so that when he first one was opened, you could then walk in and close it behind you before opening the second one, and this would then prevent Maggie's attempt of escaping past whenever someone wanted to go into the aviary.

They both looked at me as though I had three heads, which I thought was a bit rich, but rather appropriate, coming from "Medusa head"—and the "limpet" just grinned!

"Oh, never mind! Forget it!" I said. So they did.

The work was soon completed at a further sum of four hundred pounds, making a grand total of eight hundred and ninety pounds (which included the mynah bird cage), putting him in the category of a millionaire magpie.

Maggie was now the lucky resident of a brand new, stylish "Magpie Penthouse."

I began to think that I should take out an insurance plan on him and his lavish home, and maybe we ought to put a name on the door in big bold print:

MAGGIE'S MANSION

Adam and I added a few final touches of our own to the aviary, as we wanted to fully furnish it before introducing Maggie to his new accommodation.

We hauled the biggest fallen branches that we could manage to find, and most of them were laying right at the bottom of the field, and they took us quite some time to drag laboriously behind us, as the hill was pretty steep.

After a bit of coaxing, the branches fitted snugly, wedged firmly against the back of the aviary, and this gave Maggie plenty of branches to perch on. At the back of the aviary in one corner, he had a wooden platform where we could stand his food and water dishes, and above the platform, we fixed a nice big branch for him to roost on at night if he wanted to. On the floor he had a thick layer of fresh new gravel to keep it clean, and a scattering of different coloured pebbles for him to play with, and there were lots of nooks and crannies for him to hide his treasures behind, or under.

Then on one of the top branches we fitted his favourite budgie mirror, which had a little tinkly bell on it. This was about his third mirror which he used whenever he wanted to attract attention. He would either grab them in his beak and shake them vigorously, or just biff them to bits. The little bells didn't last for very long, and they soon became detached from the mirrors. I think he must have hidden them somewhere, but at least they kept him amused for a while.

Before Maggie was introduced to his new home, he went on his own "bargain hunt."

He must have somehow avoided everybody by flying silently like a moth, manoeuvring himself through a small gap in the door, which somebody must have left slightly open, thinking that Maggie was still in his cage and not lurking outside of it, forgetting that the door had been propped open, so that he could hop in and out as he pleased, but only within the bounds of the kitchen area.

"Has anybody seen Maggie?" I asked.

"Maggie?" came the reply.

"Yes!… You know?…that black and white flappy thing that makes lots of mess everywhere…lots of noise at times…disrupts everyone's lives…takes everything it sees…eats us out of house and home!"

"Oh!…that one!" came the reply with a hint of sarcasm. "Nope!"

Empty cage!

Not a sound!

Not a good sign!

Then I heard a harsh familiar sound, but a long way off!

"Aark! Aark! Aark!…Yak! Yak! Yak!"

The sound seemed to be coming from upstairs, and as I made my way up, I was keeping my fingers crossed that all the windows had been kept shut, otherwise there would be no telling what would happen if he was to escape yet again into an even bigger outside world than the one before!

I called out to him. "Maggie!… Maggie! Where on earth are you — you naughty crow?"

There was a brief moment of silence, which wasn't always a good omen as it could mean he was up to some of his usual mischief making.

I checked each room in turn, glancing quickly around with caution and not knowing what I would find. He left a trail of his fleeting visit in each room.

In my parents' bathroom he'd found the spare loo roll, which was sitting on the top of the bathroom cabinet. It was now lying in shreds on the carpet (like a trail left on a paper-chase) and right next to the shredded paper was a tube of toothpaste, which was now pitted with holes and a stream of soft white paste was oozing out and onto the pink carpet.

I hastily flushed the evidence of shredded paper down the toilet and then carefully scooped up the white paste from the carpet, trying not to rub too hard with the sink cleaning cloth, but the more I rubbed, the worse mess it seemed to make, as the paste left a frothy gleaming white patch which grew bigger as I rubbed harder!

Leaving the bathroom with its graffiti-style carpet, I made my way along the landing and peeped into my parents' bedroom. I quite expected to find more disruption with the fixtures and fittings, and I wasn't disappointed!

I thought the artificial flowers looked so much prettier in the vase, and not sticking in a higgledy-piggledy fashion on the top of the curtain rail, where some of them had been threaded quite neatly through the net curtains, which didn't quite hide the freshly stripped wallpaper, now lying in little strips on the carpet. All these new "make overs" went quite well (I thought) with my father's socks, which were hanging limply over the lampshade. Not the bedside lamp, I hasten to add, but the nice decorative pink silk one on the ceiling! Thank goodness he hadn't found Father's cuff-links, which were lying exposed in a little china trinket dish on top of the dressing table.

"Okay, Maggie, where *are* you?" I called. "Come on now, I'll count to ten, and if you don't show yourself, you just won't get any grub!"

Then I heard his sharp, rasping, croaky call; but much louder now. *"ARK!...ARK!...ARK!"*

This time his raucous retort was coming from my bedroom, and it sounded deadly intense and serious! I hurried along to my room, feeling rather apprehensive as to what little surprise there was in store for me.

I slowed down as I got to the door, feeling a shade nervous, and I peeked in cautiously, like Goldilocks about to be confronted by three angry bears out on a rampage!

I was confronted by Maggie, and he appeared to be rather flustered at being caught out red handed, by giving the familiar series of upward jerks of his wings, and the rise and fall of his crest, which he tended to do whenever he was discovered on one of his wrecking

271

or pillaging forays, and he changed his tune to a much higher, softer tone of voice—"*Cooee! cooee! tik! tik! tik! chewy! chewy! oh! oh! ooh!*"—to try to hide his naughty deed.

Maggie was chanting his usual excuses in his usual twitterings, whilst doing an unsteady balancing act on the shoulders of my favourite teddy bear called Maxwell, who stared out at me with his surprised glassy-eyes at this sudden assault. His smart black velvet bow tie had been unravelled from his neck, and was thrown to one side. My much-treasured old golliwog was lying face down on the bed, with his bottom stuck up in the air, and his smiley red lips (stuck on with velcro) were now completely separated from his face, forming a big letter "O" as it was now stuck to the backside of the soft toy Jersey cow. The white teddy hadn't escaped the rapidly stabbing beak either, as he was chucked mercilessly onto the floor right next to an upturned cuddly toy Penguin with its splayed feet sticking up in the air and his soft yellow beak bent crookedly to one side.

As I gazed upon the "toy torture" scene, my eyes inadvertently focussed on something sparkling and gold glinting on the floor. On closer inspection, and to my horror, I discovered that my valuable diamond and sapphire ring—which had been left to me by a close family friend—was lying on the carpet!

Maggie must have spotted the glittering, gem-encrusted ring (which I had obviously forgotten to put back into the jewel case), and finding it lying unprotected on a trinket tray, the temptation was too good to miss, and so he decided to confiscate them for himself.

As I stared at him, looking him straight in the eye, I noticed his eyes kept interchanging as they always did when he was about to carry out an evil act.

First his eyes would show a mother-of-pearl opaqueness (I called this his "mother-of-pearl syndrome"), then snapping sharply back to a glittering coal-black: On, off… on, off—pearl, black… pearl, black—just like in morse code. He really looked quite devilish!

One of the windows had been left open, and I am sure that Maggie's original plan before being discovered by me was to make off to the outside world carrying my ring, and I would probably have never seen my precious piece of jewellery again!

I suspected that as Maggie was about to make his move, he must have suddenly spotted all those unblinking staring eyes belonging to those very odd beings (mainly my toys), and felt that his cover had been blown, which must have provoked him into action, and to attack them was the only way to eliminate the witnesses and to destroy all the evidence.

Now that he had been caught red handed, he tried to act very coy and innocent, pretending he didn't know what all the fuss was about.

I "tutt-tutted!" as I picked up the dishevelled, sorrowful looking toys, dusted them down, and carefully placed them back in their original positions.

Maggie noticed that my attention was drawn back to my ring and was about to claim ownership. This was his prize alone, and nobody should have it!

As he crouched down in his normal position for take off to collect this shiny new find, I leapt across the floor with the speed of a gazelle to scoop up the ring before Maggie could clap his beak around it.

In synchronised motion, he sprang into the air, and with outstretched wings flapping fast and frantically in order to gain momentum, he flew towards the ring, and as I grabbed it up, I pirouetted over to the open window and slammed it shut before Maggie could change his flight course to head straight out the window. He quickly changed direction in mid-air and flew straight over towards me, then perched neatly onto my shoulder where he started to preen his feathers as though nothing unusual had happened in the last ten minutes or so!

I stood there quietly for a few moments, with Maggie still perched on my shoulder.

I needed to compose myself, and he just wanted to gaze in wonderment at the tantalizing scene outside which seemed to be beckoning to him, and his natural instincts appeared to be pulling at his heart-strings, as well as his senses, to go out there and explore all that he could see—at liberty.

Looking outside, a group of chattering, hopping and bobbing magpies could be seen out in the field, busily searching in the long grass for food, or just pecking around at lumps of earth, or even turning over the horse droppings. Magpies are not at all fussy when searching for food, and they like to rummage around like elderly ladies at a jumble sale, jostling one another for the best bargains!

Maggie watched, observing these carefree birds doing their own thing, and without the interference of humans to restrict their movements or to stop their "plundering forays."

He sat in silence, stock still, just looking and taking in all the activity going on out there, which was, for the moment, out of reach— so near, yet so far!

On the day of Maggie's first introduction to his brand new, meticulously furnished pad, the weather had definitely taken a turn for the worse.

It was very blustery, and the tall slender larch trees, buffeted by the high winds, rocked and swayed like Hawaiian dancers, and the clouds were not just drifting, they were fairly racing by, as though they were fast forwarding straight into winter, or had a very important date on the other side of the universe, and for now the sun was just a forgotten item.

Adam carried the cage with its precious contents down to the aviary with great difficulty, owing to the extreme weather conditions, and I followed on behind carrying his dish of food, with Katie bringing up the rear just to see what was going on. Bracing ourselves against the strong wind, we all followed in a dignified procession to witness the grand opening, and to watch Maggie's reaction to his newly acquired space, hoping he would approve of all the things so lovingly placed in it to keep him amused.

Humphrey stuck his head over the stable door to see what all the fuss was about, and as the cage drew nearer, he looked somewhat apprehensive, and when he reached down to touch the cage, he suddenly jerked his head up high, twitched his ears back, and showed the whites of his eyes. He gave a loud snort through his nostrils, which made poor Maggie flinch, and he started to squawk very loudly.

This was the first time that I'd seen Maggie show any signs of actual fear.

Humphrey then showed further distaste at the strange newcomer by turning his top lip up and showing off his large teeth, which made him look very comical to us, but not to poor Maggie!

I'm sure Humphrey would rather have another horse living next to him for a companion and not a silly, smelly, noisy bird!

Now owing to the fact that although Humphrey would probably be able to smell a birdie-type smell coming from Maggie's aviary, this would surely be a one-way experience, as I'm not at all sure if birds are actually capable of smelling things, which means that although birds can be "smelly" creatures, I don't think they can actually experience the smell themselves, but I could be wrong, of course!

When Maggie was finally released from his cage, he seemed to be highly delighted with his new apartment-come-play area, stroke bedroom—and it wasn't long before he started to poke into every corner.

Every nook and cranny had to be scrutinized, and it wasn't long before he found his sheltered little cubby hole, where he could sleep without disturbance if he so wished.

This new space was definitely much better than being cramped up in his old cage, and Maggie really looked as though he was enjoying his new independence, and after a while he seemed to ignore us, so we quietly crept away as he busily pecked and probed amongst the stones.

We left him on his own so that he could familiarize himself with everything that was all so new to him and give him a chance to settle down without any of us fussing around.

Happiness meant that at least some degree of peace reigned at last! Or at least for the time being anyway.

Each day the same routine was kept as the bird was taken out in early morning, accompanied by dishes filled with an assortment of food, then brought back at dusk with empty dishes.

This ritual had not gone entirely unnoticed by other neighbouring magpies. I was aware of their presence on the second day of Maggie's appearance in the aviary.

Black and white forms flitted through the bare branches of the beech trees, stalking me as I made my way to Maggie, who paced anxiously up and down as he waited for me to top up his dishes with tasty morsels left over from the meals of that day.

I counted six magpies, and I could hear them chattering noisily amongst themselves. They were soon lig-logging and hopping about on the lawn and parading in front of Maggie as he sat on his favourite branch pretending at first not to notice, and then his mood suddenly changed, and he teased them outrageously by tucking into his food with gusto, knowing that they couldn't reach him, and all they could do was stand and stare, with the crests on their heads rising and falling in sheer frustration.

If only they would accept him as one of their own kind, as this would make it much easier for his release into the wild eventually, because I didn't intend to keep Maggie caged up forever. He had a destiny to fulfil, and he was, after all, wild by nature.

The days and nights were fast approaching autumn.

Nights could sometimes be a bit disrupted when Maggie decided that "right now" was not time to go to bed, especially when it was apparent that everybody else wanted to settle down for the evening's supper and watch the television in peace.

Maggie had other ideas of his own, and he wanted the free range of the house so that he could do just what he wanted, and the only way to catch him was to herd (or lure) him into the kitchen. The next step was to make sure that everyone stood (or sat) still, and then turn off the lights, so that the room was in total darkness, but not before making sure that you had a torch with you, so that you knew just where to locate Maggie. If you called out "Maggie!" several times, he usually responded with little *"cooee!"* noises, and then you were able to switch on the torch and shine it to where you thought he was (which was usually under the kitchen table), and once found, you were then able to grab him up quickly, before he had a chance to clutter off again and thrust him into his cage.

"All right, everyone!… I've got him!… You can put the lights on now!"

This pantomime was performed practically every night, but at least he had his bit of fun, even if we didn't!

Autumn arrived with flocks of starlings.

They swooped down in close formation onto our lawn, where they proceeded to march up and down, probing into the earth with their long thin beaks, looking for small brown slugs and leatherjacket grubs. Their little throats throbbed away as they sang and chattered, with

276

their beaks held high. Their iridescent feathers dazzled in the sunshine as they began to sing their strange repertoire of songs, starting off with churring noises, sneezes, a few coughs, then a high pitch whistle starting off on a high note and then descending to a lower note.

They specialize in mimicry of all kinds of natural and unnatural sounds, depending on where they were hatched and the noises they could hear from their nests as baby birds. They particularly love to copy other birds' songs and calls, such as curlews, blackbirds, or even a cuckoo calling, and you know it's not a real cuckoo because it's still winter and not spring, so this premature cuckoo song is about four months out of season! They can also mimic motorbikes, chain-saws, or even a telephone ringing, which sounds so realistic that it can be taken as the real thing, enough to send anyone who happens to be in the garden at the time running indoors to answer it!

Bitingly cold northeasterly winds viciously wrenched the remainder of the autumn leaves off the trees. The tall poplars, standing like soldiers on parade, their long fragile branches, now almost leafless, looked more like redundant witches' brooms. The beeches and oaks stood just as proud, with their now-bare, intertwining branches extending upwards, as though accepting a standing ovation for services rendered to the cause of nature.

Winter was waiting in the wings.

It arrived with heavy grey clouds gathering over the distant hills, and as they approached, they trailed a snowy white blanket in their wake.

We were treated to our first fall of snow.

It wasn't long before the beautiful larch trees were laden with snow, their slender branches bearing the weight graciously, and when the watery sun fleetingly shone down on the shimmering snow crystals, you could see the icicles hanging in the trees, twinkling like stars, and you could hear a soft tinkling sound as they chinked together like wind-chimes.

On the same day, just a few hours after it had stopped snowing and everywhere looked just like a winter wonderland scene from a Christmas card, there came a knock at the front door. When I opened it thinking it might be early Christmas carol singers, I was confronted by a small band of children of various sizes. There was one four-year-old, one six-year-old, and three teenagers.

All were suitably clad in thick woolly hats and chunky jumpers bulging underneath their wadded anoraks and brightly coloured scarves covering half of their faces, making it difficult to recognize them.

They stood silently looking at me for a few moments, their eyes shining brightly and their noses, which were just about poking over the tops of their scarves, were shining redly.

The younger ones shifted their booted feet impatiently and in anticipation.

The tallest girl from the group—who had undoubtedly been volunteered as spokesperson—attempted to voice their request, which sounded very muffled through her thick scarf.

"Umm, cmmf wmmf pmmf bmmf ymmf fmmf, tmmf tbgmmf in plmmf?"

"Er…sorry, what was that? I didn't quite catch what you said," I replied.

The girl pulled her scarf down, and then she tried again. "Oh, we were wondering—could we borrow your fields to toboggan in, please?"

There was a look of great relief on the parts of their faces that could be seen, and they whooped with joy when I told them that of course they could, but to take great care that they didn't frighten Humphrey the pony, or to spook him with their sledges. I told them that if they made sure that he could see and hear them coming, he wouldn't panic.

They scurried off back home in a cloud of powdery snow and returned about twenty minutes later trailing their assorted sledges behind them, which consisted of something that looked like an old tin tray, another one was knocked up with bits of plank tied together with string, and there was an old zinc bath, a plastic dustbin lid for the smallest child, and one very posh deluxe model of a proper sledge.

As they plodded in the deep snow past the aviary, Maggie watched them go by with a look of curiosity, but when they disappeared just round the corner, he wasn't able to track their progress as the back of the aviary was built of wood and not wire mesh, thus preventing him from watching them proceed across the field, and because he couldn't see them anymore, he became somewhat frustrated, and he kept flitting back and forth across the aviary.

The children made their way to the second field where it sloped more steeply.

They had great fun that afternoon, sliding down the steep slope, trying to avoid the thick hawthorn hedge and trees at the bottom, and not always succeeding—then trudging all the way up again, pulling their sledges labouriously behind them in order to start the descent once again.

The younger ones were the first to tire themselves out, and they abandoned their sledges and attempted to build a snowman instead. The older ones didn't want to give in quite so soon, as they were obviously much stronger and were able to keep going, but eventually they too were beginning to slow down.

Later that afternoon I could hear a distant buzzing sound of something approaching. It was quite distinct, as it was unusually silent outside without the usual sounds coming from the occasional traffic on the top road.

Suddenly, a bright red helicopter appeared skimming over the trees, then veering round and circling the fields. The sharp slapping sounds could be heard coming from its rotating blades, sending out shock waves across the valley, cracking out like gunshot fire, breaking into the very core of the eerie, atmospheric silence. Then I noticed the logo of the electricity board printed on the side. They were obviously checking the power lines for any damage caused by the snowstorm, and as they passed over our house, I could see two men inside. One of them was holding a clipboard, and as they flew by they waved to me, and I waved back.

Quite an unusual event for us, as this was our first experience of snow since moving to Wales.

The snow clouds started to build up again just as it began to get dusk, and the next time I looked out of the kitchen window to see how the children were getting on, I was peering out at an empty space, devoid of all that busy exciting activity.

Humphrey had the field to himself once more.

I think he actually quite enjoyed the company after his initial gallop around the fields when they first appeared. They must have looked like aliens to him when they first arrived with their tin trays and planks of wood, causing him to bolt off at great speed across the field, kicking up his heels and sending chunks of solid snow in all directions, in defiance at this sudden invasion to his privacy. Now all was quiet and back to normal. Until the next time!

I hadn't intended to set Maggie completely free until the early spring when all the trees would be bursting into leaf and all the little creatures slowly crawling out of hibernation after their long winter's sleep—rubbing their little eyes with stiff little paws and wondering where they were, along with the dozy bumbling bumblebees and other insects, and the birds would also be starting their courtship. Many battles would be fought over territorial rights and competing for partners.

With my "good intention" still in its early production stage, I hadn't bargained for fate to deal a hand once more—in Maggie's favour!

On this particular day in question, there was a strong northerly wind blowing its way across the hills, and a ferocious blizzard swept down through the valley as winter tightened its grip—and hung on!

As I made my way to the aviary carrying Maggie's lunch in a bowl, and at the same time trying desperately to stop some of it blowing away in the wind and wishing I'd kept my thick leg-warmers instead of chucking them out, I wondered what possessed me to keep Maggie in his aviary on such dreadful days like this, and why didn't I keep him indoors during the cold weather instead?

When I opened the door, I could see Maggie standing on tiptoe on the shelf in his bedroom area. He was quite unconcerned about the awful weather, and he was reaching up to play with the icicles which had formed on one of his branches, tapping them with his beak as though he was playing a xylophone.

Just as I was about to enter with the food, an extra strong gust of wind caught the outside aviary door, and before I could pull it shut, and then open the second door, the force of the wind flung it hard back against the wire.

Maggie suddenly stopped playing with the icicles as soon as he saw his opportunity for a break, and without hesitation he flew straight past my head, through the doorway, and straight out into the blizzard, and there I was, staring out through the wire (from the inside of the aviary), watching that ungrateful black and white little horror disappear into the murk like a puff of smoke! His vibrating wings were sending flurries of powdery snow about his body. Then, like an icy curtain, the white stinging particles closed behind him, leaving just a ghostly image, and in a matter of seconds, he was gone completely from view. I cursed myself for allowing such a stupid thing to happen.

In a panic I dashed back outside of the aviary, almost tripping over the wooden door frame as I went, and yelled as loud as I could, *"Maggie!... Maggie!"* several times, but my voice was hopelessly lost to the howling wind.

Now what could I do?... I know!... The bell!... But not *his* little bell...he would never hear it in all this racket!

I rang the big ship's bell, with the word *"TITANIC"* etched on it.

It was fixed onto the wall just outside the back door and was mostly used to attract attention if anyone happened to be working at the bottom of the garden, or they could even hear it if they were half way across the field. It was normally used to call them in for lunch, or coffee, or tea breaks, or anything else that might need their attention.

It was worth a try!

Surely he could hear that?

But as I clanged it as hard as I could several times, I might just as well have sent up smoke signals for all the good it did, as the thick atmosphere only made it sound like a dull thud and not an ounce of an echo.

It was no use; I would just have to wait and hope that Maggie would eventually return.

I felt confident that his built-in radar system would kick in when his belly told him he was hungry, and birds don't usually lose themselves, although sometimes even racing pigeons have been found well off course, or they have become too exhausted to carry on and dropped in to recuperate.

I was hoping that Maggie hadn't strayed too far.

There was nothing more I could do.

My feet felt like blocks of ice, and my hands felt as though they didn't belong to me. I was fed up!...cheesed off!...gutted!—and thoroughly angry with myself, and with Maggie also. So I went thankfully back indoors to warm up and to prepare the afternoon tea.

As I kicked the soft white snow off my boots (before it could melt away into the thick coconut fibres of the backdoor mat) I was already talking myself out of returning once again into the bleak, mind-numbing coldness to search for Maggie.

All the time I was working around, I couldn't help but feel very anxious, as it would be getting dark soon.

The snowstorm and the gale had thankfully abated by late afternoon, and the pale watery winter's sun framed itself through the leafless branches of the beech trees.

Once the tea was over, I went upstairs to see if I could see any sign of Maggie from the vantage point of my parents' bedroom window.

Looking towards the west, the deep red orangey glow of the setting sun was slowly sinking on the horizon.

Just behind the stable block, I could see a small group of jackdaws heckling a couple of crows, who were quietly perching in the old beech tree. No doubt they were preparing themselves for their journey home to roost, and as they took off, I could see them winging their way towards that thin pale line of sky in the distance which links the barrier between twilight and nightfall.

In contrast to the setting sun and looking to the North, I could see the snow-capped hills were tinged blue where the sky was gradually darkening.

I could see small flocks of sheep huddled together for body warmth sheltering beneath the hedgerows which divided the lower meadows. They were finding some protection from the snow and the harsh cold wind.

Humphrey was patiently waiting at the field gate to be led into his stable for the night, where a big haynet stuffed full of hay and a nice big bowl of horse feed, together with a nice large bucket of unfrozen water, would be waiting for him, and not forgetting his nice clean bed of deep straw for him to sleep on.

My eyes were drawn toward a sudden movement just over the fence which divided the garden from the field.

Striding up and down in the patches of snow dug up by Humphrey, where he had pawed deep into the snow to reach the grass, were scavenging magpies! They were grouped together in a tight circle, busily turning over Humphrey's droppings, hoping to find some worms and big black juicy beetles.

Because I could see six of them, I assumed that they must have been the same ones I had seen earlier in the day outside of Maggie's aviary. My attention was diverted to another black and white object which had suddenly made an appearance, and it was lig-logging its way towards the circle of magpies.

The intruder appeared quite confident at joining in the fun and chatter with the other birds.

"There seems to be a stranger in the group!" I said to myself out loud.

To my utter astonishment!—Amazement!—And delight!—I wasn't looking at any old magpie who had decided to mingle with the group, but I was looking at one very familiar magpie.

And now there were seven!

It was, of course...*Maggie!*

- Chapter Six and a Half -
Over to Maggie

Troubles there are so much rarer...out of town!
(...is it a bird...or is it a plane?)

Well now! Fuss, fuss, fuss!... Oh deary, deary my!... Jibber jabber!... Cheep!... Cheep!... Shock, horror!... Thundering throttle thrushes! What a great cheese maker! Gob smacker head bender! Give me some form of respec'; I'm the best thing what's happened since the introduction of Duck'n'Orange!... Chicken'n'Chips!

I'm a much more flavoursome bird (in the non-edible sense, of course!) than most of 'em, and I certainly couldn't, shouldn't, or wouldn't go against me "future-teller piece," now could I?

"Onwards and upwards!" the magic future teller had fairly yelled out at me.

Now before me next great adventure happened, let me tell you of what crept into me sleepin' brain.

It appeared to me in a dream, and one that was quite horrible in its nature, so much so in fact that it made me intestines turn cold with fear, an' I was in danger of losing their contents therein.

I could see a giant reptile-like creature, and it was so hugely hideous! The scene behind me closed eyeballs locked itself seriously into me sleepy thoughts, an' thrown away the key. In fact, they were so seriously fixed there that it would need a "crowbar" to get me normal focus back again!

What was really truly amazin' to me was that it could actually fly! As I focused on it, I seemed to be looking at somethin' really ancient, something like a memory from the distant past, an' yet it had a familiar feel about it (in appearance that is!), an' worst of all, it was followin' me closely in a very strange manner, like a shadow, an' yet it wasn't one, 'coz I was also seein' it side-on, so it couldn't 'ave been a shadow.

I was suddenly aware of the fact that I was watchin' meself out there (or at least that's how it appeared to me), an' I was only just a few wing-flaps in front of it, yet it seemed to be followin' every move I made, but not actually attempting to gobble me up!

The *thing* was impressively huge, and it had fearsome reptile-like eyes staring out from its large head, which had a strange pointed crest at the back of it. The wings had odd-looking little hook-type claws attached to them, and when it opened its long, sharp, bright-yellow beak, it let out a bloodcurdling *"AARK!... AARK!... AARK!"* which pierced the air, an' also me ear drums!

When I dived down, *IT* dived down! When I soared back up, *IT* soared back up! Just about every move I made, so did *IT*! And its slow wing-beats made an impressive *WHOOM!... WHOOM!... WHOOM!* sound, but most of the time, *IT* just glided.

We flew over high mountains, and at the top of one of them I could see flames and thick smoke rising, and in the air was a thick acrid smell of sulphur.

Leaving the mountain range, we dipped down towards the shoreline and then sharply swooped back inland. Then we glided over vast lakes, where strange looking lizard-type creatures were drinking and wading at the edge, and they looked up at us as we passed overhead.

"AARK!... AARK!... AARK!" went the reptile once more as we swooped over swamplands, and then over the hot steamy earth where bubbles rose up, *pop!... pop!... popping!*

Looming up in front I could see a huge area of forests where I could hear strange noises, like loud roaring and really terrible shrieking noises, which grew louder as we approached.

As we got nearer to the treetops, I could see a mist approaching, and I began to fear the worst. I was worried about getting myself lost in this evil, supernatural land of lizards and other strange creatures!

When I looked behind me at me flying companion, it appeared to be catching up with me, with its great gawping beak open, as though it was going to devour me!

Then a very frightening thing happened.

The scales on the creature dropped off, and they floated down towards the earth. At almost the same instant, I could see some feathers suddenly start to sprout on its body, and they were black and white, just like mine!—and then these too suddenly dropped off and drifted down!

Suddenly, its huge body seemed to disintegrate in a puff of smoke, like magic, leaving me still flying, but alone and intact except for a few feathers which I'd shed in my panic to get away.

As I fled from the scene, I found that I was becoming engulfed in pelting scales and feathers, and as I tried to battle my way through the swirling mass, I found that although my wings were flapping like fury, I wasn't moving at all, not even a feather's breadth, and as I could still smell the fumes of sulphur in me nostrils, I could feel myself *choking!... choking!... choking!*

By now me feathers were a-shakin', and me quills were a-tinglin' with fear as I thought that this was it! I was surely going to die!

I was rightly glad when a sudden loud noise outside me boudoir woke me up, and I felt meself transported right back to the real world! Thank goodness!

To me knowledge, I knew nothing about this creature, so did me ancestors neglect to hand down the "legend" about this one, and if so, *why?* Or am I just a mixed-up bird having an awfully bad dream? Or was it from an "explosive eggshell" from the past? Then maybe it was yet another omen warning me of perhaps good or bad things to come!

I didn't open me eyes straight away, in case the "thing" was still there! But when I heard a familiar voice followed closely by a *clang!* then I knew for sure that it was Pinky Ma opening up that troublesome trapdoor thing so's I can make me way out to stretch me wings and then have a good look round to see what I can find.

Oh goody, goody!

Freedom here I come!

Since that tiresomely big migration I had to endure not long ago, regardless of whether I wanted to go on one or not, things were just beginnin' to look up, and so here we all are on this great big reservation with a limitless boundary stretching out as far as I could see, and at last I woz given a much more interestin' roostin' place, and it woz all for me!

It was about time for me to get out there and explore to find things to do so's to improve me status in life. An' it really bugs me that what I could really do with right this minute is a good old fashioned ant bath! Just a few squirts of ant juice under my wings would make me feel almost as good as new!

I was allowed some prime time after the daylight hours had faded outside, and given the flying space in this one big area, which was a mighty big step in the right direction.

It was that big hole in the wall ("doorway") that still eluded me, an' I woz just waiting for the opportunity for someone to forget to place that great wooden plank ("door") in front of it, but I did manage to find one or two mini-breaks (which only lasted a very short time) before I was captured again and then plonked back into me klakki.

However, there was one consolation, because from where I was perched, I was able to watch a tiny tee vee which was conveniently placed nearby.

I've become a bit of a "tee vee fanatic' (I think that's what you call it!) where I'm learnin' a lot of new words and things; in fact, I'm studying the three "L's!": Look!... Listen!... Learn!

From this little bit of learning, I eventually was able to place words to the objects in the way of the pinkies (I mean "humans"), and therefore I shall have to show my cleverness, by the way of this new speech.

For instance—they seem to end their long words with "g's" and "d's" an' (Oops!... There goes a bit of a slip of the beak already!) I should say: "a" "n" "d"—*and!*

Well, for most of the time I can manage it quite nicely thank you, and then I goes...er...I mean *go!* and forget it all over again.

Anyway, getting back to the escapade bits again. I wasn't going to give in just like that, at least not without running rings round everyone first. So when they wanted to put me back into *my cage* (do I get extra points for calling it *"my cage"* instead of *"me klakki"*?) I refused to be caught, and just when they were about to grab me up, I would take off out of reach and fly up onto a perching place where they couldn't even grab me by the tail.

Sometimes I would run wildly between, under, or through their sitting chairs and their eating tables (now aren't you all impressed with me newfound vocab, or what?), and they all got very angry at this, which thrilled me to bits I don't mind telling you! But they had just one trick to play on me which I didn't regard as fair: not at all I might add!

One of the pinkies would shout a command to another, something like "lights off!", then someone else would click off a switch and we would all end up in darkness. For poor old me, that was the end of my game, because somebody would shuffle about in the dark to find where I was hiding and grab hold of me, then joyfully shout out, "Got him!... Lights on again!" Then the nasty dazzlin' light would flicker on once more, like flashes of lightning. All unnatural in my opinion, and painful to the eyes I might add! Then I would be plonked back inside the cage again, with the cloth thingamy thrown over the top in order to keep me quiet, and me little door was then made shut tight as it was fastened with a *clang!*

Never mind, I'll show 'em what's what and who's who!

Before I made me spectacular move, there was a bit of a buzz in the air, and I could feel it!

I think that something pretty exciting was going to take place, and it concerned me—or so I thought!

It started one particular sundown time, when a strange human man with a fuzzy red beard and eyes with glass attachments to both of them, which had me wondering as to what went on behind those "globby glasses"—I was thinking, *Do they magnify his true intentions, or are they hiding a hint of evil?* But just a minute, what's that grotesquely ugly black and white thing I can see moving back and forth in them? Oh!... Huh!... It's only me own reflection...hee! hee! hee!

Well now, I hope you are duly impressed with my description of this "human man" which is much better than sayin', "There was this Pinky feller with strange hairy stuff growing on his face," etc. etc. So long drawn out and *yuky*, don't you think?

Anyway, he was brought in to look at me (which was a bit annoying 'coz I'd already settled down to sleep), and they were all looking at me in a very important way, talking to me, and also an awful lot *about* me.

The "man" had got bits of paper in his hand on which he was scrawling lots of strange looking squiggles and lines I hadn't seen before. He then left after moon-rise, but returned some days later.

He stayed outside, where he seemed to be making lots and lots of loud noises, like *clincking, clancking,* and *banging!* And from my cage, I could see a strange round machine into which this man was chucking in lots of stones, then powdery stuff, followed by water, and all the while this big drum thing was *whirring* and *churning* about, kicking up quite a din, and making me nervous system structurally unsound!

After a few days of this entertainment, he was gone and didn't return, and now I was getting somewot bored with nothing to do.

Now my opportunity for the great escape came one day, when some kind person forgot to close up the hole in the wall, and a bit of a draft blew the door open, just wide enough to leave a good size gap, and just right for me to flit through it with no special effort at all.

My future-telling piece was showing me that this is what I should do, for when I looked at it, after Ma put it back in my klak...I mean *cage!*—both of the wandy bits were pointing upwards, which was definitely a sign!

Nobody about, so off I goes!

Amazin' that nobody spotted me on the way.

It seemed to be quiet everywhere, which meant it would be much easier for me to look around without being noticed, and I could get on with my hunting without being disturbed.

I tried a few of the lower floor open spaces, but nothing of great interest there, at least nothing really new to me that took my fancy, so I hastily flew upwards.

Now this is where it got more seriously interesting.

I thought I would start with the furthest room to see if I could find something to either collect, or things to be sorted out and rearranged in a different order. It always looks so much more artistic and quite wonderful when I've finished the task, and it should really be appreciated after all the effort I put into me work But nearly always this isn't the case, and I'm *cursed* and *scolded* unmercifully, which then makes me crosser and crosser, and one of these days I will show them just how cross I can really get when crossed! Anyway, I found lots of pretty things that were put in such silly places, so I changed them over to where they should have been, and after I had done it, it looked ever so much better, and I felt very pleased with myself.

Next stop was a very small room which was much too small for my liking, and it didn't look at all cosy, but I did see a nice roll of soft paper which was attached to a metal thing on the wall, right next to an automatic fountain which gushes out lots of water whenever someone pushes a strange metal handle. I wanted some of that rolled-up paper, because it would make a nice comfortable nest in me klakki, but when I tried to peck some off, it just kept coming and coming and coming, 'till I got fed up and decided the best thing what I could do woz to shred it all up and then gather it in a nice heap to take back to me klakki. But then I realized that if I did that, there wouldn't be room left in me beak to take anything else perhaps better than this ol' paper, so I left it there. But before I left that room, I spotted what looked like a very interesting long tube, and I was rather hoping that there might be something really tasty inside, so I pecked a few holes in it only to find some very un-tasty white stuff inside, so I left that too. No matter!

Then I found a room that was really full of wondrous things! I could hardly contain me joy at hittin' the jackpot, and I let out a few choruses of: YES! OH YES! OH YES! YIPPEE!

There, right before me very eyes, were all these many-coloured stones. Bright shiny things, little china box things with easy-to-remove lids on them, and a long gold chain with a round gold disk hanging on it. I thought that this would look very nice indeed, all nice and shiny, and dangling on one of me perches. There were more tiny pretty things what I've seen Pinky Ma stick into holes in her ears. They would look even prettier in me klakki.

Oh glory be! Where do I start?

The biggest find yet!

All this little lot I'd so cleverly found could make me very own highly personal hoard *so* much bigger, and all in one fowl swoop! But which should I choose first? Lucky dip or what!?

Where on this earth did the pinkies find all this highly precious stuff? There must've been one hell of a raid to have found all this little lot for themselves!

Well, here goes anyway!

Gotta start somewhere!

Now let me see—oh yes!—wot have we here then?

Right in front of me was this little golden circlet, and stuck in the middle of it was this absolutely fabulous sparkling stonelet, which I *knew* I just had to have.

Oh so precious!—and any minute now, it was going to be mine—*all mine*!

I pounced onto the large wooden-topped piece of furniture, where bits-and-bobs are kept and where this piece of treasure was so conveniently left, so naturally I grabbed it up.

Then just as I was making my way off with me lovely loot, I was suddenly aware that I was being watched by these big, round, staring eyes—all ten of 'em, watching me every move.

I noticed there was something very strange about them, which made me quills stand all on end.

There was a sort of un-lifelike vibe about them. They just sort of sat there all rigid and unblinking, and just gawping straight at me.

When I bobbed and flicked me tail and wings at them (as is the magpie's usual custom of a greetings, aggression, or acknowledgement) they didn't even flinch or bob and bow back!

Very rude! I thought at the time.

So now was the time to have a quick vote with me brain! *Shall I? Shan't I?—Flee or fly?—Attack or retreat?*

Now I'm not one to go into a wrestling match with me conscience, owin' to the fact that I don't seem to have one, it wouldn't be of much use to me anyway, so it was the ultimate and instant decision: *Shall!....Fly!....Attack!*—that won the vote!

I can just *feel* it in me groin, now that me ammunition section is full, and I'm now ready for action!

"So let's go!—*Fly, bird, fly!*"

So looking them straight in the eye, I said to them:

> *Touchy!... Feely!... Pecky!... Squealy!*
> *Let me beak do a rrrrappy!... Tappy!... Mealy!*
> *Egg on your faces,*
> *feathers in your ears,*
> *me beak on your fury feet,*
> *brings your eyes to tears!*

Absolutely no reaction at all! Those dummy dudes just sat there with a fixed stare, and their eyes all dull and lifeless looking, not shiny and reflective, so you couldn't read their mood in them.

They seemed to be all stiff and not moving at all, and they didn't appear to be breathing either. Sort of not alive, yet at the same time, not dead either!

"I'll see if I can alter their present condition," I said to meself, but also in the hope that they might hear me.

I wanted to see if I could put a bit of real life into the situation! Spark them up a bit!

So what I did next, was to use me "cool-cat" karate moves, which worked a real treat in the past, as you already know! But first, I did give them a fair warning of what I was about to practice on them, so I said, "I'm about to convert your crutch into a crepe Suzette! Modify your brains to brunch! And your stony-looking eyes into mushy peas!"

No resistance at all, which was fine by me, so I just got on with me conversions as promised!

Now at the very beginning I thought they were just sitting there to guard the goodies, but now I'm inclined to think they must be little Gods or something, and put there just for them pinkies to worship!

Anyway, after I'd completed me good work, they looked much better, and much more practical-like!

I'd hardly rounded off me task and set everything all neat looking when I had that feelin' I'd been rumbled.

Radar alert! "Er what was down there, is now up 'ere an' creating me one almighty load of angst, and for no good reason at all!

Oh glory be! — 'ere she comes, 'er old wobbly throat's all vibratin' away, an' 'er cake 'ole moving up an' down, up an' down, nonstop screech an' booms issuing forth! An' all of it aimed at little ol' innocent me!

I woz all of a tizz, and just couldn't string me words together all proper like! She gave me such a fright!

What have I done to deserve such an earth moving confrontation, especially after all this good work what I've done, I felt all a-flusstery and bothery!

Anyhow, I woz just gonna get me that nice shiny thingy what I first saw, and I knew I must have it, if it's the last thing I do!

It wasn't the last thing I did!

To be quite frank and truthful, things did get even betterer!

Oh great joy and utter bliss!

This woz oh-so-forever real!

Like "red moon glow in a fog."

Me very own bachelor's pad!

I woz to have for me very own use (and mine alone) a big beautiful bird bunkhouse for me to stretch me wings in, and to do a bit of a feather-cleansing and bathing (now and then) and without any unnecessary interruptions I could do me bit of rummaging in perfect peace, and above all, to partake in the daily deliveries of the much anticipated beak-watering buffets!

On this eventful sunlight-time itself (which I cannot say with an ounce of truth that they chose the best of weathers, but as they're only human, they cannot be expected to be gifted with the same natural senses what we birds have), I was getting quite excited about these new airwaves I seemed to be picking up in the strong wind that was blowing through and over me feathers.

There was much out there that I would just have to be checking out — later on. But before reaching my bird palace, I was subjected to a bit of a fright.

Now I'm not usually one to submit myself, or even to own up to, any self-induced danger, but when it amounts to being introduced in direct firing range of a fire-breathing monster, then that's just what happened to me!

This dragon-type head suddenly appeared over the top of what looked like a giant-sized hutch, just as we reached it, and then it put it's head down towards me, and I thought it was about to bite me in half, but instead there was this loud snorting sound followed by what looked like smoke pouring from its huge gaping nostrils, and I'm sure I could see a flicker of flames in its eyes, but that could have been a reflection from Ma's red coat. Yes, maybe that's what it was (I hope!).

Just as we passed by the big hutch, it opened its mouth, and you could see these great big white things, what looked like bone-crunching, muscle-grinding, feather-shredding gnashers!

If I'd been a female fertilized Magpie, I would have just had a miscarriage and fired the whole clutch of eggs straight to the bottom of me cage—*splat! splat! splat! splat! splat!*

It was the most terrifying creature I had ever yet encountered (in real life that is) before, but I didn't want the "big black beastie" to think that I was a measly little coward and lacked in courage, even if I did lack in size!

I belted out just as loud as I could an almighty battle cry of *NAARK!*... *NAARK!*... *NARK!* which seemed to have little impact, I fear.

Never mind, at least I was still alive, and it didn't seem to want to kill or eat me, which was a big relief, I can tell you.

I must admit, I had seen these creatures on tee vee a long time ago, but I didn't know they were really *that* big and *that* hairy, and snorting fire and brimstone all over the place like that, and I had no idea there was to be a real one right in my back yard!

Much later on, I found out that it was some sort of servant of me Ma, and she would sit on its back, ride it all about, and it would do just what she wanted it to do, so then I knew it would not pose a threat to me at all; in fact, it might even be an asset to me at some point in time!

I decided that one day I was going to acquaint myself to this "oh so obedient one," and then I would be able to use it to me own advantage as well, but that would be in the future.

I was quite happy with my new daily routine, where I could mess and potter about undisturbed, finding places to keep me bits and pieces. Wot-nots here, me dojamaflips there, and me thingamybobs over there, and me wochamacallits can go under there!

I was taken out to me new pad every new sunlight-time, when the airwaves promised interesting moments, and lots of grub to be placed in front of me. And then I was taken back into the pinkie's klakki when sunlight-time left us for the sundown time, but just before the sun was all wrapped up and gone, and the moon begins to show itself.

It was the new sights and sounds from outside which encouraged me to plan very cunningly and carefully a well thought out strategy of my next great escape!

I just wanted to be out there to mix and blend with the elements, just as me ancestors had done. I could feel a "destiny" thing coming on pretty damn strong! But at the same time, I didn't want to cut the cord with this human attachment thing either. So I suppose you could say that I wanted the best of both worlds. I wanted me cake, and eat it too! — as is the new custom now authorized by none other than me!

It wasn't long before great numbers of the freckly and very noisy nomads, or otherwise known as "the flashy gypsy fellers of the air," suddenly swooped down from the sky.

A right greedy lot they are too!

The starlings had arrived!

They ponced about, up and down, back and forth, to and fro, as though they owned the place, flashing away their sparkling greeny, blacky, feathers!

"Hey you lot!" I called out, "Where do you think you're coming from, or going to then, without a bye or leave already?"

"Who asks?" snapped one of them.

"Well I do, of course!" I replied.

The enquirer comes goose-stepping over to me palace, and looks up at where I'm perched on the top branch looking down on the rowdy mob.

"Listen, me ol' flutter-by," he continued, "we come from here, we come from there, and we come from just about everywhere! We come from near and far, East and West, North and South! That's where!"

"Um...what's 'flutter-by'?" I asked reasonably.

"It means magpie, of course!" he answered leeringly. Then he continued more seriously. "I woz hatched in a place called 'Lunon,' me old mince-pie!" he said.

I thought it best not to ask him what "mince-pie" meant (maybe it means "pie-in-the-sky"!), it sounded a bit too hostile and meaningful to me, it was the "pie" bit that bothered me, so I just didn't ask.

"First of all, I'll introduce myself," he said, "I am Vice Admiral Cosimasivendavich, or you can call me 'Cosi' for short if you like, and my title is 'Grand Order of the Bird Watch,' but seeing as we haven't much time to waste, me old ducks, I'll introduce you to just some of the lads and lasses of the squad.

"Now then, you might well be overwhelmed by our impressive titles, but we are a peace abiding lot, and don't have call to pick fights like gladiators, not with anyone, although we do sometimes have a bit of a squabble, but nothing serious. It's just that we have to keep our group in good order, so as to survive, particularly if we're to make such long, wing-breaking journeys, and have to watch our backs against enemies such as hawks, trappers, and humans with guns! So you see, our names are divided up into two parts, and one part is taken from where we were hatched, and the other is from either our egg maker or egg layer's names as well!"

With that, he called a section of the group over for me to see.

"Step forward sharp!" he called to the first one who hopped forward smartly.

"Now this is Squadron Leader Abawabajubii, or 'Abbi' for short, he's in charge of leading and steering in front of the formation.

"Next!

"Now here we have Field Marshall Tumawumajumbalic, or 'Tummi' for short, and he's the one who gives the signal for everyone to take off simultaneously.

"Now this is Group Captain Big Belly Bird Battle Rattle, and it's his job to keep everyone in tight formation, and giving orders if anyone strays or veers off in the wrong direction.

"Right over there in the distance and the one on his own, but now making his way towards us, is Flatulence Florentino, who gives a wind check every twenty paces, or after fifty or so wing-flaps, so that when we're flying, we can adjust our air speed accordingly—oops!... Oh cor blimey!... There goes another wind check again!... Right on time!

"Here we have Rear Admiral Popodopolopolus, or 'Pop' for short, and behind him we have Air Marshall Svenslingerhook, or 'Veni' for short, and Petty Officer Bolinotollino, or 'Bolli' for short, with his first hatchling, and just recruited is Corporal Bolinatala, or 'Balla' for short."

Cosi then walked briskly on to the next row, and said, "On this side we have Sergeant Major Spreantoniosuperbus, or 'Spanner' for short, who keeps the younger ones in order, and then next to him is Commodore Palladingonzalus, or 'Palli' for short, and he checks the weather conditions well before flights across the oceans, and on the left of him is Brigadier Fergusastilbiosus, or 'Fergus' for short, and on the right of him is Colonel Zorokrackatier or 'Zoro' for short, and he lines everybody up, ready for inspection, and making sure that they always keep their flight feathers trim and clean. Then the one just striding over here towards us is Rear Guardsman Montithatchalikoluck, or 'Monti' for short, who watches out for any dangers approaching from behind."

Cosi then walked on to the next row and continued with his long list of names.

"Over there is Private Shufflestone, and beside him is the Chief Scout Chitterchatter, who keeps an eye out for any danger whilst we are on the ground, because that's when we are at our most vulnerable for one of us to be caught by Chiselbeak the sparrowhawk, or Bluskaa the peregrine falcon, or any other hawkish predators that might be out hunting!

"Now then, right next to Chitterchatter is Tracker Troylon, whose job is to spot the best feeding zones, like fields and farms with a lot of grain for us all to feed on, or the best areas for slugs and leatherjacket grubs.

"Then right at the back, keeping the younger flock in some kind of order, is Constable Bulgarlongarchadwick, or 'Bulli' for short.

"And last, but not least, is Sapper Singasongolomio, or 'Singgi' for short, who keeps us all cheerful with his singing of some of our favourite songs, which he will sing to you just before we leave.

"Now the rest of the group is made up of our egg layers, and the one in the middle of that small group over there, the egg layer with the extra bright shiny feathers, she is me mate Harlequin, who nearly got shot last season by a human, but Spindleburtontottletown, or 'Spindletown' for short, who's only just been promoted to Brigadier General, happened to be flying in the wrong flight path at the wrong time, got hit instead, poor old geezer, and so the last we ever saw of him was just a mass of feathers floating down to earth! But at least I still have my precious Harlequin!

"The other members of the flock are called Chatterlingers, and they are sometimes members from another group who just wish to join us.

"The others are late hatchlings from last year, and their given names are usually much shorter.

"Oh!… There is just one other thing I didn't mention, we all come under the code of the 'Colour Troup' and we all have our own 'Spirit Guide' in the form of an eagle, depending on your colour code. So let me explain this to you.

"Those who hail from the South (such as I) are white, and our spirit guide is the 'White Crane,' and those from the North are red, and their guide is the 'Bald Eagle,' and those from the East are yellow, and have the 'Brown Eagle,' and from the West they are black, and have the 'Black Eagle.'

"There you have our colour codes which makes it easier for us to identify one another when we all group together in one huge mass, or 'murmeration' as it's sometimes called, when we 'group and troupe the colour!'

"When we die, our spirit form is fetched by our spirit guide at the sound of a howling wolf, or the bark of a dog fox on a full moon, and then it passes through the 'Eye of the Tiger.'

"If you want to know more about the 'Eye of the Tiger,' you will have to ask Hootie! He will tell you!

"Now we don't have the time to hang around much longer for me to go through all the rest of their names, so in a minute we'll show you some of our smart moves, and a great presentation of formation flying! But first of all, what's *your* name, mate?" he asked.

After he'd rattled off all these names at the speed of spitting out cherry stones, me tongue got stuck in me beak, and for a few moments I just couldn't talk!

"I had to think fast, on account of not wanting to be overtaken by a 'verbal diarrhoea' contest, so I was wondering how was I going to impress this brightly speckled outfit of well-turned-out "star performers of the skies!"

Then I had a sudden inspiration, I replied, "I was hatched in a very select klakki area, and from a very aristocratic line of magpies, and they named me (and this I had to think up much quicker than I could say it!) Maggi-wagi-tabi-sabi-rabi-lianagalic! But you can call me Maggie for short, if you like!"

And so sure enough, I was indeed serenaded by Sapper Singasongolomio, as he perched himself on top of the cherry tree, and he trilled away merrily with his wonderfully sung song—whilst his chums and chumettes strode busily up and down, picking off good beakfulls of nice fresh juicy slugs, swiping them back and forth (in much the same ritual as used by the blackbirds) because, as they sez: "This tenderizes 'em and makes 'em much easier to go down the gullet!" And then the starlings continued to dig deep down into the earth to prise out the nice crackly, crunchy leatherjackets.

After their grand old feasty, they all took off in a fair old...*whoosh!*

As they circled overhead, they formed a great diamond shaped pattern, which then changed to what looked like one of those very fast, very loud, and very low-flying metal aereoplanes what I've been seeing just lately, and as they passed overhead, I heard one of them call out, *"United we fly!—divided we fall!"*

And then they called out their farewells:

"Achtung! achtung! mon ami!"

"Allez vous...cosi van tutti...isn't it already?"

"Bon journo mein Herr, und was is das sehr alten schtarling proverb?... Ah yes!... 'May you live in sehr interesting times!'—nicht wahr?"

"Ciao, ciao bwana!—get your kicks from route sixty-six!"

"Kalinka rules, okay comrades!"

"We'll meet again, amigo...dunno where, dunno when!"

"Tally ho!... Uniamo!—und adios pomme bastard!"

"Watch out!... Bandits at two o'clock!"

"Don't be daft!... We *are* the bandits!... And it's three o'clock already!"

"Turn to the left!"

"No!... Turn to the right!"

"Go towards the sun!"

"No!... Go towards the moon!"

"Fare thee well, my gallant knight!"

And then I heard the last one call out, "Ta ta, sweetie!"

Having bid their fond farewells, the black swirling mass rose up as one, into the air. But before they finally disappeared, they cleverly weaved many moving pictures in the sky.

In a cluster of arrow-shaped bodies of feathers and wings, they dipped and dived.

They made a picture of a cascading weeping willow, as though it was waving about in the wind, and then it changed into the ocean waves ebbing and flowing, and then the picture altered again, as they twisted and turned into the form of a great long writhing snakelike creature, with a massive horned-head, and I wasn't sure what it really woz or even what it meant!

"What's that last picture you did?" I shouted up to them.

And they called back, "This one is just for you—and it's a land monster!"

And they flew off in a spectacular formation, which created a picture of a great iron klakki (or a plane), and then they were gone, leaving an empty space once more in the sky!

Truly wonderful, and what stars they are, so very cosmic! I thought to meself, looking on with great admiration, and all misty-eyed.

Finally, here is Sapper Singasongolomio's song:

> *Churr! Churr! Churr!*
> *We sing, tra la, tra la,*
> *We travel near and far,*
> *With a nod and a wink*
> *Lets go for a drink,*
> *Where the river shines like a star.*
>
> *Our feathers brightly gleam,*
> *And we keep them oh so clean,*
> *As they glisten in the sun.*
> *When we flock each night,*
> *It's such a sight,*
> *When the day is almost done.*
>
> *There's not a slug or a bug,*
> *That can feel so jolly smug,*

As we pick them off the ground,
We chatter and cheep,
As we dig down deep,
It's quite a happy sound.

The name of the game is fun,
But we don't trust a man with a gun,
If we do see one…give a cheer!
Then all of us just disappear,
And go back the way we had come!

Soaring gloriously high,
Up high in the sky, again,
Swooping gracefully down,
Down to the ground, again,
Our wings beating fast with the rays of the sun,
We can swiftly outpace the man with a gun.

We love our food, but can be very rude,
As we bicker and fight,
If we think we are right,
Our beaks are so strong,
Although thin and long,
We sing our song.

Tra la, tra la,
Churr! Churr! Churr!—Ding Dong!

My presence had not gone unnoticed by others of my kind (magpies, that is), which didn't surprise me, as I'd already heard their strange mutterings and their quick movements as they scuffled about in the tall trees which hung over my abode. So when the "hatch! scratch! and dispatch!" brigade did finally make their own presence known to me, I was good and ready for them.

301

They arrived swiftly, but not altogether noiselessly, in much the same manner that I would have done if I'd been the one in their situation.

I am sure they would have noticed by now that I was not living and flying free like they were, and so they could see me within, therein and thereon, whilst they were on the outside of where I lived, so they were without, therefore, thereof!

Better play it cool, I thought to meself, *so as to "test the waters!" as you might say.*

I started to sing sweetly, in a very nonchalant manner.

"Cry me a river!" I warbled, and "Don't let the sun go down without a fight!" and then "Fly me to the moon!" I trilled, then rounded off with a resounding "La-di-da-di-da!" which I repeated three times backwards, and at the same time I pretended not to see them.

I think they were rightly impressed with my fearless manner and beautiful voice.

The first one to introduce himself was the biggest and most aggressive one from the mob.

He did a fair bit of bobbing, swaggering and mincing up and down. And then he approached just a few hops away from where I was perched on the inside of the wire separating us, which can always be a bit of a tricky situation, owing to the fact that to other magpies, it probably looked as though I had been brutally trapped, making them all feel insecure and vulnerable.

The big magpie looked to me as though he was the elder, and probably the "Featherhead," which means he is head of the 'Magpie State'.

The Featherhead always commands the highest and deepest respect from his group; therefore, any outsiders are well advised to take great care not to offend such high authority!

He introduced himself first, and standing very upright and haughty looking, he started off with the usual traditional greetings used when first meeting a stranger. So he began, "*Kek!... Kek!... Kek!*.... May the air flow freely with you, and the sun shine at your back!"

And I correctly replied, "And at yours!"

An then he continued, "May all your droppings be big and bold!"

"And yours!" I smoothly answered.

And then he followed on with, "And may your days not be numbered when the crows fly above you!"

"And not yours too!" I said, hoping I had responded correctly.

And he chanted on, "To grab and to hold!"

Now at this precise point I almost broke jubilantly into song with my responses, as I grew more and more confident. So then I chanted back, "The sick and the weary!"

He then chanted, "The weak and the poorly!"

I chanted, "The strong and the bold!"

And then he finished off with, "And may your farts be strong enough to light up your inner spirit!"

"And up yours!" I replied exuberantly.

I think I had passed the first test, because he then said on a much lighter note, "I am called Featherhead White Wings, and this," he said turning his beak towards a very nicely marked, and elegantly serene looking egg layer (*I wouldn't mind ruffling her feathers any day!* I thought to meself), "This is me mate, Holly, first hatchling of Ivy the Great!"

Great what? I thought, and then he proceeded with his grand introduction.

"And these are my last season's hatchlets, which is a term used when you are hatched out one season ago. They will tell you for themselves what they are called. So, come!… Come forward now!"

He ushered the others forward so that I could see them more clearly.

Two of them stepped obediently towards me, and the first one said, "I am Tizzy!" and the other one said, "I am Gizzy!" and then the other two came over, bouncing with a bit more confidence, and the first one of these two said, "I am Lotty!" and the other one said, "I am Totty!"

"Oh!" I replied, "And I am….!"—but before I could introduce myself, there was a noise of a door banging from the big house—and they all flew off!

My big lucky break came in the form of large flakes of soft white rain, which fell down as though somebody woz emptying a cartload of white feathers, and it seemed to make a soft whispering sound as it was drifting slowly down.

It wasn't long before everything got all covered over with the stuff.

On the first sunlight-time of the white fall, a flock of tiny pinkies turned up with bits of odd looking wooden contraptions, which they promptly threw themselves on, and it looked to me as though they wanted to commit suicide by hurtling down the sloping earth, head first!

They kept on doing the same thing, over and over again, I suppose because it didn't seem to kill them the first time, so they just had to keep trying!

Mad little buggers! I thought to meself.

It was then that I suddenly remembered about poor mad old Moonbeam!

But it was on the second sunlight-time of the earth-whitening rain, that I was given the chance to make an exit.

It seemed to be way past me first food fill-up time, and I was beginning to get that hungry feeling, and started to fret about whether me grub was going to turn up before me bones started to show through me feathers, and me stomach would fall out, owing to the fact there wouldn't be anything there to keep it in!

From out of the whiteness I could just make out the dark shape of me pinky ma, and she was stomping along towards me carrying my dish of food stuffs.

She was having a job to reach me, owing to the fact that a gusting bit of wind was blowing at the same time!

It was a sudden gust of that wind that became my friend and my ally!

It threw back the wooden hole filler (I mean door!), and that was it!

All thoughts of fuelling up me belly became not so important just now. And before you could say "Jack Daw," I was off!

I was now out in that swirling white mass!

At last!—I'm free once more!

The soft falling white stuff was in front of me, behind me, and on all sides of me.

I whooshed upwards, and the wind blew me sideways, but I was all the more determined to check out this new flying zone.

I made me way towards the dark outlines of the tall trees in front of me, at least these would give me cover if I needed them.

Suddenly, just above me, there appeared the dark shape of two birds flying in the same direction that I was going in.

I wasn't quite sure at first what they were, but as they zoomed down a bit closer, I could see that they were crows!

As the wind was *definitely* blowing freely, but the sun was *definitely* not shining from the back of me, and remembering vividly the words of Featherhead White Wings, I guardedly called out to them, "Er...good morrow to you, your sereneshipnesses!... My good fellow flyers!... Um... Are you flying above my?... And going the same way as wot I am going?... By any chances?"

And before they zapped off into the murk, they replied in their harsh croaky voices, sharp enough to knock the spots off sparrow's eggs, "No!... Idiot...but he is!"

And it was then that I experienced the chilling sensations as I suddenly realized that I was being tracked by—*a sparrowhawk!*—*Yoiks!*

Having eliminated some of the "big black-and-white bold stuff" (caused by me uncontrollable fear I might add), I knew that I had to act with great speed if me head was to stay attached to me body, and me stomach and heart were going to remain attached to me other remainin' bits, so I dropped back down to earth like a stone, and straight into some bramble bushes, where I knew he would have difficulty in reaching me.

Me old heart woz pumping away double time, and I could just see the hawk hovering above me, with his wings just barely trembling. And then he skimmed off!

I remained still and quiet for some time, until I thought it was safe enough to venture out.

Keeping close to the edge of the brambles and hedgerow for protection, if I needed it, I decided to explore my new surroundings, so that I could eventually claim my own boundary and flight path, as well as the most important commodity of all—the field canteen!

This white rain which had covered the earth everywhere was really something else, especially to walk on. It was oh so soft and tingly to the feet, but not especially appetizing to eat. Then I found something else that was quite remarkable about it.

As I walked towards the bottom of the slope, I could see these strange markings. Some of them were in neat rows, others were side-by-side, some criss-crossed, whilst some of them looked as though they had been dragged, and were of different shapes and sizes, and all of them were spread across the top of the white earth.

Then, when I turned back to inspect something I needed to check out, I suddenly realized that it woz *me* making these strange markings as well!

They were me own footprints! But I wasn't too sure who owned these other ones!

Spooky! me thinks, and judging by the size of some of them, I don't think I want to find out who (or what) owns 'em!

Strange noises coming from beneath me feet on the ground were beginning to get quite interesting. If I stood very still and listened hard, with me 'ead bent near to the ground, then underneath this white canopy, I could hear lots of strange sounds.

There woz a very soft shooshing, and also grinding, crunching, munching noises!

Thorn the Thrush had once told me that this sort of sound was made by worms, and they made it as they gulched and regurgitated in the earth, just below the surface, and that's how he knew just where the worm was for him to dig his beak in and pull it out, and I'm sure I heard one burp!

And then a bit further on, but not far from where the worms were having their lunch, I could hear another almost similar sound.

This time the sound was a bit louder, and seemed to be a lot more frenzied in its content of effects!

There was more of a scrunching, crunching and a gurgly, soggy sort of noise to go with it, and then another very odd thing happened.

Right before me very eyes I saw the earth in front of me heave up, just like an erupting volcano, and a funny little whiskery head appeared just above the surface. It had a long thin snout. It woz a funny little bib-snot snout, but not much in the way of eyes, and it had strange little flappy feet. Then, before I could really investigate as to what it woz, it suddenly vanished!

I wonder what that woz then?

Other sounds below the ground were very strange indeed.

There were sort of low rumblings, and I could also hear the sound of running water. I must find out what's making these!

I woz finding exciting things by the minute!

There were these big round steaming heaps that were definitely worth a close investigation, as there were some interesting sounds of activity going on somewhere inside.

As I expertly turned them over, they broke up into smaller bits, and lo and behold!... It was teeming with living, squirming things, like little juicy red worms, beetles, and other such goodies!

I'd just discovered very fresh free-range—an' very much alive!—*lunch*!

Having tasted my very first, very fresh but lively feast, I decided it woz time to test the air.

All seemed to be clear, so I took off and circled above the white earth.

The white stuff had stopped falling, the wind had dropped, and it woz so much clearer to see the surrounding earth.

It looked very strange, not just because it woz all covered in white, but that it seemed to be so much more open than from the other place we used to live.

There were many more hedges and trees (great for hunting and klakki building in), and the earth seemed to swell up and down.

It was then that I realized I was actually seeing real hills! Just like the ones I've seen on the tee vee. And the ones in my dreams!

The concrete pathways that the humans do their travelling on are much more twisty and bendy here, and much narrower.

The human dwelling places seemed to be much further apart and not all bunched together like an over-stocked rookery.

Most of the dwellings had smoke pouring out of the tops of them, but I couldn't see any flames. Perhaps they are practising some kind of ritual or something!

Looking down, I could see me own familiar territory, with me palace and Ma's place right near it, so I didn't want to go too far just yet!

I doubled back towards the point of where I had my lunch.

I drifted carefully down and landed close to a hawthorn hedge.

Out in the space where I had turned over the hot and steaming food-bearing lumps, I could see the familiar markings of Featherhead White Wings and his kin!

– Chapter Seven –
For Better or for Worse!

With Christmas celebrations now over, and the usual New Year's resolutions already forgotten and broken, spring still seemed such a long way off.

There was still much to be done, and plans were now well under way for a good-sized brick-built shed, and also a big double garage to be constructed. But before the shed and garage could be dealt with, another important issue cropped up.

Reality struck home after I received a long call from my solicitor requesting that I go and see him at his office.

I had to face up to the fact that the awful personal notes and statements for the divorce proceedings were long overdue, and they still needed to be written down. I couldn't put it off for too much longer, and also the final settlement would have to be painstakingly negotiated with, but for the present, it would all have to be put on the "back burner!"

Now that Maggie was more or less able to come and go as he pleased, everything should be so much easier, and I needed the time to be able to get on with the more important things in life, like building works, divorce, and other things—or so I thought!

Unfortunately, my thoughts lied to me!

It was decided that the shed and garage would be the first major projects to start with, which meant that Stephan would be the first workman on the scene. He would be with us for several weeks, and this time he would be working alone. But because Stephan had other jobs to complete for other people first, we would have to find another builder (or builders) to carry on with the task of constructing the two porches, one for the back and one at the front. We also needed a retaining wall at the front of the house, and finally, patios and pathways to go all the way round.

The whole of the outside work would have to be completed before decorating the house inside, which meant painting and wallpapering throughout.

The interior jobs were allocated to Kevin.

Our only hope was that everything would go smoothly and according to plan (or plans!).

Maggie was beginning to develop into a juvenile delinquent, and he was making it quite clear that he wasn't going to stand for anyone (or anything) encroaching on his sacred space. The only trouble was that his claim on space was gradually widening, and his first victim was the postman!

I had let Maggie out quite early, leaving the door to his aviary open so that he could come and go as he pleased, as there was nobody due to visit on this particular day.

I hadn't taken into consideration that the postman had not as yet called with the mail, as no doubt the icy roads would have slowed down his delivery time.

He arrived at about eight-thirty instead of his usual seven-fifteen.

I had just come out of Humphrey's stable, having fed him with his morning mix of feed and hay, and was just about to fetch him a fresh bucket of water, when I heard the van arrive, and when I looked up, I could see that it was the red postal van, but forgot that Maggie was already on the loose.

I watched the postman get out of his van, and from the stable I could hear his radio blaring away with loud music, and as he approached the front door with his handful of mail, I could hear him whistling away in tune to the music as he went, and then I heard another sound. When I looked up, I spotted Maggie on the roof, and he was lurking right next to the chimney pot.

He must have seen the postman arrive at about the same time as I did, and then he started to lig-log his way down towards the gutter, with his beak pointing meaningfully towards the unsuspecting postman—and he too was whistling, but it was a different tune than the postman's.

I stood transfixed, as I could almost anticipate Maggie's next move, but I knew I was unable to alter the inevitable outcome, so I thought it best if I just carried on as normal and act as though nothing awful was going to happen, and then with a bit of luck, perhaps Maggie might just change his mind and be distracted elsewhere.

We can always live in hope and wish for luck; unfortunately, this time it would be hopelessly unlucky!

Maggie was on top form as he swooped down and landed straight onto the poor unsuspecting postman's arm. He made a stab at the letters, sending them scattering in all directions as the wide-eyed postman frantically waved his arms about in an effort to ward of the attack.

But before I could reach the two of them, the postman had already leapt into his van, reversed at great speed out of the drive, wheels spinning as he went, and as he sped back up the lane, ironically his radio was playing "Postman Pat and His Black and White Cat."

Stephan turned up very early one morning at breakfast time to discuss the building plans for the shed.

He was sitting opposite me, and I had my back to the window, and as we talked whilst drinking our mugs of tea, I could see that he had a fixed stare on something straight over my shoulder. He seemed to be gazing at something in an almost mesmerized state, but he carried on talking as though he was in a daydream.

During the course of our conversation, I noticed that Stephan's concentration seemed to waver, and his replies were gradually trailing off.

It was only at that moment when I could see the object which had momentarily caught his attention from the mirrored reflection in Stephan's eyes.

I could see a black and white form moving back and forth, and somehow it looked very familiar.

Oh my God! I thought. *I forgot to keep Maggie in the aviary until Stephan had finished his work for the day and left the premises. Oh well, it's too late now!*

Since the episode with the postman, I would normally check the calendar daily to see if anyone was due to visit us and keep "the mad bird" under lock and key for everyone's safety. Now he was out and very much about, and very much on the prowl for his next victim!

Stephan's gawping mouth now uttered the immortal words, "Bloody Nora!… Am I seeing things, or has that bloody bird got a lump of dog shit in its beak?"

No sooner had his well chosen words so delicately tiptoed off his tongue, when I heard the familiar *tap!-tap!-tapping!* sound on the window pane, and sure enough as I turned round, there was Maggie acting out his "charm" technique, by parading up and down, then twirling round and round on the spot like "the belle of the ball" with the coyness and appeal of a blushing bride offering the bridal bouquet! But instead of offering a beautiful floral arrangement, he had sticking out of his beak like a big fat cigar, a very offensive-looking frozen lump of doggie waste! *Yuk!*

As Maggie matured into an adult bird, he was becoming more and more protective towards his territory, and he was on a constant lookout for easy sacrificial candidates who arrived at regular intervals, and he was beginning to invent clever new tactics of enticing people outside to join him as they watched his antics from the safety of the windows.

Watching attentively his comical performances, they seemed to be attracted to him like moths to a flame.

He would sing, warble, whistle, and coo ever so sweetly to them, whilst bobbing up and down as though he was curtseying graciously to them, and at the same time he would offer them a gift which they just couldn't resist, and if they were unfortunate enough to be fooled by his bluff, they wouldn't think twice at stepping outside just to take a better look at him, and say things like, "Oh, isn't he cute?" (not suspecting his real intentions), and it was then that he would pounce on his now bewildered admirer like a flying panther, sending them into a frenzy of arm flailing to try and ward off their attacker!

This sort of behaviour caused a certain amount of embarrassment to say the least, and our visitors seemed to be calling on us a little less frequently as he started logging up on his "who's next on my hit list?" campaign.

Perhaps I should put a sign up at the entrance saying:

BEWARE OF THE MAGPIE!

STAY IN YOUR CARS FOR YOUR OWN SAFETY
AND HOOT YOUR HORN FOR ATTENTION!

Maggie hadn't finished with Stephan yet, and was preparing to spring into action for his coup de grace! He didn't have to wait long.

The shed was built quickly and efficiently and looked really great with its pebble-dash walls, which Stephan applied by throwing handfuls of the small chippings from a large bucket, with the reverence of a priest blessing his congregation with the holy water.

He then fitted a nice wooden door which he painted red, and he painted the window with the same colour to match.

This smart new shed was just what we needed to store all the gardening tools in as well as dad's woodwork tools.

The window had to be left open just slightly so that everything would dry out quicker.

I could already imagine honeysuckle, roses, and perhaps even a wisteria growing all over it!

Soon it would be the turn of the spacious double garage to be built.

It was now mid-March, and we were treated to a few fine sunny days, but it was still quite cold.

From my kitchen window I could trace the wintery sun as it slowly moved round to the west. By early afternoon, the house cast a long shadow which reached over the lawn, down to the lower garden, and partly into the field. By late afternoon, there was a faint distant haze as the sky faded to a soft grey-blue colour.

The moon appeared whilst it was still daylight, and it looked almost translucent as it made its own slow clockwise orbital passage above the house, and like an apparition, the moon drifted behind— but without touching—the vapour trails left by passing aircraft which criss-crossed the sky, like "cats' cradles." Then, as if by magic, the trails vaporized into thick, wavy lines in the high atmosphere.

All too soon, the two golden globes separated in space. One was hot and brazen, and the other, cool and mysterious. They had danced their extraterrestrial dance, like a slow waltz, then slid gracefully out of sight.

Stephan told me that he wanted to start before the end of March, because he had promised to start on another job, but he didn't state on which day he was going to begin work on the garage.

He turned up unannounced on a cold icy morning.

There had been a very hard frost the night before, so everything was frozen up, and the driveway was very slippery, but none of this

313

seemed to bother Stephan as he was so used to working in all kinds of weather. He was well prepared for working in arctic conditions with his balaclava hat, thick anorak, and heavy studded boots which should help to grip on the hard and slippery ground. But he wasn't prepared for an unprovoked attack from a bad-tempered Magpie!

At first, everything seemed to be going smoothly.

I could hear from indoors the sounds of building work in progress, accompanied by intermittent whistling and singing of a very happy chappy, with the usual pause of silence for the usual coffee and lunch breaks, so I didn't take much notice, as I was kept busy with my own work.

As everything appeared to be going according to plan, everyone was happy, and Maggie was in his aviary, and hopefully he would be happy too!

But wait a minute!

Maggie *was* in his aviary!

I wasn't unduly worried that there wasn't any sign of him when I glanced out towards the aviary, as he could have been rummaging about on the floor, or maybe he was just resting up on his perch in the cubby-hole where his feed bowls were kept.

I made doubly sure that the bolt on the aviary door was well and truly shut, so there was no chance for Maggie to hinder Stephan in his work, so perhaps he was just sulking in a corner because he'd been shut in.

It was after a long spell of silence when the quietness was shattered by an ear-piercing yell.

"Get off me, you bloody sod!" More strong oaths followed.

I rushed outside to see what all the commotion was about, and I was greeted with the sight of a bulk of six feet four inches of Stephan's burly form flashing past the garden gate like a bat out of hell, with his arms flailing above his head in circles, just like the sails of a windmill, and his legs were pumping up and down like pistons, and he was huffing and puffing like an old steam engine, with Maggie in hot pursuit!

Maggie was just beginning to get the hang of sending people into animated motion!

As Stephan reached the top of the slope in the driveway with the intention of racing Maggie in order to reach his car first, and as the vehicle was parked at the driveway entrance, he hadn't taken into consideration that the surface had frozen over like an ice-rink.

Running down a slippery slope in hob-nailed boots is not to be recommended!

Poor Stephan upended in the middle of the drive, and because of his height and weight, he fell with a hefty wallop!

He limped his way indoors feeling pretty shaken up, and feeling very sorry for himself, then over something stronger than coffee to drink, he told me what had happened.

It seems that Stephan was having his lunch break, quietly sitting just inside the end stable (which happened to be the one just outside of the aviary and in full view of Maggie) and making himself comfortable by sitting on a bale of hay, when things suddenly turned nasty.

He was enjoying his ham sandwiches and mug of coffee, when he heard strange noises coming from the aviary. He got up to investigate, and it was then that he noticed Maggie was flying frantically up and down and was throwing himself onto the wire "like a mad thing." At the same time, he was making very pathetic calls, as though he was in distress. As Stephan peered into the aviary to see what the matter was, Maggie stopped immediately, and he started to make his pleading cooing sounds directly at Stephan. So thinking that I must have forgotten to let him out, knowing that I didn't keep him shut away *all* the time, Stephan unbolted the door and let Maggie out.

Unknown to him, Stephan had inadvertently just unleashed a demon straight out of Pandora's box!

At first, everything seemed quite normal, and Maggie appeared to be very pally and companionable, and Stephan even shared his sandwiches with Maggie, but this was actually his undoing, because when it came to the big chunk of fruit cake that Stephan had in his lunch box, Maggie wanted to help himself. It was at this point that everything went a bit pear shaped as Stephan tried to whip the box away so that Maggie couldn't help himself.

Now Maggie has a very short fuse, so it doesn't take much to "spark him off," and seeing that he was being deprived of something that he really wanted, Maggie began to show his true colours. He turned into an unrelenting mean-machine, finely tuned and ready to let the feathers fly, so the battling bully bird had turned into a winged crusader of "birds' rights!"

He flew onto Stephan's hand and started to peck viciously, and when Stephan tried to ward him off, Maggie flew onto his head and tried to peck at his ears through his woollen hat (Stephan told me that he thought he could hear Maggie hissing with anger at him—like a snake!), so it was then that his only hope was to beat a very hasty retreat and try to take cover in his car—with dire consequences!

How was I to know at that time, that somewhere down the line, the drive would be turned into a mini "Olympic" run for many other unlucky chosen ones who would have to run the gauntlet, especially when Maggie was out on his "workmen worrying" forays.

So new rules were laid down, which meant that "when men in white vans with ladders attached turned up, this would have to be curfew time for Maggie!"

Gareth and Huw (who reminded me of Bill and Ben, the flowerpot men) were next in line, and they turned up in a rather battered old blue van.

With trowels in hand and spades at the ready, and with a very firm promise "to build for us, two solid porches and a very *tidy* brick wall at the front of the house, and finally a *nice* path to go all around the house, as well as the two patios—in five weeks!"

What they didn't tell us was just how long it would take them, and just how "nice" and "tidy" it would be!

In reality, instead of five weeks, it took them six months! On and off! More off than on!

Right at the very start—and before proceeding with their work—I told them to *never* let Maggie out of the aviary, not at any cost, telling them that they would definitely regret it if they did, and I told them that he would probably attack them and not to be fooled by any of his cajoling.

I could tell that they were really fascinated by Maggie, and they would go up to the aviary and chat with him, and they sometimes pushed pieces of bread from their sandwiches through the wire of the aviary, which he always grabbed up greedily.

Their lunchtime visits to Maggie became quite a daily ritual, and finally one morning, Huw—the shorter one of the two—asked me if they could let Maggie out, as they were sure that he wouldn't do anything to them, because he was now quite used to them and always came up to the wire to "talk" to them as well as share their lunch with him. "So, please, could we let him out?" they asked.

I knew I had to be firm about it, and told them, "Definitely not!"

It became apparent that the temptation was too great, and I'm sure that they thought I was exaggerating, and making such a big issue about the whole business, and how could such an innocent-looking bird who only wanted a bit of company and attention cause so much mischief anyway? So like a couple of naughty little school boys defying their teacher, they went for it!

Just like a set stage, it was like a repeat performance from an old pantomime, only some of the players were different!

Once again, it was the silence that was ominous!

I missed seeing Huw (or Bill) carrying the bricks (or should I say brick, one-by-one) whilst Gareth (or Ben) trundled after him pushing a very squeaky wheelbarrow at a pace that would never have me "keeling over with dizziness," and once again, it was the ominous open aviary door that caught my attention! A touch of déjà vu perhaps?

Oh well! I thought. *I'd better go out and see what's going on, or what isn't, as the case may be!*

It turned out to be yet another incident of "men stuck in van!"—and they didn't even have to tell me what had happened! Their stricken faces with wide eyes peering at me through very steamed up windows and looking like goldfish in a bowl trying to come up for air said it all.

It looked as though they had just made a pact with the devil!

Goldfish number one (Huw) mouthed something to me through the closed window, but I couldn't hear or make out what he was trying to say. I knocked on the window and gesticulated with my hand in a circular movement to indicate I wanted him to wind down the window.

Goldfish number two (Gareth) wound it down just a fraction on his side, so I had to go round to the other side of the van to speak to him, and he poked his nose and mouth through the crack, making him look even more like a goldfish gasping for air!

"What on earth are you doing in there!?" I asked, pretending I had no idea what it was all about! "Good job I don't have to pay you by the hour, otherwise I would have had to take out a mortgage just to pay you for today's work alone!" I said mockingly. "Anyway, if you don't start back to work soon," I said, looking at my watch, "I'll have to set Maggie free for a bit of his exercise—he doesn't like being left all day!"

It was at this point that the two goldfishes jumped out of their bowl, looking very soulful and humble, and then they told me what had happened.

It seems that after they had let Maggie out, completely disregarding my instructions, he'd chased them all the way back to their van, where they were then too afraid to get out, or at least *he* wouldn't let them. Every time they wound the window down, he flew at them, then perched on the wing-mirror daring them to come out, and he bashed away at the mirror with his beak like a hooligan to show what he would do to them if they did!

At least they had learnt their lesson—the hard way!

The work was finally completed intermittently and uninterrupted and without any more hazardous incidents, but it wasn't always men who attracted Maggie's attention either!

Peggy, a local woman who lived in the next village, came to us once a week to help with the cleaning, washing and ironing.

She was a very happy-go-lucky character, quite tough and strong for her age (she was in her early seventies), but she was always willing to tackle any task without a second thought, even to climb up tall ladders to fix something if she thought it needed mending, and she also took great delight in painting the porches, and once she even painted the whole of the utility room (or outer kitchen as we call it) with bright yellow paint.

Peggy was not so much of a Mary Poppins with fluttering long eyelashes and radiating a sweet smile at everyone, but more of a Handy Mandy!

It was nothing to see her wheeling and brandishing large yard brooms along with sets of spanners, hammers and nails, electric drills, and an assortment of paint brushes, scowling and grumbling if anyone tried to stop her from taking on such heavy, and sometimes downright dangerous, jobs!

One day, when we were all sitting in the lounge having our morning coffee, there was a loud bang, which seemed to be coming from the other side of the house, and we all thought that the kitchen door had been caught in a draught and had slammed shut.

About five minutes later, Peggy came hobbling into the lounge, her eyes wide with shock and looking very sheepish, and her face had turned quite pale; she seemed to be visibly shaken.

It seems that she had decided to clean the fluorescent light in the kitchen, which had collected dozens of flies, and much against my wishes about climbing onto things that might cause an accident, she had stood up on the kitchen table so that she could reach the light more easily, but what she hadn't taken into consideration was that one leaf of the large kitchen table was extended out to make it longer, and when she shuffled her way along the table, cleaning the light as she went, she suddenly felt the table tilt, and she slid off the end, hitting her head on one of the cupboards and then landing heavily on the floor by the cooker!

Poor old Peggy was so apologetic because she had broken a section of the table that she didn't seem a bit bothered about the fact that she may have hurt herself pretty badly, but I think she was more sorry that she had disregarded my instructions about climbing up on things without anyone being near at hand in case she needed their help.

Thank goodness she hadn't hurt herself too much other than a few bruises, and she promised me solemnly that she would *never* do it again!

In spite of her steadfast attitude towards her outlook on life (which in her past had been pretty tough and gruelling by all accounts), she was really very good natured at heart, but didn't suffer fools gladly, and when she saw the funny side of things, she would explode into a gravely, wheezy laughter, which ended up in a fit of coughing, no doubt caused through bombarding her lungs over many years by her chain smoking.

When it came to blows between Peggy and Maggie, it was like a battle of the Titans!

For some reason or other best known to Maggie, he didn't exactly attack Peggy herself, but he seemed to fix his attention on relieving her of her possessions, mainly her cigarettes, car keys, or any other object that caught his eye. He would fetch them out of her handbag, which was nearly always left open when she left it in the usual place on the chair in the porch, and it was always stuffed tight, because Peggy liked to carry around all of her "bits and pieces, because you never know when you might be needing them! What with me being a Jack of all trades!" she used to say.

Arriving in her little blue Metro car, she would breeze in through the gate, always in a hurry, and banging it shut behind her, which acted as a wake-up call for Maggie waiting in the wings and ready to fly into action.

Before entering the house, Peggy would always stop to brandish her cigarette that was always stuck in her mouth, savouring the last few puffs before stubbing it out, and then she would throw it into the dustbin. This habit hadn't gone unnoticed by Maggie, and so poised for a good aim at his target, he would fly down from nowhere and deftly tweak the cigarette from her mouth just before she could remove it, and then fly off with it still glowing and alight in his beak, as though he was carrying a small beacon, and Peggy would lunge towards him, and taking careful aim with her handbag, she would swing it wildly after him. But he was too quick for her, so she never quite caught him, even though the same scene was reenacted almost every day!

Once she told me that "he nearly took me new set of false teeth as well as me fag!... Rotten little swine!"

She wasn't at all amused when, on one particular day, Maggie confiscated her car keys, and he teased her wickedly as he strutted off with them across the lawn, keeping just that tantalizing distance between them both as Peggy gave chase.

I caught sight of the drama from my bedroom window, and I saw her stout body pounding after him in hot pursuit, and I could hear her as she shouted curses at him in her gruff voice, which could be as sharp as a cheese-cutter, and on such occasions cats would scatter and dogs would cower!

"Oi!... Come back here, you thieving little sod!... I'll wring your bloody neck for you....if I can catch you...you little bugger!"

The pair then disappeared from view.

Peggy could out-swear a man at ten paces any day

When she finally reappeared, puffing from her exertion and with a triumphant look on her face, she said, "That sodding bird of yours led me a right old merry dance—just look what I've found!" She held out a plastic flower pot for me to look inside.

"I followed him into his aviary, because that's where he made for with my keys, and when I got inside, he dropped them in the far corner, and when I went over to get them, I found this little lot, so I just shoved it all into this flower pot! He must've been hoarding this pile of old fag ends for months and months!"

Then with her face still flushed, she beamed widely as she stuck her hand again into the flower pot and pulled out a small silver object. "Right at the bottom, I found this cigarette case that was given to me as a present from Jim not long before he died," she said.

Jim was her husband to whom she'd been married for forty-two years until he passed away after a long illness of cancer, so she now lived in her tiny cottage on her own.

Then finally she stuck her hand inside her anorak pocket and pulled out a large, man-sized gold wedding ring. "Now do you happen to know who this belongs to!?" she asked. "This I found wedged in a crack of one of the branches in the aviary!" She then gave a wry smile, and said, "A right little thieving magpie *he's* turned out to be!"

"Yes, you're quite right," I replied.

"It looks as though he's going to be a bit of a liability, I must admit I hadn't thought of that before, but I wonder if a magpie has ever been done for stealing!"

I found out later on, that the ring belonged to Kevin, the interior decorator-come-aviary builder.

He was overjoyed at being reunited with his ring, which his wife had bought for him in Spain whilst on one of their holiday trips, and she was so distraught when he told her that he had lost it.

He just couldn't believe that it had actually been recovered, and he couldn't wait until he got home to tell his wife the good news that the ring had been found by a magpie, so he phoned her there and then!

Maggie was now quite a hero in Kevin's eyes.

It seems that he lost it on that very wet day when he helped Stephan build the aviary.

He told me that it must have just slipped off his finger whilst he was fixing one of the wooden structures, and he thought he would never see it again, so it looks as though we actually owe Maggie an apology on this occasion, which means that it could work to our advantage, as he turned out to be not only a collector, but a "finder and keeper" of lost property as well!

So now I had a new challenge incorporated in my daily routine.

I would have to search meticulously in every nook and cranny of the aviary, just in case Maggie had been out on one of his bargain hunts again! Most of the time I would only find bits of old tat, and all kinds of oddments like hair curlers, bottle tops, a battered old Dinky toy, a tiny charm shaped like a cow (probably from out of a Christmas cracker) and even an old clay pipe!

It was now Kevin's turn to start the interior decorating, so he was really quite lucky with regards to bad weather, because if it rained it didn't matter one jot, as he would be working entirely indoors.

This meant a lot of hard work for me as well, as I had to remove all the furniture from each room to prepare for the wallpapering and painting, and then it was my job to drive to the town of Carmarthen, which was twenty-five miles away—taking my parents and the dogs with me—in order to buy all the necessary decorating materials, which meant that Kevin would be left in charge of the house (we trusted him completely), and of course, Maggie the menace!

Maggie always hated to see us drive off in the car, and he would sit just outside the front door, all hunched up and looking like a little old man, very pathetic and forlorn, as though he wasn't looking forward to another sunrise, which made me feel so heartless at leaving him, but then that was just what he wanted—to make me feel guilty.

Sometimes he would even sit on the wing mirror of the car, where he would cling on whilst I drove up the bumpy stony lane, then fly off just before I reached the main road, slowly making his way back to the house where he would wait for us to return, just like a loyal dog!

He became quite good at "mirror riding," and he even used to sit on Adam's wing mirror as he drove up the lane (at a fair pace, as he was nearly always late) on his way to work. In fact, he became quite addicted to it, and Adam would have to reverse smartly back again so that I could retrieve him from the mirror, just in case Maggie forgot to let go, as Adam wasn't too keen at having to explain at work, when asked, "Why did you have a magpie attached to your car? Was it a real one? Or was it like one of those tacky little 'Nodding Dogs'?"

It was a good thing that Kevin would be spending the whole of the day indoors, except when he had to go to his van to fetch any tools that he needed for the job, and to fetch his packed lunch and flask of coffee, and most important of all—his Mars bar!

Maggie loved his Mars bar too!

When Kevin stopped for his coffee break, he would call out to Maggie, who usually loitered about not far away when he knew which part of the house Kevin was working in (they became quite good buddies). Maggie would fly up to the windowsill, and then Kevin would open the window ever so slightly so that he could pass a small piece of his Mars bar to Maggie, who would gobble the whole lot up greedily, then come back for more, so then Kevin felt obliged to share some of his sandwiches with him as well.

One day, when Kevin offered him a piece of his sweet, apparently he opened the window just a bit too wide, so when he offered Maggie a bit of the chocolate bar, Maggie shoved his beak right into Kevin's hand and grabbed the largest portion for himself, leaving poor Kevin with just a tiny bit which was meant for Maggie!

On another day, Kevin brought his dog Jessie with him, as his wife—who usually kept the dog with her—had chosen to spend the whole day in Cardiff.

Jessie spent most of the time in the van with the radio on to keep her company, and the windows wound down to give her plenty of fresh air.

Kevin only took her out twice so that she could have a pee and stretch her legs in the first field.

Now it came to pass that there was a bit of a confrontation with Maggie!

Maggie liked dogs.

That is to say, he liked to pester and peck at dogs, usually between their toes, or any other vulnerable parts of their bodies, and sometimes he liked to sit on top of their heads, flapping his wings furiously, which would throw them into total confusion because they couldn't throw him off. They absolutely hated this horrible creature that kept on stabbing away at them, and they couldn't get away from it fast enough! It moved much too quickly, and it could fly as well!

When we returned from one of our "paper and paste" purchasing trips, we were surprised at not seeing Maggie nearby and waiting to swoop down to greet us.

"Have you seen Maggie anywhere?" I asked Kevin. "He just doesn't seem to be around." "Er...well yes!...um...he's sort of over there!" he replied, pointing a finger towards the stables.

And sure enough, there was Maggie, waddling away from us as though he hadn't noticed we were there at all, and it suddenly struck me that he looked rather odd.

His tail feathers were stuck up at a peculiar angle, with one pointing downwards and the other pointing straight up, rather like a Native American headdress—of the "Crow" tribe, perhaps?

"He looks a bit strange to me," I said. "What on earth has he been up to this time?"

It turned out that Maggie went into a full-on attack with Jessie, just as Kevin was about to put her back into the van after a run across the field, and diving down straight in front of her in his usual Arnold Schwarzenegger manner, so that he could take her off guard, he wasn't quite prepared when she actually retaliated by defending herself. And when she lunged out at him with gnashing teeth, she caught him by the tail and started to shake him, but in true Maggie style, he wasn't going to give in so easily just like that, and to Kevin's amazement, when Jessie let him go to try and get a better grip on his body, Maggie took the opportunity to fly up onto Jessie's head, and them promptly stabbed her repeatedly on her nose, and she ended up by yelping with pain, and then she beat a hasty retreat across the drive and leapt, without any hesitation, straight into the van, where she sat shivering.

Kevin said that her pride was more hurt than anything.

What was more astonishing is that Jessie was not just a little dog like a corgi or a collie, but the reckless bird had rather stupidly taken on a fully mature, black-and-tan, "in-your-face" Rottweiler!

Maggie tagged along with another "bosom buddy" to take advantage of.

This time it was a little Welsh farmer who came to harrow and roll the fields ready for spring.

Maggie was quite intrigued by the flocks of swirling and reeling seagulls, following closely in the wake of the little old red Ferguson tractor, as it trundled back and forth, up and down, watching the chain harrow drag out the dead grass and any other debris.

He didn't seem keen to join them, or maybe he just didn't like the loud din they were creating, but when they dispersed and flew off into the distance to descend upon another field which was being harrowed, he then flew down to investigate and see what the seagulls had found so interesting.

He looked such a forlorn little figure, lig-logging in his usual manner, trying to keep up with the tractor, and he even followed it through the gap and into the second field, so he was obviously enjoying himself.

At four o'clock that afternoon, I thought a nice mug of tea would be a very welcome drink for the little farmer, who seemed to be taking an awfully long time harrowing such small fields, but then I put that down to the fact that his little tractor was pretty ancient, and monotonously slow! So with my tin tray with a big mug of steaming tea on it, I made my way through the gap to see how he was getting on, and to see if Maggie was still hanging around.

I could hear the strains of "Oh Danny Boy" being sung, and occasionally the voice wavered slightly off key.

The singing was coming from the other side of the hedge, and then the tempo changed to another faster and even louder song, but this time it was sung in Welsh and was belted out with such great gusto.

The tractor, the farmer, and of course Maggie, were all having a break—but not for tea!

The odd couple were hunkered down on a large, very gnarled fallen branch of an old oak tree, which had blown down in the previous year's gale, and was conveniently situated on the margin of the second field, and made what looked like a very comfortable seat.

The two of them had been sharing cheese sandwiches, crisps, and a can of beer! Not just one can of beer...but three! Both looked as happy as Larry!

When I approached them, the one who was singing gave a big grin from ear to ear, his battered old cowboy-style hat was pulled down over one bloodshot eye, his weather-worn crinkly cheeks were flushed with a tinge of red, whilst his unusual companion, the one whose tail hadn't yet grown back to normal, was twittering and gurgling away (Maggie, of course!) and looked a bit peaky around the beak!

The little old farmer accepted the mug of tea gratefully, swilled it down in a couple of gulps, staggered to his feet, and then mumbled something like:

"Better get going now...*hic*! before it getsh dark...*hic*!...*burp!*" Then turning to his little companion, he added—"C'mon, Maggie, bach...*hic*!...jusht you show me the way to go home, boyo!" And as the farmer tottered back to his tractor, he gave a hearty rendering of "We'll Keep A Welcome in the Hillside...*hic!*" whilst the bird swayed unsteadily from side-to-side in the opposite direction towards his aviary, where he spent the rest of the afternoon to sleep off his little binge with the farmer.

Maggie wasn't the only contender for full supremacy of the sky! He could hardly compete with the R.A.F. who had permission to use the surrounding hillside as a mock battle zone.

They would appear out of the blue, as they screamed overhead with their fighter jets to carry out mock air strikes on life-sized rubber tanks, which had been placed strategically on top of Buttocks Hill shortly before the war games started.

At times they flew so low that you could actually see the pilot quite plainly sitting in his cockpit, and the noise they made was so deafening, and the tremendous roar which rumbled across the valley caused flocks of sheep—which were either new to the area or not used to aircraft noise—to scatter in all directions, which not surprisingly upset the local farmers who became very angry because they claimed that their terrified ewes were prone to abort their lambs, which was a very serious concern.

Most of the time the farm animals became used to the noise, and they didn't seem to take any notice.

This practice of low flying sometimes shook the very foundations of the house. In fact, on one occasion, the vibration was so intense that it actually shook the house to such an extent that it cracked the glass in one of the pictures in my bedroom, and in one corner of the room, a long ragged crack appeared—all of which didn't please me at all!

Sometimes the big old transporter planes were put into action, and they droned overhead at a much slower pace than the fighter bombers and were not nearly so noisy.

Helicopters were used for manoeuvres as well, so we were treated to quite an exciting air display when all of the fighting machines were brought into action, and visitors were quite envious of us having our own "air show" right on the doorstep!

They always chose a lovely hot sunny day to do battle, just at a time when you wanted to enjoy a nice peaceful afternoon in the garden, or to just relax in a comfortable sun lounger with a good book—only to be blasted out of your seat with the sudden onslaught of these noisy air machines, disregarding all those poor unfortunates who happened to be beneath their flight path.

Perhaps wars are never fought in bad weather!

Katie wasn't a bit afraid of these huge metal invaders; in fact, she thought the whole thing was great fun. As they roared overhead, she would chase after them barking madly as though she was driving them out of the garden, racing across the lawn, jumping over the gate, then following them down the steep slope of the fields, with her tail whipping round in circles like a lasso to try and keep her balance as she had to keep her head unnaturally high, so that she could follow their direction. With her ears flapping up and down, and narrowly missing a collision with bushes or any other solid objects in her way, she really looked quite comical!

I could just imagine her returning home one day, with one of these jump jet harriers, or similar, firmly clenched between her teeth, and me thinking, *What on earth am I going to do with this?…turn it into a garden feature perhaps!*

It would be a bit embarrassing if the R.A.F. turned up on my doorstep asking, "Please, can we have our plane back?…and have you seen a pilot anywhere?…only he goes with the set!"

I would have to say, "Hold on a minute, I'll just go and have a look for you!" whilst stepping over Katie as she chewed merrily away on a *very* large bone!

All's well that ends well!

Eventually these "Warriors of the Skies" moved themselves, their tanks, and their aircraft, on to other pastures.

So now they have ended up on someone else's doorstep!

Peace reigned at last!

It wasn't all doom and gloom, so thankfully we did have our fun times as well.

Maggie enjoyed going out on short trips in the car with me, but they would only be local and not too far away, like the little post office at the bottom of the hill, or to collect some freshly laid eggs at a free-range farm in the next village, and I would have to be very watchful that he didn't fly past me when I opened the car door, but at least if he did, he should be able to find his own way home. Fortunately this never happened.

He would perch on the headrest on the back seat, looking out of the back window, and not at all frightened.

He must have looked like one of those little fury toy animals that some people like to place on the back shelves of their cars.

When I took Katie and Hattie for their daily walks across the fields, Maggie would join us. He usually sat on my shoulder, hardly ever flying off, so it was quite nice to feel that at such times he could be really sociable, calm, and almost loveable, dare I say!

Sometimes he would waddle along behind me and the dogs, so we would all be following in one track, single file.

Katie would always run off excitedly if she saw a rabbit or squirrel, and she would give chase, yelping as she raced across the fields like a greyhound in hot pursuit, whilst dainty little Hattie stuck close to me. She obviously thought that she was too well bred to take part in such rough, unladylike pursuits; after all, she's an "aristocratic" poodle, and the only hunting that she enjoyed partaking in was to open the doggie cupboard with her paw so that she could drag out the goodie bag which contained an assortment of doggy chews and biscuits, and these she would scatter about the kitchen floor, so that she and Katie could help themselves.

Her other trick was when she would rake about in Mother's handbag, which she would drag off the chair, or sometimes, if she was lucky, she would find it lying on the floor, and then she would fetch everything out, one-by-one, and finally she would sniff out what she was looking for—a nice big bar of chocolate!—one of her favourite treats! Much better than a walk across the fields!

One day, on one of our walks, I saw Katie chase after a dog fox, and the two of them disappeared through the brambles with Katie barking exuberantly in a very high-pitched tone, whilst Maggie looked on as though he was making a mental note of what he must have thought was one of Katie's "shenanigans!"

She didn't return home until about two hours later, puffing and panting, with a big grin on her face, and her sides were heaving from the exertion of the chase. She was obviously very tired, extremely thirsty, but decidedly contented.

At least she enjoyed the fun of the chase, even if she didn't manage to catch her quarry!

I think that Maggie was a bit disappointed that he wasn't able to join in the fun of the chase, but he wasn't to know that his time would soon come, when he too would have some fun!

Later on in the year, Maggie was to meet another new member of the family to play with, and one who arrived quite by chance.

It was a cat!

- Chapter Seven and a Half -
Over to Maggie

...the one with the waggily tail!

"Well now, where is it you be coming from then, boyo?" asked Holly, in that funny peculiar way of speech what seems to go all sing-songy and up and down, just like a chaffinch flies, only sometimes it seems to stay up, and forgets to come down again!

"Seems that we are likely to think that you were all caught up in a gigantic "catching cage" set purposely by the pinkies, all neat and ready to lure us all in like!" said Lotty anxiously.

"And how did you get here then?" asked Ivy, shyly.

"And how come it is that you seem to be living with the pinkies then, isn't it?" inquired Parsley.

Oh gawd! I thought, *where on earth am I going to start on that particular question…or any of them?*

"Well," I said, "it's all a matter of equations!"

"What's that then?" one of them asked, unimpressed. "Is it a sickness, or a nasty dangerous animal or something…or is it….?"

"No," I said hesitatingly, "it means that I was the 'Chosen One' to be worshipped and adored by the pinkies!"

So I went into a lengthy tale (about as long as a python) and told them a bit about my past history, and how as soon as I broke out of the yolk, I yelled, "Hello great big round world, I've arrived, an' good an' ready to do the deed!"

I told them about me ma, Silver Tongue, and my pa, Mossy, and all about Moonbeam's misdemeanours, and Lacewing's green glass gatherings, and its consequences. I told them all about how the big nasty old crow, Forked Tongue, tried to turn me into a kebab, and how I was rescued in the nick of time by a pinky, who happened to be out looking for a great ruler for their kingdom, and luckily they found me! And I told them how the pinkies named me Maggie, "Maggie the Magnificent Magician!" I said as an afterthought.

Now this bit of information seemed to stoke up a whole heap of interest, so I continued.

"The pinkies know that they have got to give me lots and lots of nice things to eat, in fact they shower me with absolutely everything on earth that's edible—and more, and anything that I might crave for, and they even take me on long journeys in a big metal klakki, and that's just how I got here, purely because that's just what I wanted them to do, it's so…so globally featheralistic, don't you think?"

When I told them that I was "extra special" they thought I said "extraterrestrial"!

By now they were practically begging me to tell them more, so I told them about my journey, and about "motor cars."

"They travel at great speed, and they make a growling sound as they go along, and sometimes they make a loud call like *AARP!... AARP!* which is their battle cry. And not only that, I have even seen these metal klakkies having an almighty fight, with bits flying off in all directions, causing terrible 'clatter, tinkle, and crunch' noises, and this is usually followed by rallying cries, like a wailing sound of a stranded whale, only much more piercing, and this comes from metal klakkies arriving at great speed, flashing out bright blue thunderbolt lights; very impressive indeed! And another thing about these metal monsters is that when darkness comes, their two big eyes light up like fires of...!"

"Fires of a dragon?" somebody suggested.

"Yes!... Yes, that's it!... Like fires of a...a *dragon!*" I answered, not knowing quite what they meant.

"Oh yes!" they gasped in great awe.

"By the dragon's blood!... We have indeed seen these things!... And they are great slayers of birds!... You are so...so very brave!"

"Yes!... I know!" I replied, heroically.

I then thought it best to recite a little poem I made up about my trip called "Journeying Home" and singing it to them, it went like this:

> *I'm waiting in the pouring rain,*
> *I think I'll take this choo-choo train.*
>
> *No!—I think that's too much fuss,*
> *So now I hope to catch this bus.*
>
> *Someone said, "Go take a hike!"*
> *I said to them, "Give me your bike!"*
>
> *The other obvious choice, of course,*
> *Is just to hop onto this horse!*
>
> *Then someone else said, "It's much too far!"*
> *So in the end—I took a car!*

They asked me, "What's a bike like, and what can you do with a bus when you've caught it?"

I just told them they'd soon know what a bus would do to them if they caught it, saying that I'd seen much evidence of what a bus could do to a magpie what got in its way, particularly back on the roads where I first came from, and the sight was none too pretty—not to a magpie anyways!

This kept them silent in deep thought for a short while.

I told them how I'd seen lots of things about the whole of the world, in fact I've seen the *whole* of the universe on a magic box (I didn't tell them it's really called a tee vee!), and that I'd got my own "future teller" like no other ever before seen!

"Think big and bold, is what I always say!" I told them.

"And another thing," I said, "I can talk in different tongues, as well as Magglish. I can talk in MagDonald, MagNamara, and MagLunnen, as good as any 'Cockney Sparrer'!"

"Ooh, there's lovely!" they gasped as a chorus of deep admiration.

I continued telling them of other clever and magical things I could do.

"I can whistle a lurgy off at ten paces," I said.

"Oh, there's clever of you," said Lilly Bell, "but...but what's a 'lurgy'?" she asked, sidling up nearer, as if to pay homage to her hero (which is me, of course, in case you didn't know!).

"It's a sort of spotty songbird, like a blackbird, only its got lots of spots, and keeps on repeating the same old thing, over and over—'No you don't!... No you don't!... If you like!... If you like!... Is he?... Is he?... Is he?'—just like a thrush, and in my opinion, he's a bit of a bumless bimbo who's as slick as a moonbeam, and as rare as a worm's chilblains, and he once told me that he didn't know if he was a *he* or a *she*, and that his ever so great-great-great-great egg layer and egg maker happened to be dodos, who didn't do too well on all accounts—which made me say to him, 'no wonder you're nearly 'stinct mate,' so I sorta 'whistled 'im off'!"

"Hmm!" said Shiffely. "That sounds a right shifty one. It's enough to make your beak curl, isn't it?"

They pondered for a while, but I could tell that more questions were on the way, and they were not going to let me wriggle out of 'em that easy, so they bombarded me once more.

"Well then, if you're so clever, what shape is the wind?" asked Gizzy.

"Well, I think it's flat!" I said.

"If that's so, how do you know?" enquired Tizzy poetically.

"Just look at the trees!" I said. "When the wind blows really hard, they drop down *flat*, the grass goes *flat*, me feathers on my head blow *flat* back, and I fall down *flat* on me beak, so the wind must be *flat*!"

"Why not *round*, 'coz it goes all *round*?" asked Squiffly.

Suddenly, that particular conversation fell flat, so that was that, 'till Totty perks up with another mind-bending question!

"Okay then, does *anyone* know what *sound* looks like?" she asks.

Somehow or other, I just knew that this question was really directed at me, and not anyone else.

There followed a long, drawn-out chorus of, "No!"

Except from my of course, so I answered truthfully. "I do! It sorta looks like this!" I said. And so I got mighty busy and etched the runic signs of sounds by thinking them all out in me 'ead:

"Pretty, aint it?" I said.

Then the signs vanished!

"There!… Did you see it?" I asked them.

Then in an elongated "Nnaow!" they all twanged together with their reply.

"Well, look more carefully!" I told them commandingly.

They all nodded spellbound, as they gazed stupidly all about them.

Then I carried on whilst the going was good, "And what colour does sound look like you may well ask!"

There was a noise-free silence!

"Well, seein' as none of you is answerin' me—I'll tell you! Sound is a sort of greeny, reddy, colour, with pinkish spots, and flashes of bright yellow, that's what!—*No!*… It's not black, Ivy, it's only that colour if you close your eyes when you're listening to it. And the wind sings a lot, as you all know!"

They all nodded hard.

"And the sound of the wind looks like this: *OOOooo! OOOooo!* — and of course its colour is a glorious white, just like the sound of snow!... As, of course, even an *idiot* must know!"

They all looked at one another in stunned silence, and then they were thrown into utter confusion as they all scrambled about trying to find the sounds, just so's they could see its colours!

"Maggie bach!" Parsley chirped in "Can you tell us...umm...can you tell us...*who* had the first thought, and *who* it was that thunk it...please?"

"Well now, Parsley, me little flavoursome flower, I can tell you exactly who *thunk* the first thought!" I said. "And it was told to me by me egg layer ma, who heard it from one of her great, ever so great ancestors, and it goes like this..."

Long, long ago, even before time began, there was a big mass of "Mind" floating about, doing just about nothing at all.

Then, on one of its circles of the Universe, it thought to itself, "I'm fed up with all this floating about with just my own thoughts, and nothing or nobody to share them with, so I think I'll pass them on to some of those Earthly individuals, who keep bumping about everywhere, and all so very mindless to everything!"

Just at that moment, a thoughtless magpie happened to be fluttering and bumping about, and Mind floated down like a cloud, full of thoughts, and latched itself onto the magpie, who said, "Oh, thank you!... Ooh, I've just had a thought, and that was it. Oh, thank you!"

"That's all right," said Mind. "It's a pleasure, but now there's one thing I would like you to do for me in return. I want you to pass on *all* my thoughts to *all* other living creatures of the Universe!"

"Why yes, of course I will!" said the thoughtful magpie. "Oh...listen!... There goes me second thought.... Isn't it wonderful?"

"Yes!... Yes!... Of course it's wonderful. Now do your deed, magpie!" said Mind, wondering if it had done the right thing in letting all its thoughts go to the magpie, and then on a second thought, it said, "And mind how you go!"

"Oh thank you, Mind!" said the magpie, who flew off thinking and planning all the time.

First of all, he glided over a forest, and scanning the treetops somewhere in a jungle, he spotted an orange-furred animal, an orang-utan, who was sitting in a treetop eating a banana, not knowing why he was eating it, or even what it tasted like, and he was picking his nose, not knowing what to do with it!

The magpie alighted onto the shoulders of the big hairy creature and passed on some useful thoughts to it. The orang-utan hooted with glee.

"Yum! Yum! Yum!... This tastes really scrummy!" he said, holding out the banana. "Now I know why I'm eating it. Now let me *think*!... What shall I do with *this* then?" he said, holding out his other hand.

The magpie left the orang-utan to work it out for himself, and flew on.

He came at last to a rocky outcrop on a hillside, where he landed on a boulder, and jumping down onto the ground, he searched until he came upon a tiny mouse. So passing on a little thought to the mouse, he said, "I think you'd better run and hide quick, before an owl finds you and eats you, because I'm about to pass on a thought to the owl, which will make him very wise indeed, and he will think about catching you, then eating you!... So pass it on!"

The magpie was, by this time, thinking and scheming at an alarming rate, making up for all those thoughtless years, and he next searched out a grand old grey wolf.

"Now, brother wolf," he said, "you will be a cunning hunter, bolder, faster, and much wiser, and therefore even more successful, as I will at this very instant give you ingenious thoughts, and you will call your brothers to you on full moons, and henceforth you will all group together in packs, and with sheer cunning you will be thinking out your strategy of hunting, and also of how you are going to ambush your prey."

"I thank you for that, o' great messenger of 'thoughts' from the skies!" said the old grey wolf.

Passing over great flat lands of desert, with belts of lush looking trees, and strange looking ones as well, the magpie spotted a great big anorexic elephant, who was wandering about aimlessly, not knowing what he was doing or which way to turn or what to do with his great long trunk.

Settling on one of his long white tusks, the magpie dropped a "thought nut" on the ground in front of the elephant's trunk.

The big animal picked up the "thought nut" with its trunk, and ate it, unthinkingly.

"Aaarrr!" bellowed the surprised elephant. "I think I feel so much better now, and I think I'm going to do lots of clever and useful things with my trunk from now on, and I think…!"

"Stop! Stop! Stop!" said the magpie. "Never mind about all of what you're going to think!… Just get on with your own thoughts, do what you think, then you must go and pass it on to as many animals as you can…. Is that clear? And don't you forget what I've just told you! Now I think you'd better go and eat up your greens!"

"Oh, all right," said the elephant, and he trumpeted loud and long, "I think I will!… And I won't forget!"

And that is how Mind had the first thought, and then passed it on to one lonesome magpie.

So you see, we were the first living creatures to have the first thought, and that's just how thoughts first started, and why we are the most intelligent beings on earth. So now you know! And I'm just thinking "I'd better eat this itsy bitsy millipede before one of you lot does!"

When I was done my story, I heard one of them say, "He's so damned clever, I bet he can dance the worms straight out of the ground!"

I felt so proud of myself.

I deserved all the praise I could get!

The only one who didn't join in the fun at the gathering and seemed to keep himself several hops away from the group, but just far enough to listen in and to watch what was going on, was Featherhead White Wings.

He's a bit of an old "gutter snipe" if you ask me, and I could tell by the look in his eye that we would never see beak-to-beak about certain things!

It was beginning to get too dark to do any more hunting, so I called out to the group:

> *Cock-a-doodle-diddlydoo,*
> *sunset is red, and the sky is blue,*
> *the snow is white, dark is the night,*
> *gold is the sun, yellow the moon,*
> *silver the cobwebs,*
> *blue the lagoon.*
>
> *A pig in a poke is really no joke,*
> *as he plays in the hay all day,*
> *he giggles and squeaks,*
> *and puffs out his cheeks,*
> *then he snuffles for truffles,*
> *ho! heigh!*
>
> (finishing with)
>
> *Cock-a-doodle-dango,*
> *let us do a tango,*
> *toodle pip, bob and dip,*
> *find yourself a mango!*

"Good roosting to one and all, and see you at the next 'karaoke cuckoo-call'!" I called back as I flew off to me dwelling place.

As I departed, I heard one of them shout back to me, "Oh!... So poetic are your rhymes!... You'll make a superb 'bird bard'!"

And another one said, "By the way!... What on earth has happened to your tail?"

– Chapter Eight –

If You Go Down to the Woods Today— You're Sure of A Big Surprise!

Now that winter had thrown back its heavy duvet, fluffy white clouds chased across a soft dove-grey sky—promising sunshine and showers.

Spring was gradually spreading out its bright green covering, ready to be appliquéd with fresh new growth of bright yellow gorse dotted about the landscape, whilst the daffodils pushed their way up through the resisting earth to show off their frilly yellow trumpets, heralding a new beginning. And the sweetness of the spring air, tingled the nostrils as it drizzled its way into the senses. Little white dots could be seen jumping about on the hillsides, telling us that the spring lambs had arrived! The early "dawn chorus" erupted into song, as the blackbirds, thrushes, robins and wrens, competed in their own "Eurovision" song contest—their clear voices cutting through the sharp morning air.

A few warm sunny days in April teased the blushing pink and white cherry tree blossoms to burst open, much to the delight of the sleepy bumblebees, fresh out of their long winter's hibernation, as they slowly probed their way from flower to flower, appreciating the warmth from the sun on their soft gold-and-black furry backs.

A few days later and the blossoms had shed like confetti after a spate of high winds and lashing rain.

As the days lengthened, more bright colours began to appear.

Tall foxgloves added a splash of purple to the banks and hedgerows, competing with the equally tall rosebay willowherb, and closely on their heels came the sweet-scented creamy-yellow honeysuckle, twining sinuously through and along the hedgerows, and to round off the display, clusters of dainty pink and white dog roses, resting their own delicately perfumed heads on arching spiky stems.

I couldn't wait to get started on my work in the garden, only this time I had a fellow (or should I say feathery) helper to dead-head all the daffodils, which had by now sadly wilted.

Maggie followed me up and down the garden, closely watching my every move, chatting to himself as he hopped along.

When all the rubbish had finally been cut out and the leaves swept up and placed on the compost heap, it was time to carry out the more pleasurable task of gardening.

I could now set about planting out all the plants and shrubs I had carefully chosen at the local nursery.

I placed the pots of young tender plants into position, where I wanted to plant them, after shifting them around until I felt satisfied that I had found the right spot where they could grow and bloom without overpowering one another—because I knew that if I placed a short plant behind a tall one, it would be hidden from view, so I would have to get it just right before finally digging a hole and planting it in.

Concentrating on my work, I wasn't taking any notice of where Maggie was, or what he might be getting up to, but I soon found out that it wasn't the best policy to ignore him in the hope that he might just be behaving himself and acting like any normal bird, because that was too much to hope for.

He had been watching me all right, but whilst I'd been so meticulously planting my precious little flowers and shrubs, he would follow silently behind me, and just as carefully unplant them! All of them in little heaps, laying very bedraggled and looking very sad—on top of the earth!

It was so characteristic of Maggie to confiscate whatever you might have—if you had anything in your hand, then *he* would want it, and if you picked anything, then *he* would have to pick it too! For example, whenever Father or myself went blackberrying, then Maggie would have to come too, and he loved to pick the biggest and ripest of the juicy blackberries. He liked mushrooming too, but he didn't like eating those, but he would peck little holes in them or even shred them to pieces before you could harvest them, thus ruining the crop! This was all good fun to Maggie, but I did have an ace up my sleeve.

In order to hoodwink him, I pretended to pick with one hand, either a rotten overripe berry, or an un-ripened one, then with the other hand, pick the berry I really wanted to, but unfortunately he could anticipate my false move, and with the deftness of a sharp card dealer, he would then outwit me, and peck off the one I *really* wanted.

It's a tough life with a magpie hanging around!

If Maggie got bored with things (which he so often did), he didn't just stay in our garden, not when there were other alternative places for him to visit—and possibly disrupt.

One particular gloomy day—which had turned out to be a bit of a mixture weather wise, when one minute it was wet and the next it was tipping down with rain—there was a knock at the front door, sending the dogs into a frenzy of barking.

It was early afternoon, and I had already started to iron the clothes piled up from the week's washing—a chore which had been left for me to do, as Peggy was away on her holiday in Scotland, which meant that I would have to do them myself, and reluctantly, I waded into the great mounds of shirts, jeans, pyjamas, trousers, jumpers, towels, and the dreaded sheets (which I really hated ironing, as they seemed to go on forever), so I was hoping there wouldn't be any interruptions, and I wasn't expecting visitors for that day.

Pushing the clothes back into the linen basket and wondering who it could be, I went to the door.

I could see a bright mix of colours of red, yellow and green, looking distorted through the dimpled glass panels of the front door.

When I opened the door, there stood Ruth, our neighbour, who lived a few yards down the lane.

She looked like an oversized parrot standing there in her bright red boots, yellow sou'wester and long green mackintosh, which almost reached down to her boots, as she was really quite a short person, and well built, but she was not fat.

Ruth peered at me through her rain-spattered spectacles. She stood there like a limp rag doll, and she had a quizzical look on her face.

She pointed down at an equally comical wet and bedraggled squat little figure which stood almost at her feet, looking very woebegone. It was black and white, but not wearing boots or a sou'wester, or even a mackintosh.

"Is this your magpie?" she asked with a bemused look on her face.

"Er...as a matter of fact...yes, it is...but I wouldn't exactly call him *mine.... *I'm looking after him, and he does *live* here!" I said, "but do come in, Ruth, don't stand out there in the rain!"

"I hope you're not busy," she said. "I don't want to keep you from anything important!"

"No!...not at all!" I replied, almost convincing myself that this was true.

She came in, and Maggie waddled in after her.

Over a cup of tea and biscuits, Ruth told me about Maggie's exploits in her garden.

It transpired that the first time Maggie made himself known to Ruth was when she was squatting down in the vegetable patch picking strawberries. She noticed this magpie hovering around the gooseberry bushes, and he seemed to be weighing her up, as she put it. He then approached Ruth as she steadily made her way along the rows of strawberries and came right up to her wooden trug, which she used to collect her different varieties of fruits in—and then he brazenly flew onto the handle of the trug, and proceeded to grab up as many strawberries as he could gather in his beak before flying off with them into a willow tree, and from there, he flew down to the fish pond, and dropped them in, and took great delight in watching them bob about on top of the water, as the goldfish tried to eat them!

I didn't like to tell Ruth that he was probably planning on doing a bit of fishing, and the strawberries would be his bait!

Another day on one of his visits to her garden, Ruth said she was hanging out her clothes on the line, when Maggie flew down to her laundry basket, from which he grabbed up a pair of her best frilly knickers and started to fly across the garden with them, and when he reached the orchard, he flew up to the top branch of one of the apple trees and hooked them over a branch, well out of reach from her!

Poor Ruth had to wait until her husband, Bob, had arrived home from work, before her frilly undies could be retrieved with the aid of a long ladder and a very tired and utterly bemused husband.

Ruth told me that she had a lot of explaining to do, when she related the story to Bob about the magpie with a passion for knickers and how he'd snatched them from out of her basket, and it seems that Bob was not totally convinced about her story!

I think that Ruth was a bit relieved when I told her that this game of clothes snatching was nothing new, and had become more of an obsession with Maggie. He frequently hung around the washing line when I was hanging things out, and either he would make off with the clothes pegs from the peg bag, or he would land on the line, then walk across like a tightrope walker, then he would neatly un-peg the socks, pants, hankies, or anything else he could handle, and given half the chance, he would fly off across the fields with them, where he would deposit them in a most inaccessible spot, like bramble bushes or gorse.

I can only say that if any rambler happens to come across the odd sock or two or any other bits of undies hanging from a branch—they're probably mine!

"Another thing to watch out for," I told Ruth, "don't leave your wellies outside with the socks tucked in the tops of them, especially if they're spotted or striped ones, because if Maggie should find them, you're just asking for trouble, as this is another favourite game of his. He will snatch them from your boots, then fly off with them and dunk them in any water he can find! He's done this many times with mine. There's nothing worse than trying to put on a soggy sock!"

She laughed and thanked me for the warning, and then she said to me, "All my socks are navy ones anyway, so perhaps he wouldn't be interested in those!"

"I don't think that would let you off the hook!" I told her.

We had another mug of coffee with a biscuit, which Ruth (without thinking) dunked in her coffee, and when she saw the wry smile on my face—she laughed.

"Now I know where he learnt his dunking trick from!" I said.

Dusters became Maggie's brand new obsession—big fluffy dusters. These were added to Maggie's new collection of must haves!

He would wait for either myself or Mother to shake a duster out of the bedroom window, and then as soon as he heard the flapping noise of a duster being shaken (he probably thought it was a strange yellow bird coming in to attack) he would dive down in a flash and snatch the duster from your hand, leaving you waving an empty hand about in the air, and if anyone happened to be walking down the lane, it was rather embarrassing, because they thought that you were waving a greeting at them, so they would wave back!

The hills are probably alive with big yellow dusters fluttering about like flags in the breeze, and hanging in the hedgerows or gorse bushes (perhaps they are hanging alongside my socks and knickers as well!) or maybe they are even floating downstream, after Maggie eventually got tired of playing with them, and no doubt he would have discarded them indiscriminately, as most of them (socks, dusters, and some of the undies) were never seen again!

News travels fast in the country, and whenever the cry of, "Watch out...the magpie's on the loose!" went out—you would hear windows and doors slamming shut, and washing would be hastily whipped off the clothes lines.

It was as though a curfew had been imposed in the lane.

It wasn't long after Ruth's particular incident with "Maggie and the vanishing washing" that Bob, her husband, also suffered a minor encounter with Maggie.

Bob was very proud of his house maintenance, and his skills at building little walls and intricate pathways around the garden were greatly admired by their many visitors who came to stay on their holidays, as Ruth and Bob ran a guest house.

During a quiet spell (in between visitors) Bob began to work on a wall which was to surround his new rock garden, and he planned to lay a nice little path to extend along the base, and smaller ones on each level, to make it nice and easy for Ruth to reach her little rock-plants.

Bob hadn't exactly planned on employing a "graphic artist!"

It was Bob himself who later told me, that after he had built the wall, he wanted to complete the rockery project with a series of concrete paths, which he'd carefully planned beforehand.

On the chosen day, which was windless and comfortably warm, he started work on the first path not long after having breakfast, so after about three hours of hard labour, he stopped, and went indoors for his eleven o'clock cup of tea (he didn't like coffee) and left the first section of the path to dry off before starting on the second

After his tea break, he made his way back towards the rockery, where he caught a glimpse of a magpie nonchalantly waddling away from him—along the new path!

Now there are *two* "unfortunatelys" to this story, and the first one is: *unfortunately* Ruth had left a tin of red paint opened and (which she'd been using to paint two of her new wooden planters for her smaller shrubs), and she'd left it on top of the new wall!

The second *unfortunately* is: Maggie must have seen the pot of paint, flown down to see what it was, then tried to land on it, and in doing so, knocked the tin over, spilling a half-full tin of red paint, sending a cascade of blood-red colour to drip slowly down the new wall and straight onto the pristine white concrete path, not yet fully dried off!

To round off his handy work, Maggie had sploshed his feet in the wet paint, and was by now walking purposefully along the path, leaving little red marks as he went, which Bob said "looked like tiny red arrows, a bit like the ones you see on sign posts!"—so you could say that he definitely left his mark with the neighbours!

To stand outdoors holding something in your hand, is like saying to Maggie, "Hey!...look what I've got!"—and sure as eggs is eggs, it will attract him like a magnet, and down he will fly from his place of

hiding, and with a *thunk!* and a *grab!* — then it's up! up! and away! — minus your possessions, and you will be left standing there — empty handed!

On one of Maggie's most memorable episodes of hit-and-run missions, was the day I collected my decree absolute from the solicitor's office.

Now the solicitor's last words to me as I left his office were, "I advise you to keep these papers and documents in a very safe place, so mind where you put them, and I wish you lots of good luck for the future!"

He shook my hand warmly as I left his office, hopefully for the last time.

It had taken a long two years of an agonizing battle before a final divorce settlement was arranged, and a lot of conflicting statements drawn up by our respective solicitors, so when the gruelling procedure was finally over, it was a great relief to be able to collect my final proof of freedom from what had been a very unhappy and a very sad experience of my life. But now this was all over, and at long last I was able to move on in life and to get back to some sort of normality.

Driving back home, I felt highly elated, and pulling up at the front door, I just couldn't wait to get indoors and to kick off my shoes, then throw myself on the sofa, with a nice big glass of brandy to celebrate!

Before any celebrations could begin, there was someone else waiting for me — in the wings!

Maggie must have heard my car crunching down the stony drive and had flown onto the roof to wait for me to get out of the car, and as I stepped out, I reached in and picked up the documents, which I'd placed on the passenger seat beside me and turned to shut the door.

I hadn't realized that I was holding the precious envelope out in my other hand, as it was too big and bulky to fit into the little handbag which I took with me to the solicitor's office, so that's why it was on the seat and not in my handbag.

Maggie streaked down like a rocket and landed on my arm, but before I could stop him or take evasive action, he grabbed up the envelope, and I watched in horror as he winged his way with my important documents across the drive and headed towards the tall beech trees with the obvious intention of making his way towards the neighbour's fields and beyond — and to who knows where after that?

I screeched after him, waving my arms madly about in the vain attempt to halt him, but "the scourge of the skies" took no heed.

With the white envelope firmly clenched in his beak, Maggie disappeared over the treetops, and my elation on arriving home evaporated into thin air.

Then all of a sudden, like a homing pigeon, Maggie flew back towards me with the envelope still miraculously clasped in his beak, but ignoring me completely, as though I wasn't there.

He changed course and dived under the caravan (the same caravan which we bought many years ago and was towed by my brother's Volvo car all the way to Wales from the South of England) which was now parked right next to the gas container housed under the beech trees.

Maggie had to almost duck down to get right underneath the caravan, and I could hear him defiantly clucking at me each time I tried to call him to come out. He knew he'd done wrong, but was reluctant to give in—as usual!

When he got to the middle of the caravan, his attention gradually wavered as he became bored with carrying this "white thing" about, which was by now becoming a burden to him, and it wasn't edible either, so he decided to dump it right there—right in the middle of where I couldn't easily reach it.

Whilst he was busily engaged in other things, I had to act quickly before he could change his mind and return to the envelope again.

There was only one thing for it!

I had to scramble down onto my tummy, and in my best black skirt, white blouse, and black high-healed shoes, I pushed, puffed, cursed, and wriggled myself under the caravan, and thankfully retrieved my sacred documents, unharmed, which was more than I can say for the state of my clothes! Then I found I couldn't reverse back again, so I had to grovel and grunt my way right through to the other side.

"Gosh!" said Adam, observing my dishevelled appearance, "It looks as though you've been pulled through a hedge backwards!"

"Oh very funny!" I replied, feeling completely fed up and cheesed off!

"I've just been under a caravan 'forwards!'" I said, and Mother nearly fainted, thinking I'd been attacked or something!

This was just one of those increasingly all-too-frequent occasions that I could have quite willingly wrung Maggie's neck for him, but then I'd probably have to be at the end of a long queue of other prospective executioners!

The house was now beginning to feel much more cosy and very homely with the new carpets laid throughout, and with fresh paint on the woodwork, and colourful wallpaper in each room.

The only item of luxury left to add was a new shower.

We had two bathrooms with a bath in each—but no shower.

Everyone grumbled that we should have at least one shower in any case, but it didn't particularly bother me, as I liked to wallow in a nice hot, scented bath, with plenty of fragrant bath oils or heaps of nice frothy bubbles to sink into.

I relented, however, and eventually gave in to their incessant whingings and whinings, and arranged for someone to come and advise us on a suitable shower and with a reasonable estimate, as funds were fast running out!

On telephoning the electricity board to put forward my request to them, a cheerful lady on the other end of the line agreed to send a man out to see just what we wanted, and a date was arranged for his visit.

The day the man from the electricity board arrived was lovely and sunny as summer drew ever closer.

He arrived in his sleek, highly polished Porsche and pulled up almost silently in the driveway, and walked up to the front door.

I could see he was immaculately dressed in a black suit, with black shoes to match, and they had obviously been brushed to perfection—almost to a mirror finish. His tie was navy and white striped; it could have been an old school tie (that is to say an "old school" and not an "old tie!"). His hair (what little he had) was brushed carefully over to one side, and smoothed down with what looked like some sort of gel into some form of neatness.

As he stepped out of his car, he hesitated for a few moments and looked uncomfortably hot, so he decided to take off his jacket and placed it neatly folded onto the passenger seat, then he collected his briefcase and clipboard from the back seat of the car and rang the doorbell.

He was a soft-spoken man, and well mannered, and he seemed to take his job very seriously, but I don't think he had a sense of humour. If he did, he didn't show it, so it was very hard going to have a relaxed conversation with him, other than the business in hand, so we just kept to his routine sales-type talk.

Having inspected the bathroom and located where the shower was intended to be installed, he then produced a small brochure with pictures of various types of showers on offer, and as they were fairly limited, it didn't take long to choose a suitable model, i.e., the cheapest!

Asking me for a ladder, which I duly fetched, his next task was to climb through the small aperture into the loft, so that he could locate the whereabouts of the tank for the pipes to be connected. Having completed his search, and being satisfied with his findings, he called down to me to hold the ladder for him, and then very gingerly he squeezed his rather large frame back once more through the loft. Dusting off a few cobwebs from his shirtsleeves, we then went downstairs again and sat at the kitchen table so that he could complete his figures on his calculator.

Before finalizing the deal, his next request was a bit of a bombshell, which hit with a mega impact!

"Could I see where your electricity supply comes into the house?" he asked.

Now to me, that particular question implied, "*Which way to the gallows, please?*"

Now had I *known* that a simple request for a shower meant an inspection to be undertaken outdoors, then naturally I would have taken the necessary steps of keeping Maggie the molester well and truly locked up in his cell—but this was not to be!

Now Maggie doesn't always bother everyone in his "patrolling zone" if they linger only fleetingly—like getting straight out of their cars and coming straight to the door without hesitating—so I allowed him out of the aviary that very morning to do whatever he wanted to do (within reason) for the rest of the day.

If I'd been informed in advance the exact date that a man would be calling, then I would have told them their representative would most definitely need a boiler suit, a rolled up newspaper (to use as a weapon) and a protective helmet—hairnet optional!

Anyway, I reluctantly and cautiously led the "Un-action Man" out into the garden.

Fetching a measuring tape from out of his briefcase, and with his clipboard poised and a smart roller-nibbed pen held in his right hand, he was now ready for his final assignment.

The man stood there trying to look composed in the heat, as his crisp white shirt dazzled in the noonday sun.

Now if he had bothered to pick up his daily newspaper that very morning, and read his "STARS" for the day, it might have read something like:

> *Avoid anything black and white, and beware of a woman with an empty bird cage with its doors wide open; it could represent "a vampire at large," and if a few feathers are ruffled, don't despair, it's just a sign of a minor misinterpretation of a supernatural occurrence, and normal representation of an abnormal situation will be resolved in due course! Look out for (and try to avoid), a partial eclipse of the sun. Finally, try not to adjust your toupee or hairdo!*

The man stepped back to get a good long shot view of the house to locate where the electricity supply was connected up to the house.

He squinted up towards the bedroom windows, where the electric wires spanned across from the pole.

Making a few mental notes, he started to write things down on his pad, drawing a rough sketch of the side of the house with a few notes alongside.

I was suddenly aware of a silent dark shadow cast over the lawn, and looking up, I could see the black object, which briefly blotted out the sun, and as it swooped past the sun's rays, I could see it had flashes of white and a black tail.

It was Maggie, looking every bit like a pterodactyl!

I could tell that he was working out a strategy—whilst I was composing a silent prayer, like how to exit planet earth!

The man was quite oblivious of his pending fate as he was fully absorbed in his work, and hadn't noticed the menacing feathery projectile circling above him. After all, why should he be concerned? Plenty of birds fly around the sky all day and every day—nothing unusual in that!

The man scribbled his notes as I stepped back just a bit further behind him, so that he couldn't see me trying to block Maggie's path as he made his speedy descent towards his quarry.

I had that sinking feeling when I realized that my prayer had gone unheeded, and doing the sign of the cross had little effect either. Perhaps God hadn't tuned in that day for little pleaders like me, or maybe his direct line was disconnected, or could it be that his power batteries had just run out?

Maggie landed clumsily onto the poor man's unprotected head, and I could see Maggie's needle-sharp claws gripping into his scalp as he tried to keep his balance.

He stuck there like a limpet on a rock!

I held my breath as I anticipated an explosive reaction from the man.

I just could not believe how this sad person, with no sense of humour, could take this sort of torture and not show any emotion.

He barely flinched at the first impact, remaining remarkably composed, and yet he must have experienced a certain amount of pain.

His once-tidy hair, so carefully smoothed down, was now standing on end, as though he'd just received an electric shock. And then Maggie bounced off his head, only to land straight back down onto his shoulder, with his beak almost stuck in the man's ear, whilst he just carried on scribbling notes as though nothing untoward was happening to him.

I darted quickly to the man's shoulder, trying desperately to wave Maggie off, hoping he wouldn't notice what I was trying to do, as he neither spoke to me or even made an appropriate comment like, "Excuse me, but is there something all feathery on my head?? or "My wife wore one of these little numbers at Ascot last year."

Just any comment at all from him would have been quite normal!

Now that Maggie was still well and truly attached to the man's shoulder, like Long John Silver's parrot, he started to peck frantically at his tie, and managed to pull it to one side in a manner of disarray.

Once more, I made a futile attempt at trying to dislodge Maggie from his human perch, as I started to prance up and down like a ballet dancer from the "Sugar Plum Fairy" and wildly wave my arms at him, which made me feel ever more foolish!

I thought, *Should I at this point apologize or tell a joke—or what!?* I decided to do neither of those things, so instead, I dared myself to look slowly and cautiously into his face, side-on.

I could see the tension was now beginning to show, as beads of sweat started to slowly trickle down the side of his face and into the creases of his thick neck. Then I noticed a muscle at the side of his mouth twitch—just a fraction—as did a nerve at the corner of his left eye, which made him wink, but it didn't detract from his embarrassment when he started a bout of nervous sniffing noises issued in short bursts—almost uncontrollably.

Each spontaneous reaction seemed to set off a chain of further twitchings, sniffings, and winkings—as he attempted to shrug the invisible "thing" off his shoulders, and at the same time trying to act in a composed manner which couldn't possibly last too long.

He was now forced into a grand pantomime act of his own, as he leaped across the lawn with the agility of a pregnant elephant, and with me still cavorting in a mad fashion (like the rear-end of a pantomime horse) close behind him—giving a performance which would have done Widow Twanky proud. And as for Mr. Shiny Shoes, he now looked more like Worzel Gummage, the scarecrow.

A damp stain was gradually forming under the armpits of the man's nice white shirt.

The exertion had taken its toll!

He just didn't look the same man that had arrived earlier that day!

Maggie had now decided that he'd had his fun, and to show his appreciation of the show we had just given him, he applauded loudly with a clap of his wings as he flew back onto the roof, where he strutted and bobbed up and down with great satisfaction at having caused so much disruption—and a great deal of embarrassment for me!

I felt that now was the time to try and make amends, so I asked in a very squeaky, high-pitched voice, "Um…would you…er…like to come in for a nice cup of tea before you…um…go?"

In a very shaky voice the man said, "Yes, please…that would be very nice. Thank you very much!"

As we walked towards the house, I suddenly noticed a nasty, yellow, mushy blob with a black centre slowly trickling down the back of his shirt!

Maggie's last shot!

Oh well! I thought. *At least his smart black shoes still have their lovely shine!*

I didn't see the man again, but a fortnight later he sent along two men to fix the shower. An electrician and a plumber, and they introduced themselves as Mike and Dave.

Mike the electrician had black wavy hair and was of slim build, whilst Dave the plumber was ginger, with a short stubbly beard, and he was thick set, with a bit of a beer gut and an assortment of tattoos on both forearms.

They were so unlike their boss, being very chatty individuals, but I noticed that occasionally they would give me rather strange looks, as though there was something missing, or as though they were expecting something to happen, which made me feel a bit uneasy, and I began to wonder if there was something wrong with my appearance! I checked myself in the mirror and couldn't see anything wrong with my face; it looked about the same. I hadn't grown any horns on my head, my nose was still in the same place and without any warts worthy of a mention, and my make-up didn't appear to be smudged or anything, and I hadn't left any curlers in my hair, so everything was quite normal as far as I could see, so I was a bit perplexed!

It took half a day and endless mugs of coffee before the job was finished.

Before they left, I ventured to enquire about their boss, or "salesman" as I called him, and asked them if he was always so starchy and humourless, or was his usual approach to customers always so "low key?" They looked at one another and laughed.

"Oh yeh, our boss you mean!" said Dave, the more outspoken one of the two—"he's never cracked a joke, not with us anyway, so you could never call him the life and soul of a party, and he always looks the same, all togged up in a suit, whatever the weather, and he never lets his hair down, that's if he had any to let down!" he cackled.

"But when he turned up at the office the other week—well that's a different story! After his visit to you, it was like seeing a different person, and we couldn't believe our eyes! It looked as if he'd been in a tussle with a sumo wrestler! His stringy hair was falling about all over his face, and he looked in a right old tizz, as though he was about to break out into a nervous breakdown at any minute! Anyway, we gave him a tot of whiskey before he left the office, and he seemed a bit better after that, and he got a bit of colour back into his face.

"Strange though, but before we left the office this morning, the boss told us that when we came to this address, we should 'watch out for the "mad bird!"' as he put it, which isn't the sort of expression he would normally use, being an old-fashioned fuddy duddy! We've never heard him come out with anything like that before, so we didn't know quite what to expect when we got here, and it made us feel a bit uneasy like—know what I mean? We thought that there might be some sort of a rampant witch woman living here, but if you don't mind me saying, we think you're a very nice lady, and not a bit 'mad!'"

After that statement, I didn't know whether to laugh or feel humiliated.

I chose to laugh. Now I knew why they had acted so candidly.

I decided to show them who the real culprit was.

Taking them both down to the aviary, I pointed Maggie out to them, saying, *"There's* the rampant witch!"

I told them the whole story of what had happened, and how their boss was attacked by "the mad bird," and of his comical reaction. They laughed their heads off and swore that they wouldn't let on to him that they now knew the secret of his humiliating ordeal.

"So now you know why he's firmly bolted in his aviary," I said, and then added, "when I knew that you were coming today, I wasn't going to risk a repeat performance, as I didn't know whether you would have to do anything outdoors, so he was shut firmly inside his aviary—just in case!"

Once I'd signed their worksheet and receipt for "job done" without anymore mishaps, the two men left.

I was glad that we wouldn't be seeing anymore workmen—not for a very long time at least.

The birds had staked their individual claims on one of the nesting boxes, and were now busily collecting materials to line them with.

The blue tits had taken over most of the estate, but the nuthatches were strongly trying to gazump them, and whilst they argued over who should have what, the great tits took advantage, and moved in!

One morning, on my way over to Humphrey's stable, I noticed a little wren fly out of the shed window which was left open on the first latch so that an extension lead could pass through it whenever the workmen wanted to use it to plug in their electrical equipment.

As she flew out, I could see that she had a peacock butterfly in her beak. Now that explains why I didn't see so many big hairy spiders in the shed, as no doubt they were also part of her diet.

A few weeks later I found a little round nest filled with moss and a few downy feathers, and it was built just above the top shelf on one of the wooden crossbeams.

Several days later, she had laid her first clutch of six eggs, and they were pure white with a few reddish spots, and they looked so tiny and delicate. She seemed to be very much on her own, and I didn't see much of her mate, so she had to work quite hard. I thought at first that she must have been a lone parent, but later on I noticed another little wren entering the shed, so I assumed that it was her husband returning to help feed his offspring. He made enough noise when he did show up, clicking—*tic!-tic!*—and churring away loudly.

The male wren guarded his territory with some ferocity, and he would duff-up any other male wren who was foolish enough to enter his domain.

The swallows soon arrived too—quite early.

One of them had landed just outside the kitchen patio door, looking very exhausted, but when I opened the door to see if it was all right, thankfully it flew off in the direction of the stables, and I could see that it had a partner with it, flying alongside.

The poor things must have been very tired after such a long and arduous journey from Africa.

It wasn't long before this particular pair chose to build their special nests.

They were built with pellets of mud, which they had collected near the field entrance, and then they mixed it with their own saliva, and fibrous materials found nearby.

The nest was built on the top beam of the first stable, and looked most precarious.

The first attempt was sadly a failure, as it crumbled and fell onto the concrete floor of the stable, so they started again, but this time on another part of the beam, and thankfully they were finally successful with their nest building.

That particular year, they managed to rear three broods.

Once they arrive here, they stay with us, and remain roosting in the stable until they leave in the autumn.

The swallows are one of my favourite birds, because as well as being faithful messengers of spring, and always returning each year to visit us, they will sit on the top of the television aerial and sing their lovely twittering song, and remain there, singing their hearts out, even if I'm just below them hanging the washing out on the line. They also play a very significant role of helping to safeguard the other birds, by their distinctive alarm call which they give whenever they spot a patrolling sparrowhawk. They will often group together with neighbouring swallows and chase the bird of prey off into the far distance, dive-bombing them if necessary and at risk to their own lives, which makes them very brave little birds, so I hope that all the other little birds appreciate them!

I am able to study our resident swallows at quite close quarters, because when I shut Humphrey in his stable for the night, there sit all members of the swallow family, perched on the beam looking down at me, and they don't seem to be at all afraid of me, almost as though they know I won't harm them, and I always say to them, "Goodnight, little ones, sleep well," before giving Humphrey his last hug, and then switching off the light.

The collared doves arrive on the lawn each morning, flying noisily down to land, like miniature jumbo jets, and their smooth, round bodies remind me of Christmas pudding bowls, but they are also very pretty and cuddly looking. Their flapping wings making a resounding clapping noise, and their loud calls of, "*wheeoo! wheeoo! wheeoo!*" is a sure advertisement for any passing sparrowhawk out hunting for prey, who can only interpret this loud cooing call as, "*lunch! lunch! lunch!*"

Suffice to say, I have, on more than one occasion, witnessed a sparrowhawk streak down at great speed, then take off, clutching a collared dove with no effort at all, partly because the dove is a much slower flyer. In fact, one hawk who frequently visited our garden seemed to relish doves, and picked them off, one by one, until we were back to just two doves instead of about ten!

I did everything I could to distract Maggie's attention from the nesting community, because I knew that it wouldn't be long before he found out what magpies do naturally, and I could just picture him sliding stealthily off somewhere with a "swag bag" strapped to him, so that he could do a bit of nest robbing!

To try and manoeuvre him away from the busy mums and dads (who were constantly trying to keep up with feeding their hungry little broods) I would take Maggie with the dogs on nice long walks over the fields and beyond.

There was a particular walk which took us through a little meadow, left fallow and brimming with wild flowers, which attracted all kinds of butterflies, like the common browns, and the dainty little ringlet butterfly with wings of a dark velvety chocolate colour, delicately edged with silver, and they could be seen flitting and jiggling amongst the fluffy seed heads of the grasses. There were many other kinds of insects going about their daily business amongst the clover. The grasshoppers could be heard *"sissing"* away in the pesticide-free tall grasses.

Maggie showed a great deal of interest in all the movements he could see in the grass, and periodically stopped to investigate, but it didn't take him long to catch up with us again, as he didn't want to be left behind.

In order to get to the wild meadow and woods, we had to climb through the barbed wire which separated the boundaries of our fields and the meadow.

Eventually our path led us down to a very ancient wooded dell.

On the East side of the woodland, stood a very old Welsh cottage, now empty and deserted, and falling into decay.

The previous occupant had passed away, and the property and the whole estate was now left in trust to distant relatives.

Although the cottage was now almost a ruin, it had once been loved and cared for, and you could almost hear the laughter, and feel the happiness that must have once abounded within its walls. You could hear the rustle of small creatures, as they scuttled amongst the leaves which had fallen around the cottage, and bird song could be heard coming from the surrounding trees, and on warm sunny days, the sun cast rays of light and warmth upon the remaining window panes, as though trying to breathe life once more into the sad, lonely old cottage.

In contrast, and on the West side of the woodland and nestling on the side of a high bank, there stood an even older Welsh cottage, smothered in with a tangle of weeds and briars, and although this one had been lived-in just a few years ago, it too had been sorely neglected, but unlike the other old cottage, this one just didn't feel at all welcoming, in fact it felt quite the opposite.

It was eerily quiet, and no cheering sound of birds singing from the trees, as though they sensed bad vibes, and it was surrounded by a cold, damp atmosphere, that made you just want to pass it by, without even giving it a second glance.

Now on one of these nice long walks, something very odd took place.

The day was a very pleasant one, starting hot and sunny, so I was quite looking forward to the cool shade of the trees.

With Maggie perched on my shoulder in his usual manner, and only jumping off if he spied something interesting and worthwhile that needed investigating, and then jumping back on again when he found that it was only a waste of time, we made our way across the meadow as usual (where the children had—slid! bumped! and whooped! their way down the slippery slopes on their toboggans in the snow last winter), and then we continued on down through to the woods.

The beech trees were very old, but with smooth green bark—unlike the gnarled rough bark of the oak—and many of them had huge roots rising above the damp leafy ground, and they were covered in soft green moss, and vivid feathery green ferns grew at the base. Tiny holes were made beneath the roots of the trees where little bank voles lived, and little wrens sometimes built their nests between the boles of the tall beeches, and where the great thick trunks had grown over many years, and had fused together, like Siamese twins. Little pockets of water had formed there, creating miniature rock pools.

As we passed one of the beech trees, I noticed a tiny round nest with bits of moss poking out of the entrance hole. It could only be a wren's nest, and I was anxious that Maggie hadn't noticed it. He was sitting on my shoulder which was facing away from the tree, so thankfully he didn't spot it; or at least he hadn't betrayed the fact if he had.

The air was filled with bird song, and I could hear the two-tone wake-up sounding call of a cuckoo in the distance. His call to herald a new beginning, was once taken for granted, but now this elusive bird of Spring is heard less and less, and is now unfortunately becoming just a distant echo of the past.

A woodcock suddenly flew out of the bushes low and fast, giving an alarm call which startled me.

Then a couple of wood pigeons flew out of the trees startling me, as their wings made a loud clapping sound, and then a softer muted whistling noise as they flapped away.

A rustling noise in the dry leafy undergrowth betrayed the presence of a rabbit, and Katie was off!

Little Hattie trotted behind me, unconcerned, and Maggie just sat tight!

The woodland bit now opened out to an unrestricted view of a natural amphitheatre.

The steep slope led us downward, as we waded through a thick carpet of fan-shaped bracken, which was almost covering the zigzagging ancient sheep track, and as we made our way down the very narrow path, I was beginning to wish I'd worn my wellies and not my trainers. The thick fronds of the bracken almost tripped me up, and in parts it was so thick and tall, that I had to pick Hattie up to carry her through as she was too short to find her way, and it was becoming increasingly difficult to avoid stepping into the rabbit warrens dug out along the path. Nasty little seeds and burrs were sticking to my socks and working their way into my trainers, making it rather uncomfortable to walk.

The sun was slowly moving round, and out in the open, away from the trees, it was getting hotter and hotter in this sun-trap! Somewhere ahead, I could hear Katie crashing through the undergrowth, still after the rabbit she'd rustled up earlier, or perhaps she had picked up the scent of another one. "Oh well, never mind!" I said to Hattie, as she gazed up at me in my arms, with a disturbed look on her little face;—"we'll find her in a minute!" I cuddled her closer to me, just to reassure her, but she seemed agitated. I put her down again so that she could trot along on her own, now that the bracken was less prevalent, and the grass was much shorter here, probably cropped by the multitudes of rabbits!

Hattie kept close to my heels.

As we reached the bottom of the slope, the path now levelled off and walking became less perilous.

The path skirted a long line of willow trees, snaking round bends, enticing the walker to discover what lies just around the next corner!

The willows overhung the almost concealed stream, but the glint from the sun as it penetrated through the trees, revealed its existence.

I was transported back to my childhood days in Sussex, when we used to wander the fields and streams.

"What the heck!" I said to myself, and sitting down in the grass, I took off my trainers and pulled off my socks.

Stuffing my socks into the trainers, I tied the laces together and hung them around my neck, then carefully climbing through the overhanging branches of the willows, I stepped into the cool, gently babbling stream. It felt just wonderful!

Maggie wasn't at all keen to follow, so he flew off further along the boundary of the stream, where I could hear him calling out.

Hattie followed along the path, whimpering slightly, as she didn't want to get her feet wet.

I walked as far as I could, until a large trunk of a fallen willow blocked my way, so I had to scramble up the slight incline and back onto the path. I sat down in the grass once more and waited for my feet to dry, then I put my trainers back on.

It was as I stood up that I noticed the atmosphere had changed.

I was suddenly aware that I couldn't hear Katie crashing about anymore, and she was spending an unusually long time away from us. And where was Maggie?

The air seemed unnaturally still, and quiet, and not a branch or leaf stirred in the trees!

There wasn't a sound, not even bird song or calls!

I stood up and looked about, and it was as if I was looking at a still picture. Only Hattie was there beside me for company, and looking down at her, I noticed that the whites of her eyes were showing, and her ears were held back as if in fear. She was trembling as she pushed her body tight against my legs. 'What on earth was wrong with her?' I thought.

Although the sun was still beating down, I suddenly felt a chill, like a cold mist drifting past, and it was almost as though an unseen presence was brushing the willows, past me and Hattie, and continuing along the bend of the stream. My arms felt cool, and the hairs on the back of my neck stood on end, and there was a numbness about my head.

I shuddered.

There was a slight shushing noise, but not a breeze.

I could barely breathe with the fear of the unknown. With my eyes wide open, I didn't dare blink, in case I missed something, but I didn't know what.

There was nothing to be seen, and it wasn't as though I felt I was being watched by anyone: on the contrary—I felt I was completely alone at this moment, apart from Hattie. There was just a feeling of something quite extraordinary and unnatural. It was really uncanny and very unnerving!

Could it be my imagination running riot, or could it be something quite normal occurring at that particular time!

As I turned slowly to move away from the spot where I was standing, for what seemed hours, I heard a loud flapping sound coming from upstream.

It was a large heron, obviously he'd been disturbed from his fishing post, and I watched him as he flew clumsily past the willows, and then he disappeared out of sight round the corner.

It was almost a relief to see another form of life, and now everything else seemed to revert back to normal. The birds started to sing again, and the heat of the sun returned once more, as it circled slowly above us. I could see the graceful flight of a Red Kite as he silently glided above the trees, searching below for carrion.

Tracing my steps carefully and cautiously back along the same route, I called out, *"Katieee!...Maggieee!"*

Katie was the first to arrive.

She came bouncing out of the bracken, with her tongue lolling out, and a big cheesy grin on her face, quite unconcerned and as though she had hardly left our side for only a few minutes.

Maggie rejoined us further up the hill.

He had a different look about him—a look of contentment or fulfilment, as though he'd experienced an event of some kind.

I shall never know!

It was several weeks later—whilst visiting a local elderly lady from the village in her old fashioned Welsh cottage, and enjoying a nice cup of tea and home-made cake, whilst sitting comfortably and relaxed in a big old armchair—that we were discussing the whereabouts of nice walks to be found in the vicinity.

Megan was her name, and she had been a widow for four years, so she was now living alone.

Although she was born in North Wales, she had lived in our village for about sixty years, since the age of fourteen when she moved into the old cottage with her mother and Father. Her mother was a school teacher, and her father worked in an office for the local council.

After the death of both of her parents and then her husband, she moved back to the little cottage, after selling the larger house which she and her husband had lived in.

She said she preferred the cottage because she felt it was more 'homely' as she put it.

When she was younger, Megan used to belong to a local rambler's club, so she knew many of the footpaths, both near, and as far as the Brecon Beacons and Snowdonia, so I was hoping to glean some information about the walks nearby.

I mentioned to her the footpath I'd found in the woods just below us, and how overgrown it was, and casually mentioned to her the rather odd feelings I experienced there, and if she knew of anybody else who might have walked along the same path, and perhaps have had the same experience.

She remained silent for a few minutes before answering my question, and she appeared to be a little hesitant, as if she was unsure of her reply.

Her first words were quite unexpected.

"Did you be taking your walk on the twenty first of June?" she asked.

"Why yes, I believe it was!" I said, trying to think back.

"Isn't that the summer solstice….that's a coincidence…isn't it!?"

"Let me tell you a story," she said as she settled herself back in her armchair opposite me, but staring straight ahead, not directly at me, as though she was composing her thoughts, and a distant memory recall. She began her story.

"About six years ago—I think it was about six years—or maybe going on seven years…my!…how time flies…doesn't it? Well anyway, as I was saying, there was this young couple with two children, one little boy who was about eight years old, and a little girl who was just three years old when they first arrived.

They moved here from where they lived before—somewhere in the south of England: it might have been Kent actually, I'm not absolutely sure, my memory is not quite the same as it was, at least with dates and ages and such—but anyway, they moved into that very old farm cottage, you know the one I mean, on the west side of the woods just below where you're living now?"

"Yes!"—I nodded in agreement—"I know the one you mean, it's all deserted and looks as though it could do with a lot of renovation, but I bet it could be done up nearly as cosy as your little cottage. I have walked past it a few times, but it's very overgrown with lots of stinging nettles and thistles growing in the front garden, and looks a bit dark and dingy, but with a bit of paint and a few repairs here and there, it just needs the right family, and a bit of TLC. Anyway, what happened to the family, and why did they leave, and where did they go?"

"I'll have to work backwards with your questions!" she laughed —
"I'm not absolutely sure of the exact place they moved on to, but they
moved out of the old cottage, after living there for only two and a half
years, and they ended up somewhere in Scotland."

She cut two more slices of cake, took the smallest piece for herself,
and handed me the larger piece.

"Would you like another cup of tea?" she asked.

"Oh, yes please!" I replied, "but no sugar this time thank you!"

She then got up, dusted a few crumbs off her red-and-white
spotted frock, and went into the kitchen, and returned a few moments
later with two fresh cups of tea, and settled herself once more into her
chair.

She fished into a pocket of her cream coloured cardigan, which
was hanging on the back of her chair, and fetched out a clean white
handkerchief, and with it she rubbed her round spectacles carefully,
huffing on each lens in turn, then rubbing them up again until she
was satisfied they were sparkling clean, and then looking me straight
in the face with her grey-blue eyes, Megan re-commenced her story.

"Anyway," she continued, "let me see now: as I was saying — it's
debatable as to *why* they left, but it may be because of what happened
to their little girl Sylvia.

When they first came here, they kept very much to themselves and
didn't seem to have much time to socialize with us villagers, but that's
probably because they were kept pretty busy trying to sort themselves
out, and there's lots to do with two young children. I know that fact,
even though my husband and I never had any of our own.

It seems the husband worked away somewhere (I believe he was
an engineer) so he had to do a fair bit of travelling, whilst his wife was
a dressmaker, so she worked from home.

The little boy, Martin, went to the little junior school just up the
road here, but Sylvia was just a bit too young to start school when they
first got here, so she was left to play by herself around the cottage or
in the garden, and then it seems she took to wandering about the
woods. Her parents weren't unduly worried at the time because they
felt there wasn't any danger here, being all quiet and peaceful, but
they didn't seem to bother about the stream running there.

When the folks about the village heard about this from Martin,
when he told his friends that his little sister liked to go for long walks

on her own in the woods, which was by chance overheard by one of his friend's parents, they started talking, and saying how unwise they were to let her wander like that, especially in the Gwarffynon woods! — that was particularly taboo!"

"Oh really!…why's that?" I asked.

"I'll tell you in a minute!" she replied — "wait until I get to that bit!

So, as I was saying, they seemed to settle in nicely, and they even started to work on trying to get the cottage in order, but most of the decorating and repairs they tried to do for themselves, which took them a long time, because most of their time was spent on working for their living.

Anyway, Sylvia took herself off on her walks, and as I said before, her mother wasn't unduly worried about her, at least, not at first."

"Didn't she worry about her falling into the stream?" I asked.

"Well, I would have thought so" — she said, "but they drummed it into her that she was never to go anywhere near the stream, and it was said that she had learnt to swim at a very early age, so they felt confident enough that if she did happen to fall in, at least she could swim, and they said it was very shallow anyway, but you know in some places it is known to be quite deep, and when we have a real downpour of rain, it can be a raging torrent further upstream, so it all depends on which way you decide to go, and I certainly wouldn't let a small child of mine go anywhere near it, even if it hadn't rained!

Her mother took to asking her what she did on her walks, and thinking the little girl was playing at 'make-believe' she was amused when Sylvia told her she'd seen a 'pantomime!'

Each time she came back from the woods, she told her parents the same story: that she'd seen the 'pantomime' again!

Then one day she returned home in tears, and when her mother asked her 'what was the matter?' Sylvia told her a very strange story, and one which made them become quite fearful, and they began to wonder what was really going on in those woods!

She told them that the 'pantomime' she saw was 'Cinderella! Just like the one she saw at Christmas!'

She told them that the first time she saw the show, was when she saw the big pumpkin coming towards her, and it was pulled by very black horses, only she couldn't see their heads.

There were lots of people, in strange looking clothes, sitting inside the pumpkin, but not pretty clothes like the ones she'd seen at the

Christmas pantomime, and she couldn't see their faces either, only one of them, and she was a little girl, whom Sylvia thought must have been 'Cinderella!' There was a very big man driving the pumpkin, and it looked as though he was beating the horses to make them go very fast, only Sylvia said that she couldn't hear anything, not even when they passed right close to her, almost knocking her down, but she could only hear a strange whistling, windy, type sound as they went past. She said she didn't see exactly where they went to—they just seemed to disappear!

Why was she crying? Well, it seems that the last time she saw this pantomime, something different happened.

The 'pumpkin' came towards her, as usual, only this time she could hear noises, like people shouting and screaming, and the man driving it was wobbling about in his seat. Then, all of a sudden, the whole lot—the pumpkin, the horses, who were also making lots of noise, and the people who were now screaming and shouting—all tumbled and fell into the river, but all the noises had stopped, and when Sylvia went over to look to see where they gone, there was no sign of anything—nothing at all!

When she'd calmed down after telling them the story, Sylvia's father asked her to tell him exactly what did the 'pumpkin' look like?

What she described to him, alarmed him immensely!

The description she gave to him meant only one thing—she had seen an eighteenth century stage coach!—an apparition perhaps!"

"But why, and how could that be possible?" I asked.

"That's when Sylvia's father decided to try and find out about it!" she said; and then after another short pause, she continued with her story.

"He asked one of his friends, whom he used to go drinking with in the local pub, if he knew anything about his daughter's frightening story, or if he could throw any light on it.

His friend told him to go and see old 'Thomas the Tyres!' who lived further down the valley where he still worked in his little wooden garage repairing cars. He knew all about the local history, and if anybody knew anything, then old Thomas would!

So of course, Sylvia's mum and dad went along to have a chat with old Tom, and he was able to tell them of a tragic happening which took place in those woods at least a couple of centuries ago!

On the twenty-first of June, seventeen hundred and eighty something—a very posh wedding took place in the local church—in fact it was between the vicar's eldest daughter and a young gentleman who came from large estate in Shrewsbury, so it was a very grand wedding indeed!

Anyway, a big reception was held at an hotel on the outskirts to the village—since gone, owing to a big fire.

After the banquet and dinner at the reception was over, the bride and groom, and the bride's family, which included the vicar and his wife and their two other younger daughters—one of whom was about the age of Sylvia—set off across Gwarffynon Way (as it was then called) in a very posh coach especially hired for the occasion by the vicar.

It was arranged that the bride and groom should meet up with another stage coach at a local Inn, in order to make their way back to Shrewsbury, and the bride's family were then going to return back to the vicarage in their hired coach.

They left the hotel late in the afternoon, but the meeting at the Inn never took place.

Nobody really knows to this day exactly what happened, but it seems that before they all started on their journey across the track, the guests noticed that the coach driver was a bit tipsy, owing to the fact that he'd had a fair share of mead and a tankard or two of beer, but nobody cared much about that sort of thing in those days. So off they all went.

Now it was the driver of the pick-up coach who realized that something was wrong, because his passengers just didn't turn up, and he knew that the vicar was known to be a very punctual man, which was very unusual in those days as most folk went by the sun to tell the time, so nothing got done on time!" Megan chuckled.

'So nothing's changed there!' I thought to myself.

She continued once again on a more serious note.

"Naturally the driver of the stage coach became very concerned as it was getting very late, and darkness was setting in, and there was still no sign of his very important passengers, and as there was no form of communication at that time, he must have felt it was up to him to do something about it.

The coach driver decided to send one of the local lads on horseback through the woods, to see if he could find out what had happened. Anyway, when he got to a particular spot in the woods (about midway from the beginning of the track to the old cottage where Sylvia and her family lived) it was then that he noticed some wheel skid-marks, and deep imprints of horses hooves where they had dug deep into the mud, and the tracks and hoof marks appeared to just vanish at the edge of the river bank.

As I've said before, there is one part where the river is quite deep, and then it gradually narrows to a shallow stream, so it was the deep part where the young lad found these marks.

Now they say that the moon was very bright that night, but when the boy tried to search the river, the moon was clouded over, so he wasn't able to see anything, so he had to return back to the Inn to report that he couldn't see any sign of the coach, the horses, or the people.

The whole village turned out the very next day to do a search of the river, and it was then that the tragedy unfolded.

They discovered the stagecoach upturned in the middle of the river, and the bodies of the horses, and all of the passengers.

The villagers and the families of the lost souls, mourned their loss for many years, as they were such a well-loved family.

It is said that every year, from the twentyfirst of June, and for several weeks after, some people experience the ghostly apparition of the whole tragic event of that night, so that's what must have happened to poor little Sylvia, only she thought it was real, and she wasn't at all frightened of it until she witnessed the stagecoach lurching off into the river.

You may have had some form of an awareness of what took place, but you say you didn't actually see anything?"

Before I could give her my answer, Megan continued with her story.

"Another odd thing is: that the sightings are mostly seen during the daylight hours, but then I suppose that's because it happened in the afternoon, and not only that, whoever would go walking in those woods at night anyway? And another thing!" she continued — "haven't you noticed how the path along the river bank never seems to be overgrown? Nobody ever bothers to clear it because they obviously don't have to, and it's not as though sheep still graze there, as it hasn't been used for animal grazing for as long as I can remember. And another thing that's odd: at the entrance of both ends of the track, it's almost too thick and overgrown for anyone to walk through, even if they wanted to! It's said that the villagers wouldn't want to tamper with it, just in case the phantom coach and horses cross straight over and onto the main road!"

She stopped her narration at this point.

"Any more tea?" she asked.

It rained heavily that night, and I could hear it beating against the window pane, and my bedroom was lit up by flashes of lightning as a storm approached, followed by a distant rumble of thunder, and the wind howled and moaned around the house, as a finale to that spine-chilling encounter in the woods that day!

I think it's fair to say that I have no intention of returning to that particular walk in the woods—at least not on or around the twenty first of June!

- Chapter Eight and a Half -
Over to Maggie

who's afraid of the big bad wolf!?

"Cosmetic surgery, my friends of fun and great fortunes—purely cosmetic!" is what I shouted back to the unbelievers, who called out to me at that time when it was just before the first cuckoo's call.

"Go on then—tell us!" they said, before I sailed elegantly through the air back to me pad.

"Just how *did* you get that tail?"

In case it's slipped your memory, they were referring to when I had that rare old scuffle with that great hairy monster who was owned by a chocolate-gobblin' pinky, who was doin' graffiti stuffs all over me ma's walls in the big klakki.

"Well," I said, "there woz this earth runner the size of a troll, a right old lumpety thing who challenged me to a duel. Cor!—it was so *big, bad, and ugly!* And it had the temper of a dragon what had just swallowed a volcano. Well, it just didn't stand a chance, what with me all ready and rarin' for a good old battle, and me feathers were up, and me beak finely tuned all ready for action, so I just got in there and did the business!—No messing!

"If you think my tail is a bit of a wreck, you ought to see that old mut's *waggy piece*; there's just no comparison in my opinion. And after I'd dived in and added a few dots between its eyes, and a few dashes and gashes on its ears, I did a bit of smartly executed 'botox' work on its bum!… An'…wow…that sure did improve the posture of its proffered posterior!

"What I did to it put a generous amount of years on its prospects too! The old ragbag should be jolly grateful to me!"

This was me perky pertinent reply to the impertinent question put to me about me pathetically pointy-type tail! And that seemed to keep them perfectly quiet about it from then onwards!

Anyway, we all gathered together once more for our joint discussions, and to compare notes and everything.

They all wanted to know about me "future teller" piece and how I come by it, and could they see it? But then I thought that this wouldn't be a good idea at all—they would only want to steal it for themselves!

Then they wanted to know what it woz like, and did I keep me special treasures inside the giant pinky klakki, and were the pinkies hatched out of eggs, like what we were?

I told them that I didn't think pinkies hatched out of eggs, and I told them that their possessions could easily knock the spots off old Lace Cap's 'precious collections'!

They liked me telling them about the tiny wooden klakki, the one with the tiny wooden cuckoo inside of it, and about how it also has its own "future teller" piece, which makes musical notes every so often, and how the cuckoo calls out just before the music starts, and then he shoots back behind a little wooden trap, then to top it all, two tiny wooden fairies glide out from nowhere, twirl about like whirligigs, then glide back and out of sight again!

I told them how I did try to catch the little wooden perishers once, but me pinky ma spotted my just as I was about to land on the roof of the little wooden klakki, so she caught me and then took me away from it, and since then she has blocked me way for some unknown reason, so now I can't get anywhere near it, but one sunlight-time, I shall succeed when she's not looking! And another thing I can tell you. "Did you know that pinkies are really cuckoos of the human race?"

"How do you know, and what do you mean?" they asked.

"Because the pinkies don't build their own klakkis, they get other pinkies to build it for them, and when it's finished, they move in! Then if they don't like it there, they just give it over to another lot of pinkies, and then they move on to another klakki, a long, long way off, just like what we did!"

Then Lotty piped up, "Talking about cuckoos—let me tell you what Fox Tail did! Fox Tail is our sibling of two seasons ago, long before we learnt to suck eggs! Well then, he only went and swapped a *real* cuckoo's egg, which was already laid in a nest of the egg layer Cherry Stone, mate of Rowan Berry the song thrush, and put it into old Featherhead White Wings' nest, and swapped it for one of Lilly Bell's eggs (she's his mate) and then took one of her eggs and plonked it into Selena's nest. Well, there was a right old ding-dong after that, I can tell you, and the old Featherhead told Fox Tail he was going to punish him, and telling him, 'You are under arrest for egg stealing!'—an' then he said to him, 'Before long you will be up before the beak!'—whatever that means? Then he added a final oath, by saying to the petrified Fox Tail, 'Curses on you, thief!—May all your egg layer's eggs curdle!' which is one of the worse things that could happen to any decent law-respecting magpie. So I suggest that you don't *ever* meddle in the affairs of White Wing! He governs us all with a very firm wing! But getting back to the tale of Fox Tail. He was just about to tell White Wing what really happened, and then….!"

But before Lotty could finish her tale, a blackness descended upon us!

373

"Chink!… Chink!… Chink!… Run!… Run!… Run!" shouted Gurney, the 'slug-meister' blackbird, as he and his mate, Sweet Itch (so called 'coz of little white specks on her head) both darted under a bush!

Then a mob of sparrows, who were faffing about under a shrub, jittering and joggling up their feathers to gleaming point by dust swabbing in a bare patch of earth, suddenly took off in a cloud of dust, gibbering and jabbering in such a manner that they were about as coherent as geriatric jays! They all threw themselves like missiles into the middle of the nearest bushes, huddling closely together. Then the two swallows, Jeela and Solino, who were building their klakki in the black dragon's abode (known as Humphrey by the humans), appeared from the east side of us, and they seemed to be dive-bombing something, and all the while they were shouting, *"Get out!… Get out!… Get out!"*

"What the hell is going on?!" I shouted back, as the sky suddenly became black with a swirling mass of confused and fleeing birds of all description—flying off in all directions!

"Just slam on the wing power!—an' no tailgating!" shouted a terrified Totty, almost deafening me.

So I took off obediently, and headed blindly towards just about anywhere—like a tornado! I suddenly felt the full power of a wind blast as something flashed past me with a tremendous *whoosh!*

Then I heard a blood-curdling, "Oh shshiiiittt!!"

Finding myself miraculously outside me palatial klakki, I looked up cautiously, and I saw a flutter of feathers falling and spiralling to the earth.

Everywhere became silent. Not even the slightest of a twitter to be heard anywhere.

Then after what seemed like a whole season had come and gone (which is an awful long time), things started to come back to life again, as did the bushes, which now started to shudder and shake, where the bossy sparrow boys started arguing again, probably blaming one another for the whole thing!

Then another entirely different voice belted sharply into me poor fermenting brain (which was by now rising like a piece of dough, as if trying to unravel what had just taken place).

The new lilting voice said, "Oh the luck o' the leapin' salmon to you!—'tis a truly tollywoggle shenanigans that has just taken place, that it is—to be sure…begosh and begora!"

374

"And who the devil are you?" I asked politely.

"Why, 'tis Paddytalara McTosh, from the Emerald Isles, is the one you be speakin' to, that it is!" said the newcomer. Then he added, "And that be Chiselbeak the sparrowhawk, to whom you just had a near kiss-of-death encounter with, and didn't you just know that old Rollolong would get it?"

"Who or what is Rollolong?" I asked.

"Well, if you didn't know him then, then it's a fact you're not going to be acquainted with him now, for sure, for sure! That's him over there!... In a poyle o' black and woyt feathers, poor little tacker!" he answered. "An' him bein' such a good teef as well!"

"What's a...'teef'?" I asked.

"A teef, don't you know what a teef is?" he asked. "Well, he was such a good teef—he was good at teeving eggs and such loike," he said.

Now I understood what a 'teef' was!

"Twas a bit loike me old grand egg maker, Paddyloohara," he said. "Now he was caught teeving a hen's egg, and was spotted by the angry farmer, that he was—who shot at him, and old granddaddy Paddyloohara dropped the egg straight on top o' the farmers woife, killing her stony dead it did, to be sure, begosh and begora, 'tis true...'tis true, that it is!"

Now this story happened to be overheard by the other magpies, having returned to the scene of the crime after learning that the immediate danger had now passed, so they all started listening intently, as they were always up for a good tale.

Finding that he'd grabbed the attention of his spellbound audience, but looking a bit uneasy in case they might question him about the truth of his story, Paddytalara McTosh continued.

"Then!" he said quickly, "then—sure as eggs is eggs, there was this great big shadow suddenly appeared, an' it covered the whole of the earth it did, this huge, ever so huge, big turkey-looking eagle appeared in a god-almoity rush!"

All of us magpies gathered up closer, demanding to know the outcome, and he looked all puffed up and very confident, now that he had taken centre stage—so he continued.

"Well now—this big monster of a bird flew right down to where the poor ol' farmer was stood over his dead woife's body, stretched out his great big talons, and plucked the body up with no effort at all, then flew off with it, he did—no doubt to feed his eaglets!"

At the end of his story, we all looked at one another, perplexed, and Ivy said, "Well, I'll be plucked to the quills! Just goes to show, doesn't it! We'll just have to keep away from farmers and their eggs, wont we just? Don't fancy competing with giant turkey eagles!"

After his story, Paddytalara McTosh flew off without even saying where he was going, or even if he would be returning again, but when he was gone, I thought to meself, *What a wonderful story—teeving eggs and t'ings!... Hmm!... I wonder...!*

I began to feel a bit concerned about the possibility of meeting this character Chiselbeak again.

"Hey!" I said, "Does anyone know just how fast Chiselbeak can really fly?—just so's we can be ready for him—next time!"

"Why yes...I do!" said Holly. "He flies about...about as fast as a cuckoo's spit!"

"Don't you mean...a sparrow's fart?" asked Squiffly.

"Don't be so silly!" said Gizzy. "Whoever saw a sparrow's fart anyway!... You can't *see* that...you can only *hear* it!"

"Oh awright!... Awright!... I'm *wrong* as usual!" said Squiffly, moodily.

"Cuckoo's spit it is then.... Well that's fast enough anyway, isn't it? By the way, has anyone ever measured a cuckoo's spit!?"

"*Oh!... shut up!*" chorused everybody else.

We all parted and went our separate ways to our roosting sites.

The next sunlight hours I had planned on meeting up with the group again, so that we could have some fun!—but as I launched myself out of me mansion, I very near collided with the wren, Sikta Soffina, who had just flown out of the small "clutter klakki" (shed) window, with a temptingly juicy butterfly in her beak.

"Tic! Tic! Tic!" she scolded. "Watch out you silly magpie! I'm verrry busy! Tic! Tic! Tic! Lots of verrry hungrrry beaks to feed! Tic! Tic! Tic!"

"Ok, madam!" I said. "How's about we split the proceeds half way? And I can show you where there's lots of very podgy caterpillars to be had—fresh this season."

"Oh no!" she twittered. "Be that as it may, I fought a terrrible battle with a big spiderrr forrr this 'vanessa butterrrfly,' and I won't parrrt with it to you, not even a tiny bit!" she said—as frumpity as a humpity dumpity!

Then she darted off in the direction of the apple trees.

Her mate, Beeweaver, suddenly turned up from where he'd been hiding, under the ivy leaves.

"Never mind her!" he said. "She can be as cute as a toucan in a toupee at times, but she's a very good mate, and a very fine egg layer, and she appreciates a really top-class klakki even if it does take me several attempts at building the right one, and when she finally approves, she calls it 'as snug as a slug in slippers'—so I know when she is pleased. Did you know she comes from the long line of the 'Ishikka'?"

"No," I said, "what does that mean?"

"Well, it's a very ancient order of wrens, dating back to when the world was still very young. The first Ishikka was ordained by the great eagle, who at that time held the world on his great shoulders, he ordered that the Ishikka was to rule all the birds of the land, and he was employed to seek out the 'chickle chackle tree,' which was a very magical tree, and on the 'chickle chackle tree,' small precious stones hung from its branches. There were deep purple diamonds, golden yellow amber, and crimson red pearls, which had passed through the 'Tiger's Eye,' to give them magical powers. Each stone held a secret, or a small creature, and other things too—too numerous to mention. Some had either fairies or spiders, and others had wasps, ants, and other small creatures, and some of them even had naughty imps hidden inside, who danced about everywhere and did an awful lot of mischief wherever they went, which was very unfortunate for anyone who happened to come across them, but they were quite rare.

"The Ishikka chose very special wrens, who were exceptionally obedient, strong, sharp of wit and with a fair amount of intelligence, and they were to be sent out on a mission to find the 'chickle chackle tree,' which moved around, and so it was never found in the same spot twice.

"They were called 'stone crackers' because it was their job to find a way of breaking open a chosen stone, by whatever method they could. To do this, they would have to close their eyes, choose one of the small stones, tap seven times with their beaks, and then they could open their eyes again. They were amazed to see that the stone had changed into a crystal egg shell, and inside, they could see moving images and scenery.

"Sometimes, the 'stone crackers' might find that their particular stones held different kinds of seeds, like apple tree seeds, complete with honey bees to pollinate them, and some held sunflower and moon daisy seeds, or seeds of lemon and orange trees, or contained seeds for growing roses, lavender and also small lily bulbs. Some of the very small stones held tiny seeds of a plant called weasel's snout, and also found amongst them, were many precious seeds of healing plants.

"Now one particularly bright wren, called Kerdeeka, found the largest gemstone on the tree, which was a soft green jade. In order to crack the jade open, Kerdeeka dropped the stone from a great height, and even before it could reach the earth, it mysteriously split open straight down the middle, and out of it tumbled all the rune signs, in a burst of dazzling flashes and showers of small rainbows!

"First to show itself was the Ur rune, which gave Kerdeeka extra strength and endurance, and to help her focus more on her path of life. Then came Feoh, to give her spiritual richness so that she could help her fellow wrens to find all their food without too much of a struggle or effort. She was then shown the Thorn rune to give her authority, and she was given a sapphire to wear about her throat during her lifetime.

"Rad tumbled out at great speed, and this showed her the wheel of life, which meant she could 'go with the flow.' In other words, her lessons in life had a beginning, a middle, and an end, and she had nothing to fear as she was already quite fearless.

"Geofu meant that she was to be generous at giving as well as receiving, whilst Wynn would give her much happiness. There were many more runes, and Kerdeeka made the most of them, and she passed down their secrets to her fledglings."

At this point, there was a sudden movement in the bushes.

"Ah!" he said after coming up for breath from his long story, "Here comes Sikta Soffina—better dash! I must look busy, or she might think I've been lazy!" he said with a wink. And off he darted, leaving me thinking about insects, fairies, imps, stones, runes and other things.

I was off to see if I could find me own 'chickle chackle tree'!

"Have you seen the other magpies?" I asked Chikka the nuthatch, who was poncing about in the apple tree.

"Why yes!" he said, after he'd started stabbing away at the nuts in the little cage thing that hung from the apple tree. "I saw them making their way in that yonder pasture—right over there!" he said, pointing his beak towards the west.

"Okay, ta—an' tara!" I said, and flew off in that direction.

Joining the rabble, I said, "Bore da!"—using their own lingo—"I see you're making the most of me leftovers!"

"What's that?" asked Lilly Bell.

"Well," I said, "me an' me pinky slave (the farmer), we were out here the other sunlight hours, and he'd got this mighty fine 'insect juicer' (also known as a tractor) that scrapes across the earth, digging up all these juicy insects, just for me, that's why I know he's me slave, and I just helped myself, and then after me grand feast, he gave me some mighty fine liquid to drink that helped the sunlight-time to slow down, and then I felt me self tumble about, and turn upside down, and then all sorts of funny thoughts jimbled and jumbled about in me 'ead like! But never mind all that, what I would like to know is—is there a 'chickle chackle tree' here abouts? Because I want to find one for meself to own!"

"No boyo!—not possible!" said Holly. "You're the wrong type of bird. You have to be a wren…. It's only wrens that can be the special 'Ishikka' of the ancient order, isn't it?… So it's just not for you anyway!"

"Well," I said, "I was hoping to find some of those lovely shiny stones and all them things what's inside of them, and all them monkeys that I could chase around."

"What *monkeys?*" asked Shiffly.

"Well, you know?… All them—*chimps!*"

"Not *chimps*, you ninny!… *Imps!* They're not monkeys! They're naughty little elfy type things, only small and black, and full of mischief…. You don't want to find any of them, because if you do, then you must be *tup!*"

"What's *tup?*" I asked.

379

"It means you're just plain stupid!" answered Lotty and Totty together.

"So what's the likelihood of me even *seein'* a 'chickle chackle tree' then?" I asked, impatiently.

"Well, it's about as likely as you *seein'* a vomiting shark, isn't it!" said Holly (in the way of an answer and not in a question).

"Well, that will have to do then!" I said, not quite knowing what a vomiting shark was. "So where can I find one then?" I asked.

"Can you swim?" asked Holly.

"Don't know if I can—I haven't tried! That's only for fishes, isn't it?" I asked.

"So there you are then!" said Holly. "If you can't swim, and you're not a fish, so stop rabbiting on about it!"

I gave it some thought, but not for long.

"So let's go hunting rabbits instead!" I said.

"I know what would be a good idea!" said Gizzy. "Let's all fly down to the dingle and find old Hootie who lives in the green woodies, where he tells us all sorts of stories, like the one he told us only the other sunlight hours, the one about toady woadies who live around the damp swampy places, where the air is filled with dragons' breath (what I calls "spirit drifters"—or fog)—an' where they catch fat black slugs and things.

"Well now, it seems that at certain times of the season and different parts of the land, the pinkies collect the toady woadies up around darkness time, and then they take them from one side of the giant metal klakkies' pathways to the other, and it seems it's some kind of a ritual, to stop the toady woadies from getting squashed flat, which is all right for the pinkies, but it deprives us of some easy pickings, and there's nothing nicer when it's damp and cold, to scrape up a nice big, fat, juicy, toady woady!"

We all nodded in agreement.

I still thought it would be a good idea to hunt rabbits.

We flew down to the dingle, but we were careful to fly downwind from Chiselbeak the sparrowhawk. This was me first visit to the dingle. It looked so inviting and full of familiar sounds, and some strange ones too, that I just knew it wouldn't be my last visit there.

We flew low and fast, and I felt so exuberant, I called out, "Watch me stretch me wings to infinity!"

"Where's that?" Ivy called back.

"I dunno...but it's an awful long way!" I responded. "By the way—where's Featherhead White Wings? I haven't seen him for a few days now!"

"Oh, he's out on what he calls a very important mission," said Holly, his mate.

"He usually goes off to find new territories, or to look out for any marauding groups of magpies that might threaten our existence, and sometimes they try to break up our group, which then weakens our community, so then we have to go to battle."

I didn't much like the sound of that just now, and I wasn't really prepared to do a proper battle, and besides, I didn't want to get hurt! Not only that, I don't think Featherhead White Wings liked my very much, so why should I fight for him anyway?

We flew through the trees, then above a winding stream, then back to the dark area of trees, where we felt we could chatter quite freely amongst ourselves. From there, whilst we all scrabbled about in the leaves, there were more tales and exploits to be told, and all the while we were waiting for Hootie to turn up.

"We can trace our ancestry back to the 'Mabinogion,'" said Parsley, who hardly ever spoke.

"Magibonigon! What's that in aid of? Can you eat it? Is it animal? Is it vegetable? Or is it mineral?" I asked as I scooped up a passing black beetle.

But they pretended not to hear me.

"The *mabinogion* is about kings, princes, princesses, knights and dragons, good and evil with lots of fighting, and also about the first sighting of the famous Merlin," said Parsley.

"Sounds like a good day out," I said. "When does the season start?"

Another bout of deafness, so I tried again

"I've got a dragon—a black dragon who's really a bit of a 'dark horse'!" I said. "And I can do almost anything with it. I can even sit on its back. And this Merlin that you've just mentioned…do you mean the bird? You know? The one like a small eagle? Keeps close to the ground—hunts swift and low—like a swallow?"

"Swift?" asked Parsley.

"No…swallow," I said

They all looked at me a bit puzzled.

"No, I mean Merlin the Magician, not Merlin the bird, or a swift, or a swallow!" said Parsley, indignantly.

Our chit-chat was brought to a sudden halt when a snuffling, gibbering sound could be heard, along with lots of leaf-rustling noises in the undergrowth, and then, just in front of us, I saw one of the ugliest, and one of the most menacing looking black and white heads suddenly rear up from a hole in the earth, and it looked straight at us, bearing a set of seriously sharp looking white teeth!

"What the hell was that?!" I asked, as we all took off in a furious flurry of feathers and beat a hasty retreat.

"That is somebody you really don't wish to get into an argument with," said Totty.

"He is Seb the badger, and he can be mightily grumpy if he's disturbed when he's out hunting, and he loves the taste of meaty things! Here he comes! Now it's take-off time! Be quick!"

I didn't exactly want to say, "how do you do!" to this Seb character!

After a few rapid wing-beats, we settled once more, further down-wind from this flesh-eating 'Seb,' and I could still feel a certain amount of apprehension tingling away to the tips of me feathers, and therefore I aimed at keeping me options open for a major exit from these dark woods.

"I have never met a badger before," I said, "but I have heard about them. We had many sets where I came from, but I think most of the badgers where dug out and then brutally murdered by certain groups of pinkies, with their packs of small, short-legged earth runners (humans with dogs, of course)."

"If you really want to know and learn more about other creatures from these parts, then it's definitely old Hootie you'll be wanting to find, isn't it?" said Totty.

"So what do we do to find Hootie then?" I asked.

"Oh, we'll just have to be very patient and wait, he's not far away, but you won't hear him coming as he flies very silently, and before you know it, he's just suddenly there in front of you!" said Tizzy.

Whilst I waited and waited just for a tiny glimpse of this famous 'Hootie,' I had to be content to join in with the rest of the group and pretend to be very busy foraging amongst the leaves.

I was just beginning to feel rather bored and was about to take me leave and make me way back to me roosting place, when all of a sudden I had that funny feeling I was being stared at from somewhere just above me.

Looking up (in as casual a manner as I felt capable of), I could see there, looking down at me, but almost as though he was looking straight *through*, or *past* me—was the most odd looking bird I had ever seen!

He was big, fat, and very round, and he had the most *huge* eyes that were about the size of a full moon, and I'm sure I saw one of them wink! His beak was short, sharp, and hooked, and he perched on a branch with big yellow strong-looking talons, which I was quite envious about at the time.

His great round head swivelled right round, and I thought that any minute he was going to twist it off!

What a clever bird! I thought. *How on Mother Earth does he do that?*

Then Lilly Bell was the first to break the silence—but only in a quiet muttering whisper.

"Old Hootie is about to go into one of his spirit levels," she said.

"Whatever is that supposed to mean?" I asked.

"He goes into a sort of trance-like state," she said, "and sometimes he goes out on a 'questing,' and the latest 'questing' is to find out what's on the other side of the moon!"

"Look at him now!"

"What can you see, Hootie bach?"

The great round ball of feathers then spoke.

"I address yoohoo!... Maggie!—that is your given name!—is it not?" said old Hootie, now coming out of his trance.

"Yes! Yes, your graceship!... It is!... Er!... I mean!... Yes!... I am called Maggie!" I blurted out with a curled tongue.

"Now then," he said, "I can see that you have travelled from a fair distance, and that you have many stories to tell, or maybe you have already unburdened yourself of them!"

383

I'm sure I saw him wink once again.

"Have you told them the stories about Lace Wing and Moonbeam, and all the other tales?" he asked.

"Yes...yes I have!" I said.

"Good! Then let me tell you *my* stories!" he said. "My real name is Klogitiwhoo, 'the moon gazer'—son of Lunar Dune Twister, and second cousin to the barn owl, Soft Wing Moon Bird. My mate's name is Kyto, and right now she is tending her eggs in our nest in the hollow of a tree trunk, which is a few trees away from here.

"I am not always to be seen during the daylight hours, as I hunt at night, which is becoming more and more difficult these days as humans build more and more of their dwelling places, and they also bring in many earth whisperers (cats) that stalk at night, killing many, many, rats, mice, voles and shrews, which is our main diet, so our existence is very bleak. If only their human keepers would keep them in at night, then maybe we would stand a better chance of surviving.

"Anyway, where shall I start? What about the story about the moon itself?"

I nodded and settled myself down to listen.

"It all began after Gaea, the 'Earth Mother,' had given birth to the stars, seas, and mountains. She happened to come upon a little finch who was searching the barren meadows for seeds to feast upon. Gaea took pity upon the finch, so she gave him a small seed and told him to fly to the moon where he was to plant it.

"The journey was long and tiring, but eventually he arrived on the moon, and there he dropped the seed, which immediately sprang into life, and it grew, and grew, and grew, until the sun was born, and quite soon after it started to heat up, getting hotter, and hotter, and hotter.

"What the finch hadn't noticed was that a baby spider, which had attached itself to the underside of his wing, also dropped out and fell onto the moon.

"Now that he'd finished his quest, the little finch started on his long journey back to the earth. He had to pass through the darkness of night, the yellow glow of the moon, the pale streaks of the daylight, and the redness from the rays of the sun, and as he neared the earth's atmosphere, he met the goddess Palladin (a transparent angel), who was slowly drifting along on a carpet of feathers and lambs' wool, and behind her trailed a colourful rainbow—which was very different to the rainbows we know of today—an' it started to throw out crystals shaped like carrots, rounded at one end and pointed at the other, and they contained past memories, such as first speech, music, hunting and gathering, as well as the symbol of the yin and yang, and also there were the four elements.

"One crystal contained a fragment of earth, and another contained wind, and then another held fire, and last of all, one held a drop of water. Four other crystals captured a small piece of each corner of the globe—north, south, east and west, and also the four seasons— winter, spring, summer and autumn. There were many other things of great importance, too. The crystals shattered into small pieces as they hit the earth, and they lay hidden, waiting to be found by somebody to unlock their true secrets.

"Palladin—who was sent out to look for the little finch (after his long epic journey), by Gaea the 'earth mother'—said that he was to be named Goldfinch, and instead of being an ordinary brown finch, he was a beautiful gold of the moon, red of the sun, black of the night, and white of the day, and he would sing with a voice like an angel, with a soft bell-like quality, and that he would be a 'spirit guide' to lead all creatures of the earth who had passed away into the Garden of Paradise.

"As the warmth from the new sun heated the earth, many seeds started to grow in the meadows, and the first to grow was the sunflower, the seeds of which are loved by many birds. And the second flower to grow was the moon daisy, to brighten up the woodlands and loved by moths. Now one of the most revered flowers to bloom from seed, was the passion flower, which holds its own story, and it goes like this:

"The leaves of the flower represent the spear; the tendrils are the cords, which the one named Jesus was scourged with; the ten petals are the ten apostles, who deserted him; and the central pillar of the passion flower represents the cross; whilst the stamens are the hammers; and the styles are the nails; and then the inner circle round the centre, the crown of thorns. The white of the passion flower represents innocence, and the blue shade is a symbol of heaven.

"The passion flower only remains open for three days and then dies, but this is said to represent the death, burial and resurrection of the one crucified. This is a story of human compassion, but concerns us all, for in the end, we are all connected in spirit."

"Is the one that you say is named Jesus...was he a...a...God?" I asked.

"Why yes!... That is so," he said in a very low voice.

He then continued.

"So now that the little goldfinch had completed his task, he, and all of the other seed-eating birds, had plenty to eat for the rest of their lives!

"Now we mustn't forget that little spider who hitched a ride to the moon! It was a female spider, and she found another lonely male spider on the moon, and they produced millions of other little spiders. As time passed by, they ate all the food there was to eat, and in order to survive, they started to eat one another, and they eventually grew bigger, and bigger, and bigger!

"Now the sun became too hot for the moon, so it broke off, and the two drifted apart. As the now very large spiders tramped across the moon, faster and faster, to try and find food, it sent the moon into a crazy spin.

"*Tap!... Tap!... Tap!—Click!... Click!... Click!* went their mandibles and feet as they raced and fed. *Crunch!... Belch!... Crunch!* could be heard as they ate one another. Their footprints left huge craters across the moon's surface.

"The spiders decided to try and reach the sun, so that they could try their luck there, and started to spin great long cobwebs, which they could drift across the universe by. Some of the spiders reached the sun, so they began to weave a great cocoon of cobwebs criss-crossing around the moon, and then another one around the sun, then very gradually, they started to pull the sun and moon together again! But before the planet and star could be united once more, a bat—which was out chasing moths to eat—criss-crossed between the sun and the moon, and innocently cut the lines of cobwebs, thus setting the sun and moon free once more. Now this is why we have the eclipse of the sun and the moon, and the ebb and flow of the tides!"

Wow! I thought. *this is real sanctimonious stuff—must give this wise old bird his due!*

"Hmmhmm," coughed Klogitiwhoo the moon gazer, "You have interrupted me with your thoughts again.... I haven't finished my story yet! Do you wish me to continue?"

"Oh...oh...yes, please, your celestialship!" I said, not realizing he could actually see through me head and read me thoughts, but then with those big yellow eyes, I'm not altogether surprised.

He lifted his big feathery feet and shifted his position just a little.

"As I was saying," he continued, "now that the sun and moon were separated, they would have to be ruled by their own gods and goddesses. Ubasti was to become the goddess of the sun, and she was chosen by Seb, who at that time was the earth god. Then it was the turn of Nut, the sky goddess, and she chose Silene as the moon goddess.

"At the beginning, Ubasti took on a different guise, in the form of a semi-human, and she called herself Shamashona. She travelled about the earth on the back of a unicorn, who wore the Orion's Belt of three stars around his neck, and attached to the belt were black velvet pouches, fastened by silver clasps.

"The pouches contained different types of weather conditions, which Shamashona (or Ubasti!) would release at will. Out of these pouches poured raindrops, snowstorms, thunder and lightning, hail stones, whirlwinds, tornados, and sometimes a rainbow, if the sun and rain poured out together. Other pouches contained dreams, and upon opening, the dreams would float down on silken threads, and alight on those who were in a deep slumber. Another pouch contained terrible nightmares, and they would tumble down to earth, unloading the most terrifying and unimaginably horrible visions onto the forms of the more restless sleepers.

"If she was in a bad mood, Shamashona would create chaos by cracking a great long whip, which was covered in sharks' teeth, and as it cracked and sang through the air, it would drive packs of howling wolves into becoming ravaging beasts! And bad tempered giants, who roamed the earth at that time, were encouraged to throw huge boulders at one another in a fit of rage, for reasons that they didn't even know about, and as they fought between themselves, they created huge cracks to appear in the earth, and that's how earthquakes first started! The giants also chased goblins and dwarves from their homes, which were built beneath the earth.

"To build these underground homes, the dwarves and goblins had to toil non-stop, right through the moonlight hours (they didn't work in sunlight), in order to clear the small holes, which were blocked by mounds of earth and stone, probably left by badgers. Eventually they created a network of caves, which still exist in our time, and many have yet to be found! Now these small folk have been left homeless!

"The goblins were banished to another land, as they were not trustworthy, and nobody really liked them at all, so the dwarves were not at all sad to see them go!

"Now another sorceress in our story was Silene, the chosen moon goddess, and she too could also change herself into Sin, goddess of the night. But she was far gentler a creature than Shamashona. She wore a long flowing robe of black silk dotted with star dust, and on a silver belt, she wore a very large stone of the 'Tiger's Eye,' which was formed from bolts of lightning and dust storms in the galaxy, thus creating these magic golden-brown striped silky stones; the largest of which was blessed by Ra, the sun god, who was the first to see the stones as they fell from the sky. They didn't go unnoticed by a serpent, who swallowed them up.

"Ra chased the serpent across the sands with his pet jackal at his heels, and when he finally caught it, he picked it up by its tail, and threatened to hit it with his staff if it didn't give up the stones, but it refused.

"Ra ordered his jackal (who most of the time was a carved head on the top of his wooden staff) to bite off the serpent's head, whereby the serpent spat out the largest stone, hissing menacingly, and as it shook its tail in anger, the stones which were still remaining inside the serpent's writhing body could be heard rattling. And that is why the snake is now called a 'rattlesnake!'

"Now Ra was able to use the single (but sacred) 'Tiger's Eye' to see in the dark, as well as giving the bearer psychic powers and protection from evil, and also for bravery. It was also used to aid the spirits of the dead on their journey to the 'land of shadows.'

"Ra went on a long journey across the universe, which lasted for seventy-six years. He flew beyond 'the ring of Neptune' on the tail of a great comet as he sought out evil spirits, to whom he dealt out a very harsh punishment, and he banished them from his kingdom.

"Many moons and suns later, Ra passed on the 'Tiger's Eye' to Sin, and that is how she came into possession of the sacred stone, which she now wore on her own very long journeys. Around her neck, Sin wore a necklace made from glowing moonstones. On her forehead she wore a symbol of a crescent moon made with tiny blue diamonds.

"As she glided through the night sky, she twirled round and round on a thin silver thread, made from the cocoons of the moon moths. Gently and silently she would glide on the silver threads, and descend to the earth where she took the form of a dark shadow, blending in with the soft quietness of the night. She would glide slowly along, like a gentle breeze, and seeking out small defenceless creatures, she would help to guide them to safety from the predators who stalked them (including owls!).

"She was able to create dark shadows by cutting at the undergrowth with a silver sword which hung about her waist, so that the little creatures could run to seek refuge until the danger had passed by. She would then call out to them, in a whispering voice, 'Run!... Run!... Then you must be still and quiet, until your senses tell you that the danger has passed!'

"The two goddesses, Ubasti and Silene (or Sin) waged a battle between themselves for supremacy. The war raged on for many moons and many suns, until Ra stepped in, and he offered Ubasti the sacred Ankh, which was an ancient amulet of life.

"To Silene, he offered an ancient amulet called Nefer, which was made of red stone, and this would bring her happiness and good luck! The two goddesses were overcome with joy at such gifts, and both agreed to a compromise, that they would both share peacefully and in harmony during their immortal life, by carrying out their very important roles—in night and day!"

And so ended Hootie's long but fascinating story.

"Do you know," I said, "after hearing about all those things in your story, I fancy I could really hanker after a bit of the 'Ankh'—the much sought after stuff for life and all that kind of thing!—but I would never say never to 'Nefer' neither!"

Hootie just sat there and looked at me in what you might call 'contempt'!

Then I said, "But I'll make do with a plain old 'chickle chackle tree' instead."

The old Hootie just clicked his beak together and said nothing.

I felt a bit uneasy, so I looked about me for some kind of back-up from the mob. "Hey boys!" I called out. "Don't you think that was an absolutely fantastic story that Klogitiwhoo has just told us?"

I thought I'd better call him 'Klogi' instead of Hootie just to humour him a bit—but I was greeted by silence and an empty space!

"Where have all the others gone?" I asked. "Weren't they interested in your epic tale?" Klogitiwhoo answered. "Let me put it this way, as they've heard the story before, they don't want to hear it again! Would yoohooo…hooo?" he hooted! "Now if you would like me to, I will recite to you my mantra about the moon and sun. It's a verse which I have only quite recently composed!" he added proudly.

"Yes, please!" I said. "I would like to hear it."

"Before I do this for you," he said, "there are two small gifts I will leave you with. When we owls have feasted, we always give back to Mother Earth the small bones, neatly wrapped up in pelts, as a thanksgiving offering. Sometimes we 'throw' the small bones, in order to seek guidance, or for future telling, which is by the sacred 'sealed order of the oak!'—an' each pelt conceals a special rune.

"I do know that you are acquainted with some of the runic signs, but these are created for you to use wisely! The first one is called Daeg, which means 'daylight' (or 'sunlight' if you prefer), and it will give you great energy and protection against harmful influence—but remember, everything is given to you in good faith, and if you do not use these gifts with respect and wisdom, they will be taken from you—so beware!

"The second rune is called Ehwaz, which is left for you by my mate, Kyto. Ehwaz means 'horse,' which is a sacred animal. You are very fortunate, because your human saviour already possesses this animal, the one you call 'the black dragon,' so you are very privileged indeed. It means that you will make swift progress towards your adventures and your destiny. Your travel here was already made with great speed, so your future path will follow at a steady pace. Guard 'them well!

"I advise you to beware of Featherhead White Wings! Watch your back, for he has two sides to him! He is not a friend, but neither is he an enemy—so you must tread carefully, and fly very stealthily!

"Now here is me mantra called 'Sister Moon, Sister Sun.'"

The moon, that great yellow orb,
seemingly motionless against
the velvety black universe,
holding silent audience with her sister stars.
Are you trying to tell us which path to take?

The solitary nightingale sings his melodious
canticle, sharp notes ring out
his joy, his heart's desire.
The wolf will howl his condolence-like song,
calling his brothers and sisters,
to worship your power.

Pitching the senses into awareness.
A battle between reality and mythology.
Fortunes and misgivings.
Fear and expectancy.

Opening your gateway to philosophers,
astrologers and astronomers,
to practice their arts,
wizening up to your charms.

The moon daisy opens her petals
to bathe in your glorious light.
A silver-etched cloud covers your radiance,
your shyness, like a curtain,
closing an old chapter,
drifting slowly by, to reveal cosmic wisdom.

Silent deep shadows cast over the lands,
marking ways for the creatures of the night.
A shimmering mirrored image off the lake,
enticing the inquisitive
to touch your magic spell.

Your gentle nature has allowed man
to take his first step onto your virgin soil,
to probe your mystical powers,
why you create a never-ending
ebb and flow of the ocean's tide?

To the creative minds,
you map the future of the universal flow,
the gift of knowledge.

The approaching dawn brings down
the curtain, closing your night's
performance.

To reveal Sister Sun, rising gloriously
to her own awesome power,
awakening the spirit,
to dance to her tune of day.
The everlasting rhythm of earth's song.

Creator of life force,
worshipped by many to your warming rays.
With the power to destroy in an
unrelenting way.
Bronze adonis, golden Venus
parading in your approving glow.

Queen of the cloudless blue skies,
you do not possess that same cool beauty
to gaze upon, as Sister Moon.
Your brazen orange heat,
draws like a magnet to your hot breath.

Chasing mischievously,
your own rays casting shadows across
meadows and hills,
mocking unwary clouds,
who dare cross your path.

You rule your interplanetary space,
in the knowledge that no man
will step on to your
hostile, spitting surface.

Now darkness appears once more,
you must give up your deeds of the day,
once again,
farewell, Sister Sun!
Greetings, Sister Moon!

After his mantra, Klogitiwhoo fluffed himself up, then silently, he flew away.

– Chapter Nine –
One for Sorrow, Two for Joy

Millie was a little bundle of fluff, all black, and with two very appealing yellow eyes.

As if by fate, she was rescued as a tiny waif kitten in almost similar circumstances as Maggie when he was rescued as a baby magpie, only her tiny feet were firmly placed on terra firma, unlike Maggie, who appeared from the sky as a tiny ball of skin and feathers, and definitely not so appealing!

The rescue took place on a gloriously warm and sunny day.

I was out riding Humphrey with a friend called Jill, who was riding her horse called Tarquin.

Humphrey's coat shone as black as ebony after his vigorous grooming, and his graceful long wavy tail and mane (which is characteristic of the fell and dale breeds of ponies) swayed elegantly with the rhythm of his walk

Jill's horse Tarquin was a handsome thoroughbred chestnut gelding, with a small white diamond marking in the middle of his forehead, and his hind fetlocks were splashed with two white socks.

Humphrey and Tarquin had become very good friends and both were gearing themselves up to the anticipated gallop on soft turf in one of the nearby meadows, or to have an exhilarating race along a leafy wooded bridleway.

This particular ride was not very far from home, and it took us down a quiet lane which eventually led us through a farmyard, and then into a woodland area.

The lane itself took us past the little cottage where "Thomas the Tyres" now lived.

Thomas moved into the cottage after his retirement, and after the death of his wife, he was now living alone, so he was always pleased to stop and talk to any passers by. Whenever he heard the sound of horses hooves clip-clopping down the lane, he would always be there at the gate for a friendly chat, and a fair bit of gossip went on too, if there was anything out of the ordinary going on in the village.

I was intrigued by some of the stories he told me on previous rides past his cottage, and most of them were about local traditions of a bygone age.

He told me that when young men wanted to build their own cottages and claim parcels of land for themselves, they would choose a particular plot, either somewhere out on the hills or lower down in the valley, and on the chosen night they would have to stand on the spot where they wanted to build their home. With an axe in one hand, they would throw it as far as they could, and by measuring out from the spot from where they stood to where the axe had landed, this would be the exact area that they could claim for themselves, providing they could build the cottage in one night!

Now with the help of friends and relatives—and if the cottage was completed by sunrise or the cock's crow the following morning—the plot of land and the cottage were all theirs!

It seems that the locals were very skilled at building their homes overnight, and sometimes in rather dubious circumstances.

A row of houses in a small town (not far away) were built from stone hacked out from the walls of the local castle, reducing it to an even smaller ruin. The looters would come down from the hills with their little wooden carts pulled by their little Welsh ponies, and they would chip out the stones from the castle, pile them into the carts, then mysteriously vanish into the night. It wasn't long before little stone cottages suddenly appeared like mushrooms overnight, and they looked suspiciously familiar with their well-worn stone, which seemed to blend in nicely with what was left of the castle, which looked down on the rows of little cottages!

I don't think the planning department would approve of such goings-on today!

Thomas also told me another story about an "enemy encounter" during the second world war.

On a clear moonlit night, a German submarine silently entered as close as possible into one of our little coves, where it boldly surfaced close to the rocks. Then a small band of its crew were sent out with containers (cans, I believe Thomas told me), and they knocked on the doors of the small cottages which nestled at the foot of the cliffs in the sparsely populated hamlet.

Having fetched the sleepy cottagers out of their warm and comfortable beds, these brazen sailors requested that their cans be filled with fresh water, which the inhabitants did without hesitation, not knowing if these men would show hostility towards them if they didn't obey their urgent request. So when the containers were duly filled, their unwanted visitors calmly left, as though they were just casual holiday makers asking for a glass of water, and then, without even glancing back, they made their way back to their waiting submarine.

The submarine, with its thirsty crew, then slipped quietly once more out of the bay, and was never seen again!

Thomas was out in his garden as usual, tending his vegetable patch, and he looked up when he heard the sound of horse hooves trotting down the lane, and came over to the gate to greet us as we approached his cottage.

After exchanging our greetings, he said to us, "Why don't you try another route? Instead of taking the path to the right, go straight on, and then turn left, and you will be going past the cheese farm, then you will see a path that takes you through another wood. Keep going, over a little stream—it's only a trickle that runs across the path, so you won't have any banks to jump over!" he said with a chuckle. "And then you will be passing a little old cottage which was built about a hundred and fifty years ago, or maybe even longer, and there's only the bridleway leading to it. There's no proper road or anything, but the track is just wide enough if anybody wanted to drive a car through it, but it would be pretty rough going! It's got no electricity or mod cons, like central heating, and they still use their own spring water, which has to be pumped up by a generator."

"Does anybody live there at the moment?" I asked.

"I've heard that two hippie-type ladies are living there at the moment," he said. "I believe they originally came from the tepee valley, and some folks are saying that they are witches, but I think that's only a bit of old gossip. They seem nice enough, and they're always polite and friendly to talk to when I see them.

"Now there is something which might interest you both. Somewhere just below the old cottage and hidden down in a dip is an entrance to a cave, and it's all covered in boulders and ferns. If you can find the entrance hole, you can make your way from there, and it carries on for some fair distance. If you follow it right to the other side, it eventually comes out somewhere near the cheese farm, probably outside the old parlour, but nobody has had the courage (at least as far as I know) to actually explore it. When I was just a kid, I used to go there and play about just inside the entrance, but I imagined I could hear strange noises, so I was too scared to venture any further!"

"What did you think those noises were?" asked Jill.

"Well, looking back on it, I think it was just the wind whooshing through the cave tunnel, and when it was a really gusty day, the sound was like a roar, and I imagined it was made by a dragon! Some of the kids who used to come over from the nearby village even thought Merlin or King Arthur were holding up in there, so none of us were brave enough to go in any further to find out! Anyway, I'm not suggesting that you should try and make your way through the cave!" he said with a chuckle. "But do have a go and try that path I told you about, and you'll find you can get a bit of a gallop there!"

We thanked him for his advice and the interesting story (which reminded me very much of my own "tunnel" experience on the common back in Sussex) and then trotted onwards toward the alternative bridleway.

It was just as Thomas had described to us.

We rode past the cheese farm, bore to the left, then cantered along the track and splashed over the little stream. The horses loved it—it was new and exciting to them, so the gentle canter turned into a gallop—a race!

By the time we reached the top of the track—as it rose slightly uphill—the horses were puffing and sweating, but obviously enjoying themselves, and so were we!

We came to the small cottage which sat nestled between a high bank and the track. It looked very old, tired, slightly lopsided, and very uncared for. The cottage appeared to be almost deserted, apart from a large tabby cat sitting in the window, looking out with an unblinking stare through grimy windows. A thin wisp of smoke spiralled upwards from the single chimney pot—even though the day was hot and sunny.

We were a bit disappointed not to see the traditional witch's broom propped against the door, but instead there was a massive motorbike leaning against the wall of the cottage. So could this mean that today's witches travel with a more modern form of transport after all?

It was never officially confirmed that Tom's story about witches was true, but at least we enjoyed the ride through the wood, and we would definitely add this one to our list of "must rides!"

We came out of the other side of the woods and carried on through a farmyard until we reached the crossroads at the other end, and this road would eventually take us back home, which meant we would have ridden in a full circle.

It was as we were riding at a steady walk towards the final crossroads, that a faint miaowing sound could be heard.

At first neither of us had taken much notice as we were chatting away, and the metallic sound of the horses' hooves on the hard road almost drowned the sound out, and at the time we both thought that this distant, almost inaudible sound, was the call of a buzzard circling the blue sky above us, as their call sounds very similar to a cat's miaow.

It wasn't until we were already past the spot from whence the now more persistent, and much louder, and more plaintive sound was coming from.

"Miaow!…miaow!…miaow!" went the cry in a continuous wail, and it was getting more and more desperate and sounding less like a buzzard.

Pulling up, we both looked at one another and said in unison, "a cat!"

Getting off Humphrey, I handed the reins to Jill and walked back towards the point where we had first heard the cry.

As I drew nearer to the pitiful wailing, it seemed to be getting louder and louder and sounded as though the cat was in a great deal of distress.

At first I couldn't see anything as I scanned the bank at the edge of the road. All I could see were the wayside grasses and wild flowers, and a few holes probably made by rabbits, but nothing else.

I peered intently to where I thought the sound was coming from, and it seemed to be coming from the base of a small gorse bush where I could just about see a small hole which was almost hidden, and it was shaded by bright yellow coltsfoot and pretty blue harebells, along with tufted grasses.

I very carefully and cautiously put my hand gently inside the hole and felt something very small, warm, and fury. I tried to cup my hand underneath it, but it pulled itself deeper into the hole, so I had to grip hold of its fur firmly between my fingers and gently but firmly pull it out.

There, sitting on the palm of my hand, was the tiniest, sweetest, blackest little kitten you ever did see. Its little yellow eyes looking at me so trustingly, and no doubt it was grateful for being rescued from this horrible dark hole!

As we rode the rest of the way home (which fortunately wasn't very far), I carried the little kitten in the palm of my hand, holding its tiny trembling body against me.

So now we had a little kitten within the fold!

The little kitten was soon named, and we called her Millie.

She was full of fun and mischief and went all out to rule the roost, particularly with the dogs, who she would tease endlessly with her "pat and run" games. White carrier bags were used for playing "spooks" with, which meant you sprang into them, then tried to push your way through the other end which was sealed, so you had to claw your way back out again.

Then there was the "box and wastepaper basket" game. With these you had to jump inside, then make them turn over so that you were now underneath and hidden from view, and you had to keep very quiet and still until an unsuspecting dog came along, and out of curiosity would stick its sniffing nose just where it shouldn't be, and then you could thrust your little black legs out at lightning speed, and with tiny needle-sharp claws, swipe out at a tender nose, and as the humiliated dog backed off in submission, you would then scuttle along like a hermit crab in its shell, or do your "Dalek" impression, sending the dog into a complete nervous wreck!

Maggie and Millie didn't actually meet until much later on, as Maggie spent most of the time outdoors and was only allowed in on special occasions, and Millie stayed indoors until she was old enough to cope with wandering about the garden, and in those early few months, she seemed to prefer staying indoors.

Maybe this was due to her bad experience when she was a tiny kitten.

We shall never know whether she was abandoned as an unwanted kitten by a thoughtless person, or whether her own mother had forgotten her and left her in the hole in the bank. As she was found in an area where the nearest house or farmstead was about half a mile away in any direction, it was fairly unlikely that somebody had actually lost her, but it was worth taking a chance to find out, just in case she had somehow been transported by someone, or something, to that hole in the bank, and maybe there was a heartbroken child out there somewhere grieving for their lost pet. And so I decided that I would have to make an attempt to try and find out if this was the case.

The most obvious place to make my enquiries was the post office, for this is where all the local gossip takes place (just like the old blacksmith's forge used to do back in Sussex).

The villagers congregate and meet there to exchange all their latest news, as well as collecting their pensions and doing their last-minute bits of shopping.

As I entered the post office, the usual "Three Wise Men" — "Danny the Post" (retired), "Dylan the Baker" (nearly retired), and "Ben the Butcher" (semi-retired) — were discussing their latest topic.

Ben said, "Have you heard about poor old Gareth!... His misses has done a bunk!... Made off with 'Cyril the Eggs,' she has!... And she's left him with five kids to cope with!"

Danny said, "Well duw! duw!... Aye man!... That's terrible!... Isn't it? Boys bach!... I only hope the poor bugger wins the lottery!... Then his wife might realize where her bread's buttered!... She won't know what she's missing!"

"Does he do the lottery then, Danny?" asked Dylan.

"I dunno!" said Danny.

Then I thought I'd try with my own contribution. "Er…has anybody lost a little kitten?…a little black kitten?" I asked.

My words seemed to fall on deaf ears.

"Did you hear about Denzil and old Barney?" asked Danny.

"It was all over the local papers only the other day—quite a big headline it made too! Seems they're still arguing about who should have won what at that cattle show last year, saying that a lot of cheating went on, and old Denzil accused Barney of taking all his cattle over to his farm, and blow me, Barney then accused Denzil of the same thing, only that his cattle were now on Denzil's farm! Both denied the accusations, saying that they couldn't have done it, not only because they're thirty miles apart, but because each of their lorries were already half way across the continent, so how could they have got there?"

I tried again. "I found it just up the road from here, about half a mile away!"

My words trailed off as Danny continued.

"Not only that, but where the animals were penned in, the gates had been securely padlocked, and do you know what they're saying it was?… Bloody aliens and UFO's!… That's what transported them, just like as before!"

Now oddly enough, this wasn't the first time I'd heard about strange unidentified sightings. They call this part of Wales the "Dyfed Triangle," and quite a few well-known people have claimed to have seen UFOs, and even aliens.

A beautiful country like Wales, steeped in history, castles, myths and legends—why do they want to get themselves mixed up with aliens and UFOs? Next thing, they'll be holding "Extraterrestrial 'Fun' Days," with posters dotted on lampposts, advertising events such as:

MOON BUGGY GRAND PRIX.
FLYING SAUCER AIR DISPLAY WITH THE "GREEN MARROWS."
TAKE YOUR FAMILY ON A TRIP IN AN AIR SHIP—TO MARS AND BACK—
SENIOR CITIZENS ONE-WAY TICKET!
ALIENS' 5-LEGGED RACE.
OUTER SPACE QUIZ COMPETITION:
1ST PRIZE—STICKS OF MOON ROCK FOR KIDS—
FREE MOON SHUTTLE TICKETS FOR MUMS AND DADS!

401

All I wanted to know at that moment was a simple down-to-earth answer to a simple down-to-earth question—so I tried again!

"Hello...? Is there anybody here who knows about a lost cat?" I asked.

Old Megan propped her walking stick on the counter, then did a bit of fine tuning to her hearing aid.

"Did you say you've found a black hat?" she asked. "I lost mine only last week—blew off in the wind, it did."

"No.... I said...black *cat!*"

"Did you say black cat?" asked Ben.

"Huw Thomas at Pentre farm said he saw the big black cat...claims it tried to attack his sheep, an' he took a pop shot at it, but he missed...said it was the size of a German Shepherd dog, or a goat, and he went and reported it to the police!... So you've seen it too, have you?"

Then on an impulse, I blurted out in frustration, *"There's a thousand pounds reward!"*

I think I heard a pin drop as all eyes suddenly turned in my direction.

"Make a very good mouser for someone, too!" I added, sheepishly.

On my way home, I thought to myself, *There seems to be an awful lot of action packed into an area the size of Wales. What with aliens, UFOs, castle plunderings, wife stealing, big cats! Whatever next!*

Nobody ever claimed the little lost waif, so she's been with us for the last twelve years now.

The first time that Millie and Maggie met was when Millie had grown into a very slender, very sleek feline and had already developed her own unique hunting skills.

Her earlier victims were little shrews, voles, mice, and then as she grew bigger, she started to catch small birds, then bigger birds, and finally she graduated to bigger game still.

She came home one day (after stalking in the long grass around the edge of the field), proudly carrying in her mouth—with her head held high—a baby rabbit, swinging from side to side! How I hate it when cats catch little birds and animals—especially baby rabbits.

I have never gone out of my way to find cats—they always seem to find me! And yet we have always had a cat for as long as I can remember, and it's always been the same. They just seem to turn up on the doorstep—usually they are about six months old, which is about the length of time that people start to dump them, and after they have passed their pretty little "kittenish" stage and start to tear at the furniture or dig up the garden and bring home unwanted gifts—which are usually dead and half eaten. So why do I always end up with them?

I'm sure that word gets around that "there's a good home to be had over there! Just turn up, look all pathetic, hungry and adorably sweet—and you're in!"

Once they get their paws through the door, then that's it! Pampered and cared for—for life!

Then one day, Millie discovered quite by chance that there was a very new and interesting quarry for her to tackle—"right on the doorstep," so to speak, and it was an appetising looking—*magpie!*

Maggie was out for the day, and he was all intent on something over by the gas container where he was busily pecking away at an unseen object in the grass, so his beak was down and his back was turned away from any approaching danger, and his tail was stuck up in the air.

He was quite unaware (and therefore totally unconcerned) of Millie, who had suddenly spotted him. She started to belly-crawl towards him, occasionally stopping to judge the distance between herself and her prospective lunch!

Her eyes were fixed un-blinking on Maggie and her body was as still as a statue as her muscles tensed ready for action, and the end of her tail started to twitch ever so slightly. She crouched lower still and flattened her ears. Then she started to crawl, at first very slowly, and then jerkily—rather like a chameleon.

Maggie suddenly looked up—as though he'd sensed that he wasn't alone after all.

At that very instant, Millie had decided that this was the right moment to make her move.

She pounced!—and Maggie bounced!

The two of them pounced and bounced around to the other side of the gas container.

I feared for Maggie's life.

It was almost as if history was repeating itself—and Maggie was about to be killed by a cat after all!

I ran out of the house towards the gas container.

As I neared the scene of the imminent murder that was about to take place, I could hear a lot of scuffling noises, then angry clacking noises from Maggie, and lots of flapping and scuffling sounds, followed by a loud caterwauling howl, followed by hissing and swearing—this time from Millie!

Millie suddenly catapulted out from her place of "ambush," with her tail bristling as she sped towards the house.

I walked apprehensively towards the gas container, expecting to see a pile of feathers and a very dead magpie, but I was both shocked and relieved when Maggie nonchalantly stepped out from behind the gas container, lig-logging—and with not a feather out of place or a care in the world. He was looking as pleased as punch at having just won yet another battle of supremacy—especially over a mere "cat!"

Maggie had become quite firmly attached to Millie in a funny sort of way.

Whenever she went out on one of her hunting sprees, he would follow closely behind her and watch her every move as she tip-toed her way lightly across the lawn—in her rather unique but strange pussycat style. She walked with a springy, jerky movement, which reminded me of the Pink Panther character in the comedy films with Peter Sellers.

Poor little Millie; she tried so hard to be on her own.

I felt quite sorry for her as she tried unsuccessfully to escape his incessant intrusion in her private life, whenever she wanted to go out into the fields just for a wander around or to go on one of her hunting expeditions.

It wasn't long before *her* catches — became *his* rewards!

Her first attempts at catching small birds that she could see hopping around the lawn or in the shrubbery were rather clumsy and unsuccessful.

Before she learnt the important art of stealth tactics, she would bound across the lawn like a constipated kangaroo, launch herself noisily into the middle of the shrubbery, and a bushful of startled birds would launch themselves in all directions, leaving the wide-eyed kitty stranded in the middle of the bush, looking totally baffled, bewildered, and confused, and predictably — empty pawed!

It wasn't long before the unlikely duo formed a formidable partnership — each offsetting the other.

The hunter became the hunted, and the hunted became the hunter.

Small mice seemed to be the favourite menu for Maggie. They were easy pickings for him — once Millie had caught them and brought them home.

He would wait until she had returned home with the poor little limp body dangling from her mouth, and then he would go in for the *snatch!*

Before Millie could run off and hide somewhere to either eat her kill or play "toss-and-catch" with it — particularly if it happened to be still alive — from out of nowhere, Maggie would quickly be on the scene to stake his claim! He would lig-log towards her and then as he got nearer, he would — hop! hop! hop! — right up close behind her, and then neatly grasp her tail in his beak and pull sharply! Millie would be so taken by surprise that she would drop the creature, and before she could turn to strike out in protest — hissing and growling at her assailant, Maggie would have already popped round to the front, and then, as quick as a flash, he would grab up the prize in his beak.

Before departing, he would give one of his metallic calls, which was just a single "ha!" — which sounded more like "ta!" He would then fly triumphantly off and find a perch not too far away so that Millie could watch him in despair—her eyes showing big and round, and she would have a shocked expression on her face.

Then as a final victorious gesture towards Millie, he would proceed to devour his stolen lunch at leisure—with more than a hint of a smirk on his face!

It was almost as though Maggie had developed a form of psychic powers, as he seemed to know exactly where to locate Millie, and his hawk-like eyes seemed to be able to pinpoint wherever Millie (or any one of us) happened to be!

If he was in one of his devilish moods, he would soon flush Millie out of her hiding place, and it wouldn't be long before feathers and fur would fly, as yet another cat-bird skirmish would begin!

Maggie was learning quite fast the technique of hunting like a cat.

Skulking along the edge of the field, the pair of them could be seen creeping furtively through the long grass and towards the bushes and brambles, Indian style, and in single file.

First Millie—with her tail held straight up, as she crept purposefully along—and not too far behind her came Maggie, following closely in her footsteps, lig-logging in big strides, and also with *his* tail sticking straight up in the air!

When Millie stopped—then so did Maggie.

When Millie vanished into the thick brambles growing out of the bank—so did Maggie!

Some while later, Millie would reappear with a little mouse or bank vole in her mouth, and it was at this point that Maggie would emerge from the bank in hot pursuit and harass Millie until she was forced to drop the small creature so that he could confiscate it from her. And without further ado, he would fly off with his ill-gotten gains, leaving Millie looking very bewildered—minus her mouse!

Millie was never allowed to roam outside at night, as she was always kept indoors during the night time, so she always had to hunt by day, and therefore she was never free from Maggie.

One day, I heard terrible high-pitched screams which seemed to be coming from the stable block, so I rushed outside to investigate and to find out what was making such a terrible noise.

On reaching the stable, I was astonished at the scene which greeted me there.

There was Millie looking all perplexed and sitting just inside the stable door, and opposite her—at the far end of the stable—was Maggie, looking very smug, and there, crouched in the middle of the floor and trying desperately to hide under the straw, was a little baby rabbit!

Maggie looked as though he'd hit the jackpot, but was not quite sure how to tackle it! Millie looked on, as though she was wondering what Maggie was going to do about "the catch," knowing that he would probably claim it anyway—so she just sat there looking at it!

I picked up the poor little rabbit, who was by now trembling and holding his soft little ears flat to his head in fear. Fortunately, he appeared to be uninjured, so he was a very lucky little rabbit. If I hadn't heard his desperate screams and not gone out to the stable, then no doubt he would have ended up as a shared meal between the cat and the magpie!

Scolding the pair of would-be murderers, I shut them both in the stable so that they couldn't follow me, and I took the baby rabbit to the bottom of the field where I let it go so that it could make its way into the woods, hoping it would recover from its horrific ordeal.

This wasn't the only time that the two hunters had caught a rabbit.

Their next victim was left in the porch, but this time it was a slightly larger rabbit, and it too was trying to hide itself (behind a boot!). So the same rescue procedure was adopted, and yet another rabbit was introduced to the woods—and now there are lots of little rabbits…everywhere!

Unfortunately, one of their victims I was unable to discover in time, and I was confronted with two back legs and a little white bob tail!

The naughty pair had eaten the rest of it!

Millie eventually gave up catching birds and mammals just for herself, so each time she did catch something, and Maggie was conveniently standing by, she would just drop it straight in front of him, knowing full well that he would be his usual demanding self, and he would cluck "*ta!*" at her, then grab it up and fly off towards his aviary.

As time went by, Maggie was able to hunt for himself, and he even attempted to catch his own rabbit, but he'd injured its back legs very badly, and in spite of me trying to treat its injuries, the poor little thing died.

There were other unfortunate casualties caused by the cat and magpie, and as the hot dry summer yielded a baby boom in mice, their list of victims grew in number.

A very unusual event happened when on one particular evening, I had just returned from the weekly shopping trip, and Adam was helping me to unload the car when he called me back by saying, "Come and have a look here…. It looks as though the cat may have caught a mouse and left it there—but it does look *rather* small!"

I dumped the bags down on the hall floor and went to have a look.

The tiny lump (which looked the size of a pebble) was found on the patio in the dappled shade under the crab-apple tree, and it just lay there without moving.

I picked it gingerly up in case it was injured, and was amazed to discover that it was actually a very young mouse-type creature. Its little bulbous eyes were still closed, and it had such tiny little pink claws, so delicate that you would need a magnifying glass to see them properly.

We all went into a panic mode, not knowing quite how to deal with such a tiny infant, or even how (or what) to feed it.

Whilst Adam searched the kitchen cupboard for an empty butter carton to put it in, I managed to find a tiny dropper from one of my herbal remedies and gave it some slightly warmed milk mixed with a teaspoonful of filtered water, which it seemed to drink ravenously.

I was a bit concerned that the tiny creature may have needed something a little more solid than just milk and water, so holding its delicate body covered in baby-soft silky fur (it was then that I noticed that it had a white bib and a white patch on its tummy), I put a tiny piece of chicken (which had been boiled up especially for the dogs) in front of its tiny pink nose, and it started to chew on it with its minute kissable little "oo" shaped mouth, and it actually managed to take some of the food down.

We made a comfortable bed in an empty, clean butter carton by putting wads of soft kitchen towelling in the middle and then placing the little creature in the centre of it. Then Adam made up a hot water bottle (which I used as a temporary warmer until I could find the electric warming pad), which would then be used to keep the baby mouse warm for the night.

Having made the little animal comfortable in its new bed, Adam left me to it, and he went back outside to put the car away in the garage.

A few moments later, and I heard the cry of "Oh no!… Not another one!" Sure enough, when I rushed outside to see what was the matter, there was an identical twin to the first baby mouse, and he was about the size of the first joint of my thumb and felt very cold to the touch. He was still alive!—and now I had two little waifs to look after!

I carried out the same procedure on this little one, only it appeared to be very weak, and it was trembling with cold, and it was probably very hungry.

This little infant wasn't so willing to feed with the dropper, and as it was so tiny that there was just no way that I could have forced its little mouth open to accept the milk from the dropper, I didn't feel too confident about it's survival.

I placed it next to its sibling and took the box with its fragile contents up to my bedroom, where I placed it on the heating pad.

By the next morning, the first little mouse appeared to be quite bright, but the other poor little mite had unfortunately died. I think it probably had pneumonia through being exposed outside of its nest for too long.

To our great surprise, two more little mice were found, and both of these were discovered crawling along the patio, even though they were still blind and unable to see where they were going.

We decided to make an extensive search around the front garden and patio to try and find the nest, but it was an impossible task even though it must have been so close to where they had made their desperate attempt (like fleeing little lemmings!), at making their way into the unknown.

Adam decided to contact Jean Bryant, wife of the late Alan Bryant, who tragically and suddenly died the previous year.

Alan was the founder member of the Newquay Bird and Wildlife Hospital and had spent many years of devotion and hard work helping wildlife throughout Wales, which included seals, who often needed a great deal of attention, especially stranded seal pups, who'd perhaps lost their mums, and also seabirds who were unfortunate enough to become victims of oil spills.

Later, I was pleased to learn that Alan had been awarded recognition for his success with helping so many birds and wild animals back to recovery by the RSPCA at a ceremony in London just a few years earlier, and today, there stands a stone with an inscription on a plaque commemorating his achievements.

Adam gave Jean a description of the baby mice, and also of what we had done for them so far, and she told him that we were doing the right thing, but that it would be very difficult as the tiny mice were so young, and by the description of them it sounded as though they could have been "harvest mice." Thanking her for helping us out yet once again (she was used to us turning up with injured birds after cat or magpie damage, but mice were something new!), we returned to the "mice nursery!"

I decided that if one of them was lucky enough to survive the ordeal, I would name it…Tom Thumb!

Unfortunately, none of the babies survived, so with a sad heart and great disappointment at the failure of all our efforts to keep them alive, we gave them a decent burial.

Adam has since found out, via the internet, that little mice orphans should regularly have their tummies massaged in order to encourage them to do their toilet, so maybe that could have contributed to the first little mouse from dying after a seizure, even though at first he appeared to be recovering.

We came to the conclusion that these brave little baby mice were made orphans by either the cat, or one of the crow family, like the magpie, and in desperation for food and warmth, they had made a mass exodus from their nest in a vain attempt to find their mother.

There must be other poor little orphans out in the countryside, just like these, who have fallen victim to these killers, and out there, crawling along in their blind state, not knowing where they are going and just perishing from hunger and cold!

Nature can be so cruel at times!

One little creature I'm trying to protect from the cat and bird is a little pygmy shrew, whom I've named Nipper.

He lives under the slabs near the bird table, and each day since he first appeared as a very tiny being trying desperately—and failing miserably—to jump up into the birds' feed dish (where I always put out one or two slices of bread for the birds to feed on), I have been feeding him.

Nipper is still fed regularly three times a day.

I take out to him small pieces of bread, and any other bits and pieces, and with his little long nose twitching away, he grabs at the food when he smells it as I push it down between the gap in the slab. I can watch him dash from one side of the slab to the other, where he has obviously constructed a series of runs for himself, beneath some of the slabs which were not very firmly cemented down by the builders.

He must be so used to hearing my footsteps coming, that when I bend down to push his food through the gap in the slab to him, and if he's somewhere in the flower beds, I detect a movement in the grass, and then all of a sudden, I am able to glimpse Nipper as he funnels his way through the grass, and when he finds his first entrance to his den, his long nose starts to twitch until he finds his titbit. Sometimes he even takes it straight from my fingers.

After several days of pampering with these special treats, Nipper has grown very much bigger, so much so, that he now has difficulty in manoeuvring himself between the slabs, and I have watched him squirm and heave himself as he tries to carry his treats across from the opening and into his den.

He will have to be called "The Incredible Hulk" from now on!

Let's hope he lives to a good old age—he deserves to—however long that might be!

"What's that you say?... They're doing what?... So how many have they had so far?"

There was a frantic call from Ruth, and as she was calling me on her mobile phone from her garden, the reception was crackly, and the wind noise blew away most of her words. It appears that *my* magpie and *my* cat were exterminating some baby blue tits who had just left their nest—so could I come as quickly as I can and bring a cage or a box big enough for the two of them!

How on earth was I going to put a cat and a bird in one cage—or even a box? I would just have to deal with them in a more practical way. I took Maggie's favourite toy (his watch), knowing that he wouldn't want to lose it. And as for Millie—I just took along a saucer of her favourite dish—which was fish! As it turned out, Maggie wanted the watch—and the dish of fish! When I got there—there were the two of them, looking very guilty indeed! Millie still had a few tiny feathers stuck between her claws, and Maggie kept his blood-stained beak shut tight, as though he was trying to hide the evidence. I managed to entice the wicked pair back home with their appropriate bait. Millie followed me for her fish, and Maggie landed on my shoulder when I dangled his watch in front of him. But this episode wasn't the end of his "baby bird collecting."

Ruth told me that Maggie had started to hang around the patio doors, just waiting for the young birds to stun themselves when they flew into the patio windows, and then he would dive down, pick them up, and fly off with them onto her lawn, where she watched him as he plucked them like a chicken, and then pecked off pieces of their flesh to eat. Ruth could only run after him to drive him off, as it was far too late to try and save the little birds.

It was no wonder at all that he was beginning to get himself a bad reputation with the neighbours.

The novelty of his quaint little ways and his boisterous (but sometimes entertaining) antics, were slowly starting to wear off, until they finally reached the speed of light, and went down like a lead balloon!

As the baby birds were soon old enough to leave their nests, the parent birds were beginning to bring their offspring into the garden to be fed.

Unwittingly, they were innocently partaking in a game of Russian roulette with the crows, sparrowhawks, cats, and of course—the magpies!

Their most scary enemy was the sparrowhawk.

Every time a sharp-eyed bird thought that there was an enemy about, it would give one of their short, sharp warning signals by way of a loud *"chink!...chink!"* or a blackbird's alarm call of *"pink!...pink!...pink!"* which usually meant that a sparrowhawk was about somewhere. All the birds would then take off at great speed and dive into the nearest thick bush or hedge. Sometimes it was a false alarm, and the birds were quickly back once more to carry on feeding at the bird table, as though nothing had happened.

On the other hand, if the danger was real but had gone unnoticed, then it meant that the sparrowhawk had successfully homed in swiftly and silently and straight onto a weaker or slower bird, or perhaps an unsuspecting bird who just happened to be in the wrong place at the wrong time! But it was the right time for the benefit of the sparrowhawk, of course.

When there had been a hit on such occasions, all the other birds would disappear for quite a long time, leaving the garden very quiet from all their familiar chattering.

It would take some time before they felt it was safe enough to return to the garden once more.

I hated to see this killing going on in the garden, as it made me feel that it was partly my fault for feeding them all through the summer, and by feeding them it acted as a bait for the sparrowhawk.

A bit of a double-edged sword!

I have actually seen a sparrowhawk skilfully pluck a finch or a great tit straight off the nut feeder and in full flight!

The sparrowhawk would do this by swivelling its body around whilst still flying, and then grasping the bird in its outstretched talons, it would then fly off with its prey to a favourite feeding place, where it plucked out the feathers of its kill, and then tare at the flesh with its sharp beak.

As well as the pretty collared doves, sparrows, finches, blue tits, and especially the noisy young greenfinches piping away (all of them sounding like the incessant *'beep! beeping!'* noise made by the cash tills at supermarkets) are so vulnerable to the sparrowhawk, but I have also seen a starling fall prey to this bird.

One cold winter's morning, I was upstairs making my bed when I heard a bird screeching in distress, and it seemed to be coming from just below my bedroom window, and my first thought was that a cat must have caught a bird somewhere, so throwing on my dressing gown, I raced downstairs to the patio doors in the kitchen. As I was about to open the door to look outside, I was taken aback to see on the path a sparrowhawk with a very frightened, squawking starling trapped beneath one of its talons.

I have no idea why the hawk didn't just fly off with it as soon as the bird was caught, but it could have been that the bird's noisy screeching may have confused it momentarily, and by me opening the door, it broke the spell, and the hawk took off with the still loudly protesting starling attached to its talons.

Poor starling, it will never return for another winter!

Once a bird has been caught by a sparrowhawk, there is absolutely nothing anyone can do about it to stop it.

At least if a bird is caught by a cat, there is the possibility of catching the cat and then retrieving the bird.

I am not absolutely sure if magpies come under the sparrowhawk's menu list, although I did once find a magpie's dead body by Humphrey's bath, which appeared to be suspicious, but then why wasn't it carted off?

Although the sparrowhawk is a ferocious hunter, it is a very attractive bird.

Its back is a slate-grey colour (but the juveniles are brown), and it has a creamy white plumage, whilst its long straight-ended tail has four bands on it. The legs are yellow, and its sharp penetrating eyes are also a pale yellow.

It's such a shame that the sparrowhawk has to feed on other birds.

You could almost feel sorry for its loneliness, because whenever this predator arrives in the garden, and even if it was only wanting to rest up for a while, all the other birds suddenly disappear, but you can hardly blame them for that, as any one of them could have ended up as a potential meal!

Another near casualty that summer was a baby swallow, which could have only been a few days old, as it was so tiny and featherless, and it had bulging closed eyes.

Luckily it had landed directly in the middle of an empty feed bag left in the stable, which was folded over and left on the top of the wheelbarrow, and just by chance, it was parked right under the nest.

It was also by chance that Adam happened to go into the stable to fetch something out when he spotted the little pink blob move.

When he handed it to me, not knowing what to do with it, the poor little baby bird felt very cold to the touch, but at least it was still very much alive, so I guessed that it was found just in time, and seemed none the worse after its fall.

It took a long time (and three ladders) and three attempts when Adam finally managed to carefully manoeuvre it back into the nest, taking great care not to dislodge the carefully built mud-caked nest.

We stood back at a fair distance and watched to make sure that the parents returned to the nest to feed their young.

Our worries were groundless, as the parents soon darted back into the stable, just as though nothing had happened!

On nice, warm, sunny days—in between their dangerous spells of watching out for the sparrowhawk and diving into bushes at the first danger signals—the little baby garden birds found time to relax and play, whilst their mums and dads were busy searching and collecting their food.

The baby sparrows were the most playful.

They would follow the most dominant one who would lead them into taking part in as many activities as he could devise for them.

One game was to slide up and down the gutters of the greenhouse, pushing dead leaves and debris as they went, and then it was a game of sea-saw on the thin stems of the pampas grass, sending fine pollen dust into the air, and as each little bird landed on the same long silky flowery stem, it gradually got heavier and heavier, until the last bird landed, making the stem bounce wildly up and down like a yo-yo, and almost reach the ground.

Dust baths were a favourite occupation too, as well as splashing in the water with everybody trying to cram into the birdbath at the same time.

The cheeky sparrows thought nothing of rudely knocking all the baby chaffinches and blue tits off, so that they had all the space.

If one little sparrow picked at a leaf, or pulled a piece of tender clover out of the ground, then they would all want to pick at a leaf or a piece of clover, which was definitely a case of follow the leader!

One particular group of baby sparrows discovered a brand new game.

I watched them from the kitchen window and couldn't quite believe what I was seeing, as I had never seen this very unusual pattern of behaviour before.

At first I thought I was observing flycatchers (another visitor to our garden) darting after flies, but on a closer look, I could see that they were actually baby sparrows.

From the top of the ornamental silver pear tree, the leader started and the others followed suit, one by one.

Launching themselves upwards with their necks stretching and beaks pointing straight up to the sky, and with their little wings beating fast like pistons, they were attempting to see how high they could reach before dropping back down onto a branch to join their brothers and sisters. The really clever ones could reach quite high, where they would hover for a few seconds, and free fall back down again. One acrobat managed to flip right over into a somersault.

These little daredevils were applauded in an explosion of noisy chatter by their siblings for their great feats of acrobatics.

I imagined that they called this game "Skylarking!"

Other birds had their own funny little rituals to perform.

It was not unusual to see the doves sitting in the eucalyptus tree enjoying a spot of gentle rain, but what did strike me as unusual—and I'd never seen other species of bird carrying out the same ritual—was that they would hold one wing outstretched and slightly upwards (as though they were washing the underparts of their wings), and then they would swap over to the other wing for a minute or two to do the same thing.

I did once see a mistle thrush flapping and dipping his wings in the wet grass, as though he was bathing in the birdbath, and then he ran under the lilac tree to stand under the dripping leaves, as though he was taking a shower.

Birds can be so amusing to watch.

Young buzzards and red kites were beginning to show themselves and acted like lost infants on a beach, as they let out their plaintiff cries which echoed piercingly across the valley. They looked so ungainly on the ground as they waited for a parent bird to come along and feed them, and they awkwardly tried to walk on the stubble of the freshly mown fields, spreading out their wings and flapping them as they attempted to keep their balance on the ground, then flying onto the top of the hawthorn hedge, to compete with the others for the same branch to perch on. Usually the more dominant bird won!

Sometimes the young buzzards would spend quite a long period of time on the same spot, just waiting for food to arrive, and unfortunately their wait was often a very long one, and sometimes it just never seemed to arrive, so they would fly despondently back to the woods.

Not so long ago, a few farmers used to feed the kites and buzzards with lambs which had died on their land, and this was a valuable contribution towards the birds' survival, but since the foot and mouth and the BSE crisis, they are no longer allowed to do this, so these young birds can no longer rely on this extra kick start in life—more's the pity!

Perhaps I should throw out a few tins of doggy or cat meat?...just to help them out a bit—to give them assistance to reach maturity.

So with my keen devotion at giving these youngsters a helping hand with my own contributions, I scatter odd bits of suitable leftovers, like chicken, liver, a handful of raw minced meat, and reasonable dollops of cat and dog food.

Watching the great birds circling and calling above me, I felt well pleased with my efforts.

That is until one day, whilst putting my mother's freshly ironed blouses in her wardrobe, I happened to glance out of her bedroom window and there, stalking along the patch of earth where I had religiously placed the birds' offerings (on a daily basis), was a cunning, very well fed, big red dog fox!

A family of crows frequently visited our garden.

At first I didn't take much notice of them, as they seemed to be just like any ordinary family of crows who would sometimes turn up to greedily snatch the bread off the lawn and then fly off with a whole slice to feed their family with—making a horrible raucous sound as they went—and sometimes they would choose to kill a poor little baby bird left unattended on the lawn to fend for itself, or to pick off a sick or weak bird, like a chaffinch or a sparrow.

This particular family of crows caught my attention when I noticed the same two adults arrive together each day at about the same time.

The male was a very handsome looking crow. His feathers were a glossy black, and he appeared to be different from the other crows. He was not so loud and aggressive—more gentlemanly and regal in his manner.

His wife was a quiet and gentle creature and seemed to stay in the background.

His children seemed to be well behaved too.

I felt I had to name them, so "Mr. Crow" was Fred and his wife was named Wilma, and of course his two children were named Pebbles and Bam Bam!

Fred turned out to be a very intelligent bird, and he became used to me throwing out slices of bread, which I did at certain times of the day—just for him and his family.

When Pebbles and Bam Bam finally left to take up their own territory, and returned to the garden less frequently, Fred and his wife Wilma still religiously came each day.

Fred was quite cute, and he would sit on top of the weeping cherry tree just outside of the kitchen window, where he would stare at me through the window, willing me to throw out his slice of bread, and if he thought I had forgotten to do so, he would utter loud cawing noises at me, whilst bowing up and down with each call, which went on and on until I threw out his slice of bread for him.

Even when I opened the door to go outside, Fred didn't always bother to fly off, and waited on the top of the tree until I returned indoors, and then he would hop down and waddle over to the bread.

Fred always picked pieces off the bread, and made them into small chunks before collecting them up to fly off with, and leaving a small pile for Wilma to pick up for herself.

He was so thoughtful to his spouse and children, and for a big old crow, he was a gentle sort, and I never saw him vicious in any way, which was so unusual for a bird of his kind.

He became quite tame, and I got quite fond of him in a way.

If I had forgotten to throw his usual titbit of bread—or sometimes I would throw him a small chunk of stale cake—then he seemed to know—or somehow find out—exactly which room I happened to be in at the time.

If I was upstairs making the beds, I would have a strange feeling that I was being watched, and when I looked out of the window, there would be Fred sitting opposite the window and perched high on the top branch of the poplar tree, just staring at me as though willing me to go downstairs and give him his special treat—which, of course, I did!

Then one day, whilst driving back down our lane after a shopping trip, I noticed a black object lying on the grass verge, and as I drove past it, I noticed it moved slightly, and when I glanced in my rear view mirror, I could see that it was one of the crows.

I quickly jumped out of the car and hurried back to where the crow was still lying, and I discovered that it was Wilma.

She seemed to be in great distress and appeared to be experiencing a lot of pain.

I carefully picked her up and put her on the seat of the car, then drove the last few yards into our drive.

I quickly took her indoors to inspect her to see if she might be injured in any way.

Her head was thrust back and onto her shoulders at an awkward angle, and she seemed to be very disorientated. I made vain attempts at trying to ease her head back into a normal position, but each time I did this, she just threw her head back again.

I couldn't find any visible injuries on her, so she couldn't have been hit by a car or caught by a cat, and there were no signs of pellets, which could have meant somebody trying to shoot at her, so it was a bit of a mystery.

I tried to feed her with small pieces of bread soaked in warm milk. She gulped some of it down, but nothing seemed to help her, and she gradually got worse.

I gently put her into Maggie's old mynah bird cage and left her quietly for a while, hoping that she would recover from whatever her problem was.

When I returned to check on her, she was considerably worse, and she kept toppling over as she attempted to flap her wings.

It was then that I noticed a nasty putrid smell, and it slowly dawned on me that she was probably poisoned!

With great sadness and a heavy heart, I had to ask a neighbour to come over and put her out of her misery, as I couldn't bear to see her suffer any longer.

And so poor old Fred had lost his Wilma, but he didn't know that yet.

He still came for his slice of bread, and he still carefully and meticulously pecked pieces off, and left them in a pile for Wilma—but she never came.

He carried on doing this well into the winter, and it was so pitiful to see him watch and wait—to no avail.

Then on one cold winter's day, Fred turned up as usual and perched himself on top of the cherry tree, only he didn't appear to be his usual self. He looked very hunched up, and his feathers were all fluffed out as though he was feeling the cold.

I opened the door as usual and threw a slice of bread out for him, only this time he didn't seem to be very interested in flying down to collect it.

I watched him from the window, and felt a little more assured when I saw him pick up the bread, and then carry out his usual ritual of dividing it up into pieces, so I left him to it, knowing that he would return for some more a little later on.

Much later on in the afternoon, he did once more return, only this time he looked very unwell, and his feathers were all fluffed up, and he sat hunched up on the patio slabs just outside the kitchen door, which was much closer than he usually does. When I opened the door to throw a good handful of crumbs from a fruit cake—as I thought the fat content and sugar would help to keep him warm—he didn't even attempt to hop away from me, and it was then that I realized that there was something seriously wrong with him.

I knew that he would be wary enough to keep a respectable distance from me, which would prove to be difficult if I needed to capture him to take him indoors so that I could take a closer look to see what was wrong. I didn't want to cause him undue distress, so I didn't try to approach, knowing that this would probably drive him off anyway.

He tried to eat the cake, but he found it very difficult and only managed to eat a small piece, which wasn't enough to sustain him for any length of time, and he would need a lot more than that to see him through the cold night.

I watched as he flew off, hoping that he would return soon, and if it was dark enough, this would then perhaps enable me to catch him in order to keep him in overnight, in the hope that he would fare better by the morning.

He did return, and it was just getting dusk.

He looked sadly at me through the window, and I looked back at him, feeling very helpless, not knowing what he wanted or what I could do for him.

I threw a small trayful of scraps down for him in the futile hope that he would feed.

He hopped down and cautiously waddled over.

I didn't move as he almost came up to my feet.

He looked up at me, and it was almost as though he was saying, "Thank you for everything—thank you for your kindness—and now I have to say goodbye!"

He picked up a small piece of food, then put it back down again.

He was just too feeble and unable to eat.

I was feeling upset, and the tears rolled down my face as I looked on in hopeless despair.

Then he seemed to make a decision.

It was almost as though he had found the courage to drag himself towards his final destination, and he started wearily to waddle across the lawn toward the Berberis shrub, and without any hesitation, he hopped down towards the bottom lawn. Then I watched as his familiar glossy-black form disappeared down the bank—and then he was gone!

I never saw Fred again, and I never found his body—he must have perished that night—alone!

Perhaps he had grown too old to cope with life, and he knew his time had come.

His two offspring, Pebbles and Bam Bam barely visited the garden after he left, and whenever I opened the door to throw out a slice of bread for them, they just flew off.

They were never as friendly, and it would be impossible for them to live up to their gentlemanly father, Fred.

Eventually, they too disappeared.

I still miss Fred.

Although he still enjoyed partaking in his usual pranks, especially with Millie, and carrying out his devilish deeds, Maggie's behaviour started to change.

At first it was barely noticeable, but gradually his temperament changed.

He still enjoyed his bath in the old roasting tin, which was by now getting quite rusty, and he still flew up to Adam's bedroom window demanding that his feathers should be blow dried with the hair dryer!

The cat and bird found a new game to play—it was called "tag!"

This was carried out on the wooden five-bar gate which divided the drive from the stable and garage block.

First, Maggie would perch on the top of the gate, then Millie would slowly start to climb up using the lower bar, and then when she reached the bar just below Maggie, she would balance herself steady, and then pat out at his tail which was dangling invitingly just in front of her nose, and then Maggie would respond by reaching down on the opposite side, and peck her on the shoulder blades, which always made her leap down. Then it was Maggie's turn, and their roles were reversed, with Millie balancing on the top bar, and Maggie would jump like a professional athlete, from bar to bar until he reached just below Millie's dangling tail, which just had to be pulled, and the whole process would begin again—until the game was ended by the first contestant to become bored—usually Maggie!

Maggie still followed me about or sat on my shoulder when the dogs went for their usual daily walks, only now when he flew off to join the other magpies, he would stay with them for much longer periods, only returning to his aviary at dusk.

Sometimes when I found the time for a short break and took myself off into the summerhouse with a book, or just to rest for a while and watch the other birds feeding with their young on the lawn, Maggie would sit quietly on my shoulder like a little old man, looking all wise and very contented.

These were very treasured moments with Maggie, but sadly quite rare.

He would sometimes chatter away very sweetly, whilst I talked to him about everything and anything, and he seemed to understand what was said.

He followed me one day when I went to check on the depth of our underground spring, which was situated between the stable block and garage and ran diagonally across the fields and beyond to a destination unknown to myself.

Maggie watched in amusement as I dropped a small pebble down the sunken pipe to the spring in order to test for myself just how deep it might be, and waiting for the splash as it hit the surface. It took a few seconds before the dull *"plop"* could be heard.

He stood with his head cocked to one side, and his crest rose and fell as he tried to work out what I was doing. Then, much to my amazement, he went and picked up his own stone, brought it back to the pipe, and dropped it down. I just couldn't believe what I'd just seen.

Could it be possible that he was actually copying my actions—or was it just coincidence!

I decided to cover the hole over with a large stone—just in case!

Perhaps he'd heard the story about the crow and the water jar?

This is a lovely little story from Aesop's Fables, and it tells of a very thirsty crow who happened to come across a jar which had just a small amount of water at the bottom.

It took her a very long time to fathom out how she could reach the water to satisfy her great thirst. She couldn't tip the jar over because it was too heavy, so she had to come up with another idea. Now in frustration, she saw some small pebbles lying nearby, and she picked a few up and threw them in her anger into the jar—*splosh!*

She suddenly realized to her great joy, that the water level had risen slightly, so she quickly picked up more stones and threw them into the jar again—*splosh!... splosh!... splosh!*

It wasn't long before the water level had reached to the top of the jar, and soon she was able to take a drink.

Maggie had his own subtle "Magpie Fables" to live up to, and it's also interesting to note that crows and magpies like to dunk their bread in the birdbath before eating it, so perhaps there is an element of truth in this particular fable after all.

Although he was by now able to find his own food, he still expected all the attention, so whenever I was in the kitchen preparing our meals, he would bang loudly and call lustily at the kitchen window, demanding his share of our food—hot or cold!

He also had the knack of knowing whenever I was in the bathroom having a bath, for he would fly up onto the window sill, and with his modified goose-step, he would mince up and down, stopping occasionally to *"tap!... tap!... tap!"* on the frosted window pane, and then he would whistle, warble, and chortle, *"Cooee!... Cooee!... Cooee!... Yaw!... Yaw!... Yaw!... Chuck!... Chuck!... Chuck!"*

In order to keep the peace and to appease him, I would have to get out of the bath dripping water and bubbles everywhere—just to let him in!

He would then venture to sit on the edge of the bath where I could flick bubbles at him or place a neat dollop of them onto the top of his head like a frothy crown.

"Now then, Maggie," I told him teasingly, "you're as sweet as a nut!...or should I say...nuthatch!"

He was not amused, but did his impersonation of a penguin stranded on an ice floe—whilst I carried on wallowing blissfully... like a hippo in a lily pond!

Somebody once said, "Why don't you test him with a crystal to see if he's a she or she's a he?"

We were never quite sure what Maggie's gender really was at that time, so I thought it was worth a try. Nothing ventured—nothing gained!

I borrowed from a friend (who claimed to be a great believer in "crystal healing") one of her small crystals, which was attached to a length of thread.

Feeling somewhat sceptical about the whole idea, and checking that nobody else was about, I approached the cage where Maggie was sitting impatiently on the top perch wondering why I hadn't let him out yet!

Now what was it that I was told?…if it swings back and forth, then he's a he!…but if it swings round and round in a circle…then he's a she!

Holding the crystal above his head, I tried to keep my hand steady so that the crystal wouldn't move—so I kept it as still as I could.

I didn't have to wait long.

To my great surprise and excitement, the crystal began to tremble, and I could feel a slight vibration through my fingers as though the crystal had a life of its own!

It started to swing back and forth, and so did Maggie's head as he watched intently. And then after a few swings of the crystal, his bright eyes started to blink rapidly, which was a sure sign that he was beginning to get rather cross with the whole thing!

So back and forth meant that he really is—*a boy*!

And then quite suddenly it started to move in a wide circle, and so did Maggie's head as he nearly fell off his perch!

This means he must be—*a girl*!

But then it reverted back to swinging back and forth like a pendulum once more.

How on earth can he be both a boy and a girl at the same time?

Oh well, it was worth a try, and we were right back where we started!

I felt sure he was more of a boy than a girl anyway!

As I have already said before, Maggie's mood swings became more unpredictable as the weeks went by.

He began to show aggression towards me, which was very unusual as I had always been so careful not to handle him in a rough manner, and he was reasonably tolerant if I had to scold him verbally, and it always seemed to work with him, but I *never* hit out at him, even if he pecked out at me on the odd occasion if he was in a very cross mood.

Then I noticed the reason for his sudden aggression.

It was another magpie!

A female magpie!

– Chapter Nine and a Half –
Over to Maggie

…three blind mice…see how they run!

Isn't life a bowl of cherries and a bed of roses all at the same time?… Like it's fun *and* tedious. Fun, because there's so much to do, but tedious because I *still* can't find that elusive 'chickle chackle tree!' And another thing—what's wrong with euthanasia?

Just 'coz me an' this manky old earth whispering moggy they calls *Millie* (sounds more like *silly!*), goes out on these "chick-chasing" missions, and "squeaking-house-mouse" clearances, and on really good days we can clear up some of the "tasty wasty hoppity bunny-wunnies," making us as happy as hoopoes!

We seems to get the human population all frothing at the mouth and shrieking like rabid pixies who'd just tripped over a four-leafed clover—an' lost their charms in the middle of a cow pat!—an' all because we're just doin' our duties on a daily basis!

I can only say that me pinky ma really pushed the boat out with generosity when she provided me with me very own critter-catchin' kushti kitty-cat.

It took me some while to show the moggy just who was boss, but in time she proved just how rightly good a teacher she was to me at huntin' and catchin' all kinds of the wild stuff, especially those whiskery little squeaker fellers.

It wasn't long before I had her well and truly twisted round me beak, an' doin' all me biddin'. Long ears and squeakers were soon rainin' down about me like crows' droppings! I was soon able to show all the others just what they were missin', not havin' their very own earth whisperer to do all their food gathering for them.

I was scrabbling about under a big bush one sunlight-time, when I nearly crashed beaks with a big old crow.

"Hey, you big dilly-ducks-down!" I yelled. "Look where you're going!—This is me patch, don't you know?"

"This is not *your* patch!" he croaked back at me. "I have been outside of my egg for many suns and moons, so I was even here long before your egg layer and egg maker were hatched!"

He looked at me with his bright coal-black eyes, and it was then that I noticed just how big and powerful his beak looked, and felt jolly glad that I wasn't still a fledgling, otherwise history could be repeating itself! But I must say that this old crow looked very wise (a bit like the old Hootie!) and sort of placid as well, so I didn't feel too threatened.

He continued his lecture to me.

"I do know that you are in the keeping of humans, and that you are treated well. You are blessed with all creature comforts, for which I feel you do not fully appreciate."

"Hey, hang on a bit!" I said, "I know where my bread is buttered, and my cheese is cut, and my chicken is cooked, and me...!"

He cut in—"All right!... All right!... Maybe I was a bit too hasty with my last remark, and I suppose they wouldn't have kept you so long and given you such luxuries if they didn't *like* you. You have a lot to learn in life, little magpie, and may I suggest that you listen to your elders more attentively, and take heed at what they tell you, because it may help you to survive and negotiate life's dangers."

I wasn't too sure as to what he meant, but I *click-clicked* me beak in agreement.

He then carried on.

"I too, just like yourself, was found as a fledgling, after both my egg layer and egg maker were taken by a fox, and all my siblings perished in the same way judging by all the feathers scattered around on the earth.

"I was able to hide myself high up in a Holly bush, where this human (a man human), happened to discover me, because I think that at the time he was hunting in the tree for berries. He was known as a gypsy, and other gypsy folk called him 'Old Buzz'. It was said (by the hedgerow creatures), that he was a changeling, and that he had been switched over by the fairies for a human child, but I have no idea if this is true.

"I travelled about with him in his colourful—but very comfortable—round klakki, which the humans called a caravan. It was pulled by a black and white horse, which a lot of the birds from this area call a 'dragon'! I believe you have a horse here—one which is all black; is that correct?"

"Yes!... That's about right," I said, "but I do know it's not a dragon, and that it's actually a horse, and it's called Humphrey," I said smugly. "But what happened to you? And how did you get here? And what became of the human gypsy pinky person?"

"Well," he said, "we travelled all over the place—just the three of us. I was named Garron, and his horse was called Griff. Old Buzz cared for me very well, and he seemed to know much about earth creatures and plants, and went about collecting lots of small plants which he hung up to dry on the roof of the caravan.

"He also went out in the woods to collect small branches from certain trees, and I would go along with him, sitting on his shoulder. He would then take the branches back to the caravan, where he would work for much of the sunlight-time carving different objects out of them, and on larger pieces of wood (like oak and ash) he would carve out lifelike figures of humans, birds and animals, and then we would travel to the humans' dwelling places, where the humans would trade pieces of round silver for these objects, which made Old Buzz very happy.

"Many times, when the sun had gone down and the moon was rising, we would stay outside beneath the moon and stars, and Old Buzz would make a small fire from brushwood, and he would cook things that I would hate to tell you of, and one of these things I can inform you, were hedgehogs!

"He could whistle and imitate birdsongs as well as whistling his own tunes, and he would sing old folk songs as he called them, in a voice that could be strong and mellow, or as hearty as an oak, and sometimes it was low and soft as a dove's wing, whilst he played on a strange looking object which he called an accordion.

"Sometimes other gypsy humans would join us at a gathering, and they would bring their own various tune-making instruments, and they would join in the singing whilst other gypsies danced around the flickering firelight. This was far too noisy for me, so I would go where Griff was tethered to a tree, and I would sit on a branch above his head, hoping that the noise would soon go away.

"Old Buzz tried to teach me to speak the human speech, but I just felt it was above my dignity to try, so he finally gave up trying.

"We travelled far and wide, until we eventually arrived on an open space not far from here. There was an abundance of food to be had, and Old Buzz had no problem in catching the long-ears, and he found nuts and berries in the hedgerows, and for himself he would pick mushrooms, but these were no good for me or Griff.

"One moonlight-time, when Old Buzz went out on a long-ears hunt (bunny-wunnies), he stumbled upon a group of very rough, cruel-looking men, who were out with their short-legged earth runners.

"They were digging out badgers from a set, and when Old Buzz saw them, he tried to stop them because although he hunted creatures for food, he was never cruel to them, and never killed anything that he didn't need to eat, and he always gave thanks to the earth goddess for providing him with enough food to sustain himself, Griff and myself.

"I watched from a good distance, as something told me that danger was in the air! The strange men turned violent, and they hit out at Old Buzz with a large piece of wood, gashing his head, and he fell to the ground where he laid still for some time before he was able to move. The evil men ran off into the night, leaving poor Old Buzz to recover the best he could, and eventually stagger back to the caravan.

"He never seemed the same after that incident, and he gradually became thin and feeble from lack of food, and soon his skin looked grey with sickness, and he found great difficulty in walking. After many seasons of caring for me and the old horse, a great sadness came when on one particular night as he lay outside by the dying fire, Griff and I stood by his tired old body, and we both sensed his spirit slip away from him.

"Many groups of gypsies from all across the land turned up to say their farewells. Finally, at the end of their rituals and feasting, they burnt down his caravan, and then one of them led Griff away, leaving me stranded and with no dwelling place. I never saw Griff again, so I had no idea what had happened to him.

"I was now out in the open space and on my own, and very hungry, and not knowing what to do. It was then that a lone egg layer crow happened to find me, near to starving, and I think her senses told her that because I was 'human raised,' I was unable to follow any normal crow instincts.

"She took me under her wing, so to speak, and she told me that she was called Izabella Delarose, also known as Bellarose. She taught me hunting skills, and the ways of the crow family. She became my egg layer mate, and we have spent many happy seasons together.

"I was also taught the ways of the earth by Sedgeborn the raven, and this is what he told me:

"'We feel the earth speak to us through our feet, and we feel danger in the wind, and in the bend of a branch, or even the turn of a leaf can indicate danger lurking before us. When you hear Rowan Berry the song thrush, singing his ancient songs of deeds long ago, listen carefully, and you will hear riddles that will help you to survive, and when you see him standing very still with his head cocked to one side, he is listening to distant sounds beneath the earth—an' beyond!

"'As we gather ourselves up to prepare for our roosting time, before the sun has left us as it sets behind our backs and leaves us to darkness, we can sometimes hear the mountains roar as though the great dragon beneath the mountains is about to burst forth and devour us all, but by the goodness of the great hawk, this has never happened.

"'I have also personally witnessed a great 'iron dragon' pass by at great speed, and I quake with fear!'"

When Garron had finished his tale, I felt very proud to tell him that this "thundering dragon"! was actually a human-made object, and they call it "Concorde"! (I didn't tell him that I'd seen it on the tee vee, and seen lots of humans walk willingly straight up a stairway, and then into it!)—an' that it actually *roars* overhead at about the same time every sunset, and the only thing it could possibly eat are humans, so there's nothing for the birds to fear.

Then garron said, "There are other 'iron dragons' that fly low and fast like 'thunder gods' and they pass with a loud *roar* and a deafening *scream* as they race across the sky, and it is true that flocks of birds have been slaughtered by these great 'iron dragons'!"

We both bowed our heads in respect of all fallen birds from the strike of the dragons!

I thought to meself, *There must be a 'dragon boom' around here!* At that time, I didn't know just how close to the truth me thoughts really were!

I left Garron to ponder about Concorde and dragons, and flew off to seek out the group.

"Roll up!... Roll up! Come and see me play my magical chiming sticks!" I called.

Ma had strung these different musical playing things in the lower branches of trees such as the willows, and others were placed over an iron arch, and when the wind blew (or if I was to peck at 'em), they made wonderfully noisy musical notes.

The others wanted to have a go as well, so between us all, we made a right merry sound!

"Now I will show you another bit of magical stuff!" I said cheerfully."Follow me!"

We all flew off towards me magnificent mansion, and then I took them between Humphrey's klakki, and the one where the pinkies keep their metal klakki (car!).

I wanted to show them the big secret hole in the ground that woz recently discovered by me and Ma. As they all stood around me, I made sure that they were watching carefully, and with their full attention.

They looked on expectantly as I lifted up a big flat stone (in the manner that I'd seen me pinky ma do a few suns ago), and uncovered the big deep hole in the earth, that looked as though it carried on down forever!

"Now watch closely, and listen carefully!" I told them, "And you will hear something that is deep down in the middle of the earth, and you will be *so* envious that I am *so* lucky to have this 'earth mystery' thing, right next to me klakki!"

They stood in silent awe, even though I hadn't done anything yet.

I fetched a small round stone, then took it to the hole and dropped it down. There was a respectfully long silence, and then we all heard a very faint, and a very dull *plip!*—but not the nice clear *plop!* which I had heard when me pinky ma had done it.

So how was I to know that the long sunlight-time woz goin' to dry up the nice impressive water sound coming from down there!?

I didn't know whether to "break wind," or "break into song," so I "broke into a windy song."

> Let the dowser dowse,
> let the curlew cry,
> let the preacher preach,
> in a tomato soup sky.

> *Let the healer heal,*
> *with the hair from a frog,*
> *let the teacher teach,*
> *from the heathlands to the bog."*

There was that stony silence again, until one of them (that is to say, Gizzy) said, "Do you *know* what you have just done? You have committed a terrible deed because you have just opened up to release the great secrets of far below the earth, and now it will be opened to the sky, so heaven knows what will happen to us all. Down there is a sacred place known only to a few chosen ones, and you have probably disturbed the lair of the 'red dragon of Ffoss!' —or even the guarded domain of none other than the great Merlin!"

"Merlin? Oh, you mean the Merlin who's got a bit of an elvish attitude?" I asked.

"Yes, yes!" said Gizzy.

"And what about all these '*dragons!*' everyone keeps talking about, do they really live in these parts?" I asked.

"But of course they do!" said Tizzy.

"Let me tell you then, there was not even a murmur or a mutterings about '*dragons*' on the common where I came from, only a story about '*green stones and a rising phoenix*'" I said.

They all started to go into a bit of a panic, and ran around in circles doing a war-dance, and shouting—"*a phoenix!... A phoenix!... Oh no!... Not a phoenix as well!*"

I tried to calm them down and told them not to worry, and that there was no '*phoenix*' in Wales, but they didn't take much notice, and Lotty said in a frightened voice, "Cover the hole quickly!... The only ones who can tell you if you have released '*the mighty ones*' is either Tegrin the red kite, or Glider the heron. They will tell you if we are in mortal danger after what you have just done, and not only that, what on earth will Featherhead White Wings say if he gets to know about this? We will praise you greatly if you will go and do this for us, and we will thank you forever!"

The easy answer is don't tell Featherhead White Wings! I thought logically, but in answer to their suggestion and plea, I said politely, "Well thank you for finding so much faith in me—I'll give it a thought!" But a bit more squeakily than I intended to, I said, "You

435

know you can trust me completely, I'm as reliable and as pliable as a worm's kneecap!"

"That's just what we're afraid of!" chorused Lotty and Totty in a rather dry, drone tone.

I hastily covered the hole over with the stone, then on an impulse I added, "Now in the meantime, whilst we're waiting for something exciting to happen, let's lighten up, like a glow-worm's lamp, and sharpen our beaks, ready for action!... Does anyone want to join me on a...BTB?"

This seemed to get them motivated once more!

"What's a...BTB?" asked Lilly Bell.

"It's a blue tit bash party!" I said.

"No thanks!" said Lilly Bell. "I've just polished off a few thrushes eggs."

"But they're not very big though, are they!" I said.

"Yes, I know," said Lilly Bell, "but they're a tasty blue colour, and exquisitely marked with little black specks, which gives them a good presentation, and they have an excellent flavour. And this lot have just come back from an RR," she said.

"What's an RR?" I asked.

"Oh!... It's just a robin raid party, of course!"

I was beginning to think that these cheeky magpies were starting to talk more and more like me each sunlight-time, so I must be influencing them to me ways of thinking, even if they're not as smart as me!

"Okay," I said, "it's just me on me own then—is it?"

P'rhaps me problem woz that I'd got off from the wrong side of my perch this 'morrow!

Then Totty said, "Before we all move off to the distant pasture, let's go and sort out those two bushy-tails, in case they find and completely destroy our carefully built klakkies, otherwise our hatchling numbers will drop this season, and you know what they say, 'Seven magpies maketh a seventh heaven'!"

"Now that we're on the subject, let me tell you somethin,'" said Ivy.

"One of my ancestors, who was named Pea Pod, had a novel way of dealing with the bushy-tails. He used to collect peas from the peafields, and then he would fly over to the trees to where the bushy-tails would be busy foraging for chestnuts, hazelnuts and acorns, and then perching on a branch right over their heads, he would shoot out the peas real hard, right down onto the astonished nut gatherers, '*phut!… phut!… phut!*' scattering the bushy-tails in all directions."

"By the way, Maggie," she said, "we all know that you live in that large pinky-built klakki, but have you built a *proper* magpie klakki, or even a multitude of klakkies somewhere? And you know what they say!… 'Don't lay all of your eggs in the same klakki'!"

"Don't you mean…'Don't count your magpies before they hatch!?'" I asked.

Ivy gave me a squinty look—then flew off!

Klakkies!… Klakkies! Oh my giddy gofer!… A thought has just popped into me 'ead like a lead bullet! Here's me, all on me own, and not a single self-built klakki in sight!

Now to be more realistic and practical, I'm going to need an egg layer. I will have to go out there and find myself a mate even!

As it so happens, I have seen a flash of black and white feathers flitting flirtily through the trees, and from what I could see from where I woz perched at the time, these trendy looking feathers were set smartly on the most *beautiful* magpie I had ever seen!

I had never seen her with the group before, so she must have come from another flight zone. Perhaps she belongs to a new wandering group of magpies out looking for a new klakki-building area.

I had to make a firm decision as to whether I should introduce myself.

Shall I?… Shan't I? Hmm…tricky!'

Then, "heigh ho…an' hey presto!"

I took a big, bold step and approached her carefully, but with a touch of eager anticipation.

"I am Maggie of the far-off heathlands," I said.

"And I am Moltikala of the mountain ash," she said, "but I'm also known as 'Tilly.'"

I came…I saw…I conquered! I had actually *pulled* a bird!

"Do you come here often?" I inquired.

"No, only once in every seven moons!" she replied.

I realized I was off to a very good start!

Seven moons could mean seven little magpies after all! I thought to meself.

So this was it! Me very own egg layer! Me mate who woz a goddess, and nothing short of a pure angel! This was me lucky day!

Now I would just have to make a flying start, so to speak, but where should I begin?

Not having spent too much of me time in me own hatchling klakki all those suns and moons ago, before being rescued, I haven't much recollection of how I should build me own, but perhaps it'll come to me as I go along.

Although this nice big magpie penthouse is all comfort and fun, and somewhere to hide all me treasures in, it's no good for egg-laying and chick-rearing, so I shall tarry no longer at searching for a suitable site, and I must also go out on material collecting expeditions with me mate, Moltikala—or 'Tilly' as I now call her—but I wasn't prepared for all that unnecessary hammering I was getting from those two cheeky swallows, Jeela and his mate, Solino.

All I wanted to do was to start me own site in the tall beech tree just outside the pinkies' klakki, but every time I went anywhere near the swallows' chosen klakki site, which happened to be right at the very top of Humphrey's penthouse, they would dive-bomb me, screeching out—"*Git-out!… Git-out!… Git-out!*"—an' I would have to beat a very hasty retreat, otherwise they could easily have ruffled me very smart feathers!

When Jeela and Solino discovered that I had already started to work like a beaver on me own klakki, and that I wasn't even interested in theirs, owing to the fact that I was already a late starter, and therefore had a lot of catching up to do, they stopped pestering me and devoted their attentions to the bushy-tails, and the other magpies, of course!

One day, when we were both after the same fly and Jeela won, after a near beak-breaking experience, he settled down near a muddy puddle which he'd previously been scooping up as material stuff for his klakki, and Jeela told me about his and Solino's long journey from far-off lands, and of their great ordeals, and how glad he and Solino were at finding such a wonderful place to build their first klakki, and that this was their first season here.

It seems that after they had spent the whole of the winter months in the hot lands of a place called South Africa, he and Solino—with many thousands of other swallows—flew on their great perilous journey back north.

He then told me about their flight.

"We started off, after our gathering together with many others, having feasted enough to gain weight to endure our trip. Flying at low altitudes, we followed our course across the hot dry land, gathering food as we went, and stayed close to our own group for safety.

"Our long flight eventually took us down towards the Nile valley, but found the first part of this desert journey towards the river Nile very exhausting, as we had to endure many sunlight hours of hard and fast flying before arriving, and although most of us had already taken in as much food as we could muster, sadly some of the weaker members of the flock had already perished along the way from starvation.

"Our return journey then took us over Morocco and eastern Spain, and then across the Pyrenees, before reaching western France, and then finally flying over Britain to arrive here. There were a number of casualties on the way.

"Great storms took many lives over the oceans, where many crashed into blinding, flashing lights out in the stormy ocean, and many others dropped weak and starving as great waves drew them into the sea. High winds blew over mountain tops, carrying huge flocks helplessly to their deaths."

Jeela stopped at this point, as though he was taking time out to remember a particular incident that was a painful memory to him.

After a few moments of preening himself, he continued.

"There was a truly unforgettable ordeal that befell us all when we flew across arid desert lands. Above, to the sides, and all around us were the most terrifying 'metal dragons' screaming and roaring across the skies, breathing out fire and metal hail-stones, and there was much activity below us where huge dragons on the ground rumbled along, scorching the land with great fire-balls, sending thick black smoke into the air.

"The thunderous noise drove fear into our hearts, as we attempted to fly above the deathly beings, but many of the swallows were overcome by the thick choking smoke. I called out to Solino to stay close to me, and flew at great speed towards the edge of the dragons' battle fields. Solino followed bravely on, and at first I didn't notice that she was actually slowing down.

"As we reached an area of safety, I turned to make sure that Solino was still close to me, and it was then that I noticed that something was seriously wrong with her. Her beautiful glossy feathers had turned a dull and dusty black, and her once sparkling eyes had dulled and were slowly closing, even though she was still flying, but her wing-beats had slowed down, and she was beginning to fall behind.

"Then all of a sudden she spiralled like an autumn leaf, down to the earth, landing on the soft sand, where she lay as still as a stone. From out of a small desert dwelling, and almost camouflaged by the sand dunes, there appeared a human figure. I couldn't tell if it was a male or female, as it was clad in long earth-coloured robes, part of which was striped like a zebra, and its face was partly covered over, with just the sharp black eyes showing.

"I swooped down close to the spot where Solino fell, but kept at a safe distance. My heart beat fast as I watched in anticipation. The robed figure went over to Solino's body, which was barely moving—apart from the motion of her fast heartbeat—an' gentle hands picked her up.

"I sensed that there was nothing to fear, so I flew a little closer. The human turned Solino over onto her back in the palm of one hand, and gently rubbed her chest with a finger, and then after blowing warm breath onto her body, and cupping the other hand lightly over her, I could hear a low chanting sound coming from the human. This ritual went on for a few heartbeats.

"After this was done, the human uncupped its hands, and for a few moments Solino laid very still, but now she was the right way up, and she opened her eyes and looked about her. Her eyes were bright once more, and she started to raise her body whilst she was still in the human's hand, and after a little coaxing, she took off into the air, calling out as she went. We were overjoyed to be together once more and continued our journey until we arrived here!"

"Wow!" I said, "That was one hell of a story! Bet you wished you never left home though!"

"Ah yes...I know!" he said. "But something very strange happened to Solino whilst she was near to death. She told me that she had a very strange dream, which seemed so real that she thought it was actually happening to her."

"Can you tell me about it?" I asked. "Or will you have to tell me another time?... When you're not so busy like!"

"I will tell you now!" he said. "I will be much too busy later on, especially when our fledglings hatch out...an' I will have to start protecting them from the likes of you! So that won't be a good time!... Will it?"

"Okay, point taken!" I said. "So what happened in her dream then?... I like dreamy type things!"

"Well it happened like this!" he said.

"In her dream, she met up with her egg layer mother, Blue Streak, and her egg maker father, Black Arrow. They appeared from the direction of the sun, like two black angels, and they were flying alongside Gordina, a Sufi maiden who changes at will into a Bird of Paradise.

"Gordina called upon the goddess Iris, who harnessed Blue Streak and Black Arrow to her belt, and together they flew with Iris over the arching rainbow, and on to the other side of the universe, and into the depths of the Otherworld of the gods!"

"Is that it?" I asked. "Is that all there is to it? Didn't she see anything else, or didn't anything exciting happen to her whilst she was in her dream?"

"Why yes, of course!" he said. "She told me that it wasn't just a dream, but she was actually there, flying — or floating — alongside not only Blue Streak and Black Arrow, but many of her ancestors as well. She said she wasn't strictly flying as such, because she was lifted and supported by the others, and all the while, she could feel the breath of angels who surrounded her sick body.

"First of all, she was touched by the angel Rehael, who helped to heal her along with Hubuhiah, who eased her suffering, and then Seheiah added protection against the violent elements, whilst Mikael would aid her on the long journey north, but before she could embark on such a journey, she would have to undergo further healing.

"Three sacred ibises joined them, and they were escorted towards their destination. The rays of the sun enhanced the reddish-brown feathers of the ibises to a rich ruby glow. They flew high above the turquoise blue waters of the Nile, where crescent-shaped boats sailed in a slow and tranquil manner.

"Solino felt herself being gently carried to a magnificent temple, which was a place of healing, and as they landed, the angels and Solino's ancestors seemed to vanish into thin air, leaving her quite alone, but not for long.

"At the entrance of the temple stood ornately dressed guards, who blew a long sonorous note on elegantly curved ox-horns, which was to herald their gods and goddesses. The Mother Earth goddess Hathor, 'Eye of Re' and 'Lady of the West' as she is known, emerged from out of the darkness at the entrance to the temple, and she slowly descended the long steep steps to greet the new arrivals.

"She was adorned in her healing robes of a deep blue and gold, and a mantle of ibis feathers hung about her shoulders, and around her neck she wore a neck-plate of lapis lazuli and gold, which matched her long pendant earrings. On her head, she wore a crown of a bright red sun disc, which glowed like a giant ruby.

"The goddess Hathor stood silent, as though waiting for something to happen. Solino then heard a tremendous rumbling sound, which seemed to be coming from deep down below the surface of the sands. The noise grew louder and louder, and the earth shook violently, and then in one bolt of lightning, a figure of a very tall human-like shimmering form emerged from out of the ground.

"It was the god Thot! As the last grain of sand fell from his great shoulders, he stood there very tall and commanding, and with an air of dominance.

"When all was still, he started to beat on the ground with the long staff which he held in his hand, sending fragments of glittering sand into the air. Then holding the staff above his head, he uttered prayers in a strange ancient language, and whilst he did this, his head slowly changed into that of an ibis.

"Solino said that although there was a lot of noise and strange beings about her, she had no fear of the great beast standing before her. It was then that she noticed that one of Thot's eyes was a fiery red, but when he turned his head, she could see that the other one was a smoky blue, as though there was blindness in that eye. Thot then gave orders to one of the hand-maidens, and obediently she went over to Solino.

"Solino was carefully picked up, and then she was laid gently onto a palm leaf, which was then placed under the shade of a sycamore tree growing at the foot of the steps leading up to the entrance of the temple. Silver cups holding the essence of frankincense and myrrh were placed on small pedestals, and these were then heated up with small fragments of burning tree bark.

"Servants of the house of Hathor fanned Solino's trembling body with long white feathers from birds no longer of this world, whilst Hathor gently anointed Solino with healing herbs, which were kept in a sandalwood box, and these were steeped in oils. She then gave Solino small drops of healing waters from an underground spring which ran beneath the temple.

"The water was collected up in a jewel-studded chalice by the goddess Anuket, who was the dispenser of the cool healing waters, and this was then dripped into Solino's beak through a small hollow reed.

"Incense sticks were lit at each corner of the heated silver cups— one for the north, and the others for the south, east and west. When this was done, a hand-maiden played music on a sistrum, which was an instrument made from fruit and nut shells, strung across a wooden frame, and this she shook to make a calming rhythmic sound.

"Hathor started to shake a seed pod, making it rattle as she turned slowly towards each direction of north, south, east and west, and at the same time in a breathy whisper, she uttered enchantments and sacred prayers of healing.

"Some of her words were translated for Solino to understand, and they went like this:

As the swallow soars high in the sky,
she sings her sweet golden trill,
to the soft gentle whispering wind.

As the silvery moon beams down,
casting light on the long winding stream,
and when night descends,
as she rests in a cave,
let her soul drift,
as in a dream.

"Finally she sealed the healing ritual by placing her middle finger upon the white marks under Solino's wings, and extracting one of the marks, thus leaving her with seven instead of the eight, and holding out her middle finger with the white mark in the direction of Thot; it was then transferred to the centre of an eye of the great sacred ibis.

"This ritual took away the weakness from Solino. Almost immediately after her treatment, the head of the ibis suddenly changed back to the head of Thot, and then from the same spot where Thot had first appeared out of the ground, a great golden chariot rose up, and it was pulled by four magnificent golden roaring lions.

"Thot leapt into the chariot and whipped up the lions, and in an instant they raced at great speed into air, with sparks from the wheels flying out behind them, creating shooting stars as they disappeared into the universe.

"In an instant, Solino felt herself revive, and the dream (or vision) vanished just as quickly as it had appeared, and Solino found herself right back at the spot where her saviour of the desert had found her, and surprisingly, she was still cupped in his hands. He then lifted Solino up towards the sky and released her into the air, where thankfully I was able to join her.

"So as you know, we then continued on our long journey here without further mishap, but gradually Solino is able to remember more and more about her unworldly experience as time goes by."

"Well I'm so glad about that!" I said. "But can you just tell me something? Whilst you were doing your swooping and diving bit...did you happen to come across a 'chickle chackle tree' by any chance?"

"What...out in the desert?" he asked.

"Well," I added, "it wouldn't half be nice if I could have me own little angel! It would look nice on the top of my 'chickle chackle tree'. Which one would you suggest?"

"Why not try seeking out the angel Achaiah?" said Jeela.

"What would that one do for me?" I asked.

"It would help you work out all the secrets of nature!" he said.

"Rightyho!... That one would do nicely enough!" I said.

I left Jeela at the mud hole and went in search of Moltikala—an' perhaps an angel called Achaiah!

"Now I've got to go on a special quest!" I told Moltikala. "And it's all due to the fact that through no fault of my own, a certain 'dragon' and a certain Merlin have probably been tumbled out of their slumbers, and all because I went and dropped a little pebble down a silly little hole, so now I've got to go and seek out Tegrin the red kite, or Glider the heron, and seein' as I know nothing about either of them, except that both of them like meat, or at least Tegrin does, and I think Glider is a bit of a fish addict, so things could be a bit tricky, or fishy even!"

I headed off down towards the dell, then glided down through the wild woods until I reached the winding stream.

There woz no sign of Tegrin, as I had only seen him once, but not close enough to converse with.

Then I spotted Glider. He woz standing on one leg, and with his long beak sticking out like a riverside jetty. He seemed to be preoccupied with something near the river bank, so I approached him with a few hops of confidence, but not too noisy, so as not to disturb or distract him.

As I got nearer to him, I thought that he looked a bit of a comical character with his long orange dagger-sharp bill, and his excessively long neck was drawn down in concentration towards the water, as though he was about to spear something.

His orange eyes were extended by a black stripe, forming a "V" at the back of his head, where two wispy plumes hung down. He had black shoulder-pads, and fluffy-looking plumage on his breast, and his long legs were a sunburnt orange. *Very inconspicuous!* I thought with a slight hint of sarcasm, *but mighty handy at pulling a crowd!*

I woz beginning to wonder what he woz doing here, lurking about on the river bank!

"Hmm!... Hmm!... Good daylight to you, my lord fisher!... Guardian of the rivers!... Poacher of the ponds!... Can I just pick your brains for one minute before you spear your next silvery-scaled savoury supper?"

He slowly turned his head towards me and fixed me with a stare.

"Did you *see* it?" he hissed!

"See *what*?" I asked.

"*There!*....down *there!*....things you can *see*....yet are not *there!*" he answered in a whisper.

I looked in the direction of where his great long beak woz pointing, and all I could see woz what looked like smoke, or perhaps it woz mist, and it seemed to be rising, then gliding alongside the river, and then it disappeared!

"Nope!" I said. "All I can see is a bit of old misty, smoky stuff.... nothing else!"

"There are strange beings here," he said, "I see them often, when I come here to do my fishing, and I believe they are human spirits trapped here and not able to reach the other side, and until they are released from their earthly bonds, they will *never* find peace in this place. It is only with the strength of the 'four chosen keepers'!

"Myself, as 'keeper of the water,' Klogitiwhoo, 'keeper of the solar system,' Tegrin, 'keeper of the air,' and Seb the badger is 'keeper of the earth.' We all help to keep the balance and harmony of nature in these parts.

"I can tell that you need some questions to be answered and that you have been sent out on a special quest, but before you tell me of this, there are a few things that you should know, and remember well! Look down!...deep down into the water."

I looked down and deep!

He continued, "With deep concentration, you will see certain things that you hadn't at first noticed, or cared to think about."

I thought deeply, concentrated, and cared!

He went on, "If you move or turn over a pebble or a stone, it may have been touched by our early ancestors, or it may even have lain completely untouched by any other living thing. Stones can hold a power of their own, and certain ones must be treated with great respect, otherwise you could unleash unpleasant memories ingrained within the very core of the stone. Do you understand what I am saying to you, and does it mean anything to you?"

"Er...um...yes, I *think* I know what you are trying to tell me," I said uncertainly, and still trying hard to follow his meaning.

"Well let me tell you then!"

I let him tell me!

"If you see a very special stone in the water which happens to catch your eye, and you feel yourself drawn to it, then before touching it, or even picking it up, you must first of all ask permission from the river if you may do so, and you must ask to have protection against any evil-doing, otherwise something very unpleasant may happen to you...an' *that* wouldn't do at all!... Would it?"

I nodded in agreement, and gulped down a tremendous amount of doubt, pride, and fear, all at the same time, almost choking myself.

Glider carried on with his great teachings. "You must learn and remember, and appreciate that the river is a very sacred place to all living wild things.

"If a feather falls into the river, it carries a spirit with it, so do not pick it up! Fish do not swim in the same water twice, which means you don't get a second chance in life, and also you must remember that water gives life, and it can also take life!

"I have here in my own possession 'mood stones' which are connected with 'birds of omen.' Under my feet you will see there are stones of many kinds, and I invite you to choose one of them to take with you on your travels, so look carefully, and then let me see which one you have chosen!"

He lifted up his long toes and stepped to one side so that I could study the stones from under his feet. There woz one particular stone which caught my eye. It woz pearly white with a few black spots, and it had a blue glow shining from within. I didn't hesitate in pointing out to Glider the special stone which I had chosen. He looked at it and appeared to be pleased at me choice.

"You have chosen well!" he said. "It is called a 'moon stone' and it is dedicated to the moon goddess. It is also known as the 'traveller's stone,' and it will help to protect you against perils during your journeys, so you must wear it tucked between one of your tail feathers. It will also take you to wherever you wish to go, as it can also act as a 'dream stone,' but for this to work, you have to meditate first, then concentrate on where you wish to be transported to, and it really does work...but only if you believe in it! *All* worldly things and ideas are conceived through dreams!"

"Does that mean I don't really *exist* at all—that I'm only a *dream*—an' that everything I do is only a *dream?*"

"Is that what you believe?" he asked.

"Well I'm not so sure now!... But I thought I was real!... So maybe this is just a 'dream time' then!" I said.

"No, of course you are not just a dream!" he said, laughing at me. "We are all very real, but first we have to dream of where we want to go, and what we want to be. This may sound very strange to you, as you still have a lot to learn, but you will experience certain things that will make it more clear to you. You will just have to give yourself more time, and this special stone you have chosen also acts as a very good talisman, and it will help to bring you good fortune. You will need it with you at all times during your quest, as there could be many perils during your travels.

"On my own travels to lakes, rivers and ponds, I have seen many bad deeds rendered upon the earth. Terrible things are going on all around us. I have seen great metal dragons gouging great craters out of the earth, and these monsters are ridden and commanded by men humans wearing round yellow metal warriors' helmets, worn during their battles with the earth.

"Many of our ponds, lakes, reed beds and marshes have vanished after these great noisy dragons have passed through, depriving us of fish and other food. There are many dark suns and moons ahead for all of us birds, so act wisely, and don't throw caution to the wind. Look!...learn!...an' listen to the elders and the wise ones!

"I have told you enough, so we mustn't waste any more time! You still have a mission to accomplish, so I will guide you and show you the way to where it is said that 'Merlin the Wise One' still awaits an audience with pilgrims for the truth.

"There is a cave not too far from here, where you must seek out a tall-standing column of amber, which is pointed at the top, and inside of this yellow monolith you will see the figure of Merlin.

"Now in order to speak with Merlin, first of all you will have to place the talisman—the one which I have just given to you—in front of the column, and this will dissolve the amber to release Merlin for just a short while, but it may seem a lot longer to you—so now let's make haste! Follow me….and stay close!"

Without waiting for me to answer him, Glider took off with long, slow wing-beats—*whoom!… whoom!…whoom!* they went, and his long spindly legs extended back, way beyond his short, stubby tail, and his long neck was pulled back in an "S" shape.

The small talisman—now wedged between my tail feathers—was beginning to slow me down, and I found it a bit difficult to keep up with Glider. We flew for what seemed a life time.

Over hills, through valleys, across meadows, along a line of thick dense trees, until Glider finally started to descend. On the way down, I could see circles of large stones, and others were in uneven lines, or just scattered at random.

"What are those huge stones over there? Those ones standing and pointing upwards?" I asked Glider.

"The humans call them 'standing stones,' but they are known to us as 'giants' teeth'!" he answered

"They were lost to the giants whilst they were engaged in ferocious battles between one another, and although their teeth are still to be seen, once they were slain their bodies were either eaten by wolves, or cast into the bogs by demonic spirits. But the rest of their story is too long, and we don't have much time now for lengthy stories, so we must make haste!"

Glider soon spotted where he wanted us to land.

He glided down slowly, with his huge wings making that *whoom! whoom!* sound again, then he touched down with the grace of a tap-dancing elephant, scattering dry leaves everywhere, and I landed right behind him, spitting out dead twigs and leaves.

I must remember never to stick so close to a heron in a hurry again!

"Follow me!" said Glider. "I think it's just around the corner."

He strode out on his long ungainly legs, and I hopped behind him on my short ones, keeping at a safe distance!

"What's around the corner?" I asked.

"This!" he said, pointing to a deep dark hole on the side of a bank.

"Now that is where your destiny lies, and where you begin your quest to find out the answers to all your questions," he said.

"Do you mean I've got to go down that....that big old badger's or fox's hole?" I asked.

"That's not a *hole!*" he said."that's a *cave,* and neither a fox or a badger lives there...it's *Merlin's cave!*... And you don't have to go *down* it...you go *through* it!" he said.

"This is where you and I must now part company. I have done all I can to help you, so now the rest is up to you, and I hope you will remember all the things I have said to you, so I'm off now...back to me heronry, where my egg layer Nimble Tuft built our klakki many suns ago. Good luck!... and may you never lose your shadow! Always live well in the light, and may the gods be with you!"

With these passing words of great wisdom, and a loud croaking *aarrrk,* he was gone!

I took an over cautious peek into the cave, and it looked mightily dark and uninviting to me, but seein' that I woz out on this quest thing, I had no option but to go for it!

It woz like stepping into a huge mouth, and great long teeth seemed to hang down from its roof, with water dripping off from them ever so slowly, and landing on the floor with a *plop!* which echoed through the cave.

In I went, cautiously and carefully putting one foot in front of the other, and giving me wings a few flips up and down so as to make sure they were still in good working order, just in case I needed to beat a hasty retreat!

Well, 'twasn't so bad after all!—not too hot, and not too cold—an' funny thing woz, it started to get a bit brighter in there. Then just ahead of me, I saw where the brightness woz coming from.

Right in the centre of the cave stood a very tall column just as what Glider told me I would find, and what did he say it was made of— amber or something? Anyway, it woz a yellowy-orangey colour and there, standing right in the middle of it, with his eyes looking all distorted through trying to stare hard through the yellow stuff, woz the magnificent Merlin the Magician!

I did what Glider told me to do, and set the moonstone down on the floor of the cave in front of the column.

Almost immediately, a funny minty-green ball of light started to bounce around on the inside of the column, then suddenly it burst open, shattering the amber until it lay in pieces on the cave floor, and there in front of me, in all his glory, stood Merlin!

He woz a very tall figure standing there before me, and all clad up to the hilt in a great long black furry garment (it looked suspiciously like it woz originally attached to the back of an old grizzly bear—an' that was probably a good many suns and moons ago judging by its moth-eaten appearance) and it almost reached down to his feet. His feet were togged out in clumsy looking hessian-type clodhoppers.

Merlin's thick black hair was growing a good long way down his back, and it was tied back (just like a horse's tail) with a leather thong, and he had a long black beard to match, and on his head he was wearing a wide gold band with runic symbols inscribed on it, and down the left side of his head were two ravens' feathers fixed in his hair, and the feathers were both pointing downwards. Around his neck dangled a very large silver medallion, and inscribed on the edges were the twelve signs of the zodiac, and in the middle were stars, planets, the moon and the sun, and they were all moving in circles around one another—in the same manner of direction as does me very own future teller!

I could see that he had a longish hooked nose, which looked a bit like a beak, and his shining black eyes were as sharp as an eagle's. His long thin hands were all knobbly and gnarled, and looked like talons!

The magician looked as though he was a bit cross at being disturbed, so I thought I'd better say nice things to him, otherwise everything might go seriously egg-shaped.

"Oh dear!" I said, trying to sound very humble. "Seems I might've disturbed you from several hundreds of winklets of sleep, o' lord and knight of the mountains and caves—that is if you really are Merlin the Magician, not that there's any reason to believe that you're not!…is it not?" I said, getting my nots all tied up in knots!

Merlin then spoke to me in a very gravelly voice that seemed to echo about the walls of the cave. Now what may (or may not as the case may be) have grabbed your attention is that this was—up till then—the very first time in my life that I was able to actually *speak* in *human*, to a *human* (but that doesn't include the time when I spoke to me pinky ma, through me picture of course, because that came about much later on).

"I am indeed Merlin…but *not* a magician!" he said. "I am Merlin the Wizard!… Or you can call me Merlin the Enchanter if you so wish. Your presence here must be of great importance, as I am not usually visited by little magpies, such as you. My long meditations are usually disturbed by birds such as Klogitiwhoo the owl, or Sedgeborn the raven, or even Chiselbeak the sparrowhawk, and then there's my old friend Featherhead White Wings, who can transform himself into Khonsu the moon god, by changing into a falcon."

"So that's what he gets up to when he disappears most of the time," I said, "I thought that all this changing into godly type creatures only went on thousands of moons ago...not in our time.... So what's he want to change from one bird type to another one for?"

"It's to give him more power, and he can also travel about unseen, which means he can see for himself what is going on around his chosen space and territory, in order for him to take appropriate action to protect his flock from any danger, so to disguise himself in this way can only be very useful to him, don't you think?"

"Yes I suppose so," I said, feeling a bit inadequate at not being able to change into an all-powerful god to see me through some awkward moments.

"Now Tegrin the red kite can change himself into Apollo, and he has the power to drive out evil spirits!"

"Oh, great!" I said, making me wish I hadn't left me klakki this particular sunlight-time, and all this changing stuff is beginning to get my down, and it's making me head go all fuzzy, but then that's probably because of all those strange flashing lights from Merlin's medallion, and that green glow still coming from that ball thing what's hanging from the ceiling of the cave.

I think Merlin must've sensed that I was beginning to get a bit fired up inside, because he went over to the far side of the cave to a big round marble slab that was resting on four blue stone columns, and he beckoned me over to it.

When I looked down onto it, I could see that the centre piece woz actually a round plate of copper, and so smooth and shiny that you could see yourself in it! Pretty awesome, I thought! Then, with a short piece of what looked like a forked hazel twig (which he drew out from his black furry garment), he lightly tapped the very middle of the copper plate, which sent ripples of waves across it, and as I stared mesmerised into it, I could see all kinds of strange pictures, and they were all moving about.

"Oh!" I said. "It looks as though you've got your very own fancy tee vee!"

"What's a 'tee vee'?" he asked.

"I couldn't really tell you exactly what a tee vee is except it's a bit like this, only this is *much, much* better than the old tee vees what I know!" I said.

I just carried on looking into the copper plate movies to see what I could see! This was too good to miss, so I needed to concentrate really hard!

As I gazed into it, I could see a swirling mist (why is everything in a "swirly mist"?), and when it had cleared there were masses of images coming towards me, and they seemed to flash past me at great speed with a *hissing, swishing, whooshing* sound!

I could see eggshells, abalone shells, great boulders and rocks, flashes of lightning, rainbows, fairies and elves, mermaids and penguins, and feathers of all colours and sizes — so many, in fact, that I found myself nearly choking on them!

Then there woz a great explosion of different things flashing past, and it made me all dazzled and dizzy, frazzled and frizzy!

Then everything slowed down a pace, and I could see a picture forming in front of me just as though I woz actually there, and what I saw woz *so* terrifying, that I froze on the spot, with a great dread and a powerful fear!

It appeared to me like me worst nightmare, and as I looked at it more closely, I could see that it woz in fact the very nightmare I experienced not so very long ago!

It wasn't exactly huge, but it was about the size of a crow, and even I know what damage a crow can do!

This creature looked extremely menacing, in fact it looked quite evil as well as looking familiar in a funny kind of way, which made me feel somewot uneasy I can tell you!

As it lumbered along in a very ungainly manner — all skink like, and getting nearer and nearer, and then it opened its ugly looking excuse for a beak, and I could see that it had rows of sharp looking teeth.

I just stood dumbstruck as me feet wanted to go one way, but me wings wanted to take me another!

The very thought of being impaled on those razor-sharp gnashers sent shock-waves up and down me feathers, from the crown of me head, to the tips of me tail, and I felt me claws starting to fester and me tongue to decompose. In fact I felt me whole body was coming out in one big rash!

The hideous thing then let out a blood-curdling screech!

'Holy moses!' I thought. 'I'm glad you're only a figment of me imagination, and that you're there, and I'm here!'

I then realized that this clumsy creature couldn't seem to fly, so it wasn't the same one in my dream after all, as the one in my dream was bigger, and it was most definitely flying after me.

"What on earth is it?" I asked Merlin in a quavering voice, and at the same time trying to hide me feathery 'yeller-belly' cowardly side.

"Great Jupiter!" he exclaimed, "i think you've transported yourself back way too far, and the creature that has materialized before you is an archaeopteryx! It's a dinosaur bird! One of your ancestors from the earliest of times, and now you must accept that you are part of the chain of evolution!"

"Ah yes!" I said, "I've just remembered me egg maker pa mossy telling us about our great ancestors. None other than our billion, billion times great, ever so great-great-great, so on and so forth, uncle archie and aunty trixy—springs to mind!

Eva looshion has a lot to answer for...hasn't she! So perhaps I am after all, 'the weakest link!'"

Merlin gave out a great laugh like a thunder clap, which seemed to echo and bounce off the walls, and I just wondered what all that was about!

He then went all very serious again.

"Me thinks we'll have to try afresh!" he said.

With that, he tapped once more on the copper plate with his hazel twig which cleared the old image, and a completely new one appeared.

After yet another swirl of heavy mist wafted about for a few moments, I could then see something totally different.

At first I could see the sky woz a very pale blue, and then from out of the blue hovered a very unwelcome and unexpected spectre of Chiselbeak, the sparrowhawk!

"What's he doing here?" I asked Merlin.

"Observe closely!" he answered commandingly.

As I did so, I could see a change in Chiselbeak's appearance.

His head grew larger and flatter, and his beak became thicker and sharper looking, whilst his hawk-like eyes grew bigger and more terrifying to gaze into, and he seemed to be looking straight at me with those great piercing eyes!

Chiselbeak was now a truly magnificent falcon!

"Wow!" I said in great awe, "he's so...so...!"

"Godlike?" suggested Merlin.

"Yes…I suppose you could say that….but who, or what on earth is he?" I asked.

"You have the privilege of looking upon none other than the great god Ra-Harrakte—the sun god," said Merlin. "He has great powers, and is a great ruler over all others in the underworld. Now if you want to learn more about the ways of the underworld, look deeply into his eyes and close your mind to all other thoughts, then let yourself drift into his inner being, and you will become as one!"

Now that I've come this far, I might as well give it a go—besides, it could be good fun being someone else!

I stared hard into the blood-red eyes of Chiselbeak, alias Ra-Harrakte (I'd only just noticed that his eyes had turned a bloody red) and I emptied me brains, just as Merlin had told me to, and *that* didn't take me long to do!

Then I felt myself come over all sloppy and sleepy.

When I opened me eyes again, I felt I hadn't got me own body anymore, and I felt much stronger and bolder, and I could feel a great power surging through every feather.

Then I suddenly took off without even thinking about it!

I woz flying high!—so very high and fast, like the wind.

I could feel the air skimming over my golden feathers, as me great long wings swept back, and I flew straight as an arrow, calling out *"wheeoo!… wheeoo!… wheeoo!"*

This felt wonderful, and this "changing" bit is so very cosmic!….so very cool!—perhaps I could be Ra forever!

Hooray for Ra!

Then I felt myself searching for movement far below, scanning the ground as I went, twisting and turning my head about, not in the manner I'm accustomed to, as I normally fly quite slow and low compared to this, and I always keep my eyes straight in front of me, just looking for a place to land, usually.

Then I spotted a group of…*magpies!*

Before I could do anything about it, me wings swept back, and like a demented demon I went into dive.

I felt myself dropping down like a stone towards the magpies.

My sharp eyes had focussed on one particular magpie, and it looked an awful lot like me!

I plummeted straight onto the unsuspecting magpie, and after holding its trembling, squawking body for a few seconds, I ripped into its neck and gizzard with my sharp hooked beak.

I was utterly horrified!

My inner self started to rebel and repel against the murderous deed to one of my own kind, and my heart cried out: *"stop!... stop!... stop!"*

I felt myself rising and then falling, but without actually moving in any direction—up or down.

Then I suddenly came to and was thankful to find myself back in the cave and at the feet of Merlin.

"Why did I have to do this thing?" I asked Merlin.

"Because you needed to learn and experience some of the ways of the beings of the otherworld or the underworld!" he said. "To see through the eyes of another, and what it feels like to be on the receiving end of a sacrifice."

"What's the sacrifice for?" I asked.

"Ra, or Ra-Harrakte as he was usually known, was out on a soul-searching mission for the other gods of the underworld. He fixes onto his prey and then he gouges out their souls (usually in the throat and gizzard area), and then he carries these back in his sacred vessel called the Manjet boat, to the holy centre of a place called Heliopolis. The birds' (or sometimes animals') souls were then given to the gods.

"The magpies are sought after for their cunning and deceit, and the blackbirds are treasured for their beautiful singing voices, whilst the starlings are useful for their gift of chatter and amusement, and the song thrush has psychic powers, and lastly the doves represent peace and harmony.

"Now because he carried the spirit of a magpie within him, this is why he chose to find a magpie for his quarry. If you hadn't retreated when you did, it is quite possible that you may have been enslaved, and therefore would never have returned to this world, ever again!

"Many others before you decided to stay the course and followed through to the end, and they are now trapped in the kingdom of the underworld; and there they must stay, to the end of eternity! Because you are a mere 'mortal' bird, your very short blink-of-an-eye journey to the underworld, gave you an insight of just part of some of our mysteries through the mists of time, and of deeds carried out beyond our 'mortal world'!

"You still have much to learn, but what you have already experienced will help to guide you on your quest and your continuing journey of discovery. If you had chosen to stay within the form of Ra-Harrakte a moment longer, then you would have lost your soul to the underworld!"

I gave the Merlin a quizzical look, and so he said, "Let me tell you a little about Ra, seeing as you have just had a more than just close contact with him!

"Ra first appeared (or came into existence) on a hill which had risen out of the chaos of Nun, who was the first god from the beginning of time. Before that, he was the primordial ocean from which all things sprang forth in the ancient times. Nun (the first god), became lonely, so he sprang up as an island, and the exact spot was commemorated by placing on the island a gigantic obelisk which was known as the Benben Stone, but this shouldn't concern you in any way at this moment, as it's probably too much for your small bird-brain to take in all at once, but you might as well know the rest of the story about Ra.

"The said obelisk (or the Benben Stone), symbolized the life-giving rays of the sun, and that is why Ra is known as the sun god, but before he first appeared, his first given name was Atum, and for a great length of time he lay dormant within Nun (which I have already told you was now formed as an island), as he curled up inside the bud of a lotus flower. His eyes and mouth were firmly closed, and he held onto the bright flame of solar light, keeping it safe from the torments of chaos."

I yawned, but I don't think Merlin noticed, and so he droned on and on and on!

"Eventually Atum got bored with his inactivity, so he climbed out from the darkness, thus releasing the rays of sunlight, and from his first given name of Atum, he was thereafter known as Ra.

"Some while later, Ra became tired of his life on earth and wished to hand over his power to another, and so he chose Thoth, the moon god, to take over ruling the earth for him. Every morning, from that time onwards, Ra appeared in the east above Manu, the mountains of the sunrise, and he would travel across the universe in the Manjet boat, and with him were the gods of the creation, wisdom and magic, as his crew.

"The god Horus stood at the helm, whilst Thoth stood at the bow of the boat, defeating Ra's enemies as they went. For extra power, Ra wore Sekhmet, which is Uraeus, the double crown of the united Egypt, and is in the form of a cobra spitting flames. It is also known as the great seeing eye.

"Now one of Ra's worst enemies was Apep, a gigantic serpent who lived in the depths of the waters of Nun, and as the boat carrying Ra and his crew passed overhead, the great serpent would rise out of the water and try to destroy Ra, but the power of the gods was so great that he was cast back to the waters, where he would hide and wait until the next time!

"He was very active indeed, but there's no time to account for all his deeds!

"So now that I have given you much to think about and to ponder upon, let me try one more time to send you on your journey!" said Merlin, as I came out of my stupor, and he tapped the copper plate once more.

This time I could see lots of trees (which made me feel a bit more on familiar territory) and a twisty, snaking road, which looked as though it went on forever, and not even one nasty monster in sight.

"You must make haste and not waste any more time!" said Merlin. "I cannot help you any further, the rest is up to you, and you must try and stay on the straight path, otherwise known as the 'snake path,' but before you leave this place, might you have just forgotten something?"

"What might that be?" I asked.

"Why your talisman, of course! It's where you left it when you used it to open my amber chamber of waiting," he said.

After I had retrieved me talisman and tucked it once more behind me tail, I was all prepared to leave the darkness of the cave, but before I left, I had one more question to ask of Merlin.

"What about 'the big red dragon'?" I asked.

"Ah, let me tell you now, that one resides well below this cave, deep in the bowels of the earth, so have no fear, you will probably never encounter him in his rare rambles. Most of his time is spent sleeping, and at certain times, you can hear his heavy breathing, especially when he starts to wake up from a deep slumber, and it's then that he starts to scramble and pull himself through the underground passages, and when he pushes great rocks and boulders to one side to make himself new pathways; this creates earthquakes, and you may sometimes hear the rumbles, but they are usually not very serious ones, at least, not in this land. That's why you see so many humps and hills.

"Now, when he gets hungry—he only eats about every one hundred years—he forces himself up through the earth and then he takes either a cow or two, or a few sheep amongst a flock, causing much havoc and anger amongst the unfortunate farmers when they discover their animals who have mysteriously disappeared, and they are much baffled about the loss of their stock, and they usually blame it on some other guiltless creature!

"He has been known to travel to the far north of the country, and when he does, he changes colour from red to a dark green, and he travels about from loch to loch.

"Now I hope you find the answers to your questions, and that you will always honour 'the circle of life,' and let mother nature take its course, and embrace your destiny with outstretched wings! So tally no longer, and be courageous, little magpie. I will send my faithful servant to lead you out of here.

"He is Arkeel the raven, son of Rogonika, and he replaces Sedgeborn the messenger, who now remains in your world only, and no longer returns here. Sedgeborn is too old now, so he is retired from his duties, but he has reported back to me many important incidents during his long life.

"A long time ago, he saw an alien creature enter one of the coves not far from where you live. He had just returned at sunset to his usual roosting place on the top of the cliffs when he spotted a strange whale-type object out at sea. He watched as it approached, and then it came to the surface just near the entrance to the caves. He could then see that the thing was made of what he thought was metal or iron as he continued to watch to see what would happen next, he saw a small group of human men emerge from the top of this thing, and in small boats pushed over the side, they made their way to the shore. They appeared to approach the dwelling places in the village. Standing in a group, they banged on the doors until they fetched the occupants out, and after much talking in a strange speech with the people inside, they then came away with small drinking vessels filled with water, and then they started to carry them back to their small boats. But before they could row away from the shore, Sedgeborn wanted to make sure that they would never return, and as one of his duties was to defend the shore, he flew swiftly down, then landing onto the shoulder of one of the invaders, he pecked out one of his eyes, and he then flew off with great haste!

"The terrified strangers, wondering if they were going to be attacked again, helped the one-eyed man back into the boat, and they rowed as fast as they could out to sea to return to the iron whale, where they very quickly clambered back in. The whale then slowly sank down beneath the waves, and Sedgeborn never saw it again.

"He returned to me with the 'eye,' and with this trophy I was able to trace their course away from the land. The 'eye' is now kept safely in a small secret recess in one of the walls of this cave, and it is encased in a round glass globe filled with water from the magic pool in the land of Mabinogion, and it is held in the mouth of a golden carp. One day, if you return here, I will show you its magic powers, but it is now time for you to disappear also, before you request more stories from me!"

No fear of that! I thought.

Then he said to me, "I will light you three candles. One candle is for your past, one for your present, and one for your future, and remember, do not leave any of the special stones unturned! And now you must follow Arkeel—into the land of Mabinogion!"

"Righty ho!" I called.

Then, as an afterthought, I called out, "Oh, just *one* more final question, if you please? As your name is *Merlin*, do you happen to sometimes change into a Merlin?… you know?… the bird Merlin?… the one that flies low and?…!"

"No!"

As I turned to leave, I heard a sound like crunching ice, and when I looked back to see what it was, I watched as the fragments of amber flew back together again, with bright sparks flashing from it, and with three burning candles at his feet.

Merlin was once more encased inside of his golden yellow column, waiting to be released at another time when a wanderer, like myself, happens to stumble upon this magical cave, with its "wise old wizard in waiting"!

Arkeel then took off, and he led me straight through to the other side of the cave.

As I stepped boldly over the threshold and into the "otherworld" which now lay before me, it was then that it dawned on me that I was about to take part in me own mythology and legend-making bit, so I suppose I'll be known As—"The Legendary Magical Mythological Magpie Maggie'!

What a great story this would be to tell me future fledglings!

Arkeel called back, "Take care!… Remember all that Merlin has told you! Now I must leave you!"

He circled round three times, and then he headed back to Merlin's cave.

Well, Maggie, my boy! I said to meself, *welcome to the land of Mabinogion!*

Just as Merlin had told me, I kept strictly to the snaking path, but as I hopped along it, the path would somehow straighten itself out, and when I came to a hill, it would then suddenly become flat!

Another thing that struck me woz that it seemed some sort of quiet, without all that noisy stuff coming from all the metal klakkies clanking about, and the noisy metal machines flying about the sky interrupting me very important thoughts and spoiling me food gatherings with so much noise everywhere. The air seemed so much nicer too!

There were some different noises though, but not horrible ones, sort of nice twittering, tinkling, happy-type noises, and I could hear the croaking and burping of froggies in the swamps, and lots of *"sissing"* noises coming from unseen crickets and grasshoppers in the bright green meadows, and I fancied I even heard one long howl from a wolf!

It sounded a long way off, so I wasn't too bothered about it.

To give me some courage, I sang Klogitiwhoo's lengthy mantra, and it surprised me somewot that I woz actually able to remember it all, but it enabled me to put behind me, for the moment anyway, all those unfamiliar creatures of the "otherworld" or "underworld."

The scene then changed. I could see a river coming up in front of me, and trees grew at the edges, and there was a meadow on both sides of it.

As I drew near, I could see that there were white sheep grazing on one side, and black sheep grazing on the other.

Then a very strange thing happened.

One of the black sheep called to one of the white sheep, and when one of the white sheep crossed over the river to the other side, it turned black! As I watched in amazement, a white sheep called across to one of the black sheep, and when the black sheep crossed over the river to the other side, it came out of the water white!

Now this went on until all of the white sheep had turned black, and all of the black sheep had turned white!

My turn! I thought, so I crossed the river, just like the sheep had done, and guess what?… I came out onto the bank, and me white feathers had turned black, and me black feathers had turned white!

I had to cross over again, just so's me feathers went back to me normal black and white; not white and black!

Then I forgot which side of the river I wanted to be on in the first place!

It was on one side of the river that I came across a huge old tree, and it looked so unusual, that I decided to dally for a while and inspect it more closely.

It was no ordinary tree, and I came to the conclusion that it was definitely different.

It must be a magical tree, I thought to meself, because one side of it was all alight with fire and burning mightily, whilst on the other side of it (like it was divided in two) wasn't burning at all, and all its leaves were a bright green, and not a spark to be seen!

"Hello, tree!" I said for no good reason, but I just felt that it was aware I was staring at it, so I just thought I ought to give it some respect.

"Who are you?" said the tree.

Now before I go any further, I must add that I did find myself wondering what on earth was I doing holding a conversation with a large block of old wood, so to speak; it woz very unnerving in fact.

Anyway, after the tree had enquired as to who I woz, I decided to carry on with a bit of a tête-à-tête!

"I am Maggie of the Cerdin Wood!" I told the tree, "and I was sent by Merlin on a special quest to find certain answers to certain questions, if that's all right by you, tree lord of the forest!"

"I am called Brannon, the Tree of Life!" said the tree. "Now what is your first question you want to ask of me, little magpie?" asked the ancient perennial plant.

I looked him square in the roots and asked, "Are you, by any chances, the 'chickle chackle tree'?"

He nearly split his old trunk with laughter. *"Ho!... Ho!... Ho!... he!... he!... he!"* he cackled and boomed.

His green leaves shook on one side, and the fire sparked and crackled on the other, and his great thick roots twisted and heaved, as they were nearly wrenched out of the earth.

I didn't think my question was *that* funny!

"No!... I am not the 'chickle chackle tree.' As I have already told you, I am the Tree of Life, or 'the beginnings and endings,' if you like," he said. "Now what is your second question?"

"I was told by Merlin that I would probably never meet the red dragon, but my magpie flock expect me to either slay him, or at least scare him off a bit!" I said. "So can you tell me if I'm likely to find him in my travels here, in the wood of the Mabinogion?... And if I do, how can I deal with him?"

"Well that's a tall one!" said Brannon. "Nearly as tall as me!" he said, nearly splitting his trunk again with laughter. "Let me see now!... Ah, yes!... I've got it!" he exclaimed. "If you carry along this path, you will come to a red tree, and you will see a fountain beside it, and beneath the tree you will see a stone. This is a very special stone which is called a 'Moldavite,' and because it is of extraterrestrial origin, it is all powerful, which means you have to treat it with great respect.

"Beside the stone, you will find a shell which is filled with crystal clear water. Now if you pick up the shell, then you must take three steps backwards, and from there, you must throw the water over the stone, being very careful not to spill any of it onto the ground. When you have successfully done this, it will 'cause a great thunder, lightning, and boulder-sized hailstones, and if you are lucky and the red dragon happens to be in the right spot at the right time, then the lightning and hailstones will put out his fiery breath, and most probably kill him, but the least it could do is to frighten him off for a very long time, and he might even follow his path north and then on to Hadrian's Wall, beneath which he keeps hordes of his ill-gotten treasures! Do you have any further questions to ask of me?" he asked.

"No ta!" I said. "I think that will be enough for me to be getting on with for now, so if you don't mind...I had better be on me way."

Further along the path, I came across the red tree and the fountain which Brannon described to me, and at the foot of the tree woz the Moldavite stone, which woz dark green, and looked more like glass to me and not stone, and it had a very rough surface. Beside the stone woz the shell filled with crystal clear water.

Just as Brannon told me to do, I took three steps backwards, and took careful aim, then threw the shell with the water in it onto the middle of the stone.

At first nothing seemed to happen, then slowly the water evaporated into the stone, and then steam started to rise from it, and as it gradually cleared, I nearly laid an egg in astonishment when I saw me very own name inscribed in red on the stone, along with all me heroic deeds, like "egg collecting for the poor," "worm baiting," and "cat nipping," to name but a few, and then there was more as it told of me absolutely amazing great escapes! And then I could see something else gradually appearing before me very eyes, and when it came clear, it read something like "Dragon Removal Specialist!" Well, that's all a bit premature, but I was rather hoping that eventually it would read "Dragon Slayer!"

Never mind, beggars can't be choosers! Besides, I think the competition would be pretty strong for *that* particular title anyway!

So *that's* what Thorn Stormcock, the mistle thrush, meant when he said that me name would be inscribed on a special stone in a secret place!

I wasn't to know then that the secret place would be in the land of Mabinogion!

All of a sudden, the wind started to roar like a lion, and leaves started chasing round like mad monkeys, and then there woz a loud clap of thunder, followed by flashes of lightning, and then I had to quickly dive for cover when huge hailstones the size of boulders started to drop down, smashing through the trees and making huge craters in the ground.

After a while it all stopped, and it went all quiet again.

Wow!… That should do it! I thought. *If that doesn't turn old red into a white lump of jellied dragon, then I might as well be a froggy in a bobble hat!*

Congratulating myself on me good deed for the daylight time, I whistled and sang on me way, and carried on through what was left of the devastated forest, avoiding all the craters made by those huge hailstones.

Further along the smoke-filled path, I met up with a dainty little white songbird who was so white that she nearly dazzled me, and she told me her name was Gwynweaver. She told me that her name meant 'white witch, weaver of spells!' and I quickly said to her (thinking that I'd had enough to do with spells and things), "not today, thank you!" but being an inquisitive bird what I am, I followed her anyway as she led me out of the smoky ol' path, and onto a fresher one.

As we went along, I took the opportunity to ask her about Tegrin, the red kite, as I woz told that in the underworld, he changes into the god Apollo, and he drives out all evil spirits, and said that I would like to meet and talk with him.

Gwynweaver told me that Tegrin was a frequent visitor to the land of Mabinogion, but here he takes on the form of the Knight Owein — protector of the great King Arthur himself, who resided in a great hall not far from where we were now travelling, but we wouldn't be able to see him just now, as he was out on some errand.

Gwynweaver also told me that Tegrin sometimes changes into an owl, and then works alongside his companion Morvran, the raven, so that they can spy out over the land, but not to confuse Morvran with Arkeel, because Arkeel works strictly for Merlin.

She told me how Tegrin — in the form of Owein — had told her that many humans had persecuted the red kites, and that they were in grave danger of being wiped out from the face of the planet! But fortunately there was still hope left, as certain humans — whom Tegrin calls "brave hearts" and are known as great warriors in our world, and therefore very loyal — will defend the red kites with their lives.

Tegrin had told Gwynweaver that these brave hearts were called Gurkhas by humans, and that they were employed to guard the red kites' nests (klakkies) until all the fledglings were hatched, and had safely left their nests.

"Oh yes!" I said. "I know what gherkins are! Me pinky ma uses them with cheese in her bread stuff, and sometimes she throws me a piece, but they are not so tasty, and not only that—they make me beak squeak!"

I don't think that Gwynweaver quite understood what I meant, and she said that she'd never heard of gherkins!

When she had finished her story about Tegrin, Gwynweaver told me that there was yet another very special tree that was worth a visit if I wanted to complete my quest.

On our travel to find this special tree, Gwynweaver asked me from whence I came.

I think she wanted to know where I had originally been hatched, and where I now roosted after sunset, so I told her my whole story, which seemed to take an awful long time; but then we did have a long way to go to find this tree.

I told her about Chiselbeak and how he frequently turns up as an uninvited guest at our feeding place, only "we" happen to be the ones on his menu!

"Don't you have a lookout?" asked Gwynweaver.

"Yes, usually!" I said. "But sometimes he turns up in the guise of a dove, or even a sparrow, and when he swoops down towards us, then naturally we don't take any notice of him, and then, all of a sudden, he changes back into being Chiselbeak again, and by then it's too late...for one of us!"

Gwynweaver looked so upset about our plight that I had to change the subject, and I told her about all the good things as well as all the nice things I had collected and stored, and of my unusual life with the pinkies, and that seemed to cheer her up.

Eventually we came to a very odd-looking tree, the likes of which I had never ever seen before.

This tree had black and white round sort of disc-shaped leaves, and they seemed to be in two halves wrapped around each other, with one half white and the other black.

They made a *clink* sound as they moved against each other in the breeze, and on the very top branch, a nightingale sang.

When the bird had finally stopped its singing, I asked Gwynweaver, "Is *this* a 'chickle chackle tree'...an' does it speak?"

"No to both of your questions!" she chuckled, "and it is called a yin yang tree. This tree rules all things, and it is the very breath of nature throughout the land and the universe."

"Look at me then!" I said, "do you think I'm a yin yang bird then, 'coz I'm half black and half white just like this tree?… or do my brown toeses make me a yuk and yok bird?"

"That is so, about you being black and white, but there's no such thing as a yuk and yok, at least not in my world as I know it!" she laughed. "Let us now be more serious, and I will tell you all about the yin and yang."

So, throwing me into yet further confusion, this is what she told me: "The yin rules the earth and all negative things, like dark, water, soft, cold, deadly or still—whereas the yang comes from heaven and all positive things, such as light, fiery, hard, warm, and all living, moving things. Now do you understand me so far?" she asked.

"I think I might just about catch your drift!" I said. "So please tell me some more!" and giving a big sigh, Gwynweaver cleared her throat, then continued with her description of the yin and yang.

"The white half is yang, and it has a small seed of dark, which you can just about see if you look closely, whilst the dark side, which is yin, contains a small seed of light. Is that clear to you also?" she asked.

"Yes…I see…an' yes…it is quite clear!" I said, trying to sound intelligent and understanding.

Gwynweaver went on. "Now if you take one seed from each half of a yin, and one seed from the yang half, it will guide you out of the land of Mabinogion and into the cave of Merlin—from whence you came!

"Now to complete your quest, you must find the five elements, which are water, fire, wood, metal and earth. Now this shouldn't be too difficult for you, so this is how it works. Wood is fed by water, which covers and binds earth, and then it is cut down by metal tools, and is then ignited to give fire. So each one, in turn, destroys the other."

"So how does *that* work?" I asked, feeling me brain twisting into more and more knots.

"Well," she said, "metal cuts down, thus destroys wood, and wood is fed from (and destroys) earth, and then earth in its turn is destroyed by water, and water then destroys fire, and fire melts and destroys metal, and then the destructive cycle begins all over again."

"Excuse me!" I said, "Just hang on a mo'!… I think I've lost the plot!… So could you tell me that just once more?… I've just missed out on the first bit!"

She ignored that, and carried on with her instructions.

"Now if you can find *all five* of the elements, then you will be able to banish the red dragon from your land!"

"But how can I do that?... And what must I do?" I asked.

"If you find a piece of metal," she said, "then with this you cut a piece of wood that's on fire, and then throw it into the water where you think the red dragon is resting in the earth beneath, then the fire will destroy the water by evaporation, and this will expose the dragon from his lair, and then he will be in great haste to go in search of a fresh river, which may take him far away, and off into another land!"

I thanked Gwynweaver for her very useful tips on "how to banish a dragon in a thousand easy steps!" — an' went on my way in my search for the serpent, and other tourist attractions!

Presently I saw a glint of sunlight through the trees shining on a bright object, and as I drew near, I could see it woz a discarded suit of armour belonging to a knight of old, and it woz propped against a tree, whilst the contents therein had gone for a dippy in the river.

Now there's some metal I could use! I said to meself. *That gallant knight over yonder won't miss just a tiny piece of it!*

I could see the knight splashing merrily away, and he sounded very happy as he sang a song about battles, round tables, kings, dragons, and fair maidens in white satin.

I thought he was a very brave knight indeed, bathing in dragon-infested waters!

It wasn't just the bad dragons' breath that would put *me* off, but all those dragons' fart bubbles filled with obnoxious methane gas and breaking to the surface that would put me off bathing there!

A familiar whinnying sound made me turn, and there, tethered to a tree next to the one with the tin suit, was a dapple-grey horse, probably belonging to the knight. Only there was something very odd about it. Its right leg was a bright red colour, and the other three legs were coloured yellow, right down to its hooves, and it kept to a steady trot — on the spot!

It woz doing a spot of "fox trot on the spot"!

I called out to it, "Are you the one what can speak straight from the mouth!" (which is something I've heard the pinkies say from time to time), but there woz no reply.

Seein' that everythin' else seemed to be able to talk around here, I thought 'why not this painted-up horse!'

"Suit yerself!" I shouted at it, but there was still no response wotsoever, so I let it go on trotting on the spot. *Stupid thing! It's not goin' to get very far like that now…is it!* I said to meself.

My attention went back to the shiny suit thingy which was slowly sinking to the ground with a *clank!*

It sat there, all spread-eagled beneath the tree.

I crept over the spooky looking piece of metal work, and started to peck cautiously, so as not to make a sound, until one of the smaller bits of plating dropped off.

Picking it up, I hopped smartly back along the same path I had come, leaving the merry knight to bathe in the delightful concoction of his lethal bubble bath and loads of heavenly scents!

I felt quite smug at how very clever I had been, and I knew now exactly what I should do!

I made me way back to Brannon, the Tree of Life.

He woz still burning on one side, and on the other it woz still fresh and green.

I sneaked quietly up to him, and with my sharp piece of metal, I gently sliced a small piece of wood which, although it was still burning, didn't hurt me!

As I tiptoed away from Brannon, he boomed out, "With my compliments, little magpie!… It would have been more polite if you had asked me permission first!… But I wish you luck anyway!"

I sped off without looking back.

It woz then that I decided to take to the air, and as I flew on my way back to the yin and yang tree, I suddenly spotted from the air a faint outline of what looked like the scaly old dragon beneath the water, so I landed quietly by the bank.

Edging carefully to the the lake, I peered down into the water, and I could see his great long body all covered in scales which seemed to vibrate in the water, and at the same time making a strange long booming sound as bubbles skipped and danced over his back.

I took a gulp and then decided to go into action!

Leaning over, I dropped the burning piece of wood (which didn't appear to be hot to the touch) into the lake, and jumped quickly back.

The lake started to sizzle, and smoke started to rise off the water, and then there woz a great surge of waves hitting the banks, and more huge bubbles started to pop to the surface.

It woz like a huge battle going on down there!

Then after what seemed to take several suns and moons, the lake evaporated and dried up!

So this is it! First I used the 'metal' (from the knight's armour) to cut the 'wood on fire' (from Brannon, the Tree of Life) and then this woz thrown by me into the water with the earth below it!

Eureka! I had done it! I had completed the task! But I woz so busy complimenting myself that I'd quite forgotten about the most important thing!

One very pissed-off dragon!

I could see in an instant that things were just beginning to hot up, as the seriously bad-tempered dragon started to crawl out of the dried up crater, which woz once upon a time the lake, being his beloved stomping grounds, but now 'twas a grey desert—*all* gone—just like that—an' all done by clever ol' me!

He woz now one very outrageously upset reptile, and I could tell by his reeking bad breath that all woz not well, and he woz all out to seek revenge!

His tail started to thrust from side to side, and he drew his great red body up onto his great scaly haunches, and his menacing-looking claws started to wrench at the dried up earth on the side of the bank, and then he snorted twice through his huge gaping nostrils (just like Humphrey does!) followed by a tremendous roar which echoed right across the land, making boulders plunge down from the tops of the mountains and the earth to shake violently.

There woz a horrible gurgling, rumbling sound in his throat, like a deep, long growl, and his scales made an odd sharp clapping sound that seemed to follow down the full length of his body as his scales vibrated more loudly than they did under water in his pent-up anger.

His green lizard's eyes gleamed with malice, and then they turned red!

He started to run like a jackrabbit with a sore bum! Fast for his great bulk. And he woz running in my direction!

I didn't think quick enough to take off and fly, so I too started to run like a road runner, and sped towards the trees until I could see the yin and yang tree where I could head for cover.

I got there quicker than the dragon did, and I quietly stepped back under the yin and yang tree, in the hope that the clanking of the disc-shaped leaves, and the shaking of me black and white feathers, and me vibrating beak that woz chattering together in fear, couldn't be heard by him!

I woz hoping that he wouldn't notice me there, quaking in me feet!

I needn't have worried, because he didn't notice me at all!

He must have been hard of hearing, lacking in good eyesight, and lost his sense of smell, as well as his sense of humour!

He then let out an almighty *belch!* like a rumble of thunder, and out tumbled bits of rusty old armour plating, a few helmets, and a lance with a tattered flag still attached to it!

By the Saint George and all the other saints, this old dragon sure did know how to eat, and I certainly didn't wish to be the dish of the day!

I needn't have worried too much, because he changed his mind about galomphing through the forest, and with a final roar he turned about and went back towards the dried-up path of what was once a lake. Then at great speed, and making such a stonking great noise as he went, he made his way into the distance.

This time I decided to fly, and I followed him back to the lake bed which was still smouldering a bit. He jumped down with a large *thump!* and made his way along the wide path, with his great long tail swiping the sides of the bank which widened it even further and caused trees to crash down into it, and dragging some of them behind him as the great long roots got stuck in his scales and twined themselves around his spiny forked-tail.

As he stomped off with a resounding *thrump!… thrump!… thrump!* and leaving an untidy trail of mess behind him, I saw these huge, pure white, egg-shaped rocks just lying in a neat pile on the path—only they weren't rocks at all!—they were *dragon's eggs!*

That scaly old gink had been guarding them, and he hadn't even crushed them into tiny bits!

This can only mean one thing…somewhere nearby lurks a *hen dragon!*

Phew! I thought as he disappeared, *there goes a blast from the past!* as the great red ghetto blaster hit the high road.

My ever so great uncle Sidney Snake Snatcher would have been well and truly beak snapped (gob smacked!) if he ever came across such a gigantic lizard as this, and I'd like to see him try and throw one of *these!*

But what about the singing, swimming knight and his shining armour?

No longer could he perform his synchronized swimming with that school of oversized fish who had joined him, now that the lake was just a dried up bed of mud, so had he ended up as a piece of pork crackling all wrapped up in tin foil, for the dragon's lunch? And had the dragon also devoured the knight's candy-striped steed, as an hors d'oeuvre?

Let's hope that this little bit of unseasonable weather stuff we'd just experienced, will have stopped this masquerading monster out on his jolly jaunts searching for fast-food forays for his potential gastronomic goblin-gobblin gourmets, and his once-a-knight sprees!'

Maybe I'll see him in me own world—but I sincerely hope not!

Anyway, at least I've won me title of 'Dragon Removal Specialist!' post-haste!

After all these little minor interludes, it woz now *my* turn to leave, but before doin' so, there woz just one (or two) more things to collect.

I gently picked of a seed from each side of the yin and yang tree—one light and one dark—then flew at great speed back towards Merlin's cave, passing Brannon, the talking Tree of Life, who shook some of his branches in a farewell gesture.

As I sped onwards, a howling wind like a pack of hungry wolves pushed towards me and then behind me, and all the scenery about me started to tumble and fly about like a whirlwind.

Lots of weird-looking creatures floated past me.

There were flashes of black and white, as hundreds of yin and yang discs whizzed past me like chariot wheels, and then a lotus flower floated by with the cherubic face of Atum smiling at me, as he lay curled up in the middle of it, and he was followed by Ra, floating along on his Manjet boat, with Horus at the helm, and they were followed by an army of elves, and flying in front of them were owls, eagles, ravens who were chased by wild boars, and in front of them woz a fleeing white stag with one large antler in the middle of its forehead. Large fish swam past me in thin air, and fancy-dressed humans cavorted in their wake! Then I flew straight through a swirl of feathers and scales, and they fell all around me just like a snow-storm, and then it started to rain buckets of bits of old metal, but these were no ordinary pieces of old tin—it woz the suit of armour I'd seen a bit earlier on, and clinging to it for dear life woz the desperate-looking unclad bold knight!—and he woz closely followed by his galloping steed, who woz going so fast that its one red leg and the three yellow ones flashed brightly like streaks of lightning!

All these weird images glided or whirled at a tremendous speed in front and around me with a *clang!*—*tinkle!*—*roar!* and a *whinny!*

before they finally went *poof!*—an' vanished into a blue mist.

I think I woz mightily lucky to escape by the tip of me tail, and still be in one piece!

I kept on going for what seemed like forever, but I woz glad that the two magic seeds helped me to find the hidden entrance to the cave, and I flew without hesitation, straight through and then past Merlin, who woz still standing in the same position as when I left him.

As I flashed past, I called out, "I've done it!"

I could see his hands splayed out flat against the clear yellow amber of his obelisk chamber, and his eyes (looking like two wasps trying to crawl out of a jam-jar) gaped open in amazement as he mouthed back through the mellow yellow "well done!"—as I shot through to the opening of the cave and out into the open, and onto familiar ground once more!

Glider had left the river bank, but as I sped on up the hill and through the woodland, then over the fields, I glanced up land saw Tegrin circling overhead, and I felt a deep respect for him—the bird king of the otherworld!

I knew it was getting past roosting time, because all the crow boys were lining up on the wires, and were pointing their black bums towards the setting sun in the west.

When I finally arrived back to me klakki, it was dark, and the sky was fairly littered with sparkling stars.

– Chapter Ten –
Pipe Dreams with Feathers—
From the Dark Side of the Moon!

More plants were to be put in before the summer was out.

I wanted to plant as many buddleias as the garden could possibly cope with, as these would attract lots of butterflies and bees, and the attractive pastel shades of a passion flower would look eye catching if it was planted on one side of the front porch with a deep-blue or a snowy-white climbing clematis on the other.

Maggie took a great interest in the passion flower as he watched me dig and set the plant into the ground. Perhaps his wild instincts told him that if he waited long enough, and when eventually the flowers had gone over, they would bear edible fruits, and then he could go "passion-fruit scrumping!"

The song thrush continued to sing his repetitive song—"*tweeoo!... tweeoo!... tweeoo!—shiree!... shiree!... shiree!—gari!... gari!... gari!*"—which seemed to go on all day, but I was very grateful for his snail-clearance forays in the garden, so I wished him well!

September arrived, and the robin started to sing its sweet autumn melody once more. Blackberries festooned the hedgerows, and the blackbirds took full advantage of the sweet juicy fruits, judging by the purple-coloured droppings which I discovered dotted along the patio path, and soon the redwings would return to feast off the berries in the rowan trees, and fieldfares had just started to arrive in our fields, doing their pest-clearance duties by searching for invertebrates in the ground.

The bird feeding stations were becoming busier than Heathrow Airport at peak flying times, and their arrivals and departures were almost as noisy. Their landings and take-offs were a continuous *"whirring!"* of flapping wings, and angry *"squeaks!"* came from those who arrived at the same time—all were contesting for the same piece of food, even though there was always plenty for everyone.

The days were getting shorter, and the birds needed to build up their fat reserves to sustain them through the long chilly nights.

A renegade sparrowhawk had become a frequent visitor to our garden, picking off my poor little sparrows, along with a few blue tits, and even some of the collared doves.

It's so sickening to look out of the window to see scattered feathers and a dead bird.

One particular morning I stumbled across yet another body of a dove, and when I looked more closely at it, I could see that the wretched sparrowhawk had plucked the feathers from its neck, and had then ripped at its throat, but nowhere else. What a dreadful tragedy, to kill another bird in order to take just a small part of it and then discard the rest.

At least the poor things wouldn't be wasted.

Instead of putting their bodies in the hedgerow for the foxes or crows to take, I now place them in the middle of the field where the buzzards or red kites can feast off them. In fact, I place the cat's victims there as well, so now there's a row of different types of food for them to choose from, like dead voles, mice, and sometimes rabbits.

The fox doesn't arrive until late evening, so he has to pick whatever might be left for him.

One juvenile sparrowhawk is either loopy or short sighted!

His first failure was when he mistakenly landed on a dead leaf, thinking he'd caught a small bird off-guard—when he saw the leaf caught by a slight breeze, sending it fluttering about on the lawn—and he just stood there with one of his talons wrapped around the leaf and a rather embarrassed look on his face!

Another unsuccessful raid was when he dived into the middle of a thick Berberis bush, and all the sparrows burst out in all directions, like sparklers on bonfire night, and so he missed lunch again!

His most spectacular "mission impossible" was when he flew straight into the lounge window and bounced off in a flurry of feathers.

What had he seen this time?

It was my "Dream Catcher"—full of exotic bird feathers and hanging over the patio doors (to help prevent little birds from flying into the glass windows!).

I watched another large bird of prey one late evening, as a lone buzzard scouted across the twilight sky. He was on the lookout, in the hope of spotting a last-minute meal that might be lying in the grass below his flight-path, and as he sped across the sky, his underside flashed a silvery colour against the darkening clouds.

The approaching night sky was perfectly clear, and the stars shone brightly as the moon stole across the inky blackness as a silent witness to the events of the day, and I wondered how many little birds hadn't managed to evade capture from their feathered enemies!

It wasn't the clock alarm that woke me one particular morning, it was still too early for the radio to come on. Yet in my subconscious state, there was something out of the ordinary that was jogging my senses into wakefulness—and it wasn't music!

At first, it sounded like a distant rumble, and then it seemed to be approaching, rather like an express train passing through; the only thing is—we live nowhere near a railway!

Then I thought it might be a very heavy vehicle trundling along the top road, and yet it didn't sound like the usual familiar noise of a lorry approaching and then passing by.

What really snapped me out of my still rather sleepy thoughts, was when I noticed my display cabinet, with its glass sliding doors, had started to rattle, and my fancy collector's plates hanging on the walls were jiggling about unnaturally too, making them vibrate against the walls.

The strange sensation only lasted for a minute or two, and then all went quiet.

I began to think I was imagining things or was just having a pre-waking dream!

It was later that day I heard the news on the radio that there had been a bit of an earthquake in the Midlands, and that many people had experienced the same alarming sensations, but thankfully it was only a mini-quake!

I could see Maggie's half attempt at building a nest in the beech tree, but it now looked as though he'd abandoned it, so perhaps he was building another one somewhere else.

He was still collecting lots of strange objects, then stacking them up in a corner of the aviary, and amongst them were two very small black and white beads, or on closer inspection, they looked more like seeds, but they were quite foreign to me.

I was puzzled, I had no idea where these two beads or seeds could have come from, as they were definitely not mine, or Mother's, so where had he collected these from?

As the aviary door was almost permanently left wide open, I noticed that it was beginning to be visited by other inquisitive magpies, and they didn't waste any time inspecting all the nooks and crannies to see what they could find, and they were soon helping themselves to Maggie's dish of food, and some of his treasures as well!

If Maggie knew what was going on, I'm sure he would have chased them out, and even given them a good hiding in his magpie way. I'm not sure he could have taken on the big magpie I named Charlie White, as I've seen this rather large and imposing-looking bird setting upon Maggie, bowling him over on his back, and then pecking him viciously whilst poor Maggie squawked and screamed loudly for help! It's not the first time I've had to rush out and rescue him from the big bully.

Other times, I have seen Maggie and Charlie White getting on quite amicably out in the field, almost as though they were exchanging friendly gossip.

Maggie's appearance about the garden became less frequent as the weeks went by, and even the other magpies seemed to have made off to pastures new, so perhaps Maggie had been enticed away to join them somewhere else, and although he still returned for his food in the aviary, he was becoming more and more aloof, and he didn't even seem to be interested in playing with Millie anymore.

Visitors to the house who had heard about Maggie, and friends who had shared our fun and enjoyment at watching his antics, were disappointed not to see him about the house and garden, as he was undoubtedly the main attraction, and they always asked about him and wanted to know where he might have got to, and would it be possible to see him again?

Sometimes Maggie looked quite forlorn and disturbed, as though he was torn between two worlds and couldn't make up his mind whether he wanted to stay with us or to return to the wild completely and join the rest of the flock.

I think in some ways that he was still fond of us (in his funny way) and thought that he should still be part of the family.

Perhaps he found himself caught up in a dreadful dilemma, and I felt quite sorry for him, because there was no way I could help him on this one. All I could do was to try and keep track of him somehow and just keep on putting his food out for him in the aviary, even if his friends wanted to share it with him too!

His departure from us was a gradual process, as he would return one night into the aviary for his feed, and then perhaps the next night he wouldn't return at all, and this went on for a few weeks at a time.

Deep down I was glad that he had been accepted by the other wild magpies, because that was what I really wanted for him—to be able to live a natural life and rear his own young, as this would be the perfect goal for him to aim at, and now it was up to him, so he would have to choose which way he really wanted to go.

It would also solve the problem for us not having to keep all the bedroom windows shut whenever he was out and about, because this had been quite a problem all through the hot summer.

As magpies are known to have a cruel streak, particularly during the nesting season when they start to rear their young, I was particularly concerned that he might attack the neighbour's children if they approached him, and I certainly didn't want that to happen.

Although I still left a dish full of food out in the aviary for him in the hope that I would see him return, I couldn't understand why the dish became empty each morning, with not even a crumb of morsel left in it, and it appeared to be licked clean, in fact it fairly shone with cleanliness!

Then one morning I found out who the culprit was.

It was a little stray kitten who was found in the aviary with his face in the dish, and as soon as I approached him, he shot out of the aviary and ran across the fields like a frightened rabbit.

It took a few days before I could coax him onto the patio with a dish of proper cat food and a saucer of milk, but the poor little thing was so hungry and thirsty that it wasn't long before he let me pick him up and take him indoors to join Millie, and he has lived with us ever since.

We named him Percy—another feline menace to add to the family of pets!

He loves to sit comfortably by the fire or curled up on someone's lap, looking sleek and very fat!

There's another rather strange coincidence about Percy, which makes me wonder if it's just a twist of fate—he's a black and white cat! Is that creepy or what!

Days and weeks go by, and I have no idea where Maggie is or what may have happened to him.

He has either taken over a new territory, or maybe he was driven out by that big magpie, or he's succumbed to a sparrowhawk, or even a fox; but I sincerely hope not. He was (or still is), such a character, and we shall miss him very much, as life just won't be the same without him.

Perhaps his free spirit was up there somewhere, floating about in the aether (or so I thought at the time!), until a few years later, there was another twist to the tale, and it was quite unexpected, and came out of the blue!

I was driving back home one day from a shopping trip when I saw our good neighbours, who lived in the bungalow near the top of the lane, and they were just unloading their shopping from the boot of their car.

As I drew parallel with them, I waved in recognition, and they both waved back, but then I noticed that Alun was actually gesturing frantically for me to stop, so pulling over into his drive, I switched off the engine and wound my window down to see what he wanted.

Alun had a big beam on his face, and he told me to wait just a minute, as he'd got something to show me that he'd kept by for some time, and that he'd been meaning to catch me on one of my trips up and down the lane, but it always seemed to be at the wrong time, so he'd missed his opportunity.

He rushed back indoors, and it wasn't long before he returned.

In his hand he was waving a white envelope.

"Here we are, Louisa bach!" he said, "look at these, and see what you think!"

Intrigued, I opened the envelope and took the contents out.

It was like opening Pandora's box!

In my hand, I was holding four photographs, two of which were a little bit dark, but the subject matter stood out as clear as day, and now

I could piece together some of the jigsaw of what may have become of Maggie.

Two of the photos taken in the garden showed Maggie perched on Alun's arm, and another one showed Maggie reaching through the kitchen window, taking something from a spoon, and the other one was of Maggie, once again at the kitchen window, begging for some more food!

This small piece of evidence showed that Maggie must have (at least at some time after his disappearance), returned to our area, but not back to our house and garden.

Something must have driven him away, and for whatever reason, it must have been so overpowering for him that he was unable to return!

I feel pretty certain that the body of a dead magpie (which I'd found by Humphrey's bath one morning, and partly hidden in the stinging nettles), was not his, because the photos of Maggie were taken by Mr "L" sometime after the discovery of the body.

I would like to think that he is out there somewhere making his own way in life, but he has made such an impact on our own lives in the short time he had already spent with us, with all the fun times, as well as the sad!

I feel it was a privilege to have been part of his life.

Oh well, no use brooding, perhaps I should take up playing the piano again and tinker away on those precious ebony and ivory keys, which some people may not realize that many of the older piano's keys were actually made from the white tusks of the long-forgotten woolly mammoths. So I think I will try something appropriate. I know, how about Rossini's "The Thieving Magpie!"

- Chapter Ten and A Half -
Over to Maggie

...do birds really fly with the angels?

"Have you seen him then?" asked Shiffely, stabbing at a passing beetle.

"Seen who?" I asked in an unconcerned manner.

"Why, Merlin, of course!" answered Shiffely crossly.

"And what about the red dragon...did you see him at all?" asked Squiffly.

"But of course I did!" I said. "I saw the great Merlin, and he thought I was a very brave and gallant magpie, and he told me that I should have everything I wanted, and then he sent me on me quest to the land of Nog."

"Don't you mean the land of Mabinogion?" enquired Tizzy.

"Yes!... Of course that's what I meant to say!" I said. "Just a slip of the tongue...that's all! Anyway, as for the dragon, well I can tell you we had a good old battle going on between us, and that's a fact. I fought him across the stream, I fought him over a cliff, I fought him in the air, and eventually he ran off like a scalded mouse, and went and hid in a cave, without even a whiff of a puff, or a roar of a fire, or the tiniest bit of a steam left in him! So I definitely won that battle...good and proper!... And now he's out there somewhere, tunnelling about the underground like a mole!

"In fact, only just the other sunrise time, I thought I heard something like him doin' one of his usual rampaging about, so I bet he's cooking up something mighty cunning in his fiery snout, but before I did battle with this very same beast, I even rubbed shoulders with gallant knights in armour!" I said. And I told them about this particular knight doing his solitary sequence swimming, and his singing of romantic melodies in the dragon's lake, and of the knight's rainbow-coloured horse.

I also told them about me close encounters with Chiselbeak, and of his constant change into a god called Ra, and then he would change back into Chiselbeak again. Then there was Thoth, the moon god, and another one called Horus, and all those other cuddly god-type beings, which I can't remember too much about, and a lump of island called none other than Nun, and a special stone called Benben. And I didn't forget to tell them how I first met the queenly bird called Gwynweaver.

There was one thing that I didn't want to tell them, and that was about the yin and yang tree, because I didn't want anyone trying to steal me yin and yang seeds from me, but in the end—I relented!

One sunlight-time, when I was out hunting for a suitable klakki-building tree, so that I could start with some serious klakki building, I was confronted by Featherhead White Wings.

Looking me straight in the eye (which was pretty unnerving in any event), he said, "We must flee...all of us...before it's too late!"

"Flea, or flee?" I asked. "Do you mean flea, as in covering ourselves in those itchy little critters?... Or flee, as in 'fly the coup?' and for why should we do this? Do you think I'm an oxymoron or something!"

"Now listen to me carefully!" he said, standing over me. Then, without any warning, he threw me onto me back, and pinned me mercilessly to the ground, saying, "Humans are coming, and with them they carry small wire-covered-klakkies for the purpose of trapping as many magpies as they can, and then killing them all! We are in grave danger!"

"Hey, ged orf me, wax head!" I said. "I hear you!... I hear you...an' I'm listenin' very carefully! So what can we all do then?" I asked him. "Should we go and have some fun in the sun, play a game in the rain, or sing a tune to the moon?" I said, trying to lighten the mood.

"No time!" came his terse reply.

Looking into his eyes, I swear I could see them turn all red, and I'm almost sure I was gazing into the eyes of that all powerful one called Horus, so he must mean business!

"We must fly!....we must all leave this place before it's too late!"

"Okay then, I'll just go and pack a few of me personal belongings....shall I?" I asked. And then before he could answer, and thinking ahead of the game, I said, "Now there's me future-telling piece, me rune stones, me crystals, and then there's me magical talisman, and then there's me...!"

"*My* personal belongings!" interrupted White Wings.

"Well!" I said, "I dunno anything about *your* personal belongings...now do I?"

"You should be saying there's '*my*' personal belongings, not there's '*me*' personal belongings!" he said, scornfully.

"Okay then! There's '*me—my*' personal belongings!" I said, compromisingly.

I nearly said to him, "Give me a set of slug's teeth, and I'll chew me (oops! *my*) own words up!"—and I also very nearly said to him as an after thought, "Who's rattled your branches then, you grumpy old cupcake?" but caution held back me tongue.

"We'll help you!... We'll help you!" they called.

"Oh yeh!... you and who's army?" I shouted back.

More like they'd help themselves!—especially when I heard one of 'em mumble:

"Yum! yum!... give us a crumb!... and what's that '*something very interesting*' I can see over there?"

"Listen, aphid brains, yer all about as reliable as a worm's kneecap in a two-legged race, an' I wouldn't trust you as far as a feather can float!" I told 'em in no uncertain terms.

It looked like we were all about to split and fly the coup, so what have we got in front of us, now that everything is behind us, and the "egg-timer" has all but run out!... Which reminds me, I mustn't forget me future-teller piece! And, of course, *Moltikala!*—*where is she?* I mustn't forget my precious Tilly! She must come with me too!

Ah well, at least I've spent some quality time here and there, and I've been out-and-about on special territorial hunts for pastures new, and looking for suitable klakki-building trees, so I suppose I shall just have to get used to being without me pinky ma and her lot, seein' as she's made it very "cosy van tutti" for me.

I'll miss 'em all, no doubt.

I've just had this most *brilliantist* idea in the whole world.

If I was to find a nice tidy secret place, I could plant those two enchanted seeds of the yin yang tree, then go and fetch in a small nut shell, some of that precious water from the magic fountain in the land of the Mabinogion, and pour it onto the seeds, and I'm almost sure that I'll be able to grow me very own yin yang tree, seein' as I just can't find any sign of a 'chickle chackle tree'! And then I can sing me yin yang song, which goes like this:

I'm a yin yang bird,
in a yin yang tree;
eating yin yang seeds;
doing a yin yang pee!

In a yin yang sky,
there's a yin yang moon;
on a yin yang night,
I'll sing a yin yang tune!

First of all, I must find the cave of Merlin, and I think the quickest and easiest way to it, is down that dark long drop, which ends up in the underground stream, and eventually leads down to the river near the cave.

It was when I went over to that hole in the ground (where I threw the stone down, and heard the same splash that was the very beginning of me quest, and the long journey to the land of the Mabinogion, and then to meet Merlin and the dragon!)—that the *hit* came!

It happened as I removed the stone which covered the said hole, and bent over to peer down it, when something knocked me a crashing blow from behind, and it was powerfully painful, I can tell you!

At that very instant, I was pitched forward into the darkness, and then I found I just couldn't move, either up or down!

Then everything seemed to go all black and fuzzy!

Blimey! I thought. *I can't see anything!... Only shooting stars!... What's happening?... I think I've copped it! Oh dear!... Oh dear!... What is to become of my?... sob!... sob!*

I've not been a bad bird really! Maybe a badly bold bird, but that's different to being just plain bad! I've heard a lot!... seen a lot!... and done a lot!....much more than most birds in fact! I've had thrills, bills, and spills! "Bills" as in beaks!—"thrills!" as in excitement, and "spills!" as in a few minor accidents! So here I am!... stuck in this hole!

I don't want to die!....I'm just *too* young to die!....and there's still a lot more things I have yet to do before I die! Oh how I long for the loving care of my ma, and all those good things she has done for me, and I promise to be a much better behaved bird. And what of Tilly, and all my other friends? I want to see them all again.

Then there's all those wise words from the old Hootie Klogitiwhoo, and Glider the heron, not forgetting Merlin, and all the others from the land of the Mabinogion!

I've got to prove myself worthy of them all.

So *please*, ever so *please*, "mother of the universe!" *Please* give me a chance!... just one more time!....*please!*

Then I felt a great coldness creep over me, and me feathers began to fluff up, and my heart started to beat faster.

"Oh misery my!... Is this to be my end?" I said out loud. "Now if I see the 'great white albatross,' then that's the end of everything!... But wait a minute!... What's that I can see through the haze?"

On opening my eyes, I could just about see a dark shape, and it was moving towards me, then from the depths, just below me, a croaky voice said, "Oops-a-daisy!" followed by, "Good-day, mate!... 'owz yer doin', me old cobber?" and then it said again, "Just you ease yourself over a tiny bit! I think I can help you, mate! If you can leave a small crack, then I should be able to throw some small stones down between you and the side of this hole!"

"What's the idea of that then?" I wheezed.

"Well now, the idea is that if I can throw enough stones down, and they gradually get higher and higher, they will reach up to where you're stuck down there, and then you'll soon be able to stand on the top of them, and eventually you'd reach the top again, and be able to just step back out of the hole!"

Now it suddenly dawned on me—there's only one bird that I know of who could possibly come up with such a birdbrained, daft idea.

"Moonbeam!"—I croaked back. "Is that really...*you?*"

"Nope!" came the reply. "But try again!"

"Yes!" I said, feeling a little stronger, and a little more hopeful. "Yes!... I think I will...try again!"

Epilogue
And Finally
A Pause with A Thought for the Day!

I believe that we are all bound together, like one gigantic book of life, with so many non-ending chapters, and it's up to us to read it well, and to try and understand how nature works for us, as well as all other living creatures.

Take the trees, for instance. Birds need trees to feed from the insects which they can find in them, and also to roost or shelter, as well as to nest in them.

We need trees also, but for very different purposes. A lot of our furniture started off as living trees, and so did wooden posts and fencing, and many, many other everyday things we all take for granted, too numerous to mention here, but there is another side to the life of the trees.

They say that trees communicate, but they can make music as well.

Some of these magnificent trees are sacrificed, but rise again so that we may enjoy the beautiful sounds made by them, like the piano—in tune with the rich mellow tones of the blackbird's song, which reminds us of a beautiful summer's day in a meadow, when you want to dance with joy to the waltz in a bluebell wood.

The melodious voice of the violin seems to have the song of the nightingale embedded within the very grain of the wood, whilst the harp's melodies soothe and relax us.

The woodwind sound of a trilling flute is uplifting, and rises to the gentle twittering, like the distant song of the ascending skylark, whilst the sensual resonant sound of the clarinet entices the rose and poppy to bloom.

Go for a walk into the woods on a dewy damp morning, and take a moment to listen to the songbirds as they sing out their haunting melodies from the past—so rich and sweet—surely they must fly with the angels!

I am so glad that I've held back on using those awful slug pellets, to stop those slimy, black, blobby creatures from eating my precious plants. Those little blue granules are so full of poison, but thankfully, because I don't use them any more, I now reap the benefits of having so many happy, healthy, thrushes and blackbirds around my garden, as they appear to prosper well on these organic pesticide-free slugs for their food, and I'm sure that the hedgehogs, frogs and toads are happy about that too.

There are so many species sitting on the edge of extinction, which is a matter of concern to all of us, so every little bit we can do must surely help.

It's a case of survival for the lucky ones—a fine balance between what is to be, or not to be!

We must strive to heighten our awareness, and to make sure that those, which are dangerously close to vanishing into nothingness, are given a "kick-start" back into a safer environment, back into our lives, for us all to enjoy their presence around us once more.

We are able to feel the warmth of the sunrays pierce through the transparency of the windows of our minds as we search for our own purpose in life, anchoring us to the reason for our forever-quest, and to try and unravel the mystique, inviting us to step through the door of the world. For what we seek, then we shall find.

All this can inspire us with a primeval instinct hidden deep within our emotions.

Savour the rich heady scent of wild garlic, along with the musky smell of field mushrooms and the earthy smell of damp moss clinging to rocks and trees, and the sweet floral smell of a thick blue carpet of heavenly bluebells, or the delicate perfume of the primrose.

The leaves—once glowing with vibrant autumn colours—are now touched by early-morning frost, swirling and drifting in the wind like lost souls.

The essence of pinewood burning on an autumn bonfire lingers in the memory, uplifting the spirits, whilst winter sleeps on—fragrance free!

The sound of gentle falling rain is very therapeutic and calming.

Stand still for a moment, and listen to the sounds of nature sending out messages of peace and hope, willing us all to live in harmony, to understand what life really means, and if you listen really carefully, you will hear the true sounds of our earth, and that surely is real magic. And by weaving a rich tapestry of this life force, this surely must tell us that if we can be patient enough to take heed, and let the senses flow over us like a cool mountain stream, we can experience deep within us the knowledge of all natural things, and therefore all things are possible, and dreams really can come true!

The past is linked with the present, and the future as well.

It's also worth remembering that with every moment, every day, every month, and every year, the past drifts further and further away from us. It would be a sad day if stories of our past were to be forgotten forever, so it's important to revive them from time to time, and bring them out of the mothballs for some airing! It makes the present more fun and worthwhile to look forward to.

It's a strange thought when you realize that this very moment, too, will become past history, ready and waiting for yet another story to be told!

We have gone almost full cycle of the four seasons, and experienced the darkness of winter, and the lightness of summer, but best of all, we look forward to the new beginnings of spring, and await the return of those clowning starlings, arriving in a great black swirling mass across the sky.

They will entertain us once more, like actors in a well-known pantomime, and smartly decked out in their brightly sparkling harlequin uniforms, cutting a dash as they march up and down, probing into our lawns in their usual fashion, and searching our fields for a befitting banquet set out by mother nature herself.

I hope that one day I will look out of the window to see Maggie out there on the lawn amongst the other birds. But in the meantime, we look forward once more to the sound of the cuckoo's call, that reminds us all "to be happy as a lark!"

Now I have related my own story, and Maggie has told his own tale—from the tail of a magpie!

Printed in the United Kingdom
by Lightning Source UK Ltd.
108286UKS00001B/71

9 781413 749823